GALINA
PETROVNA'S
THREE-LEGGED
DOG STORY

Andrea Bennett graduated from the University of Sheffield in History & Russian and then spent a good part of the 'Yeltsin years' living and working in Russia. On her return to the UK she joined the Civil Service – first at the Foreign & Commonwealth Office, then the Department for International Development. A stint in local government followed, and she now works in the charity sector. This is her first novel. She lives in Ramsgate, Kent, with her family and dog.

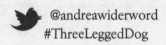 @andreawiderword
#ThreeLeggedDog

GALINA PETROVNA'S
THREE-LEGGED
DOG STORY

ANDREA BENNETT

THE BOROUGH PRESS

The Borough Press
An imprint of HarperCollins*Publishers*
1 London Bridge Street
London SE1 9GF

www.harpercollins.co.uk

First published in Great Britain by The Borough Press 2015

This paperback edition 2015
1

Copyright © Andrea Bennett 2015

Andrea Bennett asserts the moral right to
be identified as the author of this work

ISBN: 978-0-00-810840-3

Set in Sabon by Palimpsest Book Production Limited,
Falkirk, Stirlingshire

Printed and bound in Great Britain by
Clays Ltd, St Ives plc

MIX
Paper from
responsible sources
FSC
www.fsc.org   **FSC® C007454**

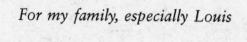

For my family, especially Louis

Author's Note

In the 1990s, there was a three-legged dog called Boroda, who wore no collar and lived in Azov with an old Russian lady who worked hard on her *dacha*.

However, everything else in this book, while inspired by my memories of the people and geography of Russia, is a work of fiction, and should be treated as such.

Contents

1. A Typical Monday Afternoon   1
2. The Azov House of Culture Elderly Club   16
3. Mitya the Exterminator   27
4. A Chase   36
5. A Visit   52
6. The Plan   68
7. Grigory Mikhailovich   84
8. A Train Ride   94
9. A Rescue   109
10. Guests   116
11. A Date with Mitya   129
12. A Letter from Vasya   142
13. Mitya's Angel   149
14. The Ministry   164
15. Deep in the SIZO   183
16. A Minor Triumph   192
17. The Cheese Mistress   203
18. The Third Way   215
19. A Dog's Life   231
20. The Return   235

21. Of Butterflies, Dogs and Men 255
22. Rov Avia 264
23. Vasya's Pussy 275
24. The Sunshine SIZO 281
25. Chickens Roost 300
26. The End of the Beginning 309
27. The End 319

Glossary 337
Acknowledgements 339

1

A Typical Monday Afternoon

'Hey! Goryoun Tigranovich! Can you hear me?'

A warm brown hand slapped on the door once more, its force rattling the hinges this time.

'He's dead, I tell you! He's probably been eaten by the cats by now. Four of them he's got, you know. Four fluffy white cats! Who needs four fluffy white cats? White? Ridiculous!'

'*Babushka*, can you hear any cats mewing?'

The two ladies, one indescribably old and striated and the other only mildly so, waited silently for a moment outside the apartment door, listening intently. Tiny Baba Krychkova bent slightly to put her ear to the keyhole, closed her eyes and sucked in her cheeks.

'I hear nothing, Galia,' she replied after some moments.

'So that's good, isn't it, Baba? That means that Goryoun Tigranovich has probably gone on holiday to the coast, or perhaps to visit friends in Rostov, and has left the cats with someone else. And that means he isn't lying dead in his apartment.'

'But Galia, maybe they're all dead! The cats and Goryoun

Tigranovich! All dead! Maybe they found him too tough to eat and they starved! It's been several days, you know.'

The older lady's face crumpled at the thought of the starving cats and the dry, wasted cadaver of Goryoun Tigranovich, and she began to sob, rubbing a gnarled red fist into her apple-pip eyes. Other doors began to creak and moan along the length of the dusty corridor, and slowly other grey heads studded with curranty eyes bobbed into view, to peer curiously down the hall towards the source of the noise and excitement. A vague hum stretched out along the length of the building as the elderly residents rose as one from their afternoon naps, whether planned or unplanned, to witness the drama unfolding on floor 3 of Building 11, Karl Marx Avenue, in the southern Russian town of Azov. Galia sighed, and offered her handkerchief over, and made compassionate tutting noises with her tongue.

'Baba Krychkova, there is nothing we can do out here in the hall. I am sure that Goryoun Tigranovich is in the best of health. He's such a sprightly fellow – and a regular traveller, you know. Just last month he was in Omsk.'

Galia didn't trip over the words, pronouncing them firmly and evenly, but to her own ears they sounded unconvincing: the last time she had seen the gentleman he had resembled a piece of dried bark dressed in a suit. 'I am sure I saw him last week, down at the market, and he was buying watermelons. People who buy watermelons are not about to die: they are enjoying life; they are robust, and hopeful. Watermelons are a sure sign. He was probably taking the melons as a present for whoever he has gone to visit. I am confident he will be back soon.'

Melons or no, Goryoun Tigranovich was a very private person, and he would not welcome being discussed in the

2

hallway by his entire entourage of elderly neighbours. Galia tried to encourage the older lady to go home.

'Why don't you go and have a nice cup of tea, and I can bring you one of my home-made buns. You'd like that, wouldn't you?'

The older lady's face did not change, but her tiny watery eyes were on Galia now.

'And if we still haven't seen him by the end of the week, we'll ask if the caretaker knows where he's gone.'

'He promised me a marrow, you know,' said Baba Krychkova over her shoulder, as she shuffled off down the corridor. Now there, thought Galia, is the real root of the problem: upset over an unfulfilled vegetable promise.

'I can give you a marrow, Baba Krychkova, and mine are just as tasty as Goryoun Tigranovich's.'

Baba Krychkova shrugged in a dismissive manner and shut her door, leaving Galia little choice but to cluck her tongue, shake her head gently and disappear into her own apartment. Boroda got up from the box under the table and greeted her with a gentle wag and a beautiful, elongating stretch.

'The grace of dogs,' thought Galia, 'is in their complete, friendly laziness. And the fact that they can't speak.'

Unlike many of her neighbours, and all her friends at the Azov House of Culture Elderly Club, Galina Petrovna Orlova, or Galia for short, almost never cried. While they glistened like sweetie wrappers chewed up by one of Goryoun Tigranovich's cats, she sat squarely on her chair, quietly bronzed, her muscular hands resting in light puffy fists on her floral-clad thighs. She listened attentively to the complaints of the others, sighed and tutted gently as they recounted tales of lives that were hard. Galia considered that she herself lived in the present, and rarely reminisced. Her concerns included her vegetable patch, good food, complicated card games and her friends. She took pride in her town and her region, and she would certainly defend her motherland against any sort of criticism that wasn't her own. She was not what one might call a sentimental person.

However, even the most unsentimental among us have to have something or someone and, in the autumn of her days, the source of Galia's completeness, and the well from which she drew her compassion, her patience, her certainty and her rest, was neither the church nor alcohol, nor gossip, nor gardening: the source of her calm was her three-legged dog.

The dog had a narrow face and graceful limbs tufted with wiry grey hair. Her dark eyes tilted over high cheekbones, recalling, perhaps, some long-lost Borzoi relative waiting on the eastern plains, under a canopy of frozen tear-drop stars. That was Galia's initial impression when she first saw the dog from a distance outside the factory, when she didn't have her glasses on. On closer inspection, however, she could find little evidence of blue blood in the mutt: limp-tailed and apologetic, she had taken up residence under a particularly rancid snack kiosk, and was scavenging for food. Galia steadfastly ignored the beast. For five days, Galia pretended the dog wasn't there and turned her head slyly as she passed to and from the vegetable patch. And then on the sixth, she saw the dog trying, with her lone fore-paw, to extract a stub of bone from under the piss-stained kiosk. Poor dog: only three legs. It reminded Galia of a feeling, like a vague sniff of something or someone that had been a long time ago and long-since departed. Something she wanted to hold on to, but could not even touch. The old lady watched the dog and sighed. The dog's ears pricked at the sound, and she stopped scrabbling. There was a moment's breathless pause in the bustling afternoon, and a long dark-brown gaze was directed straight through Galia's woollen cardigan and into her heart. Their fate was sealed, whether she liked it or not.

Galia had carefully extracted the stub of bone with her penknife and given it to the dog, who accepted it between gentle white teeth. As evening drew on, the dog followed Galia home at a polite distance, ignoring vague shooing noises that emerged, half-hearted as sun-kissed bees, from Galia's throat. The dog sat patiently outside the apartment door as dusk crept down the hall, and was still there when the ball of the sun rose on the horizon and the blackbirds broke into song. After a night of deep meditation, Galia relented and opened the door wide. In slid the dog, to sit calmly under the kitchen table, looking about her with brightly inquisitive, almond-shaped eyes.

'Dog lady, what shall we call you, eh? I wonder if you've had a name before? Probably Fido, or Shep, or Sharik or something else ugly and completely unsuitable. Well, no matter. Look at you, handsome lady, with your cheekbones and your pointy beard: we will call you Boroda, the bearded one. That'll do for us.'

And Galia called the dog Boroda, in recognition of her fine, pointy beard.

* * *

Sometimes, her broad arms thrust into a great cool bowl of pastry, gently kneading the gloop into the tastiest morsels this side of Kharkov, Galia's thoughts turned to the past. For all she insisted she lived in the present, as she got older, she needed, occasionally, to remember. Not to look for answers or mend long-forgotten quarrels, or cry and miss and reminisce, but to remind and reassure herself of who she was and where she'd come from. Rolling the pastry out into huge snowy sheets, ready to cut into hundreds of leaves to be filled, crimped and boiled, Galia sweated in the heat of midday, the small salty drops occasionally dripping into the expanding mixture below. Her brow grew wet and dark as the culinary process proceeded and memories crowded around her, and Boroda receded further under the table, claiming her cardboard box in the darkest, coolest corner.

Galia had lost her parents, her virginity and many of her teeth during the Great Patriotic War. She preferred not to relive any of those events. In a space of weeks, that seemed like her whole lifetime – but also no time at all, as time had stood still or ceased to exist or just exploded – she had grown up. This was a few weeks that, in her memory, she condensed into something untouchable and shut up in a black box. Open the box, and all you could hear was a never-ending scream and all you could see was a giant mechanical hand scratching dry bones, and all you could feel was the freezing wind of the steppe and a raging hunger. A box of memory that denied the existence of the sun, animals, trees, laughter or childhood. A box she rarely dared delve in to.

This same era of numbing change, hurt and sacrifice also brought her – like a particularly big and difficult baby under a gooseberry bush – a husband. Just like that! Again, she didn't like to brood on this fact, but she could not, for the life of her, remember how it had happened. She had been a slight girl then, with milky skin and frizzy blonde hair that she hid under a greasy khaki cap. Entirely alone and so scared she couldn't recall her parents' faces, or her own, she had somehow got slung together with Pasha and his field kitchen and a band of stragglers, way behind the front line, with Victory in Europe a few weeks off. Pasha: a little weak, a little lazy perhaps, with liquid brown eyes and a smile as wet as tripe. He kept the black box out of her sight for a while. He smiled and there was a possibility that laughter had, at some point, existed, and had meant that something was funny, not that someone was mad. He felt like a ballast, keeping her feet on the ground as the world shook and the war ended around them.

'Ah, too bad, butter fingers,' Galia muttered to herself as the last of the *vareniki* slid from her tired fingers and plopped with a puff of flour on to the floor. Boroda extended her noble neck a few inches from her box under the table, politely indicating that she would happily clear up the fallen morsel if Galia would permit.

'Go on then, *lapochka*, you may as well have it. Do a good job mind, clean it all up, my bearded lady.' Boroda's sharp pink tongue lapped up the mixture in seconds and her tail thumped gently on the wall of the box.

'No gulping, mind – even street dogs don't have to gulp!' Galia teased. Boroda flicked her a grateful glance and continued licking the floor clean with a great deal of care. The dog's needs were simple: bread, potatoes, occasional scraps of fat and bits of fruit were her staples. She, generally speaking, would not have dreamt of begging for food from the table, but if it fell her way that was a different matter. In her turn, Galia would not have thought of putting a collar around her neck. They were equals, and chose to be together in companionable quiet. There was no constraint, and new tricks were not required. The spillage all cleared up, Boroda licked her lips and then the tip of her long thin tail, and settled down to sleep.

Galia was prevented from returning to her reverie by the sudden bleeping of the phone, which brought her huffing into the hall. 'Oh for goodness' sake!' she muttered under her breath, 'is a body to get no peace in this world?' and then loudly 'Hello! I'm listening!'

'Galina Petrovna, good afternoon! It's Vasily Volubchik here,' said a confident but somewhat creaky voice.

'Yes, I know,' replied Galia with a sigh, and then, fearing she sounded rude, 'and how can I help you, Vasily Semyonovich?'

'I'm just checking that you're coming to the meeting this evening, Galina Petrovna. We have a very exciting agenda, I assure you: the Lotto draw, and . . . er, oh, er, bother, what was it? I've forgotten the most exciting thing, er—'

'Yes, Vasily Semyonovich, I'll be there. I am sure it will be most entertaining. Goodbye!' and Galia replaced the receiver with a slight frown. Vasily Semyonovich Volubchik was nothing if not determined. He had been phoning every Monday for at least three years to ensure that she didn't forget to attend the Elderly Club. And every week he promised her something exciting. So far, the most exciting event hosted by the Elderly Club had been a talk on fellatio by a local enthusiasts' group. Or did she mean philately – Galia could never recall the difference. But it had not been exciting: merely diverting, in her estimation.

She padded down the hall in her soft white slippers to wash her face and neck. She had a feeling that the evening was going to be dull. Looking back later, she couldn't quite believe how wrong this feeling had been. She had no presentiment of how her life was about to change. People often don't.

* * *

'Straindzh lavv, straindzh khaize end straindzh lauoz, straindzh lavv, zat's khau mai lavv grouz . . .'

On the east side of town, in a square box of a room with orange walls and a shiny mustard lino floor, a youngish man intoned the words of his beloved Depeche Mode without a recognizable tune. He was wearing some sort of uniform that was very clean, but still smelt to others around him of something not quite savoury. The man was making busy, precise preparations under a bare sixty-watt bulb as the sun set outside, unnoticed. His black nylon trousers, crease-free and firmly belted, sparked small currents against his thighs that made the black hairs there stand up as he moved. His regulation blue shirt was neat and pressed and tucked in snugly all the way around. It made taut pulling noises as he reached to comb his hair, which he found minutely satisfactory. He had shaved carefully, including his neck and that part of his shoulders he could reach, and had fully emptied his nose into the basin (down the hall on the left, no, second left: first left is the room of the violent alcoholic – well, one of them). He had cleaned out his ears with a safety match, and the match had then been safely placed in the bin – not in the toilet, as had happened once, by accident, when it had bobbed about in the yellow-brown water for several days, disturbing him greatly to the point where he couldn't sleep. For that matter, a match had also once been carelessly left on the bedside cabinet. But only once. The match problem had been overcome and Mitya's will imposed on the small woody sticks and their sticky pink heads. Now they always went in the bin, immediately, and he slept well.

These things he did every day, in a set order. Or rather, every evening. He turned over the cassette – Depeche Mode, *Music for the Masses* – as he did every evening around this time, and pressed play with the second finger of his right hand. He inhaled deeply and closed his eyes as the music began. He envisaged the night before him, and emitted a satisfied snort, quietly, just for himself.

Mitya was thorough. He took pride in being thorough. Thorough and careful would have been his middle names,

9

he thought, if his middle name hadn't been Boris. He frowned and paused with the boot brush poised in his hand. The thought of his middle name spoilt his mood as a bark spoils silence, and he shuddered briefly in the shadow of his thoughts about Mother. There were things he held against his mother, and his middle name was one of them. A drunkard's name, a name with no imagination: a typical Russian name. His left eye twitched slightly as he aimed the boot brush at a mental image of his mother hovering near the door, and slowly and deliberately pulled the trigger. Her green-grey brains spread out across the orange wall as Dave Gahan hit a rousing chorus and Mitya felt a tremble shoot from his stomach to his groin. Life was sweet. He had his order, he had his job, and in this room on the East Side, he was in control of his own affairs. He was Lord of all he surveyed.

There was a muffled click in the hallway, and Mitya froze, sensing trouble. He was not mistaken: a thumping beat suddenly vibrated his orange walls, snuffing out his tape like a candle in a snow storm. He lowered the boot brush and bit his lip. His neighbour, Andrei the *Svoloch*, was hosting a party, again. Soon there would be girls with too much make-up, girls with too much perfume, girls with skirts impossibly short and tights with ladders reaching up with clawing fingers towards their unmentionable parts. Girls: his neighbour was a success with them, it seemed. The younger, the better, according to Andrei, although Mitya always tried not to listen whenever his neighbour opened his ugly, tooth-speckled mouth. Mitya violently disapproved of Andrei, and his girls. He frowned at them from around his door, and when they laughed, he closed the door and frowned at them through the keyhole. They came out of Andrei the *Svoloch*'s room to go down the hall to the stinking shared toilet, and then he sometimes frowned at them through the keyhole of the toilet too, just to make his point, although this always made him feel bad afterwards. He didn't know why he did it. It wasn't like he found them interesting. It wasn't like he wanted to see them at all. They were just hairy girls, after all.

Mitya's view was that girls, and women in general – females, to use the technical and correct term – were a distraction. Men should keep their eyes on the prize and their wits about them. Girls were for when the fight was over. Or nearly over, as Mitya's fight would never be over, fully. He knew that if he ever got in the position of being in physical contact with a girl, he would make sure that she knew where she was in his order of priorities before any actual physical contact ensued: somewhere near the bottom, way down the line after work, eating, sleeping, beer, going to the toilet, Depeche Mode and ice hockey. Oh yes, he'd show her. She'd realize how lucky she was, to be in physical contact with Mitya. One day. When he had the time. When he met the right one.

Mitya's boot brush was still poised in his hand, one plastic-leather boot shiny, the other slightly dull. He collected his thoughts, pushed the girls firmly to the back of his mind, in fact out of it completely, and polished the dull boot with a frenetic stroke that turned his hand to a blur and made his neatly combed hair vibrate like a warm blancmange on a washing machine. When he had finished, the boot gleamed and small beads of sweat stood out on Mitya's forehead. He folded a piece of tissue twice and blotted away the small drops. His arm ached slightly, and his heart was beating faster.

With satisfactory boots in place, he collected his wallet, keys and comb, and indulged in a last look around the room. Everything was in its place under the glare of the bright single bulb. He was out of here, and it was going to be a long night. He felt big, and enjoyed the noise his confident footsteps made stomping on the floor. He was a man on a mission, a man with a plan. He was important. The only cloud on the horizon, so to speak, was his bladder, which was now painfully full.

In the hall, Andrei the *Svoloch* with his hateful dyed hair and cheap cologne was leaning against his doorway, smoking a cigarette with one hand and rubbing the thigh of what appeared to be a schoolgirl with the other.

'Hey Mitya, off for another night on duty? You're so fucking dull, mate! Why don't you join us for a drink? Come on – have a look at what we've got on the table? Maybe you want some?' Andrei slid his hand right between the schoolgirl's legs and she squeaked.

Mitya winced, but despite himself, he glanced into his neighbour's blood-red room. It was a scene of hell. There were women everywhere: draped over the divan, curling over the TV, straddling the gerbil cage.

'I'm going to work, just as soon as I've had a piss,' he muttered, and stomped down the corridor. Turning on a sudden impulse at the toilet door, he bit out the words, 'You need to clean this toilet, Andrei. It's your turn. I did it the last four times. I'm not doing it again!'

Andrei the *Svoloch* laughed, displaying two rows of stumpy yellow teeth, and pushed the schoolgirl back inside the red room, closing the door behind him with a hollow thud. Mitya pushed hard on the toilet door, and his nose connected with the back of his hand. It was locked, again.

'Son of a bitch.'

His swollen bladder would not be denied. The strain of keeping the pee in was bringing a film of sweat to his smooth upper lip. He had been periodically waiting to use the filthy toilet for over half an hour but every time he gave up

12

and went back to his room, the cursed toilet occupant would come lurching out and be replaced by another incontinent before Mitya could get back down the corridor. So now he had to wait, and risked leaning on the wall next to the violent alcoholic's door, his slim legs tightly bound together, hands clenching and unclenching. He hammered on the door again.

'Come out of there you stinking old tramp! I'm going to call the *skoraya* – you'll go to the dry tank!' Mitya really, badly, needed to pee.

The door opened slightly, and in the festering half-light a peachy soft face looked out at him, hesitantly. After a moment the door opened wider on its squealing hinges and out stepped, not the stinking old alcoholic with vomit down his chin, but an angel come to earth. Mitya gasped and felt a small pool of saliva collect in the corner of his mouth and then trickle gently on to his chin. He had never seen a girl so beautiful and so perfect. Blonde hair framed a delicate face with apple cheeks, a small freckled nose and eyes that seemed to stroke a place deep within his stomach. And here she was, in the stinking bog, with a twist of yellow toilet paper stuck to her perfect, peach-coloured plastic slipper.

'I'm sorry,' she lisped, looking up at him through gluey black lashes.

'No! Ah . . .' Mitya wiped his mouth with the back of his hand. 'I'm sorry, er, small female. Let me!' and he held the wobbling door open for her as she slid through the gap between it and his underarm. 'I didn't know . . . I thought you were the old man – from up the corridor. He spends . . . hours in the . . . smallest room.'

'Jesus, I'm surprised he's still alive,' joked the perfect angel with a wink.

Mitya felt something twang deep within him, like a ligament in his very soul stretching and snapping, never to be repaired. She turned slowly and swayed, tiny and ethereal, up the hallway towards the end room, and then hesitated, looking back at him from the doorway.

'Who are you, beautiful?' Mitya blurted, without meaning to make a sound, without knowing his mouth had opened, without giving his tongue permission to form any words at all.

'Katya,' she said, as if it was obvious, and she vanished behind the farthest door. The click of the latch struck Mitya like a punch in the face, and he gasped.

He took a long, slow piss and was struck by the thought that she, the angel, had been seated where his golden stream of warm pee was flying and foaming, just a few moments before. He shuddered and then, despite himself, leant down towards the toilet and could just make out a trace of her scent among the other odours rising from the dark bowl, the floor and the bin. Her scent, the musky scent of an angel, was subtle but powerful. Another hand rattling the door handle pulled him from his reverie. He pushed his way out of the cubicle, past the wobbly old man who roared something indecipherable but crushingly depressing at him, and made his way down the stairs and out to his van.

'That my life should come to this,' he thought, and aimed a ferocious kick at a passing tabby cat. He missed it by a wide margin and lost his balance for a moment, grabbing hold of the hedge to save himself and trying to ignore the muffled laughter bubbling from a bench behind it: a bench laden with small children and elderly hags, of course. 'Females, children: nothing but trouble. I've got my work,' he muttered to himself, and brushed the leaves from his shirt, ready to march off. As he did so, a butterfly bobbed up from the depths of the hedge and collided with his nose, making him flail slightly. Again muffled laughter scuffed his ears.

'What are you doing, sitting there, cluttering the place up? Haven't you got work to do?' he spluttered hoarsely over the hedge.

The babushkas looked at the small children and the small children looked at the babushkas, and then they all began giggling again, tears streaming down their cheeks.

'There, there, Mitya, on your way,' croaked a sun-kissed face pitted with tiny, shining eyes.

'Idiots. Geriatrics and idiots. You're no better than rats, laughing rats,' scolded Mitya, but not loud enough for his audience to hear. He turned on his heel towards the setting sun, and his shiny van that glinted in its rosy rays. The night was young.

2

The Azov House of Culture
Elderly Club

Galia smiled with quiet satisfaction as she finished making her way along the corridor, dishing out the steaming *vareniki* to her aged and tremulous neighbours. Xenia, hunched in the midst of a gallery of grainy pictures of her son, had been very happy to take the food. Galia had greeted the son as was expected, crossing herself in front of the little shrine devised in his memory and housed behind the television in Xenia's sitting room. Twenty years had passed, but the son's keys and school bag still lay on the cabinet in the hall, where he had last thrown them that day in July 1974 before heading off for the river, and adventures.

Next was poor Denis, with his huge bulbous nose and disfigured cauliflower ears, a bachelor of bear-like proportions. He disappeared into his apartment with Galia's offering and returned with a huge bunch of mottled grapes in exchange. Galia eyed the grapes and wondered what best use to make of them: they looked a little past their prime, but she accepted them gracefully. Baba Krychkova took the food with a little grumble about Goryoun Tigranovich and how selfish it was of him to go away and not tell her, and of course there was still no answer at Goryoun Tigranovich's door. The old Armenian was an enigma, and that was the way he liked it. There were rumours of gold, and foreign travel, and antique icons, and land deals in the Far East, but the thing was that no-one on the corridor really knew Goryoun Tigranovich at all. He gave out his vegetables and was always sober, polite and clean, but that was it. Galia wondered again whether she had been right to reassure Baba Krychkova that he was away. But it was true there had been no mewing of ridiculously fluffy white cats discernible from outside the door, and there certainly would have been if they hadn't been fed for a day or two. Galia had once seen them being fed when she popped in to exchange some garlic for a pineapple, and it had not been a pretty sight: the white cats turned in to beasts when food was involved. Anyway, it was best not to pry. The neighbour would re-appear when it suited him, or he would not.

Back in her kitchen, Galia clucked as she wiped down the plastic table top and put away her tools.

'Dog lady! Boroda! You want some fat? Come on, my lady, have a little fat, it'll help your eyes.' Galia cut small strips of grizzled mutton fat for the dog, whose eyes already shone like stars.

She laid down her knife and flopped down on her tiny stool for a moment, wiping her eyes with the corner of her apron. She observed the knife lying before her: it had been sharpened so many times the blade was now a thin arc, chilli-pepper sharp. Pasha had cut his thumb on it the day he bought it: that had brought steam to his ears. She had cleaned the wound with iodine and bound it with gauze, all the time him muttering under his breath. It had been during the funny time, when he was sick and not himself, not long before the end.

17

The half hour struck in a lazy, absent kind of way, and Galia pushed herself up from her stool. It was time for the Elderly Club. She gazed from the window out into the hot evening. She could hear laughter rising in the courtyard like bubbles in beer, and the sound of children playing. Every so often a shriek would escape the young fat girl on the bench: it'll come to no good, thought Galia, as she struggled to swat the mosquitoes dive-bombing her hair. Boroda made her way across the room and placed her muzzle gently into the corner of Galia's open hand. Galia looked down at the dog and smiled.

In the cool darkness of her bedroom, she stood in front of the wardrobe and picked out tonight's floral dress. The wardrobe contained four garments to choose from, each a different colour combination, but otherwise almost identical. This evening it would be the blue-and-white flowers, and the blue sandals over flesh-coloured pop socks. She would also take the white headscarf to keep the mosquitoes out of her hair. There was nothing like insects struggling in your hair to put you off your stride. Why had mosquitoes been created, she wondered, when their only purpose was to make other creatures miserable? But she mused only for a moment, the effort of getting her pop socks on over hot swollen ankles pushing the thought out of her mind.

Boroda, sensing it was time for Galia to go out, stood silently inside the front door, with her nose just touching it and her tail still, waiting to be let through. Then, jauntily balanced on her three legs, the dog wove her way along the corridor, down the stairs and out in to the courtyard, to sit a while under the bench and watch the children playing on the wide brown square of dry grass.

'Pyao! Pyao! Pyao! You're dead!'

Boroda made her way gingerly past the smaller, more unpredictable children and across the courtyard to the scruffy trees that hung over the swings. In a comfortably shady spot, she laid her head on her paw and twitched her long grey eyebrows. Sometimes, the children would make up a fidgeting circle around her under the tree and fashion her headdresses of wild olive leaves. She looked noble. She hoped they would stop the shooting and make her a headdress or two soon.

* * *

The lights, such as had bulbs in them, were burning brightly at the Azov House of Culture Elderly Club. The building itself was typical: concrete panelled, with large windows set high in cracked walls gazing on to parquet flooring, itself breaking away from its moorings. Forty-five women and two men, one of whom appeared not to be breathing, stood or sat at tables arranged around the walls of the central hall. At one end a plethora of spider plants hung from the top of a large serving hatch, trailing their grubby fingers across trays of moistureless biscuits, crackers and pretzels, such as could well be found on Mars. In the middle of the room, the host, chairman and general in charge, Vasily Semyonovich Volubchik, or Vasya to his friends, scrabbled through papers, dropped pens and stamped the all-important official membership cards.

Galia thought the Elderly Club was rather a waste of time but felt compelled to go, simply because she was old. There would be card games and tea, chess and arguments. And perhaps a talk on astrology or healthy eating, as if the old ones present didn't know what fate had in store for them, or what food might kill them. Galia handed her card over to be stamped, avoiding Vasya's enquiring eyes, and nodded to her old friend Zoya, whose hair had, on this occasion, turned out a violent shade of purple, and went to sit down in the corner.

'One moment, Galina Petrovna, my dear,' tolled Vasya like an old cracked bell. He was sorting through papers that kept falling from his fingers, splishing across the floor in great sheaves of hopelessness. Galia's lips pursed despite herself and her left eye twitched very slightly.

'Please, here is the agenda for this evening. I thought you might like to say a few words about cabbage root fly?'

'Really, Vasily Semyonovich? Why?'

'Vasya, call me Vasya – why stand on ceremony? We are old, and time is not our friend. We are old, so we must be best friends.'

Galia sighed at the well-worn, and totally un-entertaining, phrase. 'Very well – Vasya – but I gave a talk on cabbage root fly last spring, as I recall.'

'Yes, yes, my sister, so you did. But it is always worth reminding the people how to avoid this pest, don't you think? And I think we've had some new members join, and some depart, since then.'

Galia was not sure about any new members joining, but recalled, with a needle in the ribs from a sharp stab of missing, that a number of valued members had indeed departed.

'Yes, you are right, of course, Vasily Semyonovich.' Galia squashed the thought that all those present knew all there was to know about cabbage root fly with a firm thrust of the chin and a splash of smiling dignity. 'It will be my pleasure to speak about cabbage root fly, again.'

In truth, Vasya often asked her to speak on vegetable infection issues, and she was, although she would never admit it, quietly flattered. Vasya, for his part, considered that her talk on the Cockchafer beetle still rested in many a memory as the highlight of the Azov year, or even the decade. It had left a lasting impression on him.

He pressed a boiled sweet into her palm and a small sphere of spittle burst at the corner of his smile. She took her hand away sharply and, nodding quickly, made squarely for her seat. Through the long-closed window high above her head, she could see the pale moon rising in a blueberry sky, and vaguely wished she hadn't come. It would have been so much nicer to be at home with her comfortable slippers, the radio, a bowl of steaming *vareniki* and her Boroda curled up beside her. As she sat sucking the sweet, circling her ankles and nodding absently to the old, old lady welded to the chair next to her, a memory crept into her mind, as unwelcome as a cockroach under a toilet seat.

One moonlit evening, way back, she had done a very untypical thing. Pasha had walked out, just as she had turned to pour him more tea, it seemed to her, teapot poised in mid-air. Instead of finishing off both their dinners, she placed the teapot on the lino table cloth, put on her cardigan and shoes with shaking hands, and followed him. She could hear the repeat of his footsteps on the stairs, down the passage way, through the courtyard, then clicking briskly along the alley. Down through the old town centre she had crept, as best she could, feeling furtive but unable to stop, scuttling in her billowing summer dress, across the bridge, past the factory, out towards the flats on the east side of town. Once or twice she felt a hint of his tobacco or a lick of his hair cream clinging to the warm panels of the shops she passed: Grocery No. 5, Milk Products, Shoe Shop No. 1 . . . There was not another soul about. Evenings ended relatively early in Azov back then.

She was beginning to think that she had lost him, that he must in fact have turned off at the factory and simply hurried in to work with some important idea, or maybe an idea or two about one of the women there who wore trousers and smoked cigarettes, when a vague glinting up ahead, away to the right, caught her eye. She was on the very edge of town now, stolidly rustling forward. The half-hearted street lights had petered out 200 paces back, and only the moon lit her way. She made out the dim outline of a building site to her right, the great bulks of concrete panels stacked up like enormous playing cards. To her left lay dead fields, uncultivated, heaving, empty. She caught a vague snatch of words on the wind, and ducked down behind a dark pile of pipes. Something scuttled sharply in the heart of the pile and she recoiled with a startled gasp. With her heart beating in her ears like giant felt boots in the snow, she moved on carefully in her thin canvas shoes. The wind blew her a few words, and she recognized the speaker: it was Pasha, and he was answered by another voice. Was it a woman? Galia hadn't waited to find out. She had run home, afraid to come face-to-face with what-ever was out there on that summer night. The memory sent a shudder up Galia's backbone that travelled all the way to her eyes, making them prick with tears.

'So, Galina Petrovna, would you like to inform us of developments around cabbage root fly?' invited Vasya Volubchik. Galia was sitting staring at the moon, mouth open, eyes glazed. A silence thick as fog rolled over the crowd for several seconds, broken only by a vague slurping at the back of the room. Vasya began to fear a stroke. 'Galina Petrovna . . . Galia!' The urgent pitch of his voice finally broke in to Galia's reverie. The vision of Pasha and the building site melted and then crystallised into the faces of dozens of her fellow aged citizens, bright eyes burning into her as their rubbery gums sucked rainbows of boiled sweets into tongue-slitting shards: waiting. Galia met their eyes, and swallowed. 'Yes, Vasily Semyonovich!'

'A glass of water is required?'

'No, thank you, I'm quite all right. Just a little tired. I've been working today.'

'And the moon has a strange effect on all ladies, I am told?'

Galia twitched her lip, and took command of her faculties. She began her report, stumbling a little at first, but gradually building her case before the slumbering group. Vasya drew his chair nearer, and gazed at her from five feet away: his deafness brought him in to close proximity with ladies on a daily basis, and it was something he treasured and respected.

But Vasya was troubled: Galia looked pale, and less hearty than usual. The thought crossed his mind, as it often did, that what she needed was a man to look after her. A good, old man, a retired headmaster say, with a vegetable patch of his own, four grandchildren living more than seventy kilometres away, a fine Ural motorbike (1975 vintage) that ran like new, three pairs of good shoes, no bad habits, a lovely cat called Vasik, and at least five of his own teeth. Vasya, he was content to affirm, met all of these criteria.

But no matter how close he sat to Galina Petrovna, she didn't seem to notice him. She fed him scraps of attention, but rarely a direct look. She resisted all his advances. The flowers he had left outside her door had remained there for days, untouched. If he tried to take her hand to help her up

23

the kerb when they passed in town (he knew her routine quite well, and often managed to happen to be in the same place on the same day), she smiled but frowned simultaneously, and shooed him away with a quiet but firm tut. Once or twice he had made her genuinely angry, but he couldn't really say why. Her cheeks had flushed and her voice shook slightly as she chased him away, as if he were a cat doing its business among her broad beans. He had only been trying to help with hard work. But he couldn't be offended, and he couldn't give up.

He recognized that he was a man who needed to feel useful to a woman, and since his Maria had gone, he was at a loss as to what to do. His mastery of the House of Culture Elderly Club was, of course, a manifestation of being put to good use for women folk. And many of the women were sweetly grateful. He received bowls of fruit, and little cakes, and he never had to mend his own trousers. But the women who put on lipstick for him, and even sometimes wore sandals in summer, held no love interest for him. They were like sisters, or mothers, or even daughters. He didn't know why. A mystery of life, along with why vodka tasted so good with pickles but not with cress, and why there were no fish left in the river, not even little ones. A riddle, and a good one. Vasya sighed and rested his chin on his walking stick, enjoying the prickling of his white stubble against the old plastic handle, and the proximity of the untouchable Galia.

The oldest old woman stood up with a clearly audible creak, her mosaic brown face cracking open to produce a voice that rumbled up from her belly, or perhaps her boots, which were fashioned from the same stuff as her face. 'So, citizen, when will the drought be over?'

Galia blinked slowly, twice, before responding.

24

'*Babushka*, I do not know when the drought will be over. But if I hear, I will be the first to let you know.'

'This, this bourgeois capitalism! This is why we have a drought!'

Galia looked down at the papers in her hand and then at Vasya, who was staring at her, smiling vaguely, in a lopsided fashion. Stroke, thought Galia.

'Rubbish, crone!'

There was a rustle as forty-five heads turned slowly but urgently to take in the second speaker.

'Drought is punishment for all the years of godlessness!' the second oldest old woman rejoined, also creaking to a stand, her voice high, thin and piercing as a rusty violin in a bucket of vinegar. The recently slumbering majority heaved a collective sigh and shifted in their seats, sensing that their comfortable half hour was coming to an end.

'Citizens—' began Galia.

'There were no droughts under Brezhnev, bitch!'

'Now, ladies, now!' Vasya levered himself upright and knocked his stick on the parquet floor in an attempt to call order. No-one heard the noise, muffled as it was by the rubber tip, the collective years of hardened earwax, and the screeches and rumbles of the newly roused collective. 'Ladies, no! General discussion is not on the agenda. We haven't done the Lotto draw yet!'

Chairs scraped the floor as one after the other the members of the crowd rose to their feet, all the better to berate their neighbour. Knobbly fingers were thrust into ancient faces, and tongues that until five minutes ago had been thick with sleep were now roused to full war-cry and hullabaloo. Vasya, arms flailing, was engulfed in the onslaught, disappearing in a crush of bustling floral-clad flesh and grey hair. Galia subsided slowly into her chair with a sigh and took in the view at the window high above her head. The sky was now a deep black, hung with a moon sharp and cold as the silver arc of her peeling knife. She wished she hadn't come.

3

Mitya the Exterminator

Mitya didn't enjoy his job. No, that just wouldn't do it justice. You might enjoy an ice-cream or something trivial like that, where the feeling passes quickly and is mainly connected to your gut or some other swiftly satisfied desire, leaving you with sticky fingers and a dribbly chin, but rarely with any inner fulfilment. No, Mitya lived for his job. In fact, it wasn't a job at all. To him, as his boss observed with what Mitya felt was a somewhat insincere smile, it was a calling.

Some are called to the church to share God's word, give comfort to the sick, guidance to the sinners and enjoy the hospitality of old ladies, especially those who make good jam. And some are called to be medics, healing the sick, giving comfort to the incurable, and receiving gifts from thankful relatives when someone is helped ahead of the queue for testing, results and treatment. And some citizens, some are called to take up arms. Mitya classed himself among this latter group. He had willingly completed his national service after school and had, like many Soviet children, not really enjoyed it. The discipline wasn't a problem: Mitya enjoyed discipline, and a uniform, however ill-fitting and badly made. The food had not been a problem for him: he liked things plain. The bullying and cold had not got to him, and the military dentist had probably done him a favour by removing all those teeth. But it was the apparent pointlessness of the service that had caused him a problem. He had failed to be sent to Afghanistan: both he and his mother had been disappointed. He wrote to his divisional commander and asked why his unit was not going: there had been no response. So they had been stationed in the middle of the flat Russian steppe for two years, their only adversaries the drunken local peasants and huge clouds of mosquitoes that ruled the land from May to September.

So the army was not for him. He needed something more direct, a service he could provide locally, with immediate results, and which kept the streets clean of foreign bodies and pestilence. He became a defender of freedom from animal tyranny, a fighter against the disease and nuisance caused by flea-bitten scrag-end dogs: Mitya was a warrior against unauthorized canine infestations. Mitya could not abide a dog. Any dog he saw made Mitya feel sick, the bitter bile rising in his throat, catching at his tonsils, making him cough. But a stray dog: a stray dog made him really mad. A stray dog was an enemy of the state, an enemy of civilization: a personal enemy of Mitya. He contained his loathing through his job, and put his hatred to good use. Any stray in Azov had better be on the lookout: Mitya showed no mercy.

And as the great Soviet Union had finally fallen to pieces and was replaced by a patchwork of republics and autonomous regions, each one jostling the other, he found his own job became semi-autonomous, and he had more freedom to work as he saw fit. While he would never condone the black market, pernicious as it was, it offered up opportunities for armament and persuasion that had previously been out of the question for dog wardens. So, armed with his dog pole, throw net and Taser (not strictly standard issue, but an addition he felt was fully justified), he spent six evenings out of seven patrolling his jurisdiction in the Canine Control Van, or CCV. Mitya was the best Exterminator this side of Kharkov. And the town of Azov relied on him to keep canine vermin at bay, even if they didn't know it.

This evening, warm and sweet-smelling as only an industrial town on a river in August can be, Mitya was targeting the west side of town, the old quarter, which took in a lot of important staging posts and was always a good hunting ground. His van oiled slowly around the areas beloved of stray dogs: the collage of kiosks selling books, gum, porn, dried fish, vodka and music boxes; the back of the market, where huge bins of rotting mush drew crowds of dogs like flies, with flies as big as bears buzzing around their squirming sores; and the waste-ground outside the shabby church, strewn with begging crones and bones flung down by do-gooders for the dogs that prowled around the old women, and sometimes took a crafty bite out of them when God wasn't looking.

Mitya started the evening at the kiosks and worked his way around in a clockwise direction. He was swift with his pole: a talented snatcher. He never took on a whole pack. He would observe a group of dogs from a distance and then pick off the weaker specimens one by one as they got distracted and separated. The only way to deal with a whole pack would be by using a stun-grenade or poisonous gas, neither of which was currently approved by the state for dog-warden use, to Mitya's chagrin. The evening was warm, and Mitya's skin became wet and sour beneath his close-fitting trousers and regulation shirt. He pulled the van over and took a wet-wipe from his black plastic-leather bum-bag. It was important to try to remain clean and fresh. Mitya had no idea how doggy he smelt. No-one except Andrei the *Svoloch* ever told him, probably because Andrei the *Svoloch* was the only person he regularly came in to contact with.

With four matted mongrels already caged and whining in the back, Mitya spotted a lone dog, thin and lank, sitting in a square just off Engels Street on the corner with Karl Marx Avenue. Lone dogs were bad news: even their own canine kind could not stand them. A group of children played nearby. Mitya's stomach quivered: the dirty dog was salivating, panting like an animal, preparing to savage one of the innocents, there and then. It was Mitya's duty to spare the child and bring the dog to justice.

'Master and servant,' whispered Mitya as he dropped the used wet-wipe into a plastic bag he kept in the van specifically for this purpose, and sprang quietly on to the pavement. He took a few steps into the square and concealed himself behind a set of bins, resting his mini-binoculars on the rim, the better to observe his quarry. He watched, while the dog licked its forepaw, and he blinked, confused: the animal appeared to be a tri-ped.

'Excuse me?' a female voice behind him made him jump and drop his mini-binoculars into the open bin with a soft clunk.

'Christ! Look what you've done!' Mitya thrust his arm into the bin after the binoculars. His fingers came into contact with slime, grit, and soft-boiled cabbage and he winced. He pulled out his hand and turned on the owner of the voice.

'Oh! It's you!' He put his dirty hand behind his back and tried to wipe off his fingers on the edge of the metal

30

bin. It was the angel from the smallest room, Katya. His gaze bounced off the golden hair crowning her head and rested for a moment on her toes, which peeped out from a pair of slightly dog-eared wedge sandals. He found himself imagining his tongue curling around them, and bit on his free knuckle.

'Oh, I'm sorry! I didn't realize you were . . . what were you doing, actually?'

'I'm working, female citizen.' Mitya aimed for clipped tones, and tried not to look at the curve of her jeans.

'Oh, you can call me Katya, you know. You asked so nicely, after all.'

Mitya felt the skin on his face and neck flush hot red, and almost stuttered his response, 'Yes, but I'm working, and you made me drop my binoculars.'

'Oh shucks, I am sorry.' The girl looked genuinely contrite, her brown eyes large and serious.

'It's OK. They're only the regulation ones. Not the special night-vision ones.'

'Ooh, night-vision binoculars. Wow! Are you spying on those grannies over there?'

'No, I am not.'

'What have they done? Are you in the *Spetznaz*?'

'No, of course I'm not in the *Spetznaz*—'

'But I suppose you wouldn't be able to tell me if you were!' She smiled at him and winked in her lopsided way.

'I'm not in the *Spetznaz*, Katya. Look, I'm busy right now. What do you want?'

'Oh, it's nothing really. To be honest, I just wanted to talk to you.'

'Why?'

'Well, I'm new in town, and I don't really know anyone, except my cousin, and I like to chat. You know, just chat.

And I know you – sort of. And I was just curious about what you were doing sneaking around like that—'

'I wasn't sneaking around.'

'And you remind me of someone.'

'Who?'

'I'm not sure. But it'll come to me.' Katya smiled self-consciously and scraped her sandal across the corner of the flower bed, watching intently as the dry earth broke like brown sugar over her toes. She looked up and caught Mitya's stare.

'Look, I just wanted to know if you could tell me how to get to the cinema?'

'The cinema?' Mitya asked flatly, his face blank.

'Yes, the cinema. I've never been and I'm having a bit of trouble finding it. I've been round this block at least three times and no sign. But the tourist map says it should be here. Look – see?' She leant towards Mitya and pointed to a blob on the badly reproduced map that was supposed to represent the location of the cinema. He observed her golden hair and the way the streetlight picked up slight reddish tones in it around her ears and the nape of her neck.

'Ooh, what's that smell?' she squealed, looking up suddenly, her golden head nearly colliding with Mitya's nose.

'Sewers!' Mitya bit out, jumping back to a safer distance. 'It's always the sewers, and the bins. Look, I've never been to the cinema, but I can tell you that it is that way.' Mitya indicated the boulevard to their left with a slightly shaking finger. 'Your map is clearly out of date. Or maybe you've got it upside down – I hear women often do that. Now, I have important work to do, so, please be on your way.'

Katya looked him up and down slowly, her eyes seeming to reach into every nook and crevice of his body, through his clothes. Mitya shuddered slightly and again felt his skin flush.

'OK, thank you. But you should go to the cinema some time. They have some good films these days. You could learn a lot! Oh, and,' she stepped towards him slightly, leaning in conspiratorially, 'your flies are undone, soldier!' With a tinkling laugh and a wink she turned and ambled off up the boulevard, her hands swinging slightly, everything about her looking light and fresh and clean and happy.

Mitya yanked up his flies with his sticky hand and for a few seconds watched her progress up the street, wishing he had his binoculars: the binoculars that were languishing in the bottom of the rancid bin. He turned to examine the square: the dangerous tri-ped was still sitting there and the children were still in danger. He turned for one final glance at Katya's receding backside, and then stared at the patch of earth disturbed by her tiny, perfect foot a minute ago. There was nothing else for it: he was going to have to retrieve his equipment.

'Hey, you, Citizen Child!' he called out to a small boy playing under a bench on the edge of the square. 'I've got a task for you. I'll give you five roubles if you'll get my binoculars out of this bin.' He pointed to the bin.

'Get them yourself, stinky!' replied the small boy, before running off to find his *babushka*.

Mitya sighed, and cautiously set about climbing into the bin.

* * *

Ten minutes later, like a cabbage-encrusted stay-pressed sheriff from the old Wild West, Mitya loped into the court-yard towards the dog, his pole over one shoulder and a few

33

streaks of pork fat in the opposite hand. He had egg stains on his trousers and something unmentionable sticking to the sole of his left shoe, but he didn't care: the binoculars were again his, and now he was fully primed to bag this three-legged son-of-a-bitch.

'Here doggie doggie doggie!' he called in a strange, soft, high-pitched voice.

The children on the swings looked up at Mitya's approach. Old ladies buried their stories mid-grumble and sucked in their gums, while the little ones at their feet moved back, their snot-sticky fingers forgotten half-way between nose and mouth. Masha, the tallest and the leader of the gang, stopped stirring her dirt pie and dropped the stirring stick back on to the dusty ground, hands hanging by her sides, watching. The Exterminator's steps were unhurried, taking him gently over the ground that separated him and the dog in his sights.

'That dog isn't stray,' said Masha, bravely.

'Hush, Citizen Child. This dog has no collar.' Mitya stepped forward, and extended his hand towards the canine.

'Yes, but she's not a stray,' she persisted, doubt and fear making her voice wobble slightly, and she frowned.

'Yes, she's right – this dog is no stray!' Baba Krychkova broke in.

'It has no collar. It is illegal. And it is dangerous.' Mitya approached ever nearer, moving carefully, his feet barely making a sound.

'But she belongs to Galina Petrovna!'

'No, little girl: it belongs to me.'

Boroda, who had been dozing with the scent of wild olive all around her, woke with a start and peered up at the stranger moving slowly towards her. She felt an odd sort of twinge: she sensed pork fat, mixed with a riot of

34

other scents that made her hair stand on end. But the pork fat was the strongest, in fact somewhat overpowering. The hand that reached out to her was relatively clean and calm and sure, the finger-nails short. She hesitated, and heard a strange chorus of barking from somewhere nearby but closed off. She couldn't make it out: her hearing wasn't as good as it had been as a pup. The hair on her back was still raised, her spine tingling, but she felt safe here in the courtyard, with the old ladies and the children. She inspected the stranger more closely as best she could in the dusk. She sensed no vodka or big sticks, and he certainly didn't appear drunk. And people with pork fat were generally good, weren't they?

4

A Chase

The shrieking at the House of Culture peaked to a crescendo that threatened to crack the windows and then died down slowly, somewhat like a fire ripping through several shops and an old people's home, consuming everything in its path but now reducing to glowing embers, every so often expelling a mouthful of acrid yellow sparks and fizzes of burning fat. Vasya had corralled the oldest old woman and her gang to one side of the hall with the promise of tea and cards and the strategic positioning of some folding chairs, while the second oldest old woman and her hangers-on were hemmed in on the opposite side, being plied with biscuits and soothed with spider plants. In the middle, there was a floating ridge of ladies who had no interest in politics, history or rain, and they presided over an uneasy peace. Vasya congratulated himself on having restored some sort of order and felt the chances of successfully bringing off the Lotto draw were now not worse than evens.

As calm was restored within the hall and relative quiet ensued, a row of barking dogs broke out like sniper fire, far off on a distant river bank, giving the breeze a sharp and threatening edge as it drifted over the town. Galia, dishing out biscuits and helpful tuts and sighs to the ladies who hated Communism, hesitated mid-flow on hearing the noise. It was a good thing that Boroda was at home under the table, out of the way of those packs of stray dogs. She recalled the mutts she had seen that day outside the railway station: wild and toothy with matted fur and dripping backsides. She collected herself, and asked if anyone had any further questions about the cabbage root fly.

As she sat down after batting away a vague concern over the use of pesticides – all methods of defence must be considered – a chill ran through her as she remembered that Boroda was not locked inside the flat, but was out in the courtyard. The noise of the dogs was continuing, getting louder and then dipping away again, making no sense, like troublesome conversations in a bad dream. During a lull in the barking, the sleeping man, utterly peaceful until that point and marooned in the middle of the room, suddenly awoke with a cry and slipped from his chair on to the floor with an ominous, muffled crack. A furore of clucking broke out as twelve old ladies around him sprang from their perches to circle him like flapping chickens, or perhaps well-meaning vultures. The old man groaned as he was put in the recovery position by an old lady who had been a grocer, and then turned around and put in a different recovery position by an old lady who had been a nurse. An old lady who had been a construction worker was just about to have a go herself when Galia joined the fray, offering to straighten the old man's leg if he bit on a metal spoon. His other leg was raised, and lowered, and raised again by the construction worker, as an old lady who had been a teacher tried to get everyone else to sit down and listen to her instructions. No-one listened to Galia's offer to straighten the leg apart from Vasya, who begged her to be patient for a few moments while the construction worker attempted to find out which bit of the old man, if any, needed straightening. Galia stood by the Chairman's desk and, with nothing else she could helpfully do at that moment, selected a red boiled sweet from the bowl in front of her and popped it into her mouth. The concentrated sweetness made her gold teeth ache, but still, it was sweet.

'Turn him over!' bellowed the construction worker.

'Nooo!' groaned the old man, who Galia now recognized as Petya, who used to be around six foot six and had been an engineer: quite high up, and once very athletic. A broad, tall, dependable man, who now lay on the floor being re-arranged by a gaggle of hens.

'Citizens, perhaps we should wait for the *skoraya*? Has anyone called them? I say, has anyone called an ambulance?' Galia shouted over the melee, but there was no discernible response. She made her way out of the room, down the grand marble staircase and over to the reception desk, where a lady in a bobble hat sat knitting a blanket. 'Please call for an ambulance, Alicia Nikolaevna, there has been an accident.'

'An accident? Another one? What do you old birds do up there? That's the third time this summer!'

'Please just call the ambulance, Alicia Nikolaevna. There is a man in pain, and he needs help.'

'And it's always the men, isn't it? Why is it always the men? What do you do to them up there? Poor old Afanasy Albertovich last month, wasn't it?'

'Yes, that was most unfortunate, but please – just get on the phone, Alicia Nikolaevna.'

'I've not seen him since, you know! No-one has!'

Galia gave the door keeper a stern look, for several seconds. 'Alicia Nikolaevna, the phone—'

'Yes, yes, I'm doing it! I've just got to finish this line.'

Galia thumped her hand on the desk with a gravity that surprised both of them. The other woman slowed her knitting, completed a stitch and put it down with an exasperated sigh.

'Some old people should know their places!' Alicia Nikolaevna shrilled as she reached for the phone.

Galia strode back up the grand marble staircase with purposeful steps. Just as she reached the top, the big metal doors at the front of the building clattered open and a stampede of small feet slapped their way across the grand hallway in an awful hurry and made straight for the staircase.

'Stop, no children allowed in here! Get out!' cried Alicia Nikolaevna, jumping up from her chair and dropping the knitting and the phone to the floor.

The children slowed and glanced at her briefly, but on spying Galia at the top of the stairs surged forward again en-masse.

'Baba Galia, Baba Galia! It's terrible! Come quick! Something terrible has happened!'

Galia's jaw sagged slightly, and she wished she hadn't wished for more excitement at the Elderly Club.

'What, children?'

'He's taken Boroda!'

'Who? What are you talking about?'

'The dog van! The Exterminator! He's taken Boroda!'

'We told him she wasn't wild, but he took her with the others anyway, and put her in the van.'

'He said she hadn't got a collar on, so she must be wild. He said it's the law!'

39

'She left her headdress behind, Baba Galia! I found it in the street! Look!'

'Shut up you idiot, what does that matter? They're going to gas her!'

'No, they're going to shoot her. That's what he said.'

'No, he said they would exterminate her by all means necessary.'

Galia looked at the broken leafy headdress, her mouth open. She felt her knees buckle and dropped the metal spoon she'd been clasping for the last five minutes down the concrete steps, the sound reverberating off the marble like a mad church bell. Her kneecaps cracked on the floor where they hit, the goodly layer of flesh not enough to cushion them, and even Alicia Nikolaevna looked up from her desk with a flash of sharp interest on her face.

'Baba Galia, are you ill? You must get up and run after the van!' one of the children cried as they tugged at her shoulder.

Galia could not speak. In the deep black night enveloping the building, they heard the faint imprint of a howl as a rattling engine passed by a couple of streets away.

Vasya Volubchik let the old man's head drop with a soft thunk when he saw Galia, out on the landing, drop to her knees. This was not good. The old man would have to be left to the women. Vasya hobbled over to the door and stood hovering gently, unsure where to begin.

'Galia my dear, what's the matter? Are you ill?'

'No, *Dedya* Vasya, Boroda has been taken away by the exterminator van! They are going to gas her! She will be eaten by the wild dogs and then gassed!' Masha, the tallest and boldest, started to cry.

'My goodness, is this true?'

The children nodded vigorously, all of them now sniffling and dripping like leaky buckets.

'Galia, there is no time to waste, why are you on your knees? Get up, get up, woman!' Vasya gripped Galia's shoulders and looked into her face. He always thought this moment would be full of joy, to touch her and gaze into her eyes. But alas, it stopped him short and made his heart thump in a most unpleasant way. Because for a moment, his Galia was lost: the dependable, stolid woman had disappeared and been replaced by a frightened child dressed up as a haggard old lady with death in her eyes and her mouth wide open.

'Galia, listen to me: don't despair. Even if the Exterminator has got Boroda – and we don't know that for certain – it's not without hope. We can go after him! And, and even if that fails, I know where he lives, that Mitya the Exterminator. We can find him! Now is no time to sit on the floor. Look – the old ladies are looking at you; they think you've lost your reason!'

And indeed, the coven had, as one, ceased to minister to the old man with the broken hip, and were gathered, goggle eyed, at the doorway, watching Galia minutely, while the old man took up groaning again and pleading for a nip of vodka, or a swift death.

'But it's too late, Vasya, she's gone. She's in the van already.'

'We can chase him down! Listen. My bike is just outside. I've been tuning it all day. It's running like a dream and ready for anything. We can do it, Galia!'

And with the help of the children gathered around him, together they levered Galia upright, dusted her down and jostled her down the steps, through the clattering metal doors and out into the darkened street. At the kerb, Vasya's ancient but gleaming Ural motorbike and sidecar waited, a vision of polished chrome and blood-red paintwork.

'Get in, woman, get in!'

Galia held the ends of her headscarf close to her chin and eyed the gleaming motorbike and its deep, narrow sidecar. She knew she would never fit. Her brows drew together, and then she spoke.

'You get in, Vasya.'

She caught Vasya's eye, and held it. 'I'll drive. It's the only way.' Vasya looked from bike to woman to sidecar and back to woman, and then at his shoes. She was right.

'OK, but follow my instructions.'

'But of course, Vasily Semyonovich.'

'Listen!' cried Masha. They froze, Vasya with one foot the size of a tennis racket in the sidecar, Galia with skirt hitched above her knee, the rosy flesh oozing delicately over the top of her pop sock. The wind carried vague hints of sound, a scrap of a rasping engine, a hint of muffled furry fury which could have been the noise of a dozen wild dogs, maybe in a van, maybe in a tin can buried underground. Maybe in hell.

'That way!' shrieked Masha, flinging her right arm wildly into the air. 'Go! Save the dogs!'

Vasya folded his stiff legs in front of him in the sidecar as Galia hitched up her floral skirt still higher and, with an ease that Vasya couldn't help noticing, straddled the bike. A sandaled foot kick-started the faithful engine and then, headscarf and frizzy hair streaming in the wind, she increased the revs and took off after Mitya the Exterminator's van.

Across the bridge and the blackened oily river, past the factory, out to the flats on the new side of town they sped. Galia hadn't ridden a motorbike for at least thirty years, but after the first couple of minutes and a rather hair-raising bend or two, she discovered that it was, indeed, just like riding a bike. Vasya kept a beady eye on both her gear changing and her speed, while also trying to make out the lights of Mitya the Exterminator's van in front of them, and the exact texture of the pink flesh that was oozing at him oh-so-beautifully from the top of Galia's pop sock.

Vasya was aware at this moment that he was a truly modern man, in every sense: not only had he allowed the woman to drive, but he could multi-task, even in a dangerous and unusual situation like this. He congratulated himself, briefly, before the discomfort of being thrown violently forward and his nose coming into close contact with his knees concentrated his mind on other matters, such as the blood spots on his trousers.

Every so often they pulled over to ask teenagers snogging on benches or sniffing glue to tell them which way the Exterminator had gone. Everyone knew his van. When they reached the newest new flats, they glimpsed the van's red lights for the first time, meandering through the suburbs, looking for dogs to make disappear. Their eyes met for a moment, and then they surged onward. Hearing nothing over the roar of the engine and seeing nothing apart from those twin red lights, they gradually reeled them in, getting closer, starting to make out the back of the van through the thickening dark.

'Look out!' Vasya shrieked and Galia squeezed the brakes as hard as she could, as a shoddy-looking ambulance careering in the opposite direction zig-zagged towards them across the middle of the road, siren blaring. The bike skidded crazily and came to a stop just short of the ambulance, side on. Galia panted as the grim faces of the paramedics, sucking on roll-ups on the front seat, grazed past her nose. They were near enough to touch: no, near enough to kiss, and she could smell the interior of the vehicle. Formaldehyde and aspic. 'Kiss of death,' muttered Galia with a shudder as she re-started the engine, nodded to Vasya whose face was now the colour and texture of lumpy sour milk, and roared away.

There was no sign of the van. Galia revved the engine and sped along the nameless, characterless streets, past huge blocks of flats with dark windows like empty eye sockets. She had no idea where they were. A cold sweat replaced the hot sweat and she felt the blood drain from her face: there was no sign of them. The long, straight road was thoroughly empty. Seconds ticked by and she felt tears begin to sting the backs of her eyelids. She'd lost them.

She was about to pull over when Vasya grabbed her arm with shaking fingers and pointed to a turning to the right. Galia tutted, and muttered to herself, but followed his instruction.

'You old idiot, why would they have gone in there? That's just . . .' She trailed off, and pulled the bike up behind a stack of street bins. The van had pulled in to a courtyard between tower blocks that seemed to have become derelict without ever having been finished. She could see vague movements in the mottled darkness.

'Vasya, how did you know they had come in here, do you have special powers?' Galia hissed. She wasn't any more superstitious than most Russian women, but the old man's insight had intrigued her.

'Ha, you women, you're all the same. If a man knows something you don't, he must be psychic.'

Galia snorted quietly and attempted to dismount the bike with something like dignity, but found it a lot harder than jumping on had been. Vasya disengaged his legs from under his chin and felt the blood returning painfully to his feet. He couldn't attempt to get out just yet; he knew he'd fall flat on his nose if he did.

Galia began to creep around the bins and into the court-yard to observe the van from a safe distance.

'Galia, wait for me! Don't attempt anything on your own!' Vasya swung his feet to the ground and levered himself into a vertical position, but wasn't able to walk.

'Keep your voice down, you old fool!' chided Galia, still unhappy at being laughed at.

'I know his mother.'

'What do you mean, you know his mother?'

'I know his mother. The Exterminator's mother. And when he started coming out this way, I guessed.'

'What did you guess?' Galia was becoming exasperated.

'I guessed what Mitya the Exterminator wanted. After a busy night killing dogs, what would any good exterminator want? He'd want to go to his mother's apartment for some washing and some *kasha*. It's what any man would want, surely?'

Galia was just about to respond with some choice words when the rear doors of the van were flung open and a cacophony of howling smashed the night air to flea-bitten pieces. Vasya reached the spot where Galia stood, grimacing at the noise filling the courtyard.

'What are we going to do now, Galia?' asked Vasya with a hopeful half-smile.

'We're going to get my dog back,' Galia retorted, and marched, as well as her still-bent and swollen knees would allow her, across the broken ground towards the back of the van. Vasya sighed, words of reply flapping uselessly on his tongue like carp on a dry river bed, and hobbled after her.

'You have stolen my dog!'

'Wha—?' Mitya the Exterminator had been singing under his breath 'yorr awn, personal dzhezuz' while removing dog excrement from his boot and his ear with a special knife he kept for that purpose. The dogs were still in cages in the back of the van and he had been mulling over how to ensure that the perpetrator of said excrement never forgot his vengeance in what was to be left of its short life. The sudden appearance beside him of a solid-looking old woman with bent knees and laddered pop socks, shouting throatily and shaking her fists, was both unwelcome and unsettling.

'You have stolen my dog!'

Mitya sensed that she was angry, and possibly crazy: why else would she be worried about a dog?

'Who are you, mad woman?' he asked, his face twisting under eyes that popped with either fear or hatred, Galia was unsure which.

'You have stolen my dog!' Galia tried again, finally straightening her legs, although somewhat tentatively. The noise of the dogs in the back of the van filled her head with the sounds of nightmares. Among the howling, barking and growling, she could make out the sound of Boroda, crying softly.

'Citizen, let me explain,' said Mitya the Exterminator softly, 'all the dogs I take have no owner. It follows, therefore, that your dog is not with me.' Mitya put his excrement knife back in his bum-bag and turned his back on the old woman with funny knees. He hoped she would now disappear as quickly as she had appeared. She gave him the creeps. And he had unfinished business to attend to.

'You have stolen my dog! She's grey and has three legs and a small, pointy beard, and she is in the back of your van! I can hear her. Boroda! Boroda! I'm here, darling! Don't worry; we'll get you out, *lapochka*!'

Mitya smiled slightly to himself. The three-legged dog had been a very easy catch, once he'd got out of the bin.

'Citizen Old Woman, I only take stray dogs, diseased dogs. Dogs that should not be. I never take a dog with a collar. And your dog must have a collar, if it is genuinely your dog. So it cannot be in my van.'

'No. You don't understand—'

'Has your dog got a collar, Elderly Citizen?'

'No.'

There was a pause in the barking and growling, a silence filled only by the sound of Vasya panting as he made his way across the courtyard. He finally reached them and leant against the side of the van to catch his breath. Mitya the Exterminator turned to Galia and smirked.

'No collar? Then Citizen Old Woman, you have no dog. You need to familiarise yourself with the legislation, perhaps. End of discussion.' Mitya turned away to deal with the dogs.

'No, she is my dog. She lives with me. Boroda! Boroda!'

'No, Citizen, it is a stray. As set out in Presidential Decree No. 32 of 1994, Section 14, paragraph 3.2 – go home and read it.'

'So you admit you've got my dog? You scoundrel!'

'Now, now, Galia, my dear, I am sure Mitya, I mean the Exterminator, is a reasonable man. Maybe we could recompense you for the return of the lady's dog? We'd be happy to make a donation to any charity you'd care to name, or to cover any personal costs.' Vasya squeezed a wad of worn bank notes from his pocket and fanned them out for Mitya the Exterminator to see. Enough for some vodka and the dried fish to go with it, Vasya thought.

Mitya stared at the money for two seconds and then glanced into Vasya's face, his nostrils flaring as if the stench of dog had finally sliced into his olfactory nerves. 'No, Citizen . . . Volubchik, I don't want your money. I enjoy my job

47

– do you understand? Not everyone is motivated by money, even in these days of "freedom" and "democracy".'

Vasya began to stutter a response, but the Exterminator cut across him.

'No, Elderly Citizen! These dogs have no place in freedom and democracy. These dogs are strays, and they are unhygienic. And I will deal with them. It is my service. Now go home.'

'No, please!' Galia stepped purposefully between Mitya the Exterminator and the van. Mitya thought about shoving the old citizen roughly away, but the thought of having to touch her made his stomach shrivel. He decided that the non-standard issue Taser might be the best weapon for this particular job. Vasya gasped as he saw the Exterminator's hand reach for his holster, and made a dash, on legs still coming to life, to protect Galia.

Galia saw Vasya launch himself at her at the same moment as Mitya the Exterminator fumbled with a holster. She felt afraid, but didn't know why. Surely he wasn't going to shoot her?

A second later a screech as if from Baba Yaga herself ripped through the night. All three protagonists froze, with fear squeezing each and every heart. Only Mitya seemed to know the likely source of the chilling wail, and his head jerked towards the entrance to the flats. In a flash, a tiny old woman with a bristling chin and a brightly coloured headscarf darted out of the stairwell with something gleaming raised above her head. It took Galia a second or two to work out what it was: a sickle.

'Go to hell you son of a bitch!' she screeched in a pitch so high it set all the neighbourhood dogs off as she lunged at Mitya the Exterminator with a wicked, slashing motion. Galia and Vasya ducked on instinct, but the old woman hadn't even seen them. Her terrible eyes tracked the Exterminator alone.

'No!' he shouted, backing away, hands outstretched.

'Murdering bastard, get out of here!' Again she lunged, and the Exterminator lost his footing slightly, backing away, scrabbling like a chicken about to lose its head.

'Mother, no! Drop the sickle! It's me, Mitya! I've come for some washing!'

Vasya and Galia stared at each other, dumbfounded for a moment, unable to take in the spectacle of David and Goliath that was unfolding in front of them as the tiny woman chased Mitya the Exterminator around the courtyard, screeching like a banshee with the sickle held high over her head.

A chorus of barking from the back of the van reminded Galia that she'd come here to do more than just gawp at suburban madness. Pulling the van's battered doors wide, she peered into the murk, her ears ringing. Inside she could make out a patchwork of small cages, each stacked on the other, each housing a miserable dog, each miserable dog just a blur of heaving fur interspersed with white teeth that flashed in the moonlight. Hardly daring to touch the nearest cage, which wobbled about as if on its own accord, she spotted Boroda near the back, small and scared. Galia began to claw out the other cages one by one, placing them on the ground as gently as she could while also withdrawing her hands from the feel of claw and drool as quickly as possible. The stench of the stray dogs caught in her throat and she coughed and gagged as the cages came out.

At last she reached Boroda and heaved out the cage. Glancing over her shoulder to make sure Mitya the Exterminator was still thoroughly occupied with what was apparently his

49

mother; she tugged back the bolt and grabbed the shivering dog.

'What about these poor wretches, Galia?' Vasya pointed to the vibrating cages and their contents, strewn about the courtyard floor. 'What shall we do with these? We can't just leave them!'

'Do as you think best, Vasya, I can only care for my dog!' Galia replied over her shoulder, running for the motorbike with Boroda in her arms. 'Just do it quickly, for heaven's sake!'

Vasya looked at the miserable cages and their frenetic contents, and decided quickly. Moving them roughly round so that all the cage doors faced in the same direction, he grabbed the Exterminator's bag of fat bits from the back of the van, strew them on the ground in a brief trail leading away from him, and then, leaning over the cages from behind, drew back all the bolts and flung the doors as wide as he could. Without waiting to look, he then took to his heels and, with an energy he hadn't felt since the previous decade, hobbled unevenly across the courtyard to where Galia waited for him on the motorbike.

Galia folded Vasya back in to the sidecar and placed the terrified dog in his lap. She felt like a girl again, a feeling she could almost taste, which rose from the pit of her stomach all the way up: she had outwitted the enemy and might live forever, or just till tomorrow . . .

As they turned a wide arc to return to town, Vasya glimpsed Mitya the Exterminator falling backwards down the cellar steps into the bowels of the building, the raving old woman following close behind, the moonlight licking the edge of her sickle as it crested above her head. Towards them heaved a pack of stray dogs, howling and yapping and hungry for vengeance. Vasya felt his stomach turn over, and turned his head away. Some things were probably best quickly forgotten.

5

A Visit

'You say you know his mother?'

Galia threw the question over her shoulder.

Vasya Volubchik was finally seated on a stool at her kitchen
table, a place he had often yearned to be, but the circum-
stances this evening were far from how he had envisaged
such a visit. His legs ached like he had been kicked by an
apoplectic mule, so much so that Galia had had to half carry,
half drag him up the stairs to her apartment. The evening's
upsetting events had effectually driven all thoughts of
romance, chivalry and honour from his mind. He felt a bit
low, a bit stupid, and really rather old.

'Yes, we were quite friendly, a long time ago. She was a
happy little thing, bright as a button. She was always smiling,
singing, dancing. She helped out at my school for some years.'
Vasya's green eyes became filmy, like still ponds in bloom,
and Galia turned away again to frown at her hands as she
filled the kettle. A small, semi-stifled tut escaped her, despite
herself.

'And that was his mother we saw tonight?' Galia gave
him a sideways glance, one grey eyebrow raised.

'Yes.' Vasily's gaze skimmed the floor, and a slight movement in his papery, transparent eyelids suggested that a little drop of moisture was escaping from each eye. Galia sighed and set the chipped enamel kettle on the stove. Her match lit the gas with a comforting pop and they sat in silence, save for the soft hiss of the burning blue flame and the occasional bumbling drone of a late-night, sleepy mosquito.

'Vasily Semyonovich, I have to say, she didn't seem very happy to me tonight. In fact, she seemed—'

'Yes, she appears to have changed somewhat since I knew her. I believe grief has a lot to do with it.' Vasya cut her off, his tone a little clipped. Galia looked up sharply: she wanted to know more.

'Grief?'

'Oh, it's not an interesting story, Galia, really it isn't. Surely you are already familiar with it?'

Galia shook her head. 'I don't know the lady at all. She must keep over at the East Side.'

'It was just a little small-town heart break, you know. Her husband ran off, a long time ago, and her son is a big disappointment, obviously. That's the long and the short of it.' Vasya harrumphed for a moment or two and sniffed, folded his lopsided glasses into his shirt pocket and daintily blotted his nose on the back of his index finger. Then, carefully rolling up his trousers to knee height, he pursed his ancient lips and began tending to his shins with Galia's proffered iodine and cotton wool. Delicate blobs of green appeared on his dry skin, like moss on wintery silver birches. The pain was making him snappy, Galia thought, and the red blood spots on his trousers, now turning to a rusty brown, were also adding to his bad mood. She toyed with the thought of washing them for him, but the realization that he would be sitting in her kitchen for half the night

53

with those shins on show quickly changed her mind. She felt bad for him, but she knew where to draw the line.

'Have you heard about Goryoun Tigranovich?' Vasya looked up from his sorry shins to pose the question.

'What do you mean?'

'He's disappeared, apparently. Something to do with some questionable business with oil wells out east, I heard.'

'Oh nonsense, Vasily Semyonovich! He's gone on holiday that is all. You shouldn't believe everything that every gossipy old bird tells you, you know.'

Vasya returned his attention to his shins, and Galia felt guilty for snapping.

'Who did her husband run off with?'

'Whose husband?'

'Mitya the Exterminator's mother's, of course.'

'Oh, that. Not who, what.'

'What?'

'Exactly! Apparently, he took their entire potato harvest, a year's stock of jam, a pig, a quart of home brew and three sacks of onions. She never got over it. It affected her mind.'

'Yes, I can imagine,' Galia said quietly. She passed Vasya a cup of black tea with raspberry jam huddled in the bottom of it. The cup bore the legend 'Stalingrad – Hero City 1945!' and was one of Galia's favourites. She then lowered herself on to her stool near the fridge. When the weather was this close, and all clothes felt like warm wet sheets binding her body, she liked to sit with the fridge door open and her shoulders resting on a flannel draped over the ice box. It was usually infinitely refreshing, although this evening the frost hardly seemed to reach her tired, if not fried, nerve endings.

'Did that have an effect on . . . on . . . the Exterminator, Mitya?'

'I really don't know, Galia. He was a delight as a toddler,

I seem to recall. A cheeky, happy child – quite outgoing really. But ever since school age, well, seven or eight, he's been very odd. I remember he was always pulling the wings off butterflies and cutting up caterpillars and snipping worms into pieces . . . and brusque with his fellow learners, terribly taciturn. I thought maybe he'd become a scientist, and I did try to push him in that direction when he was small, but alas, it was not to be.'

'You taught him then, Vasya?'

'No, not directly. He was in the school, but not my class, it was just . . .' Vasya trailed off and contemplated the floor in silence for some moments, his face grim. Galia sighed and took in the vibrating, hairy moths circling the yellow kitchen lamp up above, and then glanced into the gloom under the table. Boroda was in her box, curled up, but not asleep: still trembling, and with her chocolate silk eyes wide open.

'Poor dog, poor *lapochka*!' muttered Galia, and rubbed the inside of her knees with each fist. She would be as stiff as a cadaver tomorrow. The clock in the bedroom struck midnight, and Galia longed for her pillow.

'Galia, you must get that dog a collar.' She was surprised by the sudden certainty in Vasya's voice. He had finished with his shins, and now seemed determined to get his point across.

'It's not in the contract, Vasya,' said Galia. 'She's my dog, but she's not really my dog, if you see what I mean. We found each other. She chooses to live with me, so it doesn't seem right to make her wear a collar. We choose to share our lives. We don't need to display ownership. It's not like . . .' she hesitated slightly, 'it's not like we're married, or bound in any way.'

'Galia, yes, I accept that you are not married to your dog.'

55

Galia blushed and smiled slightly.

'But you can't go through tonight's fiasco ever again, and neither can the dog. It's monstrous. You must get Boroda a collar. You must take responsibility for her. It's what civilized society insists, and there can be no argument.'

Galia wanted to argue, in fact she felt it was her duty to argue, and it was on the tip of her tongue to argue, but the battling words died in her throat and instead she took a slow sip of her tea. The day had been a trial for her, it was true. Difficult, for some reason, even before she had left the flat, even while she was cooking with all those irritating memories circling her for no reason. And then during the endless Elderly Club meeting she had felt uneasy, and not a little agitated. And after that the evening had become farcical, dangerous and threatening by turn, in a whirl of motorcycle wheels, dog's teeth and mad old ladies with sickles in their hands.

In the end, it came down to this: she had stood on a point of principle, assuming that her fellow members of society would respect that principle, and she had come unstuck. Maybe it was time to give in, just a little, to make life safer. Maybe it was time to just get a collar and be done with it. It wouldn't really hurt, would it?

'But what if she bites me when I try to put it on? Or leaves home in disgust?' asked Galia, with a teasing smile that showed a glimpse of her straight white teeth, and the gold ones that crowded round them.

'She won't bite you, and she won't leave home. That dog has more sense than you give her credit for, Galia. She is your willing accomplice, and will respect your decision. You're just being stubborn.'

Galia sighed. 'Yes, Vasya, I admit it: maybe you're right, on this occasion. There has been some stubbornness in this situation. I will get her a collar in the morning. But only if I find the time between the vegetable patch and the market.'

'And a lead?'

'A lead? Why would I want a lead?' laughed Galia, the sound throaty and warm and quite unexpected to Vasya. 'You go too far, Vasily Semyonovich!'

'Why indeed? Of course, you won't be taking her for walks or tying her up. She organises her own entertainment, I understand that. Oh well, maybe we can look at the issue of the lead next week, or next month. Towards autumn, perhaps?' Now it was Vasya's turn to trail off slightly as Galia fixed him with her steady blue gaze, and stopped laughing.

'Well, all's well that ends well, as they say!' Vasya smiled and jerked his tea glass towards the light-fittings and moths in a toast. Galia leant away from the ice box and was about to stand to join in the toast when a sharp rap at the front door stopped her in mid-flow, hand raised, mouth open, eyes round.

'Who's that?' she whispered. Boroda whined softly and stood up stiffly under the table, her claws stuttering slightly on the lino floor.

Vasya carefully propelled himself round on his stool with his long, spindly legs and peered out of the kitchen window into the warm, dark courtyard below. Once his eyes had adjusted to the depth of the gloom, he saw, lurking like a playground bully between the peeling swings and the weather-beaten chess tables, the unmistakable outline of a police car.

'Galina Petrovna, I smell trouble,' whispered Vasily, and pointed to the car with a nobbled finger.

There was another sharp rap at the door. This time the

sound was harder, as if a baton, rather than a fist, was making contact.

'Better let them in, my dear.'

'I'll let them in, in just a second. Boroda, get in the bedroom – in!' Galia shooed the dog through the hall and into the bedroom, before gently sliding her inside the wardrobe, and behind a box of old photographs. She pushed the bedroom door to, and made her way stiffly across the hall. As she reached the threshold, the door vibrated in front of her eyes as more blows echoed through the quiet building. She took a deep breath, and slid back the bolts.

In the dim orange light of the hallway, she could make out two figures: one short and stocky, a dishevelled and obviously drunken policeman, and the other taller, younger, also dishevelled and smelling of sweat and dog crap. It was, of course, Mitya the Exterminator. His eyes were glassy, and they focused on a place somewhere behind her head. Behind the visitors, she perceived a number of grey heads popping out of other doors down the corridor, and then swiftly withdrawing at the sight of the representative of the law and his companion.

'Citizens, I am sorry for the delay in opening the door, but it is very late. What can I do for you?'

'Baba, Baba, don't worry,' cried the chubby policeman in a loud voice, wobbling slightly under the weight of his friendly words and leaning on the door jamb for support. 'We know it's late, but you're welcome, very welcome . . . Do come in!'

Galia looked at him steadily and raised her eyebrows slowly. The policeman giggled and put a chubby fist into his mouth, realizing he had made some sort of mistake, but not quite able to work out what it was. The giggle gradually petered out, and he frowned instead, his glossy bottom lip protruding.

'I warn you, be careful, Baba!' he grimaced, fingering his gun holster with one clumsy hand and gesticulating towards his accomplice with the other. 'Be careful, granny, he's got teeth, this one. Oh, you – yes, you!' here he pointed directly at Galia with a puffy finger, 'need . . . to be careful! We all need to be careful!' he giggled again, and leant against the wall more heavily, breathing hard. 'Have you got any drink, Baba?'

Mitya cleared his throat, and winced, as if the action caused him pain. He should have warmed up in the car, he thought, but this drunken fool had distracted him. Now he appeared weak, nervous, mucus-ridden. The prolonged incident with his mother had, in truth, unnerved him some-what and left him feeling slightly unwell. But the fight went on, and the canine had to be brought to justice, no matter how tired and spent he was. He could sense the damp from the basement on the East Side still sticking to his clothes, and his nostrils quivered as he caught a sour whiff of some-thing, which he thought must be the policeman.

'Orlova, Galina Petrovna?' Mitya spoke, the pitch a little higher than he would have liked.

Galia nodded slowly, still looking at the greasy policeman, and wondering if she knew his mother.

'You have in your apartment a dangerous dog, which I am here to remove.' There was a pause, and Mitya coughed. 'My colleague here, as you see, is somewhat tired. It has been a long day.'

'It's my saint's day today, Baba!' chipped in the policeman.

'However, our actions have all the force of law, and he is armed. Now I call on you to stand aside so that the dangerous canine can be removed.'

'It's my saint's day every day! This modern Russia is sooooo great!'

Galia ceased examining the drunken policeman and turned her gaze to Mitya the Exterminator.

'Where are your papers, sir?' she asked softly.

Mitya the Exterminator thrust seven sheets of paper into her face the instant the words left her mouth. All stamped, sealed, laden with official signature, her address, details, birth date, star sign even. She was about to relent and vacate the door space to allow them in, when Vasya joined her on the threshold, looking flushed, breathless, excited even: in a word, a dangerous condition for an elderly man in the middle of the night.

'Now then young Mitya, we don't want any trouble here,' he began. The Exterminator's eyes became clouded and his cheeks flushed a dull red at the words. 'I am sure we can sort this out without any unpleasantness. What exactly is the complaint against the dog?'

There was a long pause, filled only with the sound of the policeman shifting from foot to foot and back again, a casual move that required a huge amount of concentration in his present state, and made the sweat drip off his stubby, turned-up nose. Mitya breathed deeply and evenly, his eyes still far off, his hands loose by his sides. Gradually, just as Galia was wondering whether he was still fully conscious, he drew his eyes back from the middle distance and re-focused on Vasya for a few seconds. He reached for his plastic-leather bum-bag and pulled out a notebook. He cleared his throat, peered closely at Vasya for a second time, and then started to read, '"That on the aforementioned date said canine did bite the official state dog warden both on the finger and on the ankle and when commanded to desist did recklessly continue to bite the official state dog warden further to said aforementioned place both on the calf and on the wrist. This being an offence under Article 27 of Presidential Decree 695 and in direct contravention of the laws of the Russian Federation, said dangerous dog is required to be exterminated forthwith before it becomes a menace to society." And that's the President of the Russian Federation that wants your dog dead, Citizen, not just me.' Mitya finished with a rush and a prolonged frown.

'But Boroda would never bite anyone, let alone an official state dog warden!' cried Galia, offended on the dog's behalf, and worried by the thought that the President himself could think so badly of her. 'She is a good dog – a shy dog. She knows what it is to be a stray and has respect for all citizens. She knows an official when she sees one.'

'A stray, you say?' enquired Mitya.

Galia hesitated, her eyes wary, not sure what answer she should give.

'But Galia, isn't that the dog, exactly the dog, that you took to the river just this evening to drown?'

Galia glared at Vasya for a second as if he had pierced her heart with a knitting needle. Indeed, he thought she might at any minute attempt to strike him, as she raised her hand in horror and leant towards him. He even took a slight step back at the look in her eyes, inadvertently stepping on the drunken policeman's bunion. This was a grave and fateful error, as he let out a howl that caused an answering howl to echo from deep within the apartment, which made the Exterminator's left eye twitch. Galia regained her composure in an instant, as if slapped, and coughed loudly to try to drown out the sound of the howl. She nodded slightly at Vasya.

'Yes, yes, Vasily Semyonovich, you're right. Gosh was that your stomach – you must be hungry. We have been so busy

61

this evening . . . The dog . . . had to go. Yes, she had turned a bit funny, and I am old, and I thought, well, I can't cope, so . . . heart-breaking as it was—'

'We dropped her in the river in a bag full of stones,' Vasya confirmed quickly, pulling the door almost shut behind him, as he heard Boroda whining in the depths of the wardrobe.

'The dog is in the river?' asked Mitya softly.

'Yes, yes,' Galia replied, eyes on his second button, hands twisting slightly in front of her. 'She had to go. I didn't really want to say . . . you know, people talk about rights for animals these days, and everything.'

Mitya removed a small red rubber ball from his bum-bag. 'In the river, you say?'

'Yes sir, in the river. About a mile down-stream from here. Where it's deep.'

'Stand aside, Elderly Citizens.' He bent towards the door.

'I say, have you got a permit to do that?' asked Vasya gruffly.

Mitya squeezed the small red rubber ball sharply and deliberately, three times. It squeaked with a raw venom that zipped up the Elderly Citizens' backbones and puckered their faces like limes. A small silence was followed by the inevitable clang of doom: a clatter of clever-stupid claws on the wardrobe door. 'Here doggie, doggie, doggie!' called Mitya in a strange, childlike voice, squeezing the ball again, and dropping a few morsels of bacon rind on the floor just inside the door.

'Now then, young man, who gave you permission to strew—' began Vasya.

'Stand aside, Volubchik,' commanded Mitya with some force, placing one finger in the centre of Vasya's chest.

The squeak and the bacon rind had worked their sensual

magic. Their long, chewy fingers of saltiness had reached out to the dog and hooked around her nose, dragging her forward almost against her will, out of the bedroom door and into the hallway, claws skittering softly on the ragged parquet despite herself, edging for the bacon rind and the door, the open door where her mistress stood talking to some familiar, but all the same slightly terrifying, guests. The dog gently scooped up the bacon rind with her tongue and chewed it with sad eyes as they watched. Then, rather apologetically, she wound herself behind Galia's legs and whined softly.

'She floats,' said Mitya, 'despite the stones: she has risen.'

'Now please, Mitya, there's no need to take the dog. I'm sure we can come to some kind of arrangement,' and again Vasya reached for the greasy wad of notes tucked into his shirt. No man could resist the call of real Russian vodka, and fish dried right there on the riverbank, surely.

'Put your money away. Officer, this is the second time in four hours that this man has attempted to bribe me, a state official and dog warden. But, Elderly Citizen, this time we have a state enforcer of the law on hand to witness it and I have no distractions to stand between me and bringing you to justice. You cannot get away with such undemocratic and anti-establishment behaviour a second time.'

Mitya waited for the chubby policeman to take action. All three of them, plus the dog, stood expectantly, gazing at Kulakov and waiting for the cop to take his cue. As it gradually became clear to all, including Boroda, that the chubby policeman was far too interested in the fluff inside his whistle and other contents of his breast pocket to take any individual action, Mitya pulled him to one side and hissed in his ear.

'Officer Kulakov, arrest the old man: he is trying to bribe

me! He is trying to bribe you, too! He is corrupting the State!'

'Arrest him? What for?'

'Look, I'll give you two bottles: just arrest him.'

'For what?'

'Bribery!'

'But all the paperwork, Citizen Exterminator, all the kerfuffle: it's really too much. It's more than my job's worth. Really, let's just go home.'

'But a crime has been committed, Officer Kulakov.'

'Ah, a crime, what crime? Oh, OK, OK . . . what was it?'

'Bribery!'

'Ah, yes . . . well, make it three bottles, and then I might consider it.'

'Very well, three it is,' said Mitya, releasing the policeman's arm and wiping a clammy, warm feeling from his hand on to his trouser leg.

'You, Citizen Old Man,' the chubby policeman snapped in a piercing tone at odds with his padded appearance and previous demeanour, like a Pooh Bear channelling Hitler at the Reichstag. 'You are under arrest. Come with me, don't struggle.'

The policeman lurched towards Vasya with quick, widely planted steps and deftly twisted the old man's arm up behind his back with a cruelty that took even Mitya by surprise. Vasya yelped as the two began an unsteady march towards the stairs. Boroda, the quickest to react to this obviously unfair behaviour, launched herself across the hallway and tackled the policeman's ankle just as he made the top of the stairs. Snarling, growling, snapping and yipping echoed from the stairwell walls as the policeman battled to free his ankle and Vasya struggled to free himself without tipping over the bannisters. Sharp white teeth sank into freckled sweating flesh and brought tears to the eyes of the policeman. Mitya could see that Kulakov was no match for this mutt and reached for his Taser, but couldn't get a clear shot. He was tempted to shoot anyway, just to see what would happen, but was knocked to the ground face down by Galia who, after several seconds of total immobility, realized that things were looking worse for everyone, but especially her friends, and charged in to call Boroda off.

'Boroda, quiet!' Commanded Galia in a voice that shook the walls. The dog released the policeman and retreated towards the stairs. Mitya scrambled to his feet and, pushing the wailing chubby policeman out of the way, grabbed the dog by the scruff. She yelped as he lifted her high into the air and suspended her over the stairwell.

'Quiet, Boroda,' commanded Galia again as the dog twisted and turned in Mitya's grasp, trying to get at least one fang into the sinews of his wrist. Mitya watched the dog's efforts, and smiled, briefly.

'Citizen Old Woman, the only thing stopping me from dropping this thing over the bannister is the mess it would make on my boots when I stepped through it on leaving the building. Uncontrolled canines are vermin, and this vermin must be controlled. I am now taking charge of this animal and it will be exterminated. You have the paperwork. It explains your rights.'

He started down the stairs.

'What rights?' shouted Galia after him, desperate.

'To the body: you have none. It will be burnt, along with other vermin,' with a half-smile, Mitya marched further down the steps with Boroda still held at arm's length by the scruff of her neck, still twisting, still whining.

'Please!' wailed Galia.

'Kulakov! Wake up and take that man to the station!

65

Three bottles, remember?' called Mitya from the next floor down. Vasya was, by this point, seeing to the injured Officer Kulakov, helping him back to his feet and offering him iodine and cotton wool, which he waved away with an oath.

'My apologies, Citizen Old Man, but it seems you must accompany me to the station. Bring any medication you may need. This may take some time. I really must arrest you, you see.' Leaning on each other, they began slowly down the concrete steps, Vasya supporting the wobbling policeman to the best of his ability. They passed Galia as she watched Mitya disappearing into the darkness with her dog.

'Go inside, Galia, and lock the door. I'll be OK. Don't worry.' Vasya shot Galia a worried look, but failed to catch her eye: she was still watching after Boroda, receding into the darkness, whimpering and afraid.

'Don't worry, Galina Petrovna, I'll be OK,' he shouted louder, 'and I'll free your dog! Don't give up hope! We live in a democracy. Dogs must be free, just as people must be free!'

The words pierced Galia's thick bubble of shock. 'Vasya, be brave,' she said. 'We'll get you out. You'll see. We'll get you out tomorrow. You and Boroda. I'll make sure of that. They have no grounds for taking you!'

'Tomorrow? We won't even have started on the paperwork by tomorrow, Elderly Citizens,' mumbled Officer Kulakov as he folded Vasya into the back of his Zhiguli police car and then took his position behind the wheel. 'OK Citizen Old Man, we're just going to have a little nap before we set off for the station, so just make yourself comfortable. There's no point us getting there before six. Nothing ever happens there before six. We may as well sleep things off here a bit, and then go in with a clear head, don't you think?'

Up in the apartment block, Galia stumbled back in to her

flat and clicked the door shut. In the kitchen, with no company save the empty dog box under the table and Vasya's tea glass, still half full, waiting for him to complete his toast to the bright future, she began to shake. The only sound now was the clock, ticking away the quiet, lonely night, with an occasional soft bong to mark the march towards dawn.

6

The Plan

Galina Petrovna did not sleep well. After struggling to undress, feeling like an old woman, maybe the oldest old woman in the town, or even in the whole of Russia, she eased her way into her favourite, most comforting poplin night dress and lay on her bed, exhausted but wide awake. She was barely able to unwind her lids and shut her eyes, let alone nod off. Her eyeballs stuck to her eyelids; there was no comfort in her head, and no restfulness in her body. She lay taut on top of the covers and stared at the top of the wardrobe door. After several minutes listening to herself breathe, she sighed and gingerly pushed herself vertical. This would not do.

With a solid determination to be sensible and not give in to needless and unhelpful despair, she tried all the methods in her repertoire to relax into sleep as the night wore on. She started by sitting at the kitchen table, wrapped in a blanket, making scratchy lists of jobs to do in order to empty her brain; then she walked the floor with deliberate, certain steps, no doubt annoying the light-sleepers downstairs but feeling the need for movement; she cleaned the kitchen cupboards, clanging about at three a.m. and finding four dead cockroaches, two bottles of tomatoes from 1975 and a mouse trap (empty); she forced down weak tea with so much added jam you could stand a spoon up in it; she had a bath with oil of lavender so strong it took her breath away; and eventually, giving in, she took a tablet. Galia wasn't one for tablets: the only discernible effect of this one was to turn her water green for the whole of the following day. Still she did not sleep.

At five a.m., after several half-hearted attempts at a gardening crossword, she went back to bed feeling cold and despondent despite the promising glow of the rising sun. She turned from one side to the other and then back again, replaying all the events of the evening and things that could have turned out differently, and most of all chiding herself for being a stubborn old idiot and not getting the dog a collar from the outset. If only she hadn't stood on a principle, none of this would ever have happened. Poor Boroda would not be awaiting execution, and old Vasya would be asleep in his own bed instead of languishing in some prison cell far across town. And slowly, once all the scenarios had been churned over and re-jigged to exhaustion and started getting jumbled up with one another in her tired mind, she absently and unwittingly turned to examining problems further back in time: situations, places and people she had left behind a long time ago. The theatre behind her eyelids was filled with scenes and characters about whom she hardly ever thought when she was busy with her garden, her card games, her vegetables and her Boroda.

She dozed fitfully, and remembered a time when she was young. Back then, when things were different, life was properly difficult and her memories of it were dark. She remembered clattering footsteps in the stairwell, and the dry choking dust coming off the unmade roads in huge silvery plumes all summer. It was a time when work was a twelve-hour day at least, and sparse summer harvests had to be made to last all winter. When they first moved in to the apartment, the electricity, which they were very lucky to have, went off in the evening. That was no great problem, as they had no fridge and no TV, and generally no need for light after eight p.m. In those days, the lazy got nothing, unless they were the bosses, in which case they got theirs and a slice of everybody else's, and more besides. She remembered her elderly neighbours: they were respected, but had nothing, and hoped for nothing, except maybe a better future for their grandchildren, if they survived. She tried to visualize the faces of some of those friends and neighbours who had gone away years ago and never come back, but the images were smudgy, lacking detail. Too much time had passed. There had been no miracle reunions, no matter what the films in the mobile cinema tried to make you believe. The disappeared did not come back.

The war had left Galia an orphan, but found her a husband, for which she was grateful. The move from active duty to dealing with the burdens of married life came very quickly. Galia found her new domestic chores rather stifling: occasionally, her heart beat fast against her ribs and she felt a little nauseous, a little trapped, a little desperate, sitting on her stool in the stuffy flat, waiting for Pasha to return from the factory.

She had no previous connection to the town of Azov: Pasha was required to work at the factory, which produced things that she was not allowed to know about, so they were posted to the town by the Regional government soon after the war's end. At first they lived in a wooden shack, along with the old lady who was the original tenant and a number of her livestock. Once the factory had been fully rebuilt, new apartments for workers were slotted together with amazing speed, and Galia knew they were lucky to be among the first to be re-homed. At first, they shared the two rooms plus kitchen and bathroom with another family whose baby girl howled all night and whose grandfather howled all day. After a year or so the others were re-housed, and Galia missed the baby once she had caught up on her sleep.

Azov was a sociable southern town: the people promenaded in the summer evenings, slapping mosquitoes from their legs and always wearing Sunday best if they had it, no matter what day of the week. In the wintertime, when the river froze over and the icy wind snarled in from the north, the locals would wrap up in all the clothes they possessed and go skating over the fishes and the weeds. Married men would seek the silent companionship of ice-fishing as long as the river would take their weight, and day and night, blizzard or sun, they sat over tiny holes drilled through the leaden surface, waiting for a bite or a nip from their own bottles hidden away under piles of bread and pork fat supplied by their loyal wives. Pasha never went ice-fishing though. Galia would have liked it if he had, but her suggestion was always met with a shrug and a sardonic smile. Pasha kept himself to himself.

Galia loved the river with its changing face and wide, sunlit banks, but no more than she enjoyed the old town walls and the crumbling fortress, red brick and fusty, which repelled invasion by no-one these days, but was chock-full of stories and ghosts. As a young woman, Galia had been impressed with Shop No. 1, Shop No. 2, the shoe shop and the newly built Palace of Culture. It seemed to her that her country was indeed building Communism and rebuilding

71

itself into a better, fairer, and brighter place. The factories and the schools that sprang up around the town were right on her doorstep. It was all new and as fresh as dew on green tomatoes, for a while. Galia felt part of this beginning and wanted to take a role in the real work of the collective, her union, the Soviet Union.

But at home, life was never simple, and it never reflected the Soviet model that, for a while at least, Galia hoped it would. When Pasha chose to sit and drink, she would stay in the kitchen and work methodically on enough *vareniki* for a month, gifting them out to the toothless old men and women from down the hall, when they were well enough to be roused by her knock at the door. When Pasha fell asleep at the vegetable patch during the harvest, she carried on, working all day without a break, and ensuring that he was shaded as far as possible so that his translucent pale skin did not peel. When he'd slap her backside with a pink hand and lead her into the shed for a glass of home brew and a cuddle, she tried not to think of her aching back but instead focused on the love that she hoped his attention signified. His stubble and the stale tang of sleep on his tongue sometimes brought a tear to her eye, but the intimate rub of bare wood on her buttocks as he moved inside her sent little shock-waves of desire through her belly and down her legs, and made her toes and fingers curl into tight knots of pleasure.

But in truth, Galia had realized fairly early on that she didn't really like Pasha at all. Once she had accepted this to herself, as a woman of principle, she became determined to make a good wife for him, as far as was possible: he was to be clean, his socks darned, meals provided, and other needs met. But despite her good intentions, it was not many years before her interest in him shrivelled like a late rose caught in a sly first frost. Once the home brew had dried up and the shed became a place where only the seedlings received any attention, she squared her shoulders and got on with other things. In time, this became her mantra: get on with things, and don't complain, and all will be well.

Pasha had started being away when he should be home almost before the wedding feast (boiled meat, potatoes, kvas and apples) had been fully digested and forgotten by all those concerned. Not that there were many guests to be had at their nuptials, most of their relatives and friends being missing, dead, in prison or building Communism elsewhere in the huge Union. Pasha's absence hurt Galia at first, but in a dull sort of way. She had expected a man who would be there, making demands on her, eating her food, sleeping with her, giving her ultimatums, making a mess and demanding her attention when she was busy. But mostly she saw the back of his head: as he sat at his desk in the main room, studying papers from the factory, fingers and stubble streaked with ink; or as he stood on the balcony staring out into the evening, smoke from his cigarette rising straight and listless into the still summer sky; or as he slept on the sofa, sucking air noisily out of the room and hiding it in the cavity of his chest like a miser hoarding candle ends. And then there was the quiet mockery of the click of the closing door, sometimes mid-sentence, sometimes just before a meal. Galia ate many meals for two alone. When she was lying on the bed waiting for him, wondering if there was something wrong with her, with her frizzy blonde hair and her pale skin, she'd finish off his pie, lick the fork, and tell herself it didn't matter. Good food, honesty, timeliness, good neighbourliness: these were worthy enough causes.

At first she would listen to the familiar bossy tones of the radio while she waited. Sometimes housework kept her occupied, or some mending. She'd watch the children playing in the courtyard between the brand new blocks of flats, occasionally shouting down half-hearted remonstrations. And she would cook, even on the evenings when he did not come home at all, she would cook. Her favourite was *vareniki* like her own mother had made. Often she bottled fruit or vegetables, and when she'd run out of her own produce she'd take in endless cherries, plums, cucumbers and tomatoes from her neighbours to do the same for them. Her life revolved around ceaseless movements and small busy tasks for the hands, her methodical steps around the kitchen comforting and repetitive like notes on the balalaika when she was learning to dance before the war, her mother looking on sternly. How had she forgotten that for so long?

Galia gradually grew from a frail strip of a thing into a powerful, square-shouldered woman. She was not obese, and definitely not round: she had her corners, and a core of strength that underpinned all her movements. She ate her meals for two in quiet solitude, stolidly, slowly and with care. She became resigned to the fact that Pasha was having an affair, or maybe several. She never heard any gossip, and didn't know who was involved, but had no other rational explanation. The woman behind the counter at the bakery always gave her a sly look. Then again, maybe it was one of the gypsy women who lived down by the river. Perhaps one of the women at the factory, one of the ones who wore trousers and smoked in the yard, had finally gained his attention. Heaven knew, young women outnumbered men four to one since the war, and some were not bothered where they scratched that particular itch. Perhaps it was her duty to share her husband? It was only her pride that was hurt, after all. But she could not get the thought to leave her head: why wasn't his home enough for him?

When Galia finally nodded off just before six a.m., her dreams were full of weird flashing scenes, strangely stilted and discoloured, as if she were back at the mobile cinema with the dirty cigarette smoke swirling about her like fog and the tinny speakers detached from the walls and clamped to her head. Faceless people talked nonsense, words coming out chopped up or backwards or speeded up, and nothing making sense. As she sat in the film dream she knew, with a creeping dread that rolled snail trails down her spine, that there was something vital she had forgotten to do. She couldn't remember what, and was frantic with worry. She had caused a catastrophe due to her own stupidity. But then the feeling faded and the face of Pasha loomed in front of her. He was shoving at her, angry, with the veins in his forehead standing out and pulsating. All of a sudden a furious bark erupted from his mouth. Pasha lunged at her, teeth bared and arms outstretched, making directly for her face. Galia woke with a start, covered in a cold sweat.

She shook herself free of the last remnants of the dream and, putting on the bedside light, made sure that her arms and legs were still in roughly working order. Her knees and ankles were stiff and puffy, and bruises had appeared up and down both legs. She needed to feel human, and needed some company. There were reasons why it was stupid to delve too deeply into the past, reason one being that the present was no place for the dead. She crept into the kitchen, made a cup of tea so strong she feared it may be poisonous, and looked at the clock. An acceptable hour to ring? Six-fifty was acceptable in Galia's book, and she telephoned Zoya, for help and support and some kind of plan.

Zoya: popular lover of culture, queen of local theatre and the arts, spinster, gossip and until very recently, Greco-Roman wrestler. Her thinning hair, spun into a brittle nest on top of her bird-like head, was a different colour every week. Tiny Zoya, hopping from friend to friend, quoting, quothing, groping for truths among all the lies, trying to find out what was making each and every citizen tick, and tock, and stop and go. She was a live-wire at most times of the day and in almost all settings. She had wanted to join the circus as a girl, but was forced to become a seamstress, or something like that, by luck or fate or the State, Galia couldn't really recall. Zoya: lover of the Zodiac, Pontiacs, Shakespeare and Lenin. She had a comment for every occasion, and an occasion for every hour of every day.

'Yes,' rasped a voice climbing out of a living grave. It was early for Zoya. 'This had better be good.'

Zoya took the news of Vasya's arrest and Boroda's removal as Galia expected she might: there was a soft thunk as she fainted against the telephone table followed by a few seconds of rustling as she revived herself with the smelling salts she always kept by her side and some choice, rather long-winded swearwords.

'How could they do this! Murdering poor . . . Vasya and Boroda! Call the police!'

'Zoya, they're not dead, and it was the police who took him. But Vasya wasn't even beaten: he's an old man. They arrested him – they just shoved him a bit, twisted his arm a little: he's like spaghetti anyway; he won't be any the worse for wear. But Boroda . . . he had her by the scruff, Zoya, and he dangled her . . . I really don't know whether she's— and Zoya, I feel so responsible! What can we do? I don't know where to turn. It's my fault. The old fool wouldn't have been involved if it hadn't been for me. And now he's arrested and I don't think he even has a change of socks with him. I haven't slept – I'm at my wits' end.'

'The course of true love never did run smooth, my dear. And what exactly was he doing at your apartment at midnight? You always told me that you didn't like him. You were very strongly of the opinion that he should leave you alone to your cabbages and turnips. I am, I must admit, thrown, very strongly, by the fact that he was in your boudoir at the dead of night.'

'It wasn't like that, Zoya. He helped me get the dog back in the first place, and he got knocked on the shins, so I had to have him in to put some iodine on the wounds. I couldn't have him walking around with septic shins, could I? What woman would do that?'

'And now instead he's arrested, and the dog taken away too. Galia, this isn't like you. Tragedy hardly ever afflicts your life. You are not a tragic woman. You never cry even, let alone feel passions, shaking you like truths falling from heaven. Unlike my own path . . . the trouble I've seen Galia, and now you add to it! My own dear mother once warned me—'

Galia looked at the clock and sighed. She didn't have time to listen to one of Zoya's histories today. She'd heard them all before, and while entertaining on occasion, this was not the occasion.

'—that the Ides of March itself was not to be denied—'

'Zinaida Artyomovna, be silent for a second!'

Again rustling, again the clink of the bottle of smelling salts and a long exhalation.

'I'm sorry, my dear, but this is an emergency, and I need your help. What should I do? How can I free Vasya from the police station? And how can I get my own Boroda back – if it's not too late. Please help me!'

'Ah, such trouble! Don't hurry me, Galia. I am near death's

door: it takes a while for the old fleas to start hopping and the ideas to start popping at this time in the morning. For the best: meet me at the Golden Sickle in an hour. We'll plan our actions then, once I've had a chance to . . . collect myself,' said Zoya in a dreamy voice, and rang off.

Fifty-eight minutes later, Galia was sitting on a hard wooden chair at the Golden Sickle. It couldn't be classed as a cafe, nor a restaurant, nor even a refectory, and it certainly was not a bistro. The food was plain, but usually edible, and that was all that was necessary. This was a place where people went to eat, not to socialise or show off, or relax. Galia sipped her tea and tried not to fiddle with the spoon as the clatter of cutlery against china jarred the air around her. The only voice heard above the metallic din was that of the cashier, barking unlikely numbers at dumbfounded customers as they queued to pay.

Galia's gaze was drawn to the man at the next table, also drinking tea but with soggy slurping sounds, and reading a local paper: heavy and oily looking, she recognized him as the deputy mayor. As she watched, he stood up slowly, sauntered to the door like a gun-slinger in the old west, and, having stood perfectly still for a number of seconds, let out a huge and juice-filled belch, the echo of which splashed off the walls, reverberating, and soaking the eaters' ears. The clatter of cutlery faltered momentarily, and then resumed even louder, before the oily man turned back into the room. He made his way back to his seat, adjusting his fly as he did so, and nodding slightly to Galia and a glowering waitress as he passed.

Galia stood to queue for another glass of tea and noticed that the framed posters of favourite Soviet holiday destinations that decked the cafe's walls had been moved around. Where once there had been a view of Yalta, there was now a vista of the Caucasus; where once the impressive war memorial at Volgograd had hung, there was now the hydro-electric dam at Krasnoyarsk: impressive, maybe, in a different way. Galia wondered absently why the management had decided to reshuffle the fly-blown decorations. Maybe it was the requirement of some by-law.

She hobbled slowly back to her seat and surveyed the crumb-laden table with eyes that ached. In the late Sixties, or maybe the early Seventies, she had taken a holiday to Volgograd. It wasn't by choice: all the women from her section at work were taken for four days on a tour of Volgograd. It was their annual holiday, and they were grateful. She had stood looking up from the windswept banks of the Volga, tiny in the shadow of the immense Motherland war memorial, and tears had trickled down her cheeks. Motherland, sixty metres high, wielding her sword, hair and gown flowing in wide waves of concrete, had left her speechless. The great dignity, this calling to the people for blood and honour and sacrifice, had moved her. She closed her eyes and remembered the dead, including Pasha. A voice inside her whispered that it might have been better for Pasha to have been blown to smithereens along with his field kitchen and liquid eyes, right there in 1945: it would have saved them both a lot of bother. A strange hiccup, half sob, half giggle escaped her and trailed off into a throaty sigh. Her comrades had nodded in sympathy and stroked her hand. They knew Galia never cried.

The second glass of tea was almost gone before Zoya arrived in a cloud of perfume with strong top notes of shoe polish, that Galia felt sure was handy for both killing flies and removing stains.

'Galia, my dear, I have solved the problem. You can relax: Romeo will be home before you know it.'

'Zoya, it's not like that, I keep telling you—'

'You have no subtlety, Galia, and I'm surprised at you. Anyway, you must telephone my cousin Grigory Mikhailovich, in Moscow. He used to be . . . in the services. I can't tell you which, it is a secret. He is old now, but he will know what to do. He will advise us on the best course of action. After all, we are weak women.'

'But Zoya—'

'Galia, you are exasperating me!' and indeed Zoya did seem somewhat exasperated: her lower jaw and her fingertips quivered with the pulse of unusual energy, and her eyes rolled in her lollipop head. 'You should never have taken this on. You should have known how it would all end. I told you the third house of Aquarius was rising in your moon. You should never have gone out last night. And that old fool Vasya – I read his palm last week, and told him to avoid excitement of all kinds!'

Galia looked into her glass of tea and sighed, her breath making small ripples in the remains of the brown liquid. So, cousin Grigory was to be the answer to the problem. Vasya and Boroda would be freed, and the world would be right. Galia had heard a lot about cousin Grigory over many years, and had assumed that he must be either dead or in a nursing home by now. She was not particularly heartened to hear that he was to be their saviour.

'But, Zoya, my dear, what can Grigory Mikhailovich do? He is up there in Moscow, we are down here in the sticks. He is an old man! His connections, when he had them – and I'm sure he did – were with people who are now very old, or, er, even dead. How can he help us? I think maybe a trip to the State solicitor's office would be of more use.'

Galia looked over at the oily deputy mayor, who was receiving something in a brown envelope from the manager of the Golden Sickle.

'Or a loan for a bigger bribe, to be honest.' Galia added.

'How can you talk of bribes? Bribery is disgraceful, and also – very expensive. In truth, sister, it very rarely works – trust me. But you don't know my Grigory. He is a sorter! He gets things sorted! Remember that holiday we went on, to Tambov?'

Galia remembered a while, and nodded. It had been a memorable excursion. Not least for the mosquitoes and lack of anything remotely fun to do.

'He wangled that for us! Oh yes, you may well look startled! He got us on that holiday: none other.'

'Well, Zoya, that was kind of him, but really, the holiday was quite dull. I said to you that I would have preferred the Black Sea.'

'You did not! You were very grateful at the time!'

Galia hesitated. 'Well, maybe I didn't say it out loud, Zoya. But the clouds of mosquitoes—'

'That was hardly Grigory Mikhailovich's fault! And he organised the House of Culture visit to the Moscow Olympics. Remember, when we couldn't get a booking for love nor money? He pulled some strings.'

'Oh yes, Zoya, I remember that. I didn't know he was involved with that.' Galia took a moment to remember: the happy faces of Azov's best as they clambered on to the coach to Moscow. The assistant vice-director of production at the factory, and his number two, had never returned. No-one knew what had happened to them: had they ever got to see the synchronised swimming?

'Zoya, that was—'

'And Grigory sorted out Pasha's visit to the sanatorium at Kislovodsk, when he was poorly. No-one else could have got that. Only Grigory Mikhailovich. Now, what do you say? He's our man, isn't he?'

Galia didn't say anything. She was somewhat surprised to learn that her old friend's cousin in Moscow had arranged for her husband to be taken away to the sanatorium for a two-month stay and her friend had never mentioned it before. She'd had forty years to say something.

'Zoya, you never told me that before. I never asked you to arrange anything for Pasha. What made you do that?'

Zoya stretched her face into something designed to look like a girlish smile, which actually made her look like a little dog – wearing lipstick – caught with its master's slipper half-eaten in its mouth.

'Ah, I've made a boo-boo, I can see.' Zoya was agitated all of a sudden. Her translucent arm shook slightly as she attempted to spoon jam into her tea, and a big red clot flopped on to the table, splattering her smock with bright, sticky seeds.

'Shit!' cried Zoya, the sound fleeing her in a crow-like caw, which again caused a brief lull in the clatter of cutlery.

'Zoya! There's no need for that language! Calm yourself, and tell me exactly how you were involved in packing my husband off to Kislovodsk, after which I might add, he was never the same again!'

'Can't,' muttered Zoya in a low voice. 'It's classified.'

'Classified?' Galia's eyebrows met her hair as her forehead concertinaed in disbelief.

'Classified. Let's not get distracted. Forget old history: it's not important. I shouldn't have mentioned it. I just wanted to . . . The vital thing – the real issue here – is saving your poor innocent dog from that evil Exterminator, and freeing your boyfriend of course. It may already be too late, Galia! Why are we dallying? We need a plan: and for that, we need Grigory Mikhailovich. There can be no doubt – no really! Look at you! You're no match for the organs of the State, are you?'

Galia briefly examined her reflection in the window and had to agree with Zoya: she was exhausted and dishevelled, and the thought of going into battle, alone, with the organs of the State, filled her with dread. She considered the options, and decided that pragmatism would have to win the day, for now.

'Very well, Zinaida Artyomovna. We will telephone your cousin in Moscow. But I want to hear more about your involvement in Kislovodsk.'

'It's classified,' Zoya rasped, screwing up her face. 'And not important. What is important is Boroda – isn't that true?'

Galia gave her friend a cool look. 'Yes, Zinaida Artyomovna, you're right. Let's go. I can't sit around here slurping tea with you all day. I've got a list of jobs to do.'

'And we have a plan to hatch,' chirruped Zoya, as both ladies rose from the table and started for the door, handbags held out like shields.

7

Grigory Mikhailovich

'Kolya!'

Mountainous at the window, bedecked in dead flies and crumbs, Grigory Mikhailovich was beginning to foam. His pale blue eyes, once so sharp they could bore holes in glass, lapped damply at a point mid-way between the dirty court-yard and the cosmos. A crumpled paper lay in his lap.

'Hey, Kolya!'

A draught fumbled at the old man's collar as the jangle of the Kremlin clock floated from the radio.

'He would be turning in his grave, if he had one,' the old man growled. 'If those bloody bastards hadn't made his mausoleum a bloody circus. Did you know, Kolya, that there are miles of tunnels, and literally scores of laboratories, hidden under the Kremlin walls, under the Moskva River itself? All stuffed full of boffins regulating the temperature and humidity, so that he only gently decomposes. Did you know? You didn't know!'

Kolya said nothing. He circled the kitchen in his brown plastic slippers, and wondered what the old man had done with the potato peeler.

'But you know what the real joke is? He is made of wax. Wax – sixty percent, maybe seventy. It's true! He was OK, not bad, just stiff, you know, until the Great Patriotic War. But then they had to take him to the Urals – Moscow wasn't safe – and, well, the Soviets aren't the Pharaohs and the preservation was . . . insufficiently robust.' Grigory Mikhailovich enunciated the phrase with difficulty, as if the words were made of glue.

'Our glorious brother, founder of our Soviet Union, the first and greatest communist state in the world! Kolya, it breaks my heart to say it, but he is well rotten. Sasha Gremyanchuk himself told me. He saw it. He did, don't cluck at me, boy, he saw it! Saw it all. His nose turned black and squishy, his fingers fell off one by one, and as for his belly, well, the gasses and everything: messy, unpatriotic . . . so they just replaced it all with wax.'

'Grigory Mikhailovich, where have you put your potato peeler? It is missing – again,' said Kolya, his nose appearing round the door-jamb, and the words delivered in his strange, high-pitched twang.

The old man fixed him with a watery stare. 'They preserved his brain though. This I know. It is no fairy story. It is there, with the boffins, under the Kremlin,' Grigory Mikhailovich leant forward slightly, 'waiting for us. We can reanimate him, Kolya. And we must! It is our duty! Comrade Sasha can help us. And old Petrov from the institute: he's a scientist. They are ready, boy!'

Kolya slid back into the kitchen, wishing that the radio had not mentioned Lenin, again. He located the peeler some minutes later deep inside the vibrating sarcophagus that passed for a fridge: it was beneath a heap of something resembling cheese, or fish. He got to work on the potatoes as the old man argued with the radio. Throwing the stinky

85

black and yellow bits on to a newspaper, Lenin's nose rose before his mind's eye. Lenin was not the only one who was rotting. He smirked and dropped the peeler on the floor, the sound echoing around the flat.

'That bloody Yeltsin. Standing on that tank in '91, cheering them on. Kill the Soviet Union! Kill it! Independence for all! Drunken bloody Urals bastard.'

'Grigory Mikhailovich, do not upset yourself. You won't be able to digest if you are upset.'

'I can't digest! Our brothers and sisters of the Soviets died for the cause. They donated their lives in their thousands to enrich the Soviet Union and he sold their bones for a bottle of vodka. He sold his mother for a shot and his granny for a gherkin. The dirty Urals bastard! Lenin would be turning! We have to raise him up!'

The old man pawed softly at his watery, blood-shot eyes and hacked a cough. A tiny glob of yellow slapped gently on to the window, clipping a drowsy fly. Kolya wrapped up the rotten potatoes and, stepping gently around the bulk of the old man, took them out to the rubbish chute. It was blocked again, and Kolya clasped his free hand across his nose. He left the package on the floor next to the chute. Perhaps someone would find a use for them.

'And that bloody *perestroika*. *Perestroika* my arse. What idiot thought up *perestroika*? Ahh, what was his name? Grom . . . no, not him . . . Pri . . . no, it'll come to me. Anyway, we didn't need *Perestroika*, we needed Lenin. He had guts and brains! Before, I mean, when he had real guts and brains, not wax guts, ha! No, he had guts! And a brain!'

Kolya examined the sarcophagus for something edible. After some time, he found a bottle of preserved mushrooms. He would pad out the potatoes with them.

'Kolya! Hey, Kolya, get me the phone will you, lad, I need to call my comrade Sasha. We must make plans. Now!'

Kolya sighed, placed the casserole dish on the table and stalked out to fetch the phone from its box in the hall. He plugged it in next to the old man. How many years' worth of wasted spittle were encrusted on the mouthpiece, he wondered.

Grigory Mikhailovich's bloated pink fingers hovered above the handset for a second, when suddenly the phone went off like a hand-grenade, making both men quiver with shock.

'My God, Kolya! It's ringing! Who is it, Kolya? Who is ringing me in the middle of the afternoon?' roared the old man, momentarily stupefied.

'Grigory Mikhailovich, you need to answer it to find out who is calling you,' replied Kolya with a smirk.

'Clever dick! Don't give me those clever-dick answers! Have some respect, you market monkey!' Grigory Mikhailovich fumbled with the phone, eventually separating the handset from the dial.

'Hello? I'm here! Hello?' Spittle plumed in every direction as Kolya retreated, too late, into the kitchen to finish supper preparations as the old man roared. A movement through the window caught his eye. A pretty girl in a red coat was walking an ugly dog in the courtyard. She was tall, and young, and gazed about her, as if she was bored, or lost.

'Yes! Grigory Mikhailovich speaking! Zinaida Artyomovna, how very surprising to hear from you! In the middle of the afternoon! But what a great pleasure, and honour . . .'

Kolya registered, absently, that the timbre of the old man's voice had changed slightly: it could have been respect, or fear, or something else entirely. He continued gazing at the young woman, and the dog, which he found a little disconcerting. It looked like the kind of pedigree canine that would pee on your shoes and fart on your dinner. It had a curly tail, a strange, pushed in nose and a very definite, pronounced frown. He wondered if this dog brought the pretty girl any pleasure at all.

'The problem is profound. I am glad you referred it to me. As you know, I have connections.'

Kolya observed the girl's chestnut hair as she stood about waiting for the dog to take a crap. Suddenly, she looked up directly towards him, and Kolya dodged back behind the window frame with a jolt, heart beating fast.

'Kolya! Get me out of this chair! We're going!'

'Grigory Mikhailovich, where are we going?'

'Boy, don't argue! Look!'

Kolya looked. In the distance, over the uniform rooftops, heavy skies were gathering.

'Get me out of this chair. We must get to the *Duma*. Zinaida Artyomovna and some other woman . . . wait . . . no, I forget her name. Anyway, they are meeting us there. We must protect them. No – wait! We must get to the *Lubyanka*! That's where they will have taken him. Of course! Dead of night, into the car – they'll have taken him to the *Lubyanka*, not the *Duma*!'

'Who, Grigory Mikhailovich? Who has gone to the *Lubyanka*?'

'Some friend of Zoya's. Some dog rustler, or breeder, or something. I don't really know, she did explain but . . . the main thing is, they took him – in the middle of the night. It'll be the *Lubyanka*. It might already be too late of course . . . they may already have beaten it out of him . . . but we have to try, boy! To the *Duma*!'

Kolya was startled by Grigory Mikhailovich's clear intent to set off for the *Lubyanka*, or the *Duma*, without dinner.

88

'But what about the potatoes?' The boy indicated the makings of the evening meal heaped on the table.

'Damn the potatoes!'

'We're having them with mushrooms,' Kolya added softly. Grigory Mikhailovich hesitated, licking his lips.

'And what about *them*?' Kolya mewed, arching an eyebrow.

'Them?'

'*Them.*'

'Them,' said Grigory Mikhailovich, blankly.

His bottom lip quivered gently as his watery eyes slid across Kolya's placid face. He thought he ought to know to whom 'them' referred, but for a long moment it escaped him. A vague recollection was just forming behind his forehead, when a sharp knock at the door made him jump, sending slight ripples through his chins and expelling the memory like a small egg from a chicken's arse.

'It's them,' purred Kolya.

'No!'

'They must have heard. You should keep your voice down, Grigory Mikhailovich. Shouting about the *Lubyanka* and the *Duma* and *them*. Things have not changed as much as you may think. You stay there, in your chair, leave them to me. Don't worry, it'll be fine. I am young, and innocent, after all!'

Grigory Mikhailovich subsided back into his chair, unknowingly curling his fingers into the newspaper. He felt dread, and didn't know why.

Having wiped his hands on his jeans and straightened his hair in the hall mirror, Kolya peered through the spy hole. With shaking hands, he pulled open the door.

'Hello.'

'Hello!'

It was the girl from the courtyard, the ugly dog at her

89

side. She was tall as a birch tree and smelt spicy as bark, her scent overpowering the rubbish chute and the dog. He could feel her heat like a radiator in mid-winter. Kolya tried to keep his eyes on her face. She peered at him from the dimly lit hallway.

'Are you the resident?'

'No.'

'Oh.' Her jaw slackened slightly below the red lips.

'But can I help you?' Kolya prompted.

'Well, I was calling round to say hello. I've just moved in next door, and I'll be having a little party later, a little house-warming. I just wanted to let the resident know, and to invite them round, if they'd like to come?'

'They wouldn't, I'm afraid. No. He's old, and sick.'

'Oh.'

In the next room, Grigory Mikhailovich was being eaten alive by worry. Clutching the arms of his chair, he heaved his weight up and forward, tottering on his great paw-like feet.

'You know, when I said I don't live here, I kind of do. He is elderly. I help him out. I'm here a lot. I practically live here, in fact. I'm his next of kin.'

'Oh. Well, maybe you could come?'

'Yes, yes, maybe I could. I definitely could, actually.'

'*Kroota!* Just bring some drink and snacks, yeah?'

'Of course! Would champagne be OK?'

'*Kroota!*'

'Yes, *kroota!*' Kolya laughed down his nose and a small blob of mucus exploded from the end of it, landing on the girl's fine red coat. 'Ah!'

With a rough stick in each hand, Grigory Mikhailovich eased himself haltingly towards the hall. He could make out a strident female voice, and Kolya, speaking softly.

'About eight, then?' the girl was unsmiling.

90

'Eight is good. Nice to meet you!'

She turned on a sharp heel and disappeared into the murk of the hallway. Kolya clicked the door shut and leant his forehead against it. His whole body felt electrified. He closed his eyes. 'I think she liked me.'

Reaching the hallway, Grigory Mikhailovich was relieved to see that Kolya was still there, and alone, although the boy was clearly in turmoil.

'Them?' asked Grigory Mikhailovich.

'*Them*,' whispered Kolya, after a brief pause.

'What happened? What did they say? Are you all right, my boy?'

'They said,' Kolya spoke slowly, emphasising every word, 'to keep away from the *Lubyanka*. They are watching the flat. If you try to leave – they will arrest us both. It seemed like they knew it all, Grigory Mikhailovich! I don't know how—'

'The walls have ears.'

'Maybe – your Zinaida, was it . . . ?'

'Zoya? No! Well . . . No, I can't believe it. She only just called from Azov. She can't be the mole. Maybe it's that skunk downstairs at the desk! He's been listening in again!' Grigory Mikhailovich collapsed back into his chair as Kolya skipped into the kitchen to light the stove. 'All the same, we have to help her, boy, we have to. The man . . . and the dog! They have been taken! Yes, the dog! We have to get them back!'

'There is a complication, Grigory Mikhailovich,' Kolya re-appeared in the kitchen doorway, 'I don't want you to worry, but I must present myself at their HQ tonight, to pay a fine.'

'A fine? That is most unusual.' Grigory Mikhailovich screwed up his eyes until they disappeared. 'A beating yes, disappearance, confiscation of property – but a fine?'

91

'Modern times, Grigory Mikhailovich: you are confused, and old. It would be best just to pay. That way, no-one gets hurt. It is a fine for . . . for an unauthorized phone call.'

Kolya whispered an amount, and Grigory Mikhailovich shoved a gnarled hand down inside his shirt, teasing out a sheaf of faded notes. Pressing them in to Kolya's hand, he wheezed 'Good luck, comrade. You must fight your own battles,' and turned to the window.

* * *

Around ten p.m., Grigory Mikhailovich was still sitting at the window with unblinking eyes, that had once been so piercing, but were now wet as carp. The potatoes and mushrooms sat in his belly, undigested and indigestible. The small bottle of Pshenichnaya vodka at his elbow was half empty, or half full, depending on your point of view. Slowly and deliberately, he reached for the crusted plastic phone by his side, and punched in several numbers, methodically.

'Zinaida Artyomovna? Good evening, it is Grigory Mikhailovich here. I am sorry for the delay in getting back to you. It was a particularly busy evening, if you understand my meaning. I have decided that your presence is required in Moscow, to help resolve the disappearance of . . . er, the missing . . . person. And your canine. No, I will hear no argument. You called on me for help, and unfortunately, when we spoke earlier, I was a little confused. I thought we were meeting you at the *Duma*, or was it the *Lubyanka*? I was hungry, to be honest. But I have had a good dinner, and now everything is clear in my mind. You must come here. Bring the other woman: the dog woman. She can help you. You are not used to cities, Zoya, not really. Moscow is a queen among cities, believe me: a queen

92

with filthy petticoats and a penchant for *blong*, as I believe the young people say. Book your tickets: unless I am much mistaken, the Green Arrow leaves Rostov-on-Don for Moscow tomorrow at one p.m. – you get in the next afternoon: it is the express.'

Grigory Mikhailovich waited patiently for the wittering sound at the end of the line to subside.

'Now Zoya, be on your guard. We've already had a run in with *them* this afternoon. You know what that means.' Grigory Mikhailovich replaced the handset, and spread the newspaper over his great bulk, the better to keep the warmth in. The black and white faces of sickly Chechen orphans stared up at him.

'Lenin would have known what to do,' he murmured to them, before nodding silently into the blizzard of sleep.

8

A Train Ride

'You may not see the prisoner, no. Citizen Old Women—'

'My name is Zinaida Artyomovna Krasovskaya, but you may call me Madam, and this is my friend—'

'Well, Madam Old Citizen,' broke in Officer Kulakov, smiling unpleasantly and displaying small, dirty teeth flecked with something greenish and soft, 'if you continue to beat your fists on my reception hatch like a hooligan, I will arrest you. I may even have to use my police dogs to subdue you, or maybe just my baton. Whichever it is, I advise you to fuck off back to your lair before it happens: you really don't want to find out how brutal this policeman can be. Leave police work to the organs of the State, hag.' Kulakov leant through the hatch and spat the words into the old lady's face.

'You filthy vermin, you have no right—'

'Madam Old Citizen, I have all the rights in the world. I am a state policeman, and I have a hangover. And you should realize,' he paused briefly to pick a small piece of green from his teeth and wipe it on his shirt, 'you should realize, and I'm surprised that you haven't already, that the more you piss me off here, the worse it will be for the other old fucker – your boyfriend, whatever his name is. The senile one. You're making life quite difficult for him at the moment. And the funniest thing is—'

'You . . . !'

'The funniest thing is, he's not even here.'

'What?'

'We transferred him to the SIZO last night. Best place for him. Old crim that he is. He'll fit right in there.'

'You monster!' shouted Zoya.

'He won't get lonely in that cell, I can tell you. He'll have company everywhere he looks. Let's just hope that they're, you know, gentle with him.'

'You jumped-up rabid sewer rat!' Zoya cried, clutching at the edge of the hatch with her gnarled finger-claws, reeling as if about to faint but fixing the policeman with a peculiar, piercing stare.

'Sshh, Zoya, don't upset yourself. Come on, there is no point in wasting any more time here. We don't want to make things any worse for Vasya. We'll be seeing him soon enough.' Galia slid her arm through Zoya's and propelled her gently towards the police station door. A prolonged confrontation with Officer Kulakov wouldn't get this important day off to a good start, and calling a representative of the State a sewer rat was not likely to make them any friends either.

'Yes, you are right, my dear. After all, we have a train to catch, don't we?' Zoya tugged Galia back towards the reception hatch. 'To Moscow, to the Ministry!' Zoya leant her face back into the hatch and slapped her hand on the counter once more, to make her point. 'To the Ministry, in Moscow!' Kulakov didn't look up, but snapped the hatch shut so quickly the sliding glass took the skin off the tip of her nose.

Walking away from them, over his shoulder, he called

out, 'Have a good trip, Citizens. Don't worry about your senile boyfriend – we'll take good care of him while you are away. He's very safe, up at the SIZO. And I hear he has deep pockets, eh – is that why you like him?'

Back in the bright, sun-drenched street, they made slowly for the trolleybus stop. Both ladies had been awake since before six, mainly arguing about what to pack in to their shared travel bag for the journey. The items they had agreed on were as follows: a hearty picnic of hard-boiled eggs, dried fish, best Doctorskaya sausage, two loaves of brown bread, fresh tomatoes, parsley and apricots from the vegetable patch, a litre of *kefir* and two bottles of cold tea; a change of clothes, a toothbrush and a notebook each. There were a number of things they could not agree on, and these included: a crystal ball, woollen mittens, a Makarov pistol, a big bag of sewing, a world atlas, a pair of opera glasses and two sets of galoshes.

It was a long time since either of them had taken the sleeper train and neither relished the prospect. Zoya had once, she reminisced, had a very interesting and prolonged encounter in the porter's cabin of such a locomotive, where ballet and the arts had been discussed at length, caviar partaken of and several toasts to Nijinsky raised. Galia switched her ears off and felt the chances of anything as interesting or remotely pleasant happening on this occasion were nil. The long, open carriages, with bunks for fifty at a time, were meltingly warm in the summer and filled with the cloying sounds and smells of closely confined strangers. Good if you wanted to trade anecdotes, play cards, make business connections, drink vodka, sing, learn dirty jokes or challenge your fellow citizens to a brawl: not so good if you were an old lady who wanted to sleep a little before hatching a plan to rescue your dog and an old acquaintance from untold horrors and in the former's case, certain death.

They took the rattling No. 3 trolleybus from the police station, sharing the weight of the travel bag by taking one handle each, Zoya still dabbing at the end of her nose and cursing the organs of the State. Although they both rode the trolleybus regularly, neither had realized how very, very slowly it meandered from Azov through the industrial sprawl towards the mainline station at Rostov. Galia's disquiet, a constant companion since Vasya and Boroda had been taken, pricked sharply as the trolleybus nosed into a pothole and bucked free from its overhead electric cable: the engine died with a deflated moan and the trip ground to a halt. The driver swore and dismounted his cab to attempt to re-attach the vehicle, now stranded and baking in the midday sun. Sweat trickled down the middle of Galia's back and she wondered whether it would be better to jump off the trolleybus right now – through the window if necessary – and forget Moscow. Why were they going to Moscow anyway? Why didn't they just go and see the State solicitor and try to sort things out? She eyed the emergency exit and calculated how much shoving she would have to do to get to it through the sweat-drenched crowd. Galia wasn't a happy shover, but the heat and her second sleepless night were conspiring to send tremors down her arms and nauseating twinges through her gut. She felt faint and wretched, and the meeting with Officer Kulakov had not helped one bit. She took out her handkerchief and blotted her forehead with quivering fingers, wondering which way she would fall in the event that her still-swollen knees gave way. On one side of her stood Zoya, who would be crushed as easily as a dry leaf in autumn, and would offer no cushion at all, and on the other – a gently mildewed man with a blooming red nose and an aura of moonshine. He wouldn't feel a thing.

A murmur of dissent began to snake through the trolleybus as the driver continued to fumble with the guide ropes which smacked against the windows and made a choir of babies break into hellish wailing. The travellers were getting restless.

'Fiddlesticks!' cawed Zoya, checking her watch for the fourteenth time, just as the engine jolted back into life with a high-pitched whine and a shudder, causing the standing passengers to wobble from the handrails like chickens in an abattoir. And now it was too late to move. Galia gritted her teeth and kept her eyes on the view from the window, of dusty streets, and high-rise blocks, and the occasional wilted lime tree. After twenty more minutes' torture, the greying duo were spewed out at their destination in a pool of assorted desperate and semi-liquefied travellers, with four minutes to get to their distant, promised platform. They caught each other's eye, and nodded as one: it was elbows to the ready, comrade.

The cavernous station, warm, stinking and curiously pink, embraced a concourse that was heaving with people and animals that buzzed and flowed dimly, forming small cells and then dissipating. There were skinny hens in home-made coops treading on each other's heads, bands of assorted small children with uniform grubby faces, towers of Chinese laundry bags stuffed to bursting with secret cargoes, wheelbarrows laden with juicy marrows and dripping watermelons, old ladies hidden behind shiny metal casks full of lukewarm sausages in pastry, packs of lame dogs guarding the quiet corners, waiting for scraps, or lucky accidents, or maybe, squinting out of their good eyes, planning a heist on the weakest old lady, the one who had been abandoned by her own pack. Pick off the weakest, my dear.

'Excuse me, Citizen, excuse me!' rang the battle cry as the ladies ploughed a straight furrow from the station entrance towards their platform: firm, unstoppable, mouths set straight and teeth clenched.

'We're for the Moscow train!' squawked Zoya.

'The Moscow train!' echoed Galia.

To anyone who didn't get out of the way: 'The Moscow train!' It was a stiff retort to all complaints about bashed shins, overturned bags and bloodied small noses. The bag handles squirmed in their palms, moist with sweat, and cut in to their flesh: but they surged on towards the platform. Galia concentrated on the collage of whirling shapes directly in front of her, keeping her steps measured and her shoulders square, but couldn't help slowing in the face of the mass of flesh. Zoya sensed her hesitancy and tugged hard on her bag handle with an angry 'Come on!' whipping Galia headlong into a cloud of gangly school children, all unfortunate hair and big teeth. When the two women emerged on the other side of the endless teeth, they had reached the Moscow platform. The station clock struck one.

'Which carriage?' Zoya shrieked, checking the tickets with one beady eye and the end of her nose with the other.

'Fourteen.'

'Fourteen?!'

'It's at the other end,' Galia added unnecessarily, hesitantly, trying to remain calm and keep walking as Zoya dropped to her sparrow-like knees on top of the bag.

'Oh my God—'

'Not now!' Galia surprised herself with her harsh tone. 'There's no time for that now, Zoya: get up, my dear!' She grabbed the bottle of smelling salts that hung from Zoya's neck and thrust it under her nose with some force. 'We'll rest once we're on the train. We can walk down the carriages. Come on!'

The acne-ridden Guard was blowing his whistle to wake

hell's sleepers as Galia heaved first the travel bag and then Zinaida Artyomovna in through the door of the first carriage and fell on top with a grunt as the train slowly pulled away.

'Are you trying to kill me, Galina Petrovna?' Zoya was petulant, flustered, and a little bit flattened.

'I'm sorry, Zoya, it was the only way. No harm done though, my dear?'

Zoya sat up and agreed, slightly sniffily, that nothing was broken. She patted her brittle spun hair back in to place on top of her head, and looked down the first of the fourteen carriages.

'You go first, Galia, you're bigger than me.'

Their progress through the smarter carriages was slow: their assorted fellow travellers were almost all standing in the aisle to wave goodbye to loved ones, or simply get a bit of air, and the ladies and their bag were an unwelcome side-show. Bumping, bruising, apologising, and stumbling, they made their way down the impossibly long train, all faces a blur now, all blurs vaguely threatening, their ears clogged with the sounds of track and wheels, and their own apologies for being in the way. Fourteen carriages later, they arrived at hard, bare bunks, cursing the bottles of tea and hard-boiled eggs, their carrying arms several inches longer than they had been at the start of the morning. The ladies looked around them: the carriage was completely open, with bunks at every available height in every direction. However, it was clean, and so far there were no obvious drunks present. They thought it would do.

They found their niche and the travel bag was stowed, with no little relief and a lot of huffing and puffing, under the bottom bunk. Next, their tickets were checked by a loudly welcoming carriage stewardess with an expansive red grin, bright blonde hair and the biggest, blackest eyelashes they had ever seen, who promised them fresh tea within the half hour. They took a seat next to each other on the bottom bunk and exhaled deeply. Soon the stewardess would be round with the tea and fresh white bed linen, and all would be a little righter with the world. Now they could just relax a little, recoup their strength and plan. The ladies' dissatisfaction with the morning gradually melted away and was replaced with a warm flowering sense of triumph and wellbeing: they had made the train, and they were on their way. In twenty-four hours, or so, they would be arriving in Moscow.

'Toss a coin for the top bunk?' asked Zoya, winking.

Galia hesitated, and then committed herself to tails. She lost the toss, as she knew she would, and placed her folded coat on the top bunk to show that it was taken. She couldn't help a slight tut at the thought of having to get up the tiny metal ladder. She knew there was a knack to it, but the knack was not hers. She vividly remembered once getting stuck half-way down when on the train returning from a holiday on the Black Sea. Her cheeks burnt as she remembered how a construction worker from Azerbaijan had had to take her on his shoulders to rescue her, as one foot had slipped ever further down the ladder rung as the other foot had remained firmly planted on the bunk. It had been many years ago, and the construction worker had been a fine, muscular fellow with a ready smile, high cheekbones, coal-black hair and nut-brown skin. She shook herself, and fixed her gaze on the occupants of the bunks opposite.

Formal hellos were exchanged with their nearest half-dozen fellow travellers. Within several more minutes the travel bag was heaved out from under the bottom bunk and, as is traditional in all countries on all continents, the ladies began to tuck in to their picnic with their home town still clear on the horizon. The food was offered around to their

101

neighbours, and the business of finding out who was who and what was going on began in earnest. The little old lady in the corner was visiting family, the middle-aged man directly across from them was an engineer visiting a university, and the pair of Chinese men across the aisle could not explain the purpose of their journey but smiled a lot and shared boiled eggs cooked in tea that were very delicious and quite beautiful to look at. There were two further neighbours, a young couple, who were occupying the very topmost, most uncomfortable bunks, and they did not say why they were travelling, and preferred not to talk at all. The young woman rolled her eyes and simpered, and the young man made gestures about Zoya's hair. Galia decided they were too young to be interesting, but old enough to have better manners.

The steaming tea, accompanied by sugar lumps wrapped in paper bearing the State railway insignia of a winged hammer and sickle, was duly delivered a little later by the grinning stewardess. The whole carriage relaxed a little, slid off its shoes and stuffed its pinkies into its favourite travel slippers. Galia was enjoying talking to the engineer across the bunk, nibbling sugar lumps between her white front teeth and chiding softly as he told her unlikely tales of bear hunting in the Urals and prospecting for gold in the distant wastes of Yakutia. Zoya, meanwhile, had read a number of fortunes to what seemed like half the carriage, exclaiming hoarsely about possible Lotto winnings, tall dark strangers, the dangers of deep water and the likelihood of Spartak Moscow winning the league. Now she was hunched between the table and the carriage side, yanking the travel bag out from under the bottom bunk. Stealthily, she unloaded from it an enormous blue plastic sewing bag. She began fiddling frantically with threads and sequins and velvet. Galia frowned slightly: the old minx had snuck that one in without her noticing.

The conversation with the engineer lulled, and he excused himself to find a place to smoke where the stewardess would not find him and beat him over the head with her long, black lashes. Galia smiled warmly at him, and then turned her attention, a little less warmly, to her friend.

'What are you sewing, Zinaida?' asked Galia after a few moments.

'The eyes,' answered Zoya in a mysterious croak.

'What eyes, my dear?'

'The eyes of a thousand-eyed sea serpent,' replied Zoya loudly, with a tut and a hint of exasperation, as if Galia was being obtuse. A dozen ears pricked up around the carriage.

'Oh,' said Galia, and wished she hadn't asked.

Three hours later, when a discussion of mythology, religion, politics and serpentry between almost the entire back half of the carriage had been brought to a relatively peaceful conclusion, and the crowd had dissipated, Galia took a boiled egg from the travel bag, smashed its shell on the edge of the table, and leant in to Zoya's right shoulder.

'I keep thinking about Pasha's visit to Kislovodsk, Zoya, since you mentioned it yesterday. I had no idea you arranged that for him. I thought it was the doctors. He was sick, after all. Tell me more. Why were you – and your cousin – involved with my Pasha? And why didn't you say anything?'

'No-one was involved with your Pasha, Galia. You've got entirely the wrong end of the stick.'

'So why did you need Grigory Mikhailovich to send him to Kislovodsk, then? He's not a doctor, is he?'

Zoya snorted, and licked her lips with a sharp, reptilian tongue. 'No, he's not a doctor.'

'So . . . ?'

'So, Galia, I knew Pasha was sick. Anyone could see that he was . . . not right. It was a favour to you. I wanted to help.'

103

'Well, yes, he wasn't "right". I was told it was . . . cancer, that it affected his mind.' Galia's voice became a whisper, and she looked over her shoulder as if saying the word might summon up the cancerous devil himself. 'That's what I was told.'

Zoya continued to sew, keeping her eyes on the velvet and beads, and then cocked her head to one side. 'Then that is what it was, Galia,' she said, with a sudden, direct look.

'But why was it a secret?' Galia asked. 'Why didn't you tell me, all this time?'

The young couple smooching long-distance across the top bunks looked down suddenly, frowning and hard-eyed. Both women ignored them.

'Galia, this is hardly the place! Do you remember how difficult it was back then to be referred for any sort of treatment? For any kind of holiday? It was beyond my powers to get him that place at Kislovodsk: I had to ask Grigory Mikhailovich to step in and . . . use his influence. And that is all classified! I should never have mentioned it.'

'Yes, but you have now, so it is too late to backtrack, my dear. I was – am – grateful.'

Zoya looked Galia in the eye again, leaning back to focus her gaze, assessing her.

'Pasha was at Kislovodsk for a cure,' she rumbled, eventually. 'But it never came.'

'Yes, that I know, Zoya. But at least you tried.'

'I'm not sure you—' Zoya's voice rustled like paper in her throat, and she broke off to cough loudly.

'And I'm also a little surprised,' Galia continued. 'You never liked him, did you?'

Zoya shuddered slightly at Galia's words.

'Did *you* like him, Galia?' she asked.

104

'Well of course I did!' Galia whispered fiercely, suddenly rather cross. 'Yes he worked very hard, and left me alone a lot, and had nasty habits. We didn't really talk, I have to admit—'

'That's not all you didn't do, so I heard?' Zoya interjected, smiling slightly, but her eyes like pebbles.

'That is none of your business!' Galia huffed, plopping her hands into her lap and turning to the window for a moment, before turning straight back to her troublesome friend. 'He was a difficult man, and annoying, but he was still my husband, Zoya. And his death . . . his death left me all alone.'

Galia's tone was harsh against the cosy backdrop of the carriage. The Chinamen looked up from their game of cards to stare at the old women, catching the sadness if not the actual meaning of their words. The other travellers had gone peculiarly silent.

'But you had your friends, Galia.' Zoya patted her hand slightly, but the action lacked conviction. Galia found it irritating.

'I had my friends, Zoya. But I didn't have . . . oh, you wouldn't understand.'

'Oh, wouldn't I? Why are you so sure of that?' Zoya rasped, and stood up swiftly, throwing on her kimono. She stalked off to the end of the carriage, a pack of Malboro clenched in her scrawny hand.

Galia's mouth dropped open, and she felt almost tearful. She hadn't thought about Pasha's death for years, and now a chance comment by her friend had brought all sorts of strange emotions bubbling to the surface like gasses in a stagnant pond. She didn't like these sensations: she liked her routine, and her certainties. And she didn't like upsetting her friend. She rested her head against the side of the carriage and closed her eyes, wishing that she had a warm furry body next to her to stroke.

*   *   *

As nightfall approached and the queue for the two toilets grew longer and more disgruntled, Galia and Zoya sat on the same bunk, an uncomfortable and rather lumpy silence stretching between them like a poorly mixed pudding. Galia resorted to studying the world atlas to try to focus her thoughts. Zoya sewed eye upon eye on to the thousand-eyed sea serpent, occasionally humming a jolly seafaring song that Galia knew was supposed to make her think that all was well. She knew she had offended her friend somehow, but didn't understand why. Maybe they had talked enough for one day, and dredged over too much old history. The carriage was becoming restful, dark, soporific. The queues gradually melted away like the late evening shadows, and the tea urn hissed softly in the corner.

'*Blin!*' cawed Zoya as a handful of serpent eyes splashed over the carriage floor around her feet, rolling in every direction and making directly for the crevices and corners where no human finger would ever be able to retrieve them. 'Sorry!' she grinned as the young couple on the topmost bunks looked down at her with a mixture of disdain and something uncomfortably close to pity. Zoya began to scuffle about on the floor, and Galia sighed, shutting the atlas and easing herself on to her knees to help.

'Serpent eyes, everywhere! That's the influence of Jupiter on Uranus, I'd say. Oh yes, Galia, you may scoff, but it is all in the stars. I say, careful, young man!' Zoya's cry caught the attention of the sailor striding back from the toilets, and he turned his head towards the noise just as he put his left foot straight into a puddle of beads. He skidded as if on buttered skates and flew up in the air with a whoosh, becoming momentarily horizontal and level with the Chinamen's heads as they looked up, startled, to see him flying by their card game before crashing to earth with a tearing sound followed by an agonised howl. Splintered shards of eye-beads were scattered across the entire carriage like pellets from a shotgun. '*Blin!*' cawed Zoya again, softly this time. Both women bent their heads to collect up the evidence.

The carriage stewardess was upon them in a matter of seconds, arms held wide and head swaying heavily from side to side, taking in the situation, breathing deeply, and not grinning. Her eyelashes took in the injuries sustained, and wavered in Zoya's direction on detecting the smashed beads.

'You, young man, get up and stop playing the fool. There's no harm done. You're a sailor, aren't you? So stop crying like a little boy. Your mama's not here to help you, but I am. Go into my compartment, take your trousers off and I'll bring you some iodine. Come on!' and she levered him upright with one arm, dusting him down with the other.

'And you, *Babushka*, should know better than to have glass beads in a train carriage. They are a controlled substance. Read the regulations, please.'

The young sailor groaned and held his backside, his eyes watering, before being propelled down the aisle by the stewardess. Zoya pretended to cry and faint and lay back on her bunk to wait for the furore to pass. Galia and the Chinamen cleared as many bead shards as they could, fingers prickled by the broken glass and plastic.

'OK, no more tea, people. It's bedtime now,' commanded the stewardess as she poked her golden head out from her compartment. The carriage drew a collective sigh as she

107

turned off the tea urn and dimmed the lights, before disappearing behind her door. Zoya lay on her bed humming a sea shanty, but occasionally remembering to groan softly. She held a crystal ball in her tiny hands and squinted into it, sometimes smiling, sometimes stern. Galia decided it was definitely time to call it a night, and gingerly mounted the tiny metal ladder to her bunk on the next level, feeling a twinge of vertigo nip along her spine before her second foot had even left the floor. She eased herself into a horizontal position and nudged the crackling pillow into the crook of her neck. It was very warm on the bunk, and even the thin sheet laid over her legs felt too heavy. But the rhythm of the train worked its magic, rocking her gently from side to side, and despite the late-night card games and conversations going on around her, she felt her eyelids becoming thick and heavy, and her thoughts muddled. She said a quick prayer, to no-one, for her Boroda and that old Vasya, and nestled into the arms of sleep. It had been a very long day.

plastic-leather bum-bag – the most important part of his work apparel. His Wednesday evening playing of *Violator* had not lifted him as it usually did: the music failed to pierce that strange bubble that had encompassed him. His mood was low, and Mitya growled at scuttling cats as he passed them on his way out. He had work to do, but somehow this evening it seemed a burden rather than a pleasure. Something was definitely wrong. He wondered whether he needed more vitamins: maybe he should buy some apples at the market, or see if his mother had any cabbages still in store.

The full moon touched a sheen on Mitya's hair as he crouched behind a bench in Children's Play Park No. 4. He could hear a muffled mewling, and knew the time was almost right: the mongrel puppies would show their shivering pink noses and take his bait any minute now. He'd taken their mother on Monday – and then lost her again, along with all the other canine vermin he'd controlled that night, during the painful incident at his mother's. Unconsciously, he passed a gloved hand across the bruises on his backside, still swollen and sore. She had never understood his choice of profession. Sometimes she just treated him to silence, and sometimes she was more demonstrative of her disapproval. The sickle was a new touch though, and one that troubled him. Maybe this was the cause of his lack of sleep. This, and the knowledge that dangerous dogs had been set free to once again terrorize local children and infect society with stray-ness and wild eyes. Maybe dispatching these puppies, combined with an apple a day, would re-invigorate him.

The puppies must be on the verge of starvation now, Mitya calculated. They were holed up underneath the park keeper's equipment store: a wooden panelled construction on concrete feet that Mitya did not have the keys to. The park keeper himself was nowhere to be found. Mitya suspected that he was now a resident of Drunk Tank No. 2, but had decided against making a call to find out. The drunk tanks never answered the phone anyway, and it was unlikely that the old fool would be able to find the keys even if he could remember his statutory duties concerning the park. So, Mitya couldn't get in to the store, and he couldn't get under it without a spade, so the puppies would have to end their cowardice and come out of their own accord, with the help of a little bacon fat.

The pups' mewling continued, and Mitya realized that he was clenching his jaw. He released the pressure and his teeth roots seemed to blossom slightly, making his eyes water. He shut them lightly to collect his thoughts, but in the darkness behind his lids he imagined babies crying, their pink faces all screwed up and dribbly. Unbidden, a vision of the round, pink face of a small child rose up before him and he was back in the milk queue at kindergarten, trying to keep his place in the line. Gosha was round and fat with empty blue eyes. Gosha was always pinching his arm and then pinching his milk, making him squeal and cry just like . . . just like a puppy. Then the teacher would slap his knees for being a coward.

He opened his eyes and looked at his watch: he couldn't see the time as the face was cracked, another consequence of Monday's fiasco. He thought of his mother, spittle flying from her mouth as she charged him, curses flying like witches about his head. Had she ever been different? He had a memory, or maybe it was a dream, he couldn't tell: a scene, just a snatch of quiet life: she was young looking, still with teeth and a smile that made him happy. In this vision, she was cooking lunch for them both, and there was someone else there, who made him very happy. A hairy someone. With white teeth and big brown eyes. A someone with a bark,

111

lying contentedly in the sunlight that streamed in through the kitchen window.

Mitya shook himself and pressed his short, neat nails into the palms of his hands. His teeth tore a ragged little hole in the corner of his bottom lip as he listened to the puppies crying and scrabbling under the storeroom. A trickle of warm, salty blood wrapped itself around his bottom teeth and he spat on the ground. Perhaps a gas pellet would do the trick. Not strictly regulation issue, but useful in situations like this. They would be stunned and then would die peaceful deaths overnight. He pushed himself upright and began to make for his van, eyes on the dusty path in front of him. He turned the corner from the park and walked straight into a small form. Her hands flew up to cushion the impact, her fingers brushing his nipples under the taut nylon of his shirt, as her nose pressed into his sternum. She smelt salty and familiar. He jumped backwards from the contact.

'Oops!' He could see the whites of her eyes in the moonlight. 'Oh – we meet again!'

'Katya!'

'You'll be thinking I'm following you!' She laughed and held a hand to her neck. Mitya's eyes touched the top of her head and then travelled up her legs from her shoes, eventually resting momentarily on the hand still resting on her collar bone. She looked delicious. He looked down at his own shoes.

'Are you?' he coughed. 'No, I didn't mean that. I don't know why I said it.' Mitya's heart was bursting in his chest, and there was a roaring in his ears like a sewer during the spring melt, or the sea perhaps. His blood pressure must be low, he thought. He definitely needed more vitamins. 'I won't be thinking about you at all, Katya. I am busy.'

'Oh, OK. I'm sorry.' Her smile faded and she shrugged, turning to go.

'Why are you out so late on your own?' Mitya asked abruptly, without meaning to.

'Oh, I've just been to class – night school. I'm studying to be a teacher. I was just thinking about children and the funny things they do. There was a boy, Vadik, who—'

'I have to get on, Katya.'

'Oh, right. What are you doing here so late, anyway?'

'There are some puppies, living in the bottom of that equipment store. I must deal with them.'

'Oh, puppies? You're going to rescue them! How sweet. You're such a good guy.'

'No, Katya, I—'

'I knew there was something about you that I liked. I'm an animal lover too—'

'Katya, listen—'

'I don't care what Andrei says, I knew you were OK!'

'What?' Mitya's eyes opened wide and he stopped breathing momentarily. The girl put her head on one side and smiled.

'Oh, nothing. That guy, Andrei, who lives on the corridor. He was just chatting to me, trying to get me to go round for drinks or something. I just . . . well, it's nothing.'

'Katya, don't ever go into Andrei's room.' He stared with eyes like marbles, the intensity startling Katya so that she backed away unconsciously, one small foot hiding behind the other as she wobbled slightly on her platforms.

'Yeah, it's OK. I know he's a bit, well, you know, dodgy, we were just talking in the corridor—' she shrugged.

'Promise me? Don't ever go in there. He's bad, really bad.'

Katya met his gaze and saw honesty there.

'Yes, OK, I promise. If you let me help you rescue the puppies.'

'But Katya, I—' Mitya's voice became a whisper. He really

113

needed to cough but couldn't let rip. He took a breath in and began to choke on his own phlegm.

'Oh my! Here you go!'

She reached up and thumped him hard on the back with her tiny fist. Mitya staggered slightly and stopped coughing. His eyes were watering and a film of sweat had broken out on his pale skin. Without his bum-bag, he had nothing to wipe them with except his fists. He felt stupid.

'Oh look, take this, puppy.' Katya retrieved a printed cotton handkerchief from her handbag and reached up to wipe the tears from Mitya's eyes. 'Do you have asthma?'

'No! Look, get off will you?' Mitya batted her hand away and straightened his belt and hair with hands that were not entirely steady.

'So, is it a deal, Mitya? I can hear those puppies now. I think they need our help.'

'Very well Katya, you can help me, er, rescue the puppies.'

'Oh, that's great. Thank you.' And she reached up on tip-toe and kissed him on the cheek. 'I wonder what happened to their mother? Maybe a car accident or something?'

'Katya, I—'

'No, I know, there's no point speculating. We just have to get on and get to it and do what we can. Have you got a torch, Mitya?'

Mitya hesitated.

'Yes, I've got a torch, and a sack.'

'You won't need a sack. That's not the right equipment for puppies. Maybe a box, if you've got one, with a jumper in it – just something to keep them warm.'

He thought for a moment. 'I have a body-warmer in the van.'

'Yes, yes that's great. Get it and we can wrap them up in that until we get them to the rescue centre.'

'Rescue centre?' Mitya's brain flipped over as he realized the enormity of what they were doing: these dogs would have to be taken somewhere, alive. He shut his eyes as he tried to remember where there might be an animal rescue centre in Azov.

'You must know where the local rescue centre is? We can't just take them home, can we? Cousin Marina won't like them, that's for sure.'

'No, Katya, you're right. Just a moment,' Mitya walked stiffly to his van and, after a moment's hesitation, pulled out his black polyester body-warmer, and a town guide that he kept in the glove compartment. He clicked his torch on and slowly shone its yellow beam down the columns of information, the words forming on the pages like tiny spiders emerging from the shadows. 'Here it is: we must take them to the sanctuary on Rosa Luxembourg Embankment. Apparently they deal with . . . . puppies and things like that. I think I know the place. It is frequented by elderly female citizens and fierce children.'

Katya giggled.

'Children aren't really fierce, Mitya: they're just less afraid than we are. Mostly. Right, let's go get those puppies.' She clapped him on the back and set off with a jangle. Mitya watched her for a moment, spat on the soft dust of the path, and then followed her. Together they disappeared into Children's Play Park No. 4, one small and humming, almost skipping along, and the other walking slowly with dragging steps into the darkness, rather like a man to the gallows.

10

Guests

'Moscow!'

The stewardess heaved down the gangway like a fresh blonde tidal wave, sweeping away the last straggling items of bed linen and returning them to the huge pile already filling her own private compartment. Some of the passengers gave her boiled sweets or coppers of change as a tip. Zoya eyed her suspiciously from her perch on the end of the bunk.

'She has the fifth house, Leo, rather strongly. She needs to watch her step . . . it'll end in no good: it is the Pleasure House.'

'I didn't know you disapproved of pleasure, Zoya?' asked Galia softly.

'It's not that: it's just her, with what goes with her. She needs to watch out.'

Galia shrugged, Zoya's mysticism lost on her. The travellers had spent a weary morning quietly witnessing folds of biscuit-coloured countryside speared by the occasional grey town, as they read improving books, or argued with their neighbour. All were now creased, parched and famished.

Galia rummaged in the travel bag again but could find nothing more to eat or drink. Zoya watched her with piercing black eyes.

'Moscow!'

'As if we didn't know we were arriving in Moscow. Does she think we're stupid?' Zoya complained in a low voice.

She had not slept well. Her bunk had been full of glass beads and no matter how many she removed from the mattress or the folds of her skin, there was always one more to be found. It made her resent the stewardess, for no particular reason, but with a vengeance that glowed in her eyes and made her rather pernickety this Thursday lunchtime. She picked a final few splinters of serpent's eye from her bird's-nest hair, and leant over the table, resting her forehead against the cool glass of the window. 'I hate trains,' she muttered to no-one in particular.

Galia, on the other hand, was feeling pretty chipper. She had slept quite well, all things considered, and had had a productive morning. The world atlas had, on reflection, been a good choice. While it wasn't quite as useful as a map of Moscow might have been, she had refreshed her knowledge on a wide variety of subjects, including mining, wheat production, the political map and the relative populations of the various world powers. She felt knowledgeable, and a little less like a small woman from a small town. She was a citizen of the Soviet Union. Well, a citizen of the Former Soviet Union, at least. Nothing could daunt her, and there was more to life than vegetables and neighbours. There was wheat production, for a start.

The train had been slowing softly since the dog-eared outskirts of Moscow, and its progress now was almost imperceptible. There were no clicks and no clacks, and not even any detectable swaying: just the gentlest of leaning motions, subtly forward, in tiny increments of movement. They were inching their way, for miles on end, through far-flung deserted stations where only ghosts flitted, and empty plots where once they had been building Communism, but now only rats scuttled across broken tarmac. Galia felt her stomach turn and, momentarily losing her new found confidence, wondered what they were doing going to Moscow, and whether her poor dog and Vasily Semyonovich were still breathing. And then, quite suddenly, without a single glimpse of the Kremlin or St Basil's, there was a jolt and the blonde stewardess thrust the carriage door open.

'Moscow!' she bellowed triumphantly, flinging her arm into the air like a ringmaster at the circus. Galia half expected a fanfare to follow, but all she got was a bark of 'This way!' from Zoya as she scurried down the aisle and on to the platform, before Galia had even got to her feet. Scooping up the travel bag and both their coats, Galia said her farewells and made her way out into the sticky Moscow afternoon.

She stood a moment on the platform and took in a big breath of the grand capital's air. It grazed the back of her throat and made her cough slightly. She turned to ask her friend which direction they should take, and saw Zoya racing across the platform in the opposite direction to what she perceived to be a glowing exit sign high in the concourse wall. Zoya was cutting across the human flood flowing down into the exits, like a rat swimming in a sewer, heading for higher ground, little legs pumping, eyes glinting.

'Wait! Zoya! Wait!' Galia hurried after her, the bag bumping painfully on her knees. 'Wait!' Zoya was disappearing under a 'no entry' sign on a side-door. Galia plunged through the crowds and reached the door, which had already swung shut. Feeling guilty and looking over her shoulder, ready to be harangued by an army of imagined station guards, she shoved hard and slipped through the door. She passed through a dark little cleaners' room and through another door covered all over with dirty hand prints and foot prints and then – in a flash – she was out in the open, following Zoya up the railway tracks. The full force of the Moscow smog hit Galia's senses now: her throat tickled and her eyes felt bloated, as if the lids no longer fitted over them: every time she blinked she took a microscopic layer off her eyeballs. The sky was a heavy yellow, hung with a dog blanket of humidity and the sharp rasping stink of a million throbbing car engines. Her skin felt damp and sticky.

'Zoya, wait! Why are we walking up the track? Wouldn't it be safer to get a taxi? What if a train comes?'

'Safer? Ha! You don't know Moscow, do you, Galia? That station concourse is a death trap. Bursting at the gills with murderers, rapists, spies, terrorists. Christ, how little you know! Much better to walk up here and cut across, through the alley and then up to the Garden Ring Road.' Zoya gasped for breath. 'It's not far from there. This is the way we always used to come. I've done it many times. Don't worry, the trains don't come up here. And if they do, we'll hear them.'

Galia struggled with the bag and their two coats as her friend hopped over the concrete sleepers in front of her. Tall buildings backed on to the railway line on both sides, their blank eyes empty and silent. Zoya was babbling about visiting the theatre while they were in Moscow.

'I have a friend, you know, who works at the Bolshoi – she may be able to get us tickets. That would be a treat, wouldn't it, Galia? And it would be a shame to come all this way without taking in some culture, wouldn't it?'

Galia struggled with the bag and nodded at her friend, deciding against telling her that ballet at the Bolshoi was the last thing on her mind at the moment.

'Of course, there is also the Maly Theatre, across the road, you know?'

Galia didn't know, but she nodded.

'The Maly has more plays, you know, but a bit of Chekhov never goes amiss, does it?'

Galia made no response apart from to tut quite sharply as her shin brushed past a bedraggled stinging nettle.

'Galia, I do think you could muster up a little more enthusiasm for culture, you know. I mean, I know we're here to save the dog and your boyfriend and all that, but without culture, our lives are meaningless anyway, I think you'll agree.'

'Uh-huh,' murmured Galia, stopping for a breather and stretching out her aching back. The sky was clearing slightly and the sun's rays began to pierce through the smog. As she stood surveying the sky with her hands pressed into the small of her back, Galia felt a faint vibration begin in the rails under her feet. It gradually travelled up her legs towards her chest.

'Zoya!' Her friend was up ahead of her, scampering over the tracks, talking about *The Seagull* and completely oblivious to the world around her. The tracks began to vibrate more strongly and Galia felt a whistling hum in her ears. She heaved the travel bag up on to her shoulder and looked down the tracks over it. The Urals Express was lumbering towards them, hissing dirt and steam, not fifty metres away.

'Zoya! Oh my God!' Galia jumped sideways and scrabbled

120

up the embankment, dropping the coats as she went. Zoya finally stopped and looked over her shoulder, and then, squawking like a startled chicken, began to run up the tracks, hopping from rail to rail.

'My God, Zoya, get off the tracks! Get off the tracks!' Galia waved to her friend with frantic movements. Still Zoya hopped along, seemingly attempting to outrun the Urals Express in an escapade that was only going to end in a rather grim, messy failure.

Galia hitched up her skirt and sprinted, as best she could, alongside the track until she reached her confused friend. She grabbed her shoulders and heaved, with all her might, to the side. They landed in a large patch of stinging nettles just as the engine clattered past them, blind and enormous, pulverising their coats into the rails and throwing a continent's worth of dust and rubbish into their hair and faces. The noise drowned out, but only just, the prayers and curses emitting from Zoya's troubled beak.

'What the hell were you doing?' asked Galia. 'Trying to outrun the Urals Express? Have you gone mad?'

'I don't know. I was confused. It would have been OK. Why are you sitting on me? Get off!'

'You should be thanking me,' muttered Galia as Zoya drew out the smelling salts.

'What about our coats?'

'Well, I can't even see them, Zoya. I think they've gone with the train.'

'Yes. I think you're right.'

'Well, we'll just have to hope it doesn't rain.'

'Yes, Galia.'

'At least we're OK, aren't we?'

'Yes. We're OK. I have learnt a lesson from this, Galia,' said Zoya solemnly.

121

'What's that, Zoya?'

'Don't let your friend carry your coat, and always keep some knickers in your pocket!' Zoya grinned, taking her spare knickers (shiny, crimson) from her pocket and mopping her forehead with them. Galia sighed, and took her by the arm. 'Come on. Which way now?'

The ladies climbed the embankment and trickled softly behind a range of large, brooding buildings that Galia found rather threatening, but Zoya seemed barely to notice. There was evidence of human habitation in the rubbish-strewn yards backing on to the tracks, but no people. They climbed through some low bushes, and came out in an alleyway, which turned into a road, that led them up towards, and then under, the roaring Garden Ring, the capital's inner ring road. Once inside this barrier, they were within spitting distance of Moscow's glowing core. Zoya could almost smell the culture, and her teeth chattered faintly. The back roads meandered quietly, and the walk became almost pleasant. They passed open windows in ancient buildings from where the sounds of piano and oboe dappled the pavement like sunlight, where black cats cast shadows over complacent mice and sophisticated Muscovites discussed poetry and science in loud, forthright voices while stirring sugar into their tea.

After ten more minutes they came to a tree-spattered boulevard with a green pool cutting a fresh, dark line along the middle of it. It was idyllic, save for the twin lanes of cars and trucks wrestling with each other on either side. Above the smog of the traffic, Galia could make out a pulsating cloud of starlings wheeling over the busy Moscow streets.

'Here we are, Galia. This is it. That is Grigory Mikhailovich's building over there.'

122

Zoya waved a vague hand in the direction of a hulking block that seemed to scowl into the sky on the other side of the boulevard. The windows were blank, and reflected no light.

'Let's hope he's in,' Galia said quietly.

After some trial and error with the building numbers, courtyard numbers, door numbers, corridor numbers, Zoya's patchy memory and the various bobble-hatted guardians of the building, the ladies eventually struck on the right door. A long silence was followed by more silence, which was followed by some not inconsiderable sighing from Galina Petrovna.

'Don't sigh so!' chided Zoya. 'He's in, I tell you. It just takes him a while—'

At that moment a bolt was drawn back, laboriously and with much clanking, and the door, very slowly, sank inwards.

'State your business!' commanded a thick voice, a voice of phlegm. Galia peered in at the door, but could see nothing.

'Grigory Mikhailovich! Cousin! It is I, Zinaida Artyomovna, and my friend, Galina Petrovna, as arranged!'

There was a brief pause, filled only by the sound of breathing, slow and even and wet. Then there was a sudden explosive inhalation, like a brick being thrown into a millpond.

'Oh! Ah! Yes! Ladies, ladies, I was beginning to wonder whether you would ever arrive. I have been waiting a long time, it seems.'

'Apologies, Grigory Mikhailovich. There was a bear on the line,' said Zoya drily, and in an unnecessary tone, Galia thought. She looked again into the blackened doorway, and made out a pair of eyes so startlingly blue they reminded her of those of a husky, or a mad man. She was enveloped in a bright, hard glance that made her feel rather self-conscious. She coughed and looked at her sandals, and was released again.

'Do come in, Galina Petrovna, it is a pleasure to meet you, at last,' rumbled Grigory Mikhailovich. Moving towards him through the doorway, Galia was conscious of a variety of tide-marks of what could have been gravy on the front of the old man's threadbare shirt, and what appeared to be fish bones sticking out of his beard, which pressed sharply into her forehead when he kissed her, and left tiny indentations that she could feel with her fingertips. Zoya bustled in after her, reaching up on scrawny shanks to kiss her cousin noisily on both cheeks, twice.

The front door groaned shut, and Grigory Mihkailovich led the way. His apartment was dark and cool as a cemetery in October. The block had evidently been put up during the 1950s – the Soviet boom years – and reflected as much: high ceilings with moulded roses and real crystal chandeliers; caramel-coloured parquet that gulped down the clack of footsteps; respectable oak doors that swung languidly into each lofty room, and windows stretching to the ceiling with five inch double-glazing. The solid pedigree of the building was evident, but, on closer inspection, all was decay with Grigory Mikhailovich. The chandeliers were dust-encrusted; there were dunes of flies collected between the panes of the windows, and the dull parquet swallowed light as well as sound.

The old man led them, with slow, halting steps, from the grand hall towards the main reception room. As they moved, they passed numerous doors, all half-open, and behind each one, Galia could vaguely make out either a tumult of shadowy, moth-eaten chaos, or plain echoing emptiness.

124

'Come in to the den, and we will plan our campaign.'

Galia had been hoping for a glass of hot tea, at the least, but dared not ask. She tried to catch Zoya's eye, but her friend was making directly for the huge table in the middle of the room, covered with maps, paperweights, directories, empty cups, broken radios, ashtrays and choc-ice wrappers.

The hot day collapsed into a sultry evening and, as a multitude of flies and moths circled the yellow bulbs of the chandelier above their heads, so they began to plan the next day's events. Grigory Mikhailov scrawled out long notes to himself with a squeaky pencil about which connections, at which ministries, they would need to prevail upon. There was a long discourse on whether there would be different approaches for dog and human? Different, of course, in the end: the dog was wild, the man wasn't wild, he was just desperate, and old. The dog wasn't as old, but was a Class 3 Invalid, so perhaps there was merit in approaching that section too? The Ministry of the Interior, the Justice Ministry, the Minister for Old People, the Minister for Stray Dogs . . . no, there was no Minister for Stray Dogs, strike that. Make a connection to find out the right minister whose portfolio would include Stray Dogs, who were Class 3 Invalids. It went on for hours, backwards and forwards, misunderstandings, anecdotes, everyone forgetting their train of thought all at the same time and looking at each other blankly, wondering who would take control. Each time someone recovered, after several seconds or sometimes minutes. Oh, so they did actually steal the dog back from the Exterminator? And the dog did actually bite Officer Kulakov, and several times? And who was the mad woman with the sickle? Was it a state-provided sickle, did Galina Petrovna think? Had the paperwork handed to her included a Form No. 372c signed by the required parties? Galia

opened the travel bag and brought out all the documenta-
tion, much of it now studded with glass serpents' eyes and
Urals dust. 'Oh dear, that will never do,' rumbled Grigory
Mikhailovich. Galia pursed her lips, and Zoya pretended
not to have heard.

They were offered no food or refreshment of any kind.

Galia had wanted to ask about Pasha and Kislovodsk,
and thank Grigory Mikhailovich for his help, but every
time she collected her thoughts and screwed up her
courage, either Zoya or Grigory Mikhailovich would
make some sort of breakthrough in preparing their case
and the words would be forgotten for a few minutes again.
Her own bit of ancient history seemed to have no place
in the discussions raging around the table. She felt silly
for wanting to bring it up. She gazed at the old map of
the Soviet Union hanging on the wall, and picked out
Azov, a tiny speck on the mid-western side. She felt a
sudden urge to go home.

'Right! That's all settled then!' crowed Zoya, triumphant,
beaming.

'Is it?' asked Galia.

'Galia, you really don't have the necessary physical and
mental stamina for this, do you, my dear? I can see you are
thinking of your vegetable patch and your dog.'

Galia blushed slightly as she stumbled over a denial. 'No,
I was just thinking about how large our old Soviet Union
was, that's all.'

'Ah, bless!' said Zoya a little acidly, and started rolling up
maps and sorting papers in to alphabetical order. She hopped
around the table, hands darting to and fro, as Grigory
Mikhailovich stood silent and still, the great heaving of his
chest every so often as he drew air in and then expelled it
with a whistle the only indication that he was living. His bright

126

blue eyes were unfocused now, his puffy hands limp by his sides. Galia wondered again whether this old bear actually had any influence with today's 'new Russian' ministries.

'He would have known what to do, mark my words.'

'Who would, Grigory Mikhailovich?'

The old man turned his eyes to Galia and stared through her for at least thirty seconds, before a switch flicked somewhere within the mysterious and calcified network that was his brain, and he remembered exactly who she was. He blinked.

'Ladies, I will bid you goodnight,' roared Grigory Mikhailovich, suddenly lumbering towards them, and somehow herding them towards the door without them knowing it, their small, backward steps taking them swiftly towards the open doorway. 'It is late, and we have a busy day tomorrow. Make yourselves comfortable. Sleep where you like. I generally do.' And with that, Grigory Mikhailovich closed the door in their faces, shutting them out in the echoing gloom of the hall.

'What does that mean?' asked Galia, her voice wavering slightly.

'Well, I suppose it means we find a room and go to sleep in it,' said Zoya, looking a bit baffled herself. 'He's an old man, he's probably forgotten—'

'Forgotten how to have guests,' broke in Galia.

'Yes.' Zoya sat, briefly, on a sagging chair in the hallway, and gathered her thoughts. A swift sniff on the smelling salts gave her the necessary boost, and away she went, pecking her way into one of the rooms leading off the hall, to build a nest.

'I am so looking forward to the Bolshoi,' she said with an almost girlish simper as she pressed the door shut.

'Zoya?' called Galia, but there was no answer, just a vague humming of some Soviet aria, and the sounds of her friend settling down for the night. Galia rubbed her eyes, and then remembered that she shouldn't rub them. Her belly was empty and growled like a feral kitten, but she was too tired and unhappy to brave an expedition to the old man's kitchen. She took a deep breath, and set off reluctantly to find a bed.

11

A Date with Mitya

Mitya stroked his right arm with the fingers of his left as he stood in the centre of his room, hot and sticky as a baker's crotch. He still carried the marks left by Monday's meeting with the three-legged dog, and the coming-together with his mother. He didn't mind though. He had hardly noticed the itching as the cuts had turned to scabs and then begun to dry out. Indeed, Mitya's mind was elsewhere.

Katya: the girl with the lopsided smile and the musky smell. He tried to remember the exact scent of her, and unthinking, raised his own hand to his face, sniffed his fingers and gently licked their tips. She was everywhere in his mind. All day he'd seen her out of the corner of his eye in every street, when it wasn't her at all. The nerves had leapt in his chest when he saw any woman who was approximately the same height and colouring. He'd almost run after a small blonde in the market this morning, until he realized it was a babushka in a wig. He saw her everywhere, except where he wanted her to be: at his door.

He stood in his room, gnawing a freshly clipped finger-nail, and replayed, again, their first meeting in the toilet, their subsequent meeting by the bins, and then last night, in the dark of Children's Play Park No. 4. He recalled every detail, every word, look and sigh. He replayed the image of her jean-clad rump in the air as she stretched out over the ground and under the equipment store, dragging out the half-starved, crying puppies one by one. She had been so brave, so cheerful, and so organised. She had not minded their mess and fuss: she had been wholly intent on getting them out and making them warm. She had snuggled them into his black body-warmer and they had rustled about in its man-made cosiness, seeking a teat for milk. Together they had taken them to the Rosa Luxembourg embankment, where Mitya had waited outside the window as Katya had handed them over to the salivating elderly female citizens, whose eyes glowed as the little bodies were counted in.

How long he stood there in his room, heart hammering and mind blankly replaying the scenes of the previous day, he didn't know. But when he came to, he realized with painful clarity that staying in and ironing his uniform tonight, his night off, was out of the question. Tonight, in this warm Azov evening, he needed action and company and the sights and sounds of other people. His own company was not enough this evening. He felt like his brain might explode. Town would be busy, and he wanted to be somewhere where lights shone and music played and the wind blew through the trees. He struggled free of his dressing gown as if it was crushing his very soul, and stood panting and naked, save for a pair of white socks and brown rubber flip-flops. The place where his mother had caught him with the sickle throbbed, and he stared at the long thin scab for a moment. A noise in the doorway startled him.

'You want to fucking shut your door, you fucking dog-murdering weirdo!' cackled Andrei the *Svoloch* from the threshold. Mitya had just enough time to consider that what Andrei the *Svoloch* had said was in fact true, before he added. 'Hey Oxana, want to come and see something funny? Come and look at this loser!'

In one movement, Mitya leapt across the tiny room and crashed against the door, slamming it shut with his body just as a toxic cloud of cheap perfume and big orange hair appeared to engulf Andrei. What was wrong with him? How could he make a mistake like that? He never left the door open. And then a thought chilled his soul like a shadow across a baking Black Sea sunbather: had he wanted to be caught naked in his room? But perhaps not by Andrei? That girl was having a strange effect on him. His routine was empty and unsatisfactory, and his flesh was on fire.

What Mitya needed, he realized as he gazed down at his feet, was a drink. He opened the pressed cardboard wardrobe and pulled out his usual evening wear: snow-washed blue jeans, brown loafers, red T-shirt and chunky-knit green button-up cardigan. He frowned and sniffed the cardigan: it was not fresh, but it would have to do. He felt better once everything was in place: he felt more like the real Mitya, more in control. Nakedness had a tendency to make his mind race, to make him feel like he was someone else, or maybe no-one at all.

He collected up his wallet and keys and, having made very sure he had properly locked his bedroom door, left the communal flat. The music from Andrei the *Svoloch*'s room party was echoing down the stairs, but Mitya hardly heard it. At least the angel wasn't there. She had promised. He heard a strange squealing coming from Andrei's room and hurried down the steps, putting the communal flat to the back of his mind. Tonight was going to be special.

* * *

The Azov Bar No. 2 – 'Smile Bar!' – was Mitya's habitual spot for informal social interaction. Until fairly recently it had been a typical old-style bar, simply called 'Bar No. 2' and it had contained no seats, just a selection of dirty round tables littered with chipped, empty glasses and spit. The drinks menu had been simple: flat, fishy tasting beer, or vodka. But then as the spirit of hedonism so evident in Moscow and St Petersburg had gradually trickled downstream to backwaters such as Azov, local businessmen had, eventually, recognized an opportunity: what Azov really needed was a proper bar with leatherette sofas and expensive fizzy beer imported from Italy, or at the very least, Poland. So now over-plumped, shiny red couches jostled blistering white plastic tables and a newly tiled floor, that became slippery when wet, for the drinkers' attention. Taking the place of surly, grizzled old Borya, whose charm had been limited to barking political songs and beating up the more feeble customers, there were now young, attractive, surly waitresses who chewed gum and forgot to fill orders, and mostly sat around in packs, looking bored. The vast majority of customers eked out each drink to last approximately two hours.

Mitya liked the smell of the bar, it was unusual yet familiar: cleaning fluid and new plastic, seasoned with parmesan and hormones. The strip lights scarring the ceiling were an eye-piercing white and bounced beams like lasers off the collage of mirrors hanging on the walls. A jungle of plastic flowers and shrubs around the doorway completed the bright, confusing effect.

Mitya squinted as he swaggered in the glare of the bar, taking in the jumble of drunken faces with as nonchalant a glance as he could muster: small groups of tired middle-aged men leered hungrily at larger groups of young girls; large groups of young boys taunted small groups of young girls; young couples gazed into each other's eyes in word-less wonder, or stared with mute boredom into the dark mosquito buzz of the street. Mitya was unsurprised to see Petya Kulakov at the mauve-and-green studded bar, leaning heavily on another comrade, known as Big Vova. Both the policemen were liquid with sweat and Mitya could sense their hum from the doorway, above the parmesan and the cleaning fluid.

He negotiated the plastic jungle and laser beams, albeit with a slight throbbing at the left temple, and arrived at the bar with a sense of quiet triumph.

'What do you want?' a pouting waitress with raven black hair acknowledged his presence while examining her long, purple nails.

'A beer – lager.'

'Small? Big?' the effort of speaking seemed to pain her, and she rolled her eyes seeking divine assistance.

'Big.' Mitya felt he really should add a quietly muttered 'bitch' to his order, but knew if he did he would never receive the beer tonight or any other night, so kept quiet.

'Hey, Mitya, hey-hey-hey! How you doing, brother?' Petya Kulakov lurched into Mitya's personal space and slapped him on the back with a tepid, damp hand.

'Good, thanks, Kulakov. Just taking a break from business, you know.' He cleared his throat and made a lunge for his beer, wishing Kulakov would stand further away from him. He had to make a kind of limbo move to drink his beer while avoiding a collision with Kulakov's baby-soft jowls, and he could feel the spirit fumes vaporising from the policeman, making his eyes water. He would never understand how people could drink vodka. At the back of his mind he wondered if Kulakov might just spontaneously combust when he lit the bent fag stuck to the corner of his lip.

'Business, business: we are all businessmen now! How's your business, brother? How are those doggies doing? Howling, I should think?' Kulakov giggled for no reason.

'Yes, the dogs are doing good business. Well, they're not, but I am, if you see what I mean,' said Mitya, without a trace of a smile.

'Ha, you're great, Mitya! I love you, brother.' Kulakov giggled even more uproariously. 'But seriously, business is business. I'm glad you walked in: I have something – a little thing, just little – I need to discuss with you.' Kulakov winked.

'Business?' squeaked Mitya, and cleared his throat, inwardly berating himself for not doing a warm up and gargle back home. It was the angel's fault, in actual fact: she had driven his usual preparation far from his mind. But he couldn't be angry with her. 'What kind of business?' This time it came out as a cold, harsh question, just the way he had intended.

'We share a secret, you know, you and I?'

'A secret?'

'Yeah, yeah, it's our secret.'

'I don't know what you're talking about.'

'Aw, Mitya you know! It's your . . . family secret.' Kulakov winked again, and nudged Mitya in the ribs.

'I don't know what you're talking about,' Mitya repeated, louder, attempting a dismissive tone, and nearly succeeding. He turned away from the drunken policeman and surveyed the bar, squinting in the light.

'Don't try to push me out, little brother. Mishka, Mitya,

I know your secret.' Mitya turned and Kulakov looked straight into his left eye, and as he did so, Mitya had the distinct and uncomfortable feeling that there was, in fact, some sort of secret. But he didn't have the faintest idea what it was.

'You're drunk! And you're talking shit!'

'No, now come on, you know I'm not talking shit. Kulakov never talks shit, brother. That's rude. Come on: finish your beer, I'll buy you another. And don't worry; it can probably stay our secret, if you want it to. And I'd assume you want it to. It doesn't have to go anywhere, brother. You know, just . . . make me happy, keep me sweet. We can negotiate.'

Mitya took a swig of beer and desperately searched the forgotten corners of his memory ready to drag out and shoot anything he had done or anywhere he had been that wouldn't stand up to Kulakov's scrutiny. But he was satisfied: since adulthood, there was nothing in his past that could be useful to Kulakov. He lived a blameless life, devoted to his calling. He generally avoided girls, he was never drunk, he didn't take drugs or bribes or talk to local government officials. He didn't even cross the street if the lights told him to stay put.

'Kulakov, I have no secrets, and I don't need your stupid, made-up, alcoholic's lies. It's the vodka in your brain that's telling you secrets. You should dry out a little. I know a good place where your sort can go, you know.' Mitya was pleased with his response, delivered in a deep, firm tone, eyes straight ahead. He took another swig of beer and was about to change the subject when Kulakov's face erupted with a strange, high-pitched howl and he drummed the bar with both palms, like one of those wind-up monkey drummers, and woke a slumbering waitress.

'Ha ha! You're so funny! Your mama would be proud. Of that, at least, she would be proud. Mad as a fucking Siberian Snow Goose she may be, but she'd love that firm tone of yours. It's a shame you can't use it on her, keep her under control a bit. I hear she's completely unmanageable. We might have to bring her in to the station some time for a bit of treatment, you know? But actually, you're completely wrong. This one, this secret, is very interesting, and it actually concerns your mother too, God rest her soul.'

'She's not dead, Kulakov.'

'No, but she will be when this one gets out! She'll die of fucking heart failure!' Kulakov's voice dropped to an oily whisper, 'I think you will be very interested in having this one kept to ourselves, you know. Especially if you want promotion, or actually, to hang on to your job, or your flat, or anything, really. And if you want your momma to be . . . calm.'

Mitya narrowed his eyes, despite himself. What kind of secret could Kulakov be talking about?

'I don't know what you're talking about, Kulakov. I'm just an ordinary guy.'

'An ordinary guy? Oh Mitya, you're so modest. You're the town's best dog exterminator! The only exterminator, it's true, but the best, oh yes! No, but anyway, it's not you, it's a family member that I've heard about. Take a guess?'

'No.' Mitya leant over his beer and tried to move his elbow away from Kulakov's soft, damp caress. There was a slyness in the policeman's eyes that was threatening to swallow him up. He concentrated on the small purple bowl of dry roast nuts in front of him and selected one that was evenly brown and rounded. He wished Kulakov would go away.

136

'Hey,' Kulakov sighed in Mitya's face, so close that he could taste the policeman's vodka breath mingling with the nut crumbs in his mouth, 'don't you want to get that promotion? You're not such a young man any more: you want to go up the ladder a bit? You need to impress your bosses.'

'I don't care about promotion, Kulakov,' said Mitya, 'I enjoy my job.'

'You want to impress the girls a bit, maybe, with that promotion? I hear you're not much with the ladies. The guys were saying they thought you were one of those queers, you know, a gay boy, but I said no, not our Mitya. He's straight as the day is long, it's just,' Kulakov sniffed at Mitya's thick green cardigan. 'It's just, you smell of dog shit. Did you know that? You always smell of dog shit. Do you really want to spend your whole life smelling of dog shit and being bitten on the ankle by those mutts? Sooner or later, you'll find one with rabies, or she'll find you. You know that, don't you?'

Mitya glared into his beer and stuck another dry nut between his teeth.

'You really need a promotion, brother, so that you can get a desk job and dream up strategies for dog extermination rather than having to involve yourself. It's the way of the world, brother. And for a promotion, you need to impress. And to impress, you need good family.'

'OK, OK, what is it? What is it about my family that you so want to tell me, Kulakov? Just say it, and then fuck off.' Mitya couldn't help it. The jibes about smelling of dogs and getting the desk job had got to him. He did his best every night to extinguish the pungent scent of dog crap on his body and clothes, but it was difficult, with no light in the shower cubicle and only one ancient washing tub between the ten of them in the communal flat. He did his best, but the Omo wasn't great and he couldn't afford the Ariel. Yes, he did his best, but in the end, he was a man fending for himself, he had no time to write extermination strategies being out on the road so much, and sometimes, just sometimes, he missed that female touch. She would take care of the shit smell, if he had an angel . . . she would iron his shirts while he made up plans. She would be proud of him.

'Well, now, Mitya, firstly: mind your language. I'm a patient man, and your friend. But I am also a member of the organs of state. And you, as a dog exterminator, are not. I could have you arrested for telling me to fuck off. So just, you know, be nice. You don't tell me to fuck off, my little dog-killing friend!' Kulakov ran a chubby finger down the side of Mitya's face and pinched his chin, playfully.

'What is it you want to tell me, Kulakov?' anger and frustration gripped Mitya's throat and his question came out in a soft, strangled croak.

'I want to tell you,' Kulakov leant in to Mitya's face, smiling like an old nanny, eyes focused on the wall behind him, 'that we've got your daddy – that is, your real daddy – in the SIZO. He's a common criminal! Now, what do you think of that?'

Mitya's reply was to punch Petya Kulakov right between the eyes with all the force he had and then to keep punching the soft bag of plumpness as it slumped against the bar, blood spurting from eyebrow and nose. He was dully aware of the piercing screams let out by the coven of bored-looking waitresses, but it was just a noise. Kulakov and Mitya fell to the floor with a crack and slap of skin, bone and fat on tile and glass, just as Big Vova came lurching out of the toilet with his zipper open and his fists ready. Smile Bar! patrons scattered like cockroaches as Mitya knocked Kulakov's head against the green and mauve studs of the bar, while the latter gurgled and tried to gouge Mitya's eyes out with his stubby, fat fingers

Big Vova moved quickly: he pulled Mitya off his friend and floored him with a punch that caused trinkets to tinkle against each other in his mother's apartment on the other side of town. Then Vova kicked him in the stomach like he was scoring a goal against those Spartak Moscow bastards, briefly stopping to acknowledge the cheers of the crowd in his head before hoisting Mitya back to his feet to punch his face a few more times. All the while Kulakov was crawling about on the floor, whining for him to hit harder and lower while he scrabbled about searching for his two front tooth caps. He found the shiny metallic teeth under a stool and shoved them back on to the blackened stumps in the front of his mouth.

'Let's kill him.' Kulakov clapped his hands together as Big Vova threw Mitya back on to the tiles. The barmaids watched in silence, as what remained of the customers trickled away into the night. The stereo continued to play, and Mitya, curled up into the fetal position as boots thudded around him, was vaguely aware of Depeche Mode in the background: 'Master and Servant' had always been a shitty song. Both policemen spent a happy few minutes kicking the stricken exterminator until they were too tired and breathless to go on.

When the two policemen were spent, Big Vova ejected Mitya through the fluorescent plastic jungle and out into the Azov night, where he lay on the pavement, face down, while the mosquitoes and moths colonised his capillaries and his green cardigan respectively. He had not felt his flight through the air, and only barely recognized the thump of his face against the walkway. He was dreaming, barely there: seeing dogs floating in a darkness that was deep and all around him: old dogs with scarred, grizzled faces and open sores; top breed dogs with clicking, wobbly hips and hideous holes in their skulls; mother bitches with dozens of swollen teats and tired faces; hungry puppies with their ribs sticking through scant fur and infections eating up their eyes. And somewhere behind them all, an old dog, whose name was Sharik, wagging his tail and holding a red rubber ball in his mouth, looking at him with love.

'Sharik, Sharik, come here, boy!' Mitya called in a high-pitched voice. The dog seemed unable to come to him. He called again, but the dog began to whimper and shake. It tucked its tail between its legs and started limping around, the red ball still in its mouth, but the dog lost and frightened.

'Sharik, Sharik, come here, boy! Good boy!' Come on then!' But the dog was going the wrong way, heading for somewhere very, very dark, and never-ending. 'Sharik, come back!' Mitya tried to call again, but his mouth wouldn't move. 'Come back!'

He felt something cool on his cheek and the doggy blackness wobbled and became studded with fuzzy orange lights. He could taste blood in his mouth and he gradually felt, with his fingers and nose and shins and hips and belly, that he was lying in a pool of vomit.

'Hey, are you OK?' a soft voice hovered above his head. He couldn't open his eyes, but he recognized that scent, despite the blood and the sick and the street. It was his angel.

'What happened to you, puppy? You're not having a good night.'

'I found my daddy,' he whispered through throbbing split lips, before slipping back under, into the dark.

12

A Letter from Vasya

Wednesday or Thursday, I think, but maybe not

My Dearest Galina Petrovna,

I thought I'd drop you a line to let you know that I am
well and that things are going all right here, although I
can't speak for Boroda, as we are being held in separate
establishments, as far as I understand it.

Life here in the SIZO is most interesting so far. I was
transferred from the police station to the SIZO after
roughly twenty-four hours in the police cells, and I've
been here two days – I think, although there aren't
many windows, and I don't have my watch, so it is
somewhat difficult to tell. It is all rather confusing, as I
am sure you can imagine. As you may know, SIZO
stands for *Sledsvenny Izolyator* (Remand Prison) so
the idea is that I will be held here while the organs of
state control investigate my crime and decide to bring
formal charges, or not. Judging by Officer Kulakov's

performance on the night of my arrest, the investigation could take many, many months and involve many, many reports, not to mention a large number of counter-signatories and bottles of vodka. I don't hold out much hope of being out before New Year, I fear. In which case, I think I will have to hand over stewardship of the Elderly Club to another willing pair of hands (yours maybe?), and of course provision will have to be made for Vasik. I had a dream about him last night, Galia. It was just like I was at home. He had his little fluffy face in his bowl and he was scrunching up sardine spines with great relish. He really is a precious little fellow. I do miss him so.

Anyway, let me tell you a little about life here. The corridors are somewhat long and dark, and there is a bad odour about the place, as you may imagine. The cells are even darker than the corridors, and very poorly ventilated. We are not held in small cells, this is not the case at all: the cells here are large, like classrooms, and hold fifty people at a time. However, there is only room for half that number to lie on a bunk at any time. The rest await their turn by leaning on the walls, or shuffling about from one side of the room to the other, although this appears to cause great annoyance to some of the inmates, and resulted in a fight and bloodshed last night. My fellow inmates have been very welcoming so far, and shown a healthy interest in my case which is, in general terms, a bit different from most of theirs. It appears that I share this cell with a large number of burglars, hooligans, rapists, fraudsters and poisoners. I feel that dogs were unlikely to have been involved in many of their cases, and cats even less so.

In the cell walls there are a number of windows, but there are metal shutters closed over the windows permanently – I believe to stop prisoners from passing messages between the cells or to the outside world. As a result, it is very stuffy in here. There is one toilet: it is in the corner of the room, and shielded from view by a rather ragged brown curtain. Next to it there is a small sink. This is all we have for a cell of 50 men. There are no other washing facilities, as far as I can make out. Needless to say, some of my fellow prisoners could do with a good scrub and a shave. I try not to make a point of this though, much as it pains me. I know it is not technically their fault that they are unwashed. I have not mentioned it to them. I think that is best, don't you?

So, what else to tell you? The walls are brown and mottled: there is damp here and there, and a few posters and newspaper cuttings, some drawings even, that serve for entertainment. I may add to the drawings if my fellow inmates allow, although I'm not sure we will have similar tastes in terms of decoration. Maybe I could attempt the Goddess Venus, to bring a spot of higher culture to the cell, or a cartoon of Vasik.

Despite the number of people in the room, this is a lonely place. Some of the men have been here for over a year, and are still awaiting trial. Some have been told that they now have tuberculosis, as a result of living in these conditions. It is a type of tuberculosis that cannot be cured: it has mutated within the prison system and now can withstand any of the drugs that doctors try to treat it with. Not that much treatment goes on around here, I believe. Some of the men with this awful disease, Galia, are little more than boys. There are one or two that I recognize from my days at School No. 2. They cough like beggars, and have a haggard look, with burning eyes. I must admit I have tried to keep my distance from them: I know I am old, and my life is almost over, but I have no desire to shorten it still further. Am I wrong in this?

What other news do I have? My friend Yegor Platkov was allowed to bring me this paper and a pen. I am allowed to write one letter a week, but it must be seen by a Prison Officer before it can be sealed and sent. There is regular food, served up in our cell by trusties who generally have sores and are the most dishevelled of the lot. The quality is very poor, and the food is, mainly, unidentifiable: we are, after all, relying on the State's charity. They tell me that this SIZO has a new and slightly flamboyant Kommandant and that changes are afoot, but I have not witnessed anything that could be called progressive or flamboyant so far. I do know that if and when one is found guilty and sent off to prison camp, the conditions there are far better, as they are properly equipped with workshops, kitchen gardens, farms and factories. They are designed for the long term, while these SIZOs are meant to be holding pens. The start of the sausage machine, as it were, ready to feed the system and spit out reformed characters in due course. I believed in the system once, Galina Petrovna. But I must admit, now I am not so sure that it can produce anything apart from misery, and better-qualified criminals. I can only hope that my case comes to trial soon and that, one way or another, I

145

can get out of this dungeon before the tuberculosis or the rats get me.

But let me reassure you, dear Galia, that the other prisoners are treating me with a great deal of respect, generally, and I have not been mistreated at all, so far. I am a grandfather to them, so I hope that as long as I can keep my mouth shut and my eyes on the floor, I will be all right.

Yegor communicated to me that you have departed for Moscow to try to free both Boroda and me. Thank you, dear lady: you are so valiant, and so brave! If only I could be as strong as you, I would burst out of these prison walls with my bare hands! As it is, I miss my pussycat Vasik, and my neighbours, and of course, your good self. What will the Elderly Club have to say about all this, I wonder? I am shaking just thinking of it. But it can't be helped. Even if I survive SIZO, of course, and prison camp, I will have to disbar myself from taking any role within the club, as I will have a conviction for bribery and corruption. Perhaps you will not want to know the likes of me when I am released: I cannot tell, but I could not blame you if that were the case. I may even arrive back in my old life with a convict's tattoos: I have so far escaped an etching, but only by a whisker. When my neighbour, Shura, wakes from his sleep I fear he may once again be quite determined to adorn me in some way. Maybe I will ask for a picture of my puss Vasik: I do miss him so, and he has been my constant companion these last ten years. Do you think you could pop in to see him on your return from the great capital? I'm sure he would appreciate it.

146

I miss the sunshine already, and I miss the air. Has it been three days? Not a long incarceration so far, but it seems to be sucking the life out of me at a pace. It would be so sad to die here, in this cell, never having seen the sunshine or smelt the wind on the river again. I'm sorry, Galia, this letter was meant to be hearty and uplifting, but as you can see, I am a coward, and instead of sparing you and buoying you up I am weighing you down with my own fears and cowardice. Please forgive me.

I wish you God speed on your journey, and good luck with your mission to Moscow, although I cannot believe in my heart of hearts that anything will come of it. We are very small, small fry out here in Azov, and I am sure no-one in Moscow will give two hoots about an old man and a dog with three legs, no matter how good her manners.

Take care of yourself and young Zoya while you are there. I will be thinking of you. Thank you for not forgetting me: it would be easy for you to leave me to rot, a silly old teacher, worth nothing to anyone.

Vasya re-read the letter in the dim light of the bulbs hanging despondently from the crusted ceiling a couple of metres above his head. He sighed, and shifted his feet on the sticky floor beneath him. He noted the handwriting, here clear and neat, and there turning spidery and blotted. Then he screwed up the paper into a ball and thrust it under his bunk. Staring into nothing, he gritted his teeth and firmed up his chin, and waited to go to sleep. He was no coward, and he refused to send such a whining epistle to such a strong lady. Tomorrow,

13

Mitya's Angel

Mitya wiped his face with the proffered towel, and felt the wet ghost of someone else's ball sack smear across his mouth and nose. He retched again, pressing his forehead hard against the floor. His stomach was tight and empty, and all that came up was bubbles of rotten air in a series of loud, echoing belches that shook his lips, head, chest: his buttocks even. He realized that he was sprawled on the familiar lino of home, but he felt greasy and swollen, shining and shaking despite himself. He was not in control. He cleared his throat gingerly, feeling the sting of bile on his tonsils.

'That's not my towel!' he whispered through paper-white fingers, guarding his mouthful of wobbling teeth, keeping his eyes closed against the harsh orange light and wavering shadows around him. He couldn't remember the journey home, wasn't sure who he was with, didn't know if he was still in danger of further kicks and punches. But he wasn't going to use a towel that had been anywhere near Andrei the *Svoloch*'s scrotum, that was for sure. He was not in control, but he had his standards.

'Oh, shucks, puppy, I'm sorry. I found it in the bathroom, there wasn't much to choose from, really. I just thought you needed something to have a wipe with. I didn't realize, you know: a towel's a towel in my book. Not that I keep a book about towels . . . take it easy though, hero, no puking on the lino, OK? Your landlord won't be happy. And neither will I. I'm not so good with puke.'

Katya leant over him. For a moment he could sense her warmth covering him, hear her breathing softly through her nose, feel her scent in a warm cloud passing over him, and he felt a sense of calmness creep from a point in his chest through his vital organs and out towards his tightly curled fingers and toes. But no sooner had the feeling brushed through him than the room shifted sideways suddenly and his stomach lurched into his throat again. And now she was very far away, like a distant planet out of his orbit, shadowy, unknown, untouchable on the other side of the room. Mitya tried to draw his legs up towards his head: he desperately wanted to curl up into a ball and become a small nothing melting into the floor, but the pain in his abdomen and hips stopped him moving more than an inch or two and left him splayed out, gangly and vomit-flecked under the orange light, eyes rolling for cover.

'You surprise me!' He aimed for tough, but his voice came out a thin rasp with a high note of sob at the tail-end. He breathed deeply to contain the sob as it threatened to break his bruised ribs, and gradually he calmed the churning that was tying his insides into sticky knots. Gingerly, he began to push himself up into a seated position with his back propped against the wall, and he breathed in deeply again, feeling his diaphragm relax as he did so. He leant his elbows on his knees, bracing against the waves of nausea that washed up his throat as he gained a vertical position, and gradually the pieces of the evening collected in his mind like leaves in the corner of an autumnal courtyard. He noticed the rip down the right leg of his snow-washed jeans, and the mass of thickening reddish-purple bruises blooming on his forearms. He relived the feeling of his knuckles connecting with Kulakov's pudgy, slimy face.

Katya clanked a green metal bucket down between Mitya's shaking legs and brushed his sticky hair across his forehead, her warm fingers licking the damp from his skin. She put the tip of her index finger to her lips and sucked it gently. 'You're in a bad way. I think I should call an ambulance.' She lowered her hips to the floor and squatted, warm and low, looking across at him, taking in his bruises and pallor. Mitya turned his head away, unable to look at her directly, squeezing his hands between his knees in an effort to stop them shaking.

'Don't do that. I don't need a doctor. I just need to sleep.'

'Well, I don't know. What if you croak in the night, eh? I couldn't live with myself. You might choke on your own vomit or something. It happens.'

Mitya opened both fat eyes a fraction to look at his angel, just momentarily, with an attempt at cool. He didn't know it, but it was just like the look a dog, recently kicked, gives anyone without boots on. She paid no attention: she was digging in her bag for a cigarette and talking in her lisping, slightly accented voice.

'OK, look, here's the deal, puppy. I'll stay with you for an hour or so, until you're a better colour, and you completely stop puking. You know, like living flesh kind of colour. You're still really pale. And I don't think I can leave you like that.' She found a soft pack of Pall Mall in her bag and extracted one. 'I don't think you should smoke, even if you want to. Really, I know men like to smoke and be macho and all that but I don't think it will make you feel better. Do you have any iodine?'

'No.' Mitya could only manage the one word, and this time his voice emerged clotted and thick. His brain roved slowly behind his eyelids, trying to make out what she was doing, and eventually he slid another glance along the floor in her direction, letting his eyes creep slowly from her naked brown ankles to her knees and then towards her belly and breasts, barely covered by her very small skirt and T-shirt.

'What happened in there, puppy? Did you forget to pay your bill or something?'

Mitya's eyes snapped back down to the shiny mustard lino, unusually trailed with his own saliva, and he clasped his hands across his knees again.

'It's not . . . you wouldn't understand.'

'Uh-huh.' Katya blew smoke over her shoulder towards the open window. 'You sure I wouldn't understand?'

'It was nothing to do with a bill. No-one understands.'

'Aw shucks, Mitya, no-one understands. You bet, baby. Especially if you don't tell them about it.'

Katya tutted, stubbed out her cigarette and reached into the pressed card wardrobe, eventually pulling out a brown blanket emblazoned with huge posies of garish red roses. She snuggled herself into it for a moment, turning her head to breathe in its scent, and then unwound it from her shoulders and placed it carefully across Mitya's back.

'There, that'll keep you warm. I think you're in shock, you know. I remember something about that from school. You should lower your head and raise your legs.'

'I'm not raising my legs.' His tone was decisive.

She shrugged. 'OK, it's up to you. It would make you feel better. But keep the blanket on for a while. It's something to do with blood pressure, or something.'

'You're not a nurse then, Katya?'

'No, I told you: I'm studying to be a teacher – kindergarten. But I've done lots of things. Anyway, if you've got no iodine, we're a bit stuck. Probably tea is what you need. Tea is a great healer, isn't it? Or is that time? Maybe both?'

Mitya didn't reply. His head was pulsating and the noise coming through the wall from Andrei the *Svoloch*'s room was interfering with his ability to think or feel. It was taking over his mind, in ripples, and drowning out Katya's words, although he was trying to listen, and wanted to hear. His eyelids closed as the beats thudded from the wall through his chest and into his brain, dragging him under with their awful currents, making him sleep like he would never wake up.

'You said, when I found you . . . you know, on the pavement . . . you said something about finding your daddy?' Katya looked at Mitya from under her lashes, and saw him start as her words reached him.

He jerked wide awake again, the blood draining from his face and his ears tingling, burning hot. A frown pulled his mouth and eyebrows into a deep, grim X as his eyes fastened on the edge of the bucket, driving rivets into it. Katya looked around his orange box room for some tea, and cups, and sugar.

'No tea. No questions. Just leave me!' Mitya pulled the blanket tight across his shoulders and laid his head on one of the garish red roses.

'Don't shout at me, puppy. I just saved your life, don't forget. And you need some tea. But I didn't mean to pry. We don't have to talk if you don't want to.'

153

She started to hum, a comforting sound just audible above the noise from next door. The brief rush of adrenaline faded as quickly as it had come, and Mitya found he was too weak to argue. He realized after breathing in, with a sharp pain, and breathing out, with a dull ache, that he didn't want her to go anywhere. He eased himself away from the bucket again and leant back against the vibrating wall. He was aware this time of Andrei the *Svoloch*'s voice in the room on the other side, braying among the pounding disco beats, bleating like a cloven-hoofed Benny Andersson. Garish visions surged into his head and he could almost feel himself being pulled into the nightmare next door by invisible hands sprouting through the orange wall and gripping him with childish fingers under the rough brown blanket. He struggled to keep his eyes open and avoid the dream, but it was getting dark around him, and the arms were small, but wiry and very strong. His breath choked in his throat as he tried to open his eyes, to shout out, but found himself paralysed.

'Hey, you really like Depeche Mode, I guess?'

Again, Katya's words brought him back from the brink, and again he was ready for a fight. His jaw clenched as his eyes swivelled and focused on her, ready to fend off sarcasm, irony and disapproval. Mitya was wholly unprepared for what he saw: she was leaning over his tape collection, sincere, enthusiastic, long hair hanging in golden ropes around her perfect, sunny face. She looked up and smiled.

Mitya realized, with a dull thump of the heart, that he was deeply in love, and his life was over.

'Like is not the word . . . Katya,' he began in a low voice. 'Like is not in my vocabulary. I don't like things. Liking is—'

'I love them too. I went to see them play in Moscow a

couple of years ago. It was fantastic. The best day of my life.'

Mitya shut his eyes and imagined the best day of Katya's life. He liked it. He loved it. He could feel it in his bones and see it before him just like he had been there. It was a sunny day in the bright capital, spent with friends and candy-floss and flags and Depeche Mode and hot dogs and clean jeans and new socks and order and fresh air and neatness and love. In short, it was a day full of laughter and certainty. But it wasn't his. It had never been his, and could never be his. His best day had involved dog extermination. He was sure it had.

'You should go now.'

Katya turned, startled, and the spoon in the cup she was holding rattled.

'Go on – I don't want your tea, or your pity. Fuck your best day! You don't fucking love Depeche Mode!'

She looked at him intently, holding his gaze until he had to look away. His breath came in a half sob and Mitya ground his teeth to try to stop it.

'You can be rude, that's fine: you're upset about something. You may even have a head injury and contusions. But you're getting tea whether you like it or not, Mitya. You need something to settle your stomach. I'll go when it's made. And for your information, I do love Depeche Mode.' Katya turned away after her speech, busying herself with tea preparation and humming a disjointed medley of Depeche Mode songs that battled for Mitya's attention against the beats coming through the wall.

He felt small. He sat perfectly still listening to the sounds of the girl making tea. He dreaded the moment the sounds would end, and hated himself for it. He knew he couldn't bear for her to go, couldn't bear the thought of sitting there alone, in his orange box, with the spattered lino and the sounds of Andrei the *Svoloch* shagging broken child-whores next door. He couldn't bear to sit comparing her best day with his best day in a contest that might well have him prising himself out of the window frame and splatting on to the cool hard tarmac four storeys below before the dawn broke. He couldn't bear for her to look at him, couldn't allow himself to look at her.

A teaspoon tinkled in a cup.

'Here you go. Drink it while it's hot.' Katya put the steaming mug on the floor next to him with a careful hand, and got up to collect up her things. She moved slowly, methodically, and he watched her surreptitiously, willing her to move more slowly, to turn in to slow motion, to become a permanent fixture, just to stay. Momentarily he imagined her waking up next to him, and wondered what she would look like, smell like. But before he knew it she was heading for the door, and a feeling close to panic covered his skin with goose bumps and brought bile to his throat once more.

'Katya, I'm sorry, I didn't mean what I said.'

'I know, puppy.' She turned and put her head on one side, and waited.

'I . . . I do want . . . your help. Can you help me?' It came out as a hoarse, high-pitched whisper, and Mitya struggled to clear his throat, too late, as ever.

'Yes, of course I can. What's the problem?' Katya the angel came back, and shone her light on him.

Mitya's eyes filled with tears, and he looked up at the ceiling, blinking furiously. 'I'm not sure. I can't really tell you. But there are things I need to do. And I think I need to do them now.'

Katya's eyes were round and wide, and she salivated

slightly as she replied, 'Cool. I'm cool with adventures. And I'd like to help you, of course. My life is so boring, really.'

Mitya glanced at her face, looking for any trace of sarcasm. There was none.

'But why, Katya?'

'You are my friend, Mitya. You're a funny guy. You come over all tough but . . . I saw your face when we were saving those puppies. I saw the care you took with them. You're a good man.'

Mitya thought about this, and closed his eyes again. He heard her come back towards him, drop her bag and sit down on the floor. He listened to her clicking through his cassette collection, humming, and decided that he liked it. It was strange, but also weirdly familiar, as if she had always been there, doing that, but just in the next room, just out of reach, just out of his earshot.

'Where are you from, angel? You don't live here, do you? I'm sure I've never seen you here before this week.'

'I'm here staying with my cousin: she's got a room at the top of the hall. She's the big lumpy girl with bad skin and several chickens – you might have seen her? Her name is Marina. To be honest, I don't really like her. But I needed a place to stay while I study, and she's all I've got.'

'What do you mean, all you've got?'

'I'm an orphan. I'm a no-one.'

'Where are you from though? You're not from Azov? I've never seen you here before. I think I would have . . . remembered.'

'No. I sort of grew up everywhere, but I'm from nowhere really. I've lived in lots of places: lots of homes; lots of towns. I like Azov though. I wouldn't mind coming from Azov. It's a friendly place, isn't it, puppy?'

'Don't call me puppy, Katya. You can call me Mitya.'

'Mitya-the-Exterminator. Yes, I know.'

'You know?' Mitya was stunned.

'My cousin told me that was your name. I prefer puppy.'

Mitya looked at his feet under the blanket, and the worn patch in his white sock, and wondered just what the cousin had told Katya about him.

'What do you exterminate, Mitya?'

Mitya hesitated for a long moment.

'Memories, Katya. Memories.'

She looked at him and unleashed her lopsided grin. 'You're a real Russian man.'

'You think? I don't even drink vodka.'

'A man who can be maudlin without a drop of spirit, is a Russian man indeed,' she laughed. Mitya smiled back, and as the muscles in his face stretched and moved, he realized he could not remember the last time he had smiled for real, at another human being, sharing something.

'So, Mitya, are we going to have a little adventure?'

'Adventure? I'm not sure. I have to get it straight in my mind. And I can't think with this excuse for music going on so loud!' He banged the wall with his fist, and winced as the scabs forming on his knuckles made contact with the orange wallpaper and left tell-tale rosy smears on its surface.

'I have headphones. Look – take them from my Walkman, plug them in here, listen to Depeche Mode, plan our adventure. It's not so hard, Mitya. Don't give up before you've started.'

Stretching out a stiff arm, Mitya took the headphones and put them on. Why had it never occurred to him before? Instantly, Andrei the *Svoloch* was banished from the room and Dave Gahan and the lads were in the centre of his brain. Katya passed him a pencil from the desk and he started, slowly, to draw up a list of things to do, to make him sane. Mitya didn't put pen to paper often: the writing was spidery, and the list was necessarily short.

When the track ended, he took off the headphones and was transported back to the crushing despair of Andrei the *Svoloch*'s reality. He dropped the pencil.

'Well, there's the list, angel, but you know, actually, it's all shit.'

'What is, puppy?'

'My life. It's too late. I've fucked it all up. It's not like it's meant to be. We all hate each other. It's all a waste of time: a waste of life.'

'It doesn't have to be.'

'Yeah, yeah, like there can be a happy ending.'

'There can be.'

'No, you don't understand. There can't be a happy ending. I'm just incapable now of making any sort of ending of this mess. I don't deserve better, and I can't make it better.'

'That's not true.'

Mitya looked away from her, turning to the wall.

'Everyone can make things better.'

'You're naive.'

'And you're making yourself into a loser.'

'No, *they* made me into a loser. They did it.'

'They, whoever they are, just made a start, and you are doing the rest yourself. It doesn't have to be like that. I don't care who you are: it's not a done deal.'

'Maybe it's all I deserve. You have no idea of the thoughts that go through my head. I scare myself sometimes. You don't know me, and I don't know what I'm capable of.'

'And you have no idea what goes through my head. You call me angel: I'm no angel, puppy. But I know I'm worth more than this. And so are you. We all are, Mitya.'

159

Katya swigged a mouthful of his tea and rubbed her forehead with her short, slightly bent fingers.

'We're all worth more. You have to respect yourself . . . you know, I work with little kids, and they all deserve to have good lives.'

'They won't get them though, will they?'

'Some will . . .'

'And some will become alcoholics, and some wife beaters, and some fraudsters, and some hooligans.'

'And some doctors, and teachers, or, you know, architects and things like that. Interior designers.' Katya was looking around the room again. 'I guess you like orange, puppy?'

'It reminds me of the sun,' replied Mitya, unsmiling. He screwed up the paper he had been writing on and threw it at the bin.

'Why?'

'It's just a list. Forget it. There's no point.'

Katya picked up the ball of paper and smoothed it out carefully.

'Don't read it!'

'Well I can't read it, can I, puppy? Your writing's all over the place! So you'll have to tell me, Mitya – where do we start?'

Mitya drank down what was left of his tea and grimaced as it hit his empty stomach. He stifled a belch with his fist and looked, for a long time, at the angry red marks on his knuckles.

'I told you, Katya, there's no point. It doesn't matter.'

'And I told you that there is, and it does. I'm not going till you tell me where we start. Really! Stop playing with me. You called me back: now deal with it. I can't just leave you now. You remind me of some of the kids at the school, the really naughty ones, all brave and tough but actually . . .'

Katya knelt and leant towards him, showing her little white teeth in a smile that crinkled her eyes but was lit by the glow of determination rather than laughter, '. . . but actually, they need my help more than anyone else. Although it nearly kills you to ask, eh?'

It was a look that Mitya recognized from the other significant women in his life: namely his grandmother, mother and his former primary school teacher, Miss Kryzhanovskaya. He wiped a blob of congealed blood from the inside of his nose, and realized further resistance was futile.

'OK, OK, whatever. If you really want to waste your time . . . We start, sweetness, with a visit to the SIZO, if you're really . . . up for it.'

'The SIZO?'

'The remand prison.'

Katya laughed. 'I know what a SIZO is, thank you, puppy. I've been before, but not in Azov. Tell me where it is, and I can take you there on Saturday, if you're well enough. I have a car.'

Her face took on the mystical aura of an ancient saint at the announcement of her ownership of a car.

'Where did you get a car from?'

The saintly look snapped off, and Katya frowned slightly.

'Never you mind: cars come and go, but the main thing is – it's mine, for now. I have the key and everything. I have a licence. I have diesel. And you can't argue.'

Mitya had no intention of arguing.

'Can't we go tomorrow though? It's quite . . . urgent. The visit I have to make. I'm not sure I can wait until Saturday.'

'Well, I have to study tomorrow, Mitya. And I don't think you'll be up to it, to be honest. Saturday will be OK. Trust me.'

And strangely, Mitya did trust her. The tea had made him

sleepy, and shock and exhaustion were weighing down his eyelids and tugging at his sore limbs. The shaking had worn off and been replaced by a heaviness that felt hot and sweet and heavy, and like it would go on forever. With stiff, careful movements he pushed himself up from the floor and collapsed forward, in slow motion, on to his narrow, orange bed, face first, his eyes closing as soon as his head made a furrow in the taut nylon pillow. With an effort, he turned his head to one side, to squeeze out a few words.

'We'll go to the SIZO. But you won't like it. And neither will I.'

'Like, not like – that's not the point, is it? We're making a start. And to be honest, it's got to be better than helping cousin Marina wash out her smalls in a bucket, hasn't it? I think so, anyway. Goodnight. Sleep well. Sweet dreams, Mitya!'

She looked back at him from the door, but could only see the back of his head, his short hair bristling on his collar slightly as it moved with his deep, even breathing. Katya clicked the door shut. Andrei the *Svoloch* was waiting in the corridor, leaning against his door frame.

'Katya, honey pie, where have you been all evening? We missed you, we've been having a ball. Sveta's got *vint*, and we're all getting, you know, really sexy!' Andrei was stoned, as usual, as were all the other inhabitants of the room. Katya walked on by, as she'd promised she would, and went to listen to cousin Marina's tales of her day at the cheese factory.

Back in the orange room, Mitya never heard the door shut, or Katya's goodbye: he was already dreaming of dogs, and balls, and wells. And shouting, and tears, and a summer's day that started so well, but ended somewhere else. And something Mitya couldn't see, something behind him, or in

162

the corner of his eye, a presence that was definitely there, but intangible. A something that brought him out in a cold sweat and drew an icy finger down the length of his spine. Someone that made him look behind, although he didn't want to look, and keep on running. Run but don't trip! Keep running, Mitya. Run, Mitya, run!

14

The Ministry

Galia woke early, as always. It took a few moments for her to remember where she was. She was struck by the quiet all around her. She could not believe she was in the middle of a capital city with a dual carriageway not twenty metres from the building. There was a remarkable stillness in the apartment, and even the dust in the air, glowing golden in the morning sun, was completely still, suspended on threads of soft silence. She gently peeled her face away from the plastic-coated pillow she had found the night before, and rubbed her cheek, waiting to hear footsteps and the usual communal morning movements before getting up. There was nothing. She sat up gingerly, aching a little from the unusual sleeping arrangements: she had chosen an army-issue rubber lilo with rough khaki blankets on top and a couple of relatively clean pink towels underneath to stop her sticking to the rubber, and said plastic-coated pillow. She was still convinced it hadn't been a bad choice, but she had slid off the lilo several times during the night, and at one point had woken up with it on top of her. Her dreams had not been the most restful.

She leant back against a tower of old journals and mulled

over the plan for today, ticking off the list in her head of ministries and ministers that they had discussed the previous night, and thought about looking for a city map to start making a route.

When, at eight a.m., the apartment was still blanketed in silence, her impatience got the better of her. She tiptoed out in to the hall, and then peeked into every room for a sign of life. She tried all the doors, and even the store cupboard (which gave her a fright), but could find no sign of Grigory Mikhailovich at all. He had disappeared.

Zoya was curled up on a large, French-style high-backed sofa, snoring softly under a vibrating pile of greatcoats, fur hats, long-johns and other assorted old clothes. Galia shook her roughly by the shoulder.

'Zoya! Zoya, wake up!'

Zoya groaned and tried to shake free of Galia's clutch. 'Get off me, don't touch,' she muttered half asleep, 'I'm a state servant!'

'Zoya! Wake up! Grigory Mikhailovich has gone!'

'Fanny fed the butter to the pig!' was Zoya's only response, delivered in a plaintive and high-pitched wail.

Galia tried shaking her again, and the pile of old clothes spilled over the floor, leaving Zoya's puny body covered only by a red velvet flag emblazoned with Leonid Brezhnev's bear-like face.

'Oh Lord!' exclaimed Galia, momentarily horrified, and sitting down sharply on top of a pile of old cake boxes, she realized too late.

'Don't panic, Galia, don't panic. I expect he's in the bathroom,' croaked Zoya, suddenly lucid and stretching stiffly beneath Brezhnev's musty embrace.

'No, Zoya, he's not anywhere in the apartment, and . . . and . . . his bed hasn't been slept in.'

165

Zoya opened an eye and peered at Galia. 'What bed? Anyway, how would you know if his bed had been slept in, Galia my dear? He rises early, my cousin Grigory. Always has done. When we young—'

'I've been awake since before six, Zoya, and I have heard nothing: no-one has moved. No-one has come in, and no-one has gone out. You're telling me he's got up and gone out at five, are you? That old bear? I doubt he can actually get out of bed on his own, his joints are so bad.'

'Oh, I didn't know you were so keen on surveillance, Galina Petrovna. You surprise me!'

'I'm just trying to tell you that he has not gone out this morning, but he's not here either.'

'So – what? You're saying we imagined him, are you?'

'No. I don't know what I'm saying. But I've waited for two hours to get up and I've got all sorts of plans and things to do and questions to ask and then when I do get up – he's not here. What are we to do? We can't go to the ministries on our own, can we?'

Zoya swung her pale lilac feet to the floor and arranged Brezhnev into a makeshift toga.

'What we will do, Galia, is have some breakfast, and then get going.'

Galia gave an exasperated sigh, coaxed the ill-fitting borrowed slippers back on to her swollen feet, and followed her tiny friend into the kitchen. When she got there, Zoya was standing at the table, looking theatrical.

'There is a note, Galia my dear – your search for evidence wasn't very thorough, was it?'

'What do you mean?'

'He left a note. He will meet us at the Ministry of the Interior, at nine a.m.'

'But how . . . ?' Galia was aware that her mouth was

hanging open in an elongated 'o', but she didn't understand what was going on.

'No time for breakfast then,' said Zoya, taking a bottle of pills from her handbag and popping two down with a glug of greenish looking *kefir* that she found in the rather threatening-looking fridge. Then she hopped nimbly past Galia and back to her nest with a chirpy cry of, 'Once more unto the breach, dear friends, once more! Screw up your courage, woman!'

Galia frowned, and set off back to her own patch next door to find clean pop socks and a headscarf. It promised to be a long day. And the prospects for success seemed to be diminishing considerably. She heard a dog howl somewhere in the block, a muffled cry, lonely and despairing, and felt a shiver run down her spine.

* * *

Over twenty years before, Galia had visited Moscow on a works cultural trip. She had been rushed past Red Square and Lenin's Tomb, the Moscow Museum and the Kremlin. The glinting ancient monuments studded with modern memorials to the glory of the Soviets had intrigued her, the warm rosy flesh of reality replacing the black and white bones of pictures that had smattered the pages of shared books at school. The buildings had still seemed mysterious, otherworldly and never to be touched. But the visit had largely been spoilt by the efforts of their zealous guide. She felt herded as her group moved, as a single unit, from one stop to the next, with no time for questions, or individual exploration, or even for talk between the holiday makers. Idle chat between group members had been ruthlessly shushed by the guide. Other special sights had included the grey mass of the Hotel Rossiya – the biggest tourist hotel in the world – and Bassein Moskva, the biggest open-air swimming pool in the world. She hadn't liked it, this modern stuff: it was brash, hard and unwashed. The hotel was full of roaches and inedible food, bad smells and rude staff. And the swimming pool had steamed in the autumn sky like the depths of a chlorine-impregnated hell. Every so often she glimpsed the faces of sinners writhing under the noxious clouds, their mouths wide, hands raised in silent entreaty. But mostly Muscovites had struck her as rude and self-important, and best avoided.

Now, in the 1990s, it was even worse. The Metro was bursting with adverts full of women with huge white teeth and disposable nappies. Every poster on every street corner was trying to sell the citizens shares in this or that diamond mine, oil company or chocolate factory. The roads, be they sweeping boulevards or the narrow crooked lanes that strained to connect them, were crammed with filthy cars jostling for position, and none of them going anywhere. The shops in the city centre were bursting with the kinds of things that few honest people could afford, and no-one needed. And in among all the grandeur and twenty-four-hour consumption, old ladies stood in ragged rows around Metro stations, trying to sell any old thing in order to buy a crust of bread: a single shoe; some well-used laces; a spoon.

'Zoya. Hey, Zoya!' Galia nudged her friend and shouted as their Metro carriage roared through a tunnel several tens of metres below the *Lubyanka*, 'which is our stop?'

'Relax, Galia, I've got it all under control. It's the next one.' Zoya had been busy eyeing a couple across the carriage from herself, wondering what they saw in each other. One of them was studying a 'What's On' guide to Moscow, and Zoya wished she had time to take a look. She was entranced by this new Moscow. She loved the mass of bright colours, the bustle, the quiet music seeping from cafe doorways and the hullabaloo of street performers, the well-groomed young people with their deodorant and leather shoes, the little dogs and exotic foreign students smelling of expensive perfume and tobacco. Moscow was home to dozens of fancy theatres, there were ballet schools around every corner and great collections of art galleries and historical museums at every turn. Zoya hoped she was not going to have to spend the whole day traipsing around dust-laden ministries full of people who should have been buried long ago: it would be a shame not to get a nose full of culture while they were here. The Metro train plunged deeper into the rattling darkness, making Zoya's ears pop and for a moment the lights flickered and the carriage was bathed in a weird half-light. Who knew, it may be her last chance.

To exit the station the ladies rode an escalator that was so long they almost forgot what they'd got on it for by the time they approached daylight. Turning to look back down at her friend, Galia was stabbed by a sudden feeling of vertigo that spread from her stomach in to her legs and then into every extremity. She was shaking by the time they had fought their way out of the busy station and into the bright Moscow morning.

Back on the surface, the Ministry of Internal Affairs turned out to be a plain building on the Garden Ring: solid, squatting square and grey in the sunshine, it looked uninviting, and uninteresting. Galia swallowed back a taste of disappointment that the ministry wasn't housed in one of Stalin's sky-scrapers, the Seven Sisters. She had a long-standing respect for the hugely sinister buildings, rocketing sun-ward from a broad launch pad of certainty that the Soviet Union is, was, and ever shall be, eternal. Gothic and glowering, at

169

least they had presence, Galia thought, unlike this third-rate shiny-suit of a building. Zoya hopped ahead of her and grabbed her wrist with a tenacious, claw-like grip. 'Come on, Galia, don't lose heart now. We can do this. I read the cards this morning, and all the portents are good.'

They found the correct door on their fourth attempt, which they both felt was quite good going. 'I told you the portents were good,' whispered Zoya.

As each oak door, complete with brass handles, seemed to stand at least twenty feet tall and weigh at least 200lbs, they were panting by the time they stood before the rather shabby reception desk at 'Internal Affairs: Southern (Non-Caucasus)'. The desk was littered with forms of various colours, shapes and thicknesses, many of which appeared to have been partly filled in and then abandoned. A pale, slender young man with watery red-rimmed eyes checked their papers and took their names.

'Would you like a reference number?' he asked without looking up.

'Do we need a reference number?' countered Zoya, screwing up her nose inquisitively.

'Well, it depends on you. This ministry is a modern Russian Federation state organ: we don't treat people like numbers. President Yeltsin has decreed that everyone is to be treated as an individual, and has abolished compulsory reference numbers.'

'That's good,' said Galia, smiling at the pale young man.

'Yes it is,' he said, still without looking up.

'So why might we want a reference number?' asked Zoya with a frown.

'Well,' said the young man, finally putting down his pen and raising his eyes to look at them, 'in the new Russia, it is all down to individuals' choices. You can choose not to have a reference number, and just join the queue. Or you can choose to buy a reference number, and join the queue.'

'Buy?' both ladies said as one.

'Yes, buy. This is capitalism, after all.'

'Why would we want to buy a reference number and join the queue?' Galia asked, puzzled.

'Well, it just depends on how much queuing you want to do.'

'What if I don't want to queue at all?' Zoya replied.

'Then you will need to buy the Platinum Rate reference number.'

'And if I want to queue for an hour.'

'For an hour you will need the Gold Rate reference number.'

'Saints preserve us. This is just legal bribery, isn't it?' Galia rolled her eyes towards the beige-painted ceiling.

'Elderly Citizen, this is capitalism; customer service, merit-ocracy, individual wealth. Now, would you like to buy a reference number, or not?'

'My cousin, Grigory Mikhailovich Semechkin, will be joining us shortly,' Zoya enunciated in clipped tones, leaning over the desk as far as her sparrow-legs would allow her and scanning the young man's eyes for a flicker of fear, or recognition, or life. There was none. 'So you can stick your reference number up your samovar until then.'

'Sit there,' he said blankly, pointing across the hall.

Galia took a seat next to an extremely broad, ruddy-faced woman. As she nodded to the woman she noticed that every tiny vein in the woman's face was bright crimson and clearly visible. She was momentarily fascinated by the intricate network of lines that made up her neighbour's face, and traced the network with her eyes from nostril to cheek to lip and hairy mole. Then, with a rush of colour to her own face, she realized how closely she was examining the poor woman. She was probably a farmer or construction worker or similar. She probably didn't even own a mirror. She had probably spent her whole life toiling in the fields so that the people of this city could put bread in their mouths and flush their toilets in peace. Galia turned in her seat so that she looked straight ahead instead. She wondered if they should have invested in a reference number: numbers were still very important, and if you didn't have one, you didn't really exist, despite what the young man with the red eyes had said about meritocracy. She looked down the corridors to the left and right: they were lofty, brown, echoing, and very, very long. She could not even make out the ends of either corridor; it was as if they went on for ever, a never-ending repeated pattern of brown door, brown wall, strip light and shiny floor: no people, no curves, and no life.

Zoya was bored already. She had examined all the people she could see from here, and found them wanting. There was nothing of interest in their faces, clothes or speech. They were the usual crowd. She took out her sewing bag from beneath her rain poncho: she had insisted on wearing it despite the sun and heat: she predicted rain, and with her coat gone, the plastic poncho would have to suffice.

'Oh Lord, Zoya, don't be sewing eyes on a thousand-eyed serpent in the Ministry of the Interior. It's just asking for trouble. Put it away – now!' Galia's eyes were wide as she hissed at her friend, trying not to draw attention to herself, and only succeeding in the opposite. All heads turned their way with a rustle of manmade fibres and a slight puff of dandruff.

Without raising her head, Zoya's eyes moved stealthily across the dough-pale faces with their blackcurrant-eyes staring blankly in her direction, and with a sniff indicating

172

both hurt and mild discomfort, quietly put the sewing bag away. 'These people aren't ready,' she conceded to Galia. 'This ministry isn't ready. Might be, you know . . . hmm,' and trailed off with a sigh which slipped into a vague hum of something slightly stirring, and ancient.

An hour later, there was still no sign of Grigory Mikhailovich, and Zoya began to pace, her tiny bird-like feet making sharp click-clacks on the polished granite floor. The dough zombies watched her progress, their heads moving in unison first to one side, then to the other, like spectators at a very, very slow tennis match, with no points scored. Galia had attempted, for some time, to concentrate on the crossword that had been in her pocket since before the train journey, but it was now just a mess of boxes and letters and scribbles that offended her sense of correctness. She screwed it up and tossed it in to the over-flowing bin.

'Well done!' said Zoya, 'crosswords help no-one. Whatever the problem, crosswords are not the answer. Like ironing: ironing is never the answer. Or golf.'

'Stroke,' thought Galia, but said nothing, keeping her eyes on her folded hands in her lap. A door opened in the middle-distance of corridor number one, to the left, and a man in a grey suit emerged. Tension in the waiting area mounted to fever pitch: jaws flopped open, eyelids twitched, the crowd held its breath: and then it dissipated, as the man shuffled slowly away in the opposite direction, leaving them with nothing but the echo of his steps.

Some time later, but no-one could really be sure when, as time does funny things in ministries and seems to slow down or stop altogether at some points (especially during lunch hour, which is often two or three hours, and not at lunch-time), the young man took a phone call, and looked in Zoya's direction. He talked very softly, so that they could not make out the words, but only occasional S and T noises, and the odd smirk.

'He's talking about us!' Zoya whispered, excited yet fretful, like a toddler at a fairground who needs a wee. 'You'll see. We'll be next. But where is Grigory Mikhailovich? He must be here for the meeting. We can't possibly do it without him.'

'Zoya, I think we can. After all, he's not really contributed much so far, has he?'

'What do you mean?'

'Well, we got off the train without him, we found our beds without him, we had our breakfast, or rather didn't have our breakfast, without him, and we got here without him. I don't really see what your cousin's contribution to our mission is, Zoya.'

'Well, that's gratitude, isn't it?'

'To be honest, I have found him . . . quite disappointing.'

Galia knew that these words would annoy Zoya, but she couldn't help it: they were true.

'You snake!' hissed Zoya, leaping theatrically away from Galia as if she had indeed rattled her tail and dripped venom. 'You're so ungrateful!'

'Sit down, Zoya! Sit down, and tell me what I have to be grateful for, my dear, and I'll do my best. But you know, you tell me nothing, so I just have to say it as I see it. And I don't see *him* – do you?'

'He'll be here,' Zoya muttered and took a draw on her smelling salts and looked at her watch.

The boy behind the desk had put down the phone and was scribbling something on a piece of lilac-coloured paper.

'Purple paper – you see?' nudged Zoya, her eyes shining excitedly. 'Something will happen now!'

About an hour later, nothing at all had happened: no-one

174

had been seen, and no-one had left. Zoya had resorted to seeing how long she could hold her breath for, watching the second hand go round on her neighbour's watch and occasionally feeling rather light headed when it got towards a minute. Galia had spent her time watching Zoya, and wondering why her cheeks were going from grey to ashen to ruddy every so often.

Eventually Zoya rose, with a slight wobble, and looked towards the great oak doors.

'I'm going for a smoke, Galia. Get me in if anything happens.' And with that she stalked out of the ministry and in to its grounds, where rotting plaster urns full of sand and dog ends beckoned the kippered smokers out of the building to have a puff in the yellow summer air. Zoya took in a lung full, and felt a little better.

In truth, she had to admit that she was becoming concerned. Where was her cousin? Why hadn't he made the agreed meeting point? It had been his idea to meet at nine, after all. And most pressing of all, why had he taken her Makarov pistol? She had hidden it deep in the depths of the travel bag, but there was no sign of it there this morning. Her fingers gripped the filter of her cigarette tightly: a bear with a gun was always a bad idea.

* * *

It was mid-afternoon, and the heat in the corridor hung heavily on the ladies' shoulders and eyelids. The sun, just visible through the grimy windows, bathed in a sulphurous smog. Ragged-looking birds sat coughing in the branches of the single tree that graced the gardens of the Ministry of the Interior, and the red-eyed young man behind the desk had been replaced by a stout middle-aged man with greased-down

175

hair and no neck, whose eyes were fighting a losing battle with his cheeks. One day the cheeks would win completely, thought Galia, and he would be blind. He would be the amazing eye-less bureaucrat.

'Do you ever think about death, Galia?' Zoya had been sitting staring at the floor for at least fifteen minutes, and Galia had feared something like this was coming.

'Of course I think about death, Zoya. But not every day. And not while I'm at the vegetable patch, or cooking, or playing with—' her voice caught in her throat, 'or playing with Boroda, and the children out in the yard.'

'I bet you think about it at the Elderly Club! It is unavoidable. It is staring you in the face, everywhere you look.'

'No, that's not true, Zoya. At the Elderly Club, I see life. Old life, yes, but life all the same. I see people carrying on, doing their best, enjoying medium-difficulty puzzles that do not require too much manual dexterity.'

'I see a bunch of old prunes who are idling out the last of their days with crosswords for children and collections of ailments as long as that tapeworm Sasha Smirnov had. Ha! Do you remember him? He came running out of the clinic—'

'You're just fed up because we're waiting.' Galia broke in quickly, anxious to avoid the tapeworm story.

'Sasha Smirnov. He was a nice man, wasn't he?' Zoya's eyes were far away and damp looking. 'You would never have guessed he had a tapeworm, would you? He looked so solid, not at all scrawny. Mind you, you used to feed him quite regularly, didn't you, Galia? He liked your *vareniki*, I seem to remember.'

'He did Zoya, he did. But not as much as he liked your séances. He was a regular at your flat for a while, wasn't he?' Galia smiled at the memory of seeing Sasha Smirnov, broad and red as a barn door, squeezed behind Zoya's tiny wooden table, surrounded by bright-eyed, smiling women, all intent on calling up the souls of their dead husbands, fathers and sons. She had never taken part in these events, but had simply stopped by to drop off spare apples, or garlic, or mint, and to observe for a moment. Sasha Smirnov, biting into an apple, his big white teeth belying his advancing years, and his apparent robustness masking the secret of the worm embedded in his intestines. Sasha Smirnov, who had brought Zoya beads and scarves from far-flung markets, and had trotted after her through the streets of Azov, his loyalty noticed by all except Zoya, apparently. Sasha Smirnov, who came running out of the clinic looking like he had seen the devil, and who had moved away shortly afterwards.

'He was useful to have around the table; I can't deny it, Galia. He attracted spirits well, and gave comfort to many women.'

'Did he give you any comfort, Zoya?' Galia smiled as she asked the question, already knowing what her friend's answer would be.

'There was nothing of that sort between us, I assure you. My destiny was my own to fulfil – that's the way I wanted it. I could never share all my secrets, Galia, with a man.' Zoya took Galia's hand in hers and squeezed it slightly. 'But I missed him when he went. He was . . . a reassuring presence, if you see what I mean, like the rings on Saturn.'

'I see, Zoya.' And Galia thought she saw what her friend meant. Both ladies fell silent for a minute.

'Do you remember that holiday we took, Zoya, to Chelyabinsk? I was thinking about that the other day. Well, thinking about all my holidays, really. But for some reason that one made me laugh out loud, while I was standing there washing up. Boroda came in to see what was going on – I think she thought I was having a funny turn.'

'Ha, Chelyabinsk! Yes, I remember. The mud spa that had no running water.'

'Ugh! And the four-hour visit to the tractor plant . . .'

'Oh my! The picnic in the woods when we were eaten alive by insects.'

'And the visit to the collective farm where they had no vegetables to show us. I was so disappointed.' Galia laughed.

'And the planetarium? I loved the planetarium.' Zoya directed a wistful gaze out of the window, towards the yellow skies.

'Oh yes, the planetarium. The display got stuck and the narrator had to tell us about Orion six times in a row because he wasn't allowed to change the script.' Galia giggled at the memory. 'I could recite it off by heart for a while: 'Orion is a prominent constellation located on the celestial equator and visible throughout . . .'

'Yes, but I loved it. The planets, Galia, the universe . . . all around us, in Chelyabinsk. Full of mystery, and possibility, and enormousness . . .'

'I suppose so, Zoya.' Galia did not want to admit that she had thought the stuck planetarium rather a disappointment. 'It all seems like so long ago now.' She yawned and stretched. 'And here we are, in this atmosphere that is making us maudlin, as if the solar system never existed. Government buildings are always depressing. They make you feel like death is round the corner. It's the way they are designed, I think.'

'I want to go to the moon, Galia. Will you come with me?'

Galia turned a quizzical smile-frown on her friend, who was still staring out of the window. 'Of course, Zoya, but we can't go just yet – we have got to finish this little adventure first.'

Zoya's head snapped down, and she shook herself slightly, returning her eyes to the scene around her. She sighed. 'Old people shouldn't be made to wait in government buildings.'

Galia nodded in agreement.

'I am sure if we had access to the figures we'd find out that the death rate for over Seventies rises exponentially after an eight-hour wait on a hard wooden chair in a draughty brown corridor waiting for the third secretary's underling to turn up,' Zoya went on. 'And my arse is numb, totally numb!'

The ladies had been waiting a long, long time. The Third Secretary Internal Affairs: Southern (Non Caucasus) was clearly having a very busy day. Now new people fought their way in through the heavy oak doors every so often, mopping their necks and foreheads with damp handkerchiefs as they waited self-consciously at the desk. Their time of arrival had no bearing on when they were actually seen. The anxiety in the waiting area rose to breaking point each time a bureaucrat emerged slowly into the corridor and clicked their way with deliberation, and sometimes a detour or two, towards the waiting area. The bureaucrats would bark out a reference number, and that would be it. Some people arrived and were seen within an hour. Some were sent straight back out again. But by late afternoon, no-one seemed to have waited as long as Galia and Zoya. The crimson-faced farmer had been seen by two. She did not, however, return. Maybe she was still in the building somewhere, being interviewed or filling in papers with scratchy pens, in the right order and the right colour, which made sense to no-one except the functionaries themselves. Galia shut her eyes and her head began to nod. Pictures passed before her closed eyes of piles of paper, pens that didn't work, clocks on the wall and magical numbers, snarling policemen and whimpering dogs. The whole system was a mystery, and the man with the insider knowledge to unlock its secrets, the esteemed Grigory Mikhailovich, had steadfastly refused to put in an appearance. A small tear trickled from the corner of Galia's right eye, and she gave herself up to a little sleep. Sleep was what she needed, a drop of restorative shut-eye, and a chance to forget about Moscow and dream about her garden and Boroda.

*   *   *

Across town, the man himself, the bear with wolf's eyes, was having a good day. The glossy black ZIL limousine had oiled round the corner at the allotted time and he himself had, by the filmy skin of his gold-capped teeth, made it to the corner of the road to meet it. Good days were seldom in this clapped out excrescence of what had been his life. He savoured the juice of it and cherished the feeling of mild success, at least of nothing having gone painfully wrong, in the depths of his cavernous, badly sprung chest. The odd good day kept him going when otherwise the only appointment on the horizon was with death, or worse, with one of Kolya's totally indigestible stews and clever-dick conversation.

Grigory Mikhailovich held Kolya in his heart along with the memory of his grandmother, Grigory's cousin Elizaveta, and did his best to educate the boy on his long-dead relative's behalf. But the boy's cooking was really beyond his worst imaginings. Worse than anything the NKVD had ever dreamt up. Worse than the worst years of the 1970s and 80s when rice was looked upon as a luxury and the value of a food was measured by its fat content alone. The fattiness of those years clung to Grigory Mikhailovich's arteries like a warm, thick overcoat, but still he survived, dumbfounding his doctors and former colleagues alike.

One by one, his former underlings had succumbed to strokes, heart attacks, freak accidents, brain tumours, piles as big as plums and warts with their own, hidden agendas. And Grigory Mikhailovich had outlived them all, to his own chagrin, to become an old man, cared for by a young relative who had little conversation and no interest in anything other than the study of electronics, imported arty films and girls.

So, the ZIL had come early, and Kolya's re-re-fried pasta had stayed locked in the fridge. The rest of the day had proceeded with great ease, and all had gone to plan, as far as Grigory Mikhailovich could recall. His early morning trip to the banya had been very welcome, and he felt utterly refreshed, if very hungry, after having sweated, sploshed and napped there for a few hours. But at the back of his mind, he had a nagging suspicion that he had forgotten to do something – like turn off the kettle, or put the cat out, but not exactly that. Maybe Kolya would be able to remind him later. Lunch at his club had been fulsome, and the drive around Moscow's boulevards afterwards had been slow enough for him to digest fairly well by the time he reached home.

Once back at the apartment, Grigory Mikhailovich had determined to make his own tea, since there was no-one home to do it for him. Waiting by the stove, he noticed a note on the table, in his own hand. He reached out for it slowly, struggling to recall what it might say. As he read the brief words scrawled on it, he remembered, fully and vividly, the night before, the plan, and the reason that the two ladies, Zoya and the other, quiet one, were staying at his flat. He turned the gas off, heaved himself back in to the hall, and picked up his briefcase. He entered the combination, and checked inside: everything was in order, including the pistol he'd pinched from Zoya's travel bag, for some reason he couldn't now recall.

He took the crusted plastic phone from its box in the hallway and plugged it in to the jack. The line buzzed, and he pressed in the numbers with a certainty that rarely visited him.

'Come for me, now. I have business.' He threw the receiver back down and made for the door, his blue eyes gleaming. The game was on.

15

Deep in the SIZO

Immersed in the yellow light dripping from the over-ripe bulb above his head, Vasya turned the pages of the book, slowly and with some care. Its ancient leaves crinkled softly, here and there stuck together with dubious substances, and in other places so well-thumbed that they were almost translucent, like dead butterfly wings between his shaking fingers. The pictures on the pages were grainy and dark; old-style reproductions that reminded Vasya, on a certain level, of the school books he'd formerly worked with, which gave the people depicted in them an alien, or perhaps corpse-like, air. Vasya had never really minded poor pictures before: the badly stuffed faces were neither here nor there, and he hadn't dwelt on it. But now, in this cell full of murmuring shadows and physiognomies that were only half visible, or only half there, he wanted bright colour and clean lines, and innocent smiles that reeked of minty freshness and apples. The cell felt like a living reproduction of the book's pictures: Vasya craved the comfort of bright lines to reassure him that the outside that he remembered was, indeed, real. How long had he been in this stinking room?

'Good, isn't it?'

Shura leant in closely over Vasya's shoulder, his sweet, rotten breath fanning the old man's cheek and leaving it filmed with a nutty moistness. Vasya turned his head to nod and smile in his jovial way and found his nose almost touching that of his neighbour and bunk-mate. He looked into a pair of pale eyes. Shura, a young man technically, looked like he had lived his life chained up in the yard, or down in the bins at the station, or in the process of falling off the platform at the trunk line station. His skin was pale marble over his chest, but from the neck up and over his hands it was flapping and ravaged: flesh hung off his features in sagging red dollops, soaked in vodka, smashed by fights. His flat nose was almost as wide as his forehead and spread into the remains of high cheekbones. Shura smiled.

'This book is amazing, young man. I haven't seen one like this for many, many years. In all my time as a teacher, we never had books quite like this. Where did you get it, my friend?'

'Here. It stays here.' Shura reached out for the book and took it from Vasya's hand. 'I can use it to buy stuff. See?'

Vasya thought he saw: Shura could use guardianship of the book to barter for things. Shura's eyes were still on his own: this he had recognized as a slightly disconcerting habit of his neighbour: the eyes locked on to a human target, and shone, and didn't let go. He was there, minutes after a conversation had ended, still watching, still waiting, unblinking, slightly twinkly, too intimate, too close, like he was trying to see in to Vasya's mind and sniff what he found there.

'Tonight is Friday,' said Shura.

'Yes – is it already? My goodness! Friday!'

'We like Fridays.'

'Yes, well, I do. I usually go to the Elderly Club on a Monday and a Friday. On Mondays we have the Lotto and talks from formal speakers, who often concentrate on vegetable matters or environmental issues, and then on Fridays we do fun things like watch films or read poetry or have a tea dance.'

Shura stared at him with probing, knowing eyes and gently stroked his hand.

'Of course, I find the dancing a bit difficult, but I do my best. You know, there aren't that many men of my age still available to take a lady's hand for a Friday afternoon tea dance.' Vasya was aware that he was babbling, but could not stop, the gaze from Shura's eyes spurring him on, despite his efforts to concentrate on the head of his walking stick and not to look. 'Perhaps when you get out, Shura, you'd like to pop along. Although of course, you are nowhere near elderly. But maybe you could be an honorary elderly person for an occasion. I'm sure,' here Vasya stumbled slightly, knowing he was talking nonsense, 'I'm sure you would enjoy it. And the tea is really very good. Biscuits too, sometimes even cake.' Vasya stopped, and cleared his throat a little. He wondered if Shura would think he was being sarcastic. He hadn't meant to be. He just couldn't stop his mouth from talking when he was nervous. And Shura's eyes were making him nervous. He briefly speculated on why the prisoners liked Fridays, but then thought better of it.

'Elderly Club. You think I'd like it, really?'

Vasya nodded in a sheepish, half-hearted way. Shura wouldn't like Elderly Club.

'Maybe you're right. I don't know though: clubs were never really my thing. I like my own entertainment. I was thrown out of the Pioneers. I was no good.

'Really?'

185

'Really. I killed cats.'

Vasya jumped visibly, but tried to control his disgust.

'Oh, well, that's not good, Shura, but it's never too late. No, really. There are plenty at Elderly Club who have, well, perhaps not succeeded in life quite in the way they planned. But still, they are alive, and now want to enjoy themselves a little, as long as their health holds out and they can make it up the stairs.'

'These lads,' Shura waved a drooping hand towards the men ranged silently around them, limp and smelly, like dirty rags, 'these lads aren't going to make Elderly Club. They aren't going to make elderly, full stop. I'm not going to make elderly.'

'Well, you never know, Shura. If they get to prison camp and work hard and don't drink or take drugs or fight, maybe all will be well. There is no reason to think that life is over just because—'

Vasya stopped short. His neighbour had pulled off his vest and was languidly displaying an array of silver-red scars that chopped through the smooth pallor of his stomach, abdomen and lower back.

'I got these already in life, old man. You like? I don't like . . . I remember how I got these. How many times do you think I'm going to survive that? What kind of club do you think I'm going to with marks like these? The hell club, that's where I'm going to.'

Vasya swallowed, and his eyes filled with tears.

'And who knows what's going on, on the inside,' Shura chuckled and stroked a raw red hand over his belly, a shudder running through him, along the bed and, much to his disquiet, into Vasya.

'But surely . . . the prison wardens don't beat the convicts any more?' whispered Vasya.

'Ha, this has nothing to do with the wardens. It's not the wardens you have to look out for.'

And Shura winked and laughed long and low, till his shiny blue eyes watered and Vasya thought he might faint, so strong was the stench of tooth and death. Shura noticed his pallor.

'Don't worry, old man. You won't be going there – there'll be no prison camp for you. You'll be safe here with us, with the boys. We'll look after you. We like you. You'll stay here.' Shura's arm snaked around Vasya's shoulder, squeezing painfully in a gesture meant to be comforting, but which somehow just didn't hit the spot, a bit like the chicory coffee the school canteen had served up, but much, much worse. Vasya tried not to look into the blue light of Shura's gaze, and tried not to think about school coffee.

A metallic clank and the shuffling of dozens of ill-shod feet heralded the opening of the cell door to allow the evening meal to be served. The warders shouted hoarsely to the prisoners to stand away from the door and to keep their hands and everything else to themselves. Stale air flowed in from the corridor and carried with it the distinctive smell of buckwheat porridge and meat stew. The shadows on the walls stretched and shrank as the lights swayed with the air currents, and added a note of sea-sickness to Vasya's already burgeoning nausea. His stomach had never been his strongest asset, he readily acknowledged, but this was odd. This food was exactly what had kept him on track every day for almost forty years as a teacher, but now, in this cell, the smell seemed to represent loss and death and made his stomach draw tight as he sucked in his lips to keep from gagging.

'Here!' Shura disengaged his arm and shoved a metal dish containing the evening's meal towards him.

'Thank you, Shura, but I'm not really hungry tonight.'

'You have to eat,' Shura's eyes rolled down over Vasya's puny chest and legs, 'you have to eat, oldie.'

'You're right, I will try. But tonight, food just doesn't seem the right thing. My head is full of memories, and maybe, well, yes, definitely, regrets. I am not hungry. I have done bad things, Shura.'

'You don't say. What kind of things?'

Vasya immediately regretted his statement.

'Just . . . things. Nothing really bad, obviously, I don't want you to think that I'm—'

'Like me?'

'That's not what I meant. But no, I'm not much of a criminal. I just . . .' Vasya's voice trailed away, and he attempted to take a chew on a lump of gristle from the grey stew rolling gently around his dish.

'I'm a family man, you know,' said Shura unexpectedly.

'Really? Well, I didn't have you down as that, Shura. Tell me more.'

'Not much to tell, oldie. The wife is a mad bitch: she drinks. She drinks, and she does not stop.'

Vasya nodded and chewed more fiercely, until his jaw ached.

'I have a son, but I don't see him. They won't let me near him. He lives with his *babushka*. And he doesn't even write. It's like I was never there, but I remember. I used to bath him.'

Vasya attempted to swallow the gristle, and coughed hard as it stuck in the back of his throat.

'Come on, oldie, don't croak during dinner, it'll cause a fuss.'

Vasya took a gulp of stale water from his mug and freed the lump. He laid the dish on the floor, now all the more convinced the evening's concoction was not for him.

'That's very sad, Shura. I feel your loss. But I'm sure she takes good care of him.'

'Oh you are, are you?' Shura's super-personal gaze bore into Vasya.

'I only meant that a grandmother's love is a strong bond, and . . . and I'm sure you shouldn't worry about the little mite.'

'He's fourteen. I don't worry about him anymore. He survived his mother, he'll be OK. But I've been away from him for so long. I can't even remember his face properly now. I can't remember his voice.'

Vasya looked at his feet for a long time, minutes even. He wanted to speak, but for once he couldn't find any suitable words at all.

'You going to eat that?' another grey neighbour muttered and tapped his dish with an enquiring spoon. Vasya shook his head and the dish disappeared across the floor as if on strings.

'I'm sure you did your best, Shura. And I'm sure his grandmother has done a fine job.'

Shura snorted, and turned over to begin a game of cards with his neighbour on the other side. Vasya reclaimed the bunk and sat absently observing his cellmate, while small groups of headless bodies began to shuffle restlessly from one side of the room to the other: it was getting close to the time when the evening swap-over occurred. It was not an orderly process. On previous evenings, Vasya had begun to feel a little nervous at this stage in the proceedings, but tonight he was completely oblivious. He stared at his feet, and tried to remember the logical reasons for why he had done bad things. There must have been reasons: at the time, they must have seemed solid, convincing even. But now, looking back, he couldn't remember any of them. When he

189

looked into the dirty bucket of his own past history, all he could see was the muck floating on top: the results of his actions, all the consequences, both real and imagined, bobbing to the surface like dead rats. He put his head in his hands, and breathed hard through his nose.

Much later, when he had been asleep sitting up for some time, his neighbour shook him roughly by the shoulder.

'I have to tell you something.'

'What?' Vasya's mouth was sticky with sleep.

'I have to tell you something, oldie.'

'Shura, forgive me, but it is late. Maybe we can talk—'

'No, it's bothering me. I have to tell you. I didn't tell you the whole truth . . . about the scars.'

'What do you mean, Shura?'

'About how I got them.'

'So it was the prison wardens after all?'

'No,' The sudden look in Shura's eyes made Vasya's heart lurch. There was no doubt: such a concentration of pain, fear, hurt and above all, shame, could not be mistaken. 'It was my wife.'

'Your wife?' Vasya was horrified.

'You can't believe it, can you? I told you: she drinks. And when she drinks, she goes wild. I don't know, I just drink and sing and steal and fall over. But she turns into an animal. Look!' Again Shura raised his vest, and this time, close up, Vasya could make out among the lattice of marks something that made him shudder: little arcs of silver scars, a recognizable pattern: human teeth marks.

'Wretched, Shura, but how can this be?'

He shrugged. 'I loved her: she was my mate for life. But remember, oldie: people are animals. I learnt it. She bit chunks out of me, threw bottles at me, stubbed her cigarettes on me. She terrified me, and I . . . took it. And when I couldn't

190

take it any more, I left. And I left him . . . to her. I deserve to be here. It was babushka who saved him. Oh yes, I should be dead for what I've done. And soon, I expect, I will be.'

Shura turned away and, pulling the rough brown blanket around him, curled up on the bunk. Vasya felt his emptiness growing inside him from the pit of his stomach right up to his throat and beyond into the ends of his hair and finger-nails. He was an empty man: a shell, a nothing, a less than nothing. A useless tear squeezed from his left eye and he rubbed it away with a gnarled hand, open mouthed. He looked upwards with a jerk, desperately wanting to see heaven, but saw only cobwebs, soot and ancient porno-graphic images scrawled on the walls. There was no comfort, no clean lines, no twinkling stars, no God. He looked down again, and thought hard about himself.

He still didn't feel brave. He still didn't deserve Galina Petrovna. He was beginning to doubt that he ever would. But he wasn't an animal. Shura was wrong: people did not have to behave like beasts, or carry their guilt with them till death. There were things that could be done. He picked up his pen and paper, and began to write again, this time with a certainty that had been lacking before. He wrote only the truth, with no extraneous words or explanations, and begging only that the reader finish reading before making up their mind. On and on he wrote, until his mind was at peace and he was able to curl up on the bunk next to Shura, spooning him almost, and go to sleep with a clear mind and an empty heart.

16

A Minor Triumph

Zoya felt the ZIL limo approach before she saw or heard it. She had been hovering near the heavy oak doors for a long time observing a small child whom she felt, quite strongly, may have been an Egyptian high priest in a former life. She had been trying to get a good look at the child's ears to see if her hunch was correct, all the while attempting to formulate a subtle question as to whether the child had ever visited Heliopolis, when a tingle began at the back of her neck and made its spidery way down her spine, all the way to her girdle. The tingle made her sparse, purple hair stand up straight on end, and set her nose quivering.

'Galia,' she said, loudly but conspiratorially, winking her left eye at her friend who was dozing and dribbling slightly on to the shoulder of her own floral print summer dress.

'Galia!' This time she added a piercing note, not unlike the gulls that dive-bomb the few remaining wizened fishing boats that ply the deserted waters of the Sea of Azov. Galia started with a cry of 'Shoo! Dirty creature!' and all heads turned her way. Zoya motioned her with a frantic, claw-like hand to come over to the door.

'Something is about to happen. I know it!' Galia looked around her at the dappled white and red dough faces, and stood, straightening her dress and wondering what and how much she had said in her sleep. She had dreamt of Pasha and Boroda, and even Vasya. Poor Vasya, with his own teeth, his cane and his little kitty cat, and his endless offers of friendship and companionship that she had steadfastly ignored. She found a boiled sweet in her skirt pocket, and, popping it into her dry mouth complete with cellophane wrapper, and wondered whether the waiting room was bugged.

'Galia! Move your backside!' hissed Zoya, prompting a quizzical look from the high-priest-come-small-child at her feet. As Galia reached the window next to the heavy oak doors, the ladies saw a shiny ZIL limousine draw up to the kerb. Zoya chirruped and clapped her hands, swirling dust motes so that they glistened in curls between the heads that nodded in the weak afternoon sun trapped by the ministry's hallway. Galia drew a sharp breath as Grigory Mikhailovich clambered slowly and gigantically from the back of the car, with the help of a small man wearing a smart dark uniform and a peaked cap. And then, using two sticks, the old bear began the laborious trek up the path to the ministry, swaying rhythmically, scattering pigeons and clouds of spittle with each slow step forward. The clap of each shoe hitting the flagstones seemed to produce in Zoya an answering quiver deep within her chest, and her shaking hands clasped Galia's moist arm.

'He's here!' she whispered.

'I can hardly believe my eyes!' said Galia.

'You should have more faith!'

'You might be right,' said Galia with a smile, and hugged her friend.

193

They turned to the sea of faces behind them.

'He's here!' cried Zoya, triumphantly. 'Make space for Grigory Mikhailovich! He will need a seat, or possibly two. You child, get up from that chair! There's no Egyptian sun priest in you, you snotty baggage, I was quite mistaken. Go and play in the corridor, go on!' The child's mother looked up briefly from her crossword and tutted as Zoya shooed the reluctant small boy from a chair. His bottom lip started to quiver.

'Put out your hands. Here you go.' Zoya took a handful of glass beads from her pocket and poured them into his hands.

'There, that's all you need. You have fun with those. But don't tell anyone I gave them to you. And don't eat them.' The boy looked at the handful of beads, and with slow and precise movements, took one between his fingers, examined it, and then inserted it into his left nostril.

'That's the way, Sun-Ra, that's the way!' Zoya spun him lightly on his heels and pushed him towards the corridor while Galia cleared crumbs and dead flies from the now-vacant seat.

A long drawn-out sigh from the oak doors heralded the arrival of Grigory Mikhailovich. All heads turned as his massive form paused, silhouetted in the doorway, exuding a subtle yet unmistakably earthy scent of mothballs, buckwheat, vodka and pickles.

'Ah, ladies, ladies, good afternoon. Citizens, all!' sighed Grigory Mikhailovich and gave a nod that encompassed each and every one of the warm, over-dressed bodies filling up the entrance hall. He sat heavily in the recently vacated seat, spreading his knees wide and disturbing farmers' wives on either side of him.

The portly man with the cheeks behind the desk, whose

194

eyes were now almost as red as his predecessor's, watched Grigory Mikhailovich suspiciously, while trying not to pay him any attention at all.

'We need to see the Deputy Minister Glukhov,' boomed Grigory Mikhailovich from his seat, directly to the man with the cheeks.

'You must approach the desk and sign in, citizen,' replied the man in a strangled whisper, without meeting Grigory Mikhailovich's eyes.

'No, you don't understand, we need to see the Deputy Minister.' And Grigory Mikhailovich turned the fingers of his right hand into a strange, twisted shape, the fingers overlapping.

The clerk was unmoved. 'I am afraid that is impossible. He is out of the city. He is fishing at his dacha. It is August, citizen: all the ministers, deputy or otherwise, are away.'

'You don't understand, cursed spawn of Satan. This is Grigory Mikhailovich Semechkin, and we must see the Deputy Minister,' said Zoya, making for the reception desk with a little jump at the clerk. Galia thought she might be about to bite his nose, so close did her friend manage to come to his face.

'It is not possible, madam. He is out of the city.'

'No, you don't understand, we must see the Deputy Minister,' and Grigory Mikhailovich reached inside his shirt with a bear-like paw and drew out some sort of pass on an old piece of rough string. The pass caught the sunlight, and the chubby bureaucrat squinted, and read, and then started slightly, his face pallid. A magic button had been pressed by an invisible finger.

'The Deputy Minister Glukhov is at his *dacha* fishing for all of August, but I will see what I can do. Please be seated, madam.'

Zoya retreated and Grigory Mikhailovich made himself fully comfortable in the chair, while Galia observed the bureaucrat. A sickly sheen had broken out on his glowing cheeks, and she felt he looked distinctly peaky: unwell, even. She hoped there would be no need to call an ambulance on this occasion, and concluded that bad diet in the young had a lot to answer for. A lack of roughage and an over-reliance on imported processed foods could have a terrible effect on the body as a whole. She nodded to herself quietly and watched as the clerk picked up the heavy plastic phone and made a number of short, stuttering phone calls.

'Approach the desk, please.' His voice was soft when eventually he addressed them again.

'Young man: I can no more approach that desk than I can recall *Laika* from her orbit. It is far too late for that. My knees would not allow it. Be a decent sort, and come over our way to impart your news.' Grigory Mikhailovich did indeed appear to be suffering with his knees.

The clerk stared at the papers in front of him for several seconds, and then, without looking up, raised himself from his chair with a squeak of damp plastic and made his way, eyes fixed on the floor in front of him, towards Grigory Mikhailovich's knees. Zoya looked at Galia and winked.

'The Deputy Minister Glukhov, Roman Sergeevich, is very disappointed to have to disappoint you, but he is currently in a meeting with the Minister and the Deputy Prime Minister at his *dacha*, and therefore no meeting with you is possible at present. However, the Deputy Minister Glukhov, Roman Sergeevich, requests that perhaps you would like to phone this number at eight p.m. tonight to discover his whereabouts and maybe agree on a way forward with the . . . with the . . . situation that you find yourselves in, which is currently unclear to Glukhov, Roman Sergeevich, but which he assures me, I mean you, that he has the utmost interest in resolving. Forthwith, in fact.'

'Eight p.m.? Ladies, what do you think? Will our situation still be resolvable at eight this evening?'

'I sincerely hope so, Grigory Mikhailovich, but in truth, I cannot say,' Galia was disappointed, and her bottom lip trembled slightly. Still, it was some sort of progress, and therefore not to be sniffed at. 'I can only hope.'

'Tell your Glukhov that we will call him at eight. And that we all, most sincerely, hope that it will not be too late.' The shrinking bureaucrat and his cheeks were dismissed, and Grigory Mikhailovich held out a puffy hand to Zoya. 'Come, cousin, come Galina Petrovna, we have wasted enough of the day with these good people. It is time to be swallowed by the city for a little.'

The oak doors swung shut behind the departing trio, and the young man behind the desk heaved a silent sigh of relief.

* * *

The air in the flat hung heavy and stale over the table, still strewn with maps, official orders and biscuit wrappers. Zoya and Grigory Mikhailovich had been playing poker for what was left of the afternoon, both smoking cigars that made Galia's eyes water. Any plans for cultural visits had been swept aside by Grigory Mikhailovich who insisted, with grave intensity, that his knees really could not entertain the thought of any more walking, and that all Moscow's finest cultural sights would be shut, since it was August and anyone with any whiff of education in them would be out of town and in the country. Galia felt a long way from home. She had tried to phone through to Azov, to Yegor Platkov, to get some news of Vasya or Boroda. Each time she tried, her stubborn fingers punched in the numbers and she refused to believe all the telephone lines between the capital and her southern town could be truly full, buzzing like flies all the way across European Russia. But each time there would be a long, agonising pause once all the numbers were dialled, followed by a high-pitched whine: unobtainable. She had checked several times that the phone was actually connected to the system correctly, but all appeared to be as it should be. She stopped short of enquiring whether he had actually remembered to pay his bill, and the suspicion that he hadn't clung to her shoulders. Calls in town were free, but long distance always had to be paid for. It was a worry, on top of all her other worries, that now seemed stacked up on her back and high enough to reach the ceiling, if not the sky.

Galia stood by the window in the large reception room, looking out in to the courtyard. There were no children playing, only a tattered collection of old people decking out the benches with their grey, and brown, and yellow faces. Galia felt a wave of hopelessness engulf her, and let it break slowly over her head. Instinctively, she reached into her pocket for a boiled sweet, and pushed it quickly into her cheek. Sometimes, a little taste of home was very necessary. She eyed the poker players, puffing furiously on their cigars, cards fanning their faces, eyes set. She counted her blessings: at least they were both sober, and still fully dressed.

'Grigory Mikhailovich, it's nearly eight. I think we should call. Don't you?' Galia was itching to get on with the task. Waiting around in the flat didn't suit her at all. The old man frowned at her through a cloud of smoke and coughed with a wet, rattling sound that shook the window frames and made her want to fetch a mop.

'Nearly eight, you say, Galina Petrovna? Well, in that case, let the dog see the rabbit!'

Galia placed the telephone on the table in front of Grigory Mikhailovich as he passed one paw into the recesses of his shirt and scraped around among a seemingly endless collection of pieces of string, keys and torn up newspapers that were stuffed inside his vest. Galia looked away, and caught Zoya's gleaming eye: her friend was gloating over a pile of winnings that included cash, and buttons, and matches, and what looked like a few dead beetles, but couldn't have been.

'He's a bad loser, Galia, for such a frequent one!'

'Ah, here we are, ladies, here's the number. Oh no, not that one, that's, well, never mind. Ah, here it is! Not in there at all, but in my important numbers pocket. I sometimes think Kolya is right when he says I am becoming confused. But then I think – oh fuck it! You only live once!' Grigory Mikhailovich roared with laughter and Zoya joined in, jerking up and down like a puppet on a string. Galia didn't see what was so funny, and tapped her watch in his face.

'Please, Grigory Mikhailovich, we must hurry. Vasya and Boroda are relying on us. They are relying on you!'

A dog barked in the courtyard and was answered by a sharp yap from a neighbouring window.

'Galina Petrovna, you are right, as ever. We will continue with sobriety.' And the great fat fingers began to slowly pick out the magic numbers. Galia held her breath, until she began to feel lightheaded and remembered to breathe, deep and slow, and to pace. Zoya crouched low next to Grigory Mikhailovich and craned her neck to hear every word. Galia couldn't bear to listen to one half of the conversation. What would the Deputy Minister say, disturbed from his meetings and fishing trip and *dacha* to discuss an old man and a dog banged up miles away in the dusty south west. Galia couldn't imagine that it would be positive. She watched the ugly dog in the courtyard straining on its leash to bark at a passing OAP, and wondered whether Boroda was still breathing somewhere, still blinking her dark eyes and observing people with her canine understanding, or whether Kulakov and Mitya had dispatched her already. She closed her eyes momentarily, and then jumped out of her skin as Grigory Mikhailovich thumped the receiver back on to the cradle.

'He's gone clubbing.'

'Clubbing?'

'Clubbing!'

'How very unusual? Seal or deer?'

'No, you stupid old trout, clubbing – he is in town, at a club, drinking and dancing and, and that kind of thing.'

Zoya shook her head, uncomprehending.

'The Deputy Minister Glukhov is not at his *dacha*, he has returned to town to go clubbing. Apparently, we are not to tell anyone. Our lips, as it were, must be sealed.'

'Oh, what are we to do, Grigory Mikhailovich?' Galia began to shout slightly. 'He promised that he would speak to us tonight, and we have to return to Azov tomorrow. I can't stay here any longer. I really can't. I have my vegetable patch to see to, and—'

'Galina Petrovna – may I call you Galia? Galia, your vegetables will not run away, and neither will they wilt. Your true love will be freed, and your dog will be returned to you – perhaps, God willing. We are to meet him there. We will go clubbing, and all will be well.' Grigory Mikhailovich's tone was certain, booming, calm: he seemed in control, and Galia felt, for a moment, comforted.

Zoya clapped her hands and a smudgy smile stretched from ear to ear.

'A club! A night club! In Moscow! I must change! Have you any sequins, Grigory Mikhailovich? I feel we must fit in.'

'Zoya, control your eagerness, cousin. I'm afraid the club in question is not one of Moscow's finest. There is no gold to be found at this place. It is . . . on the Bohemian side, if you know what I mean.'

Galia shook her head. 'I don't know what you mean, Grigory Mikhailovich.'

'He means there are cockroaches and no toilet doors, at a guess,' said Zoya, crestfallen.

'I think you are likely to be right, Zoya,' the old man concurred.

'Grigory Mikhailovich, I don't mean to be rude, but I am surprised at your knowledge of Moscow's night clubs. Do you go often?' Galia was curious.

'I never go myself, how preposterous! But I know things, Galia. And I also know a youth who goes to clubs. I must telephone to Kolya, and he must come with us. I fear we'll never get through the face control without him.'

'The what?' Zoya put a hand to her face and pulled worriedly at a lip and an eyebrow.

'Kolya will know what to do. He should have been here by now, anyway. He's idle, and conniving, and stupid, but he'll have to do. He is my own flesh and blood, after all. Now, ladies, have a look in the dressing room and see if there's anything you can find that will make you look a bit more . . .'

'Bohemian?' panted Zoya.

'Yes. I will do the same. I'm sure I had a fez around here somewhere.'

And with that Grigory Mikhailovich raised his great weight

from the table, stubbed out his Cuban cigar on a fifty-years-of-Communism commemorative plate, and lumbered towards the hallway.

'I don't like this,' whispered Galia.

'Culture, adventure, salvation – and vodka!' cackled Zoya. 'What's not to like?'

17

The Cheese Mistress

The pool of sweat collecting beneath Mitya's eyes gave
him the brief impression, when half-way between sleep and
wakefulness, that he was drowning in a salty orange sea. It
appeared to him that a wave of sticky, unctuous fluid had
become stuck to his face, with no tide to take it out, and
he could almost feel the crabs scuttling around on the sand
of sleepy dust that collected thickly around his eyes. He
began to feel slightly sea-sick and pushed his eyelids open
slowly, before peeling his face away from the pillow with
great care. His whole body was covered in a rich layer of
moisture, and even the air that he pulled into his aching
lungs was warmly damp. Reaching up a swollen hand to his
cheek, his fingertips felt the indentations left on it by the
coarse man-made fibres of his bed linen. The skin felt a bit
like a cheese grater. His stomach squeezed and he focused
his eyes with some difficulty. Through his narrow slit vision,
framed above and below by the pinkish insides of his eyelids,
he eventually spied the clock. It was almost midday. He turned
over and stared at the shiny polystyrene ceiling tiles. Today
was Friday: he was supposed to be on duty. It was, in fact,

his duty to be on duty. But today, Mitya the Exterminator was going to go astray.

There was a mood about the room that struck him as odd, and at first he couldn't work out what was wrong. He lay still. The sun dappled the wall as the breeze played with the edge of the nylon curtain, and somewhere an elderly citizen addressed his radio in formal tones. Then Mitya realized: there was complete quiet in the communal flat. No volcanic roaring from the no-name alcoholic, no disco beats leaking out of Andrei the *Svoloch*'s vibrating walls, no cat fights tearing up the tattered hallway and threatening to make his ears bleed. A bird twittered in the green pool of the courtyard and the silver birch tree washed its branches in the breeze. There was peace. Mitya closed his eyes and opened his ears: beyond the hum of his blood cells pulsing across his eardrums, he could make out a female voice, humming. It was Katya. She was humming 'Enjoy the Silence'. He was sure she was. His facial muscles relaxed into a gentle smile and he opened his eyes again. A dog began to bark in the courtyard below. He wondered at the sound: what was that creature saying? Perhaps it was saying 'Get up, Mitya. There's work to be done.' And perhaps it was just barking because it had no other business to do.

'Is the reason dogs can't talk because of the shape of their mouths?' He remembered asking his mother once, a long, long time ago, back in the times of chat over lunchtime and brown bread and butter. She had laughed. She had laughed so much that she cried and Mitya had felt a little stupid, although he'd smiled also. But she had not answered the question. Perhaps, because she did not know.

Mitya showered in the communal bathroom down the hall. He was barely able to clamber into the bathtub, and holding the shower above his head was torture to his bruised shoulders. The entire washing process was even more unpleasant than usual given the stiffness of his body, and on a number of occasions his face came dangerously close to touching the fecund walls of the chamber when he attempted to reach his various sore spots. Once clean and dry, he dressed in the only presentable set of clothes he now had – his winter ensemble of heavy purple wool trousers and a grey long-sleeved shirt – and these made him sweat anew. He looked at the trousers: they seemed wrong. Maybe he could make a visit to the commission shop today and try to get something second-hand, something a little more suited to the heat. He needed some shorts, perhaps. He bent down to do up his shoes and found he could barely reach his feet. He forgot about issues of clothing as he struggled with his laces, and again he thought of his mother. Then he made for the door.

In the corridor, he could no longer hear the humming. But he was sure it had been Katya: he had felt it in his soul and felt her fingers strumming on his heart. He hesitated, and then slowly approached the magical door at the end of the corridor. He had never really noticed it before – could not recall seeing anyone go through it, apart from her, the other day. He reached out a hand and knocked, gently, hesitantly. All was quiet. He felt empty. He cleared his throat and tried again, slightly louder. He heard a muffled clanging and his heart thumped slightly. He wondered what she was wearing today, and whether her hair would be tied back in a pony-tail, or loose around her shoulders. He felt a great need to touch her.

A great belch shook the door on its hinges before it was pulled open roughly, and before him towered a lumpy girl with bad skin and enormous red hands. She smelt strongly of cheese.

'What?' she roared. Mitya took a step backwards, despite himself.

'Hello. Is Katya home?'

'Katya?' She looked somewhat outraged.

'Yes, Katya.' Mitya tried to curve his lips into a smile to persuade the girl that he meant no harm.

'What would you want with Katya, eh?' She squinted her eyes and smiled in a particularly unpleasant way, leaving her mouth half open, her creamy-coloured tongue protruding and dripping saliva on to the floor. She slurped slightly, and wiped her mouth on the back of her slab-like hand. Mitya took a gamble.

'Are you her cousin, Marina?' Again he tried to smile.

'What sort of a stupid question is that, Mikhail Plovkin? Are you pretending not to know me?'

Now it was Mitya's turn to leave his mouth half open. He must have met her at some stage, but he had no recollection of it. Maybe in the kitchen at some point: if he was tending to his imported ramen noodles, he might not have taken her all in? Or if coming out of the bathroom – he would have been sure of averting his eyes. He sensed that it was important to try to continue to be civil.

'No, of course not – you are Marina. Of course. You've done your hair differently, perhaps?'

Marina snorted.

'She's not in.' The girl fed him the information like a piece of cheese rind.

'Ah. Thank you, I'll—' Mitya turned to move off towards the front door.

'You can come in for a cup of *kvass*, if you like? You look like you need one.' He stopped, suspended in the hallway by her words. He turned his head towards her, trying to avoid looking at her directly, but still uncomfortably aware

206

of the pitted pink smudge of her face and that drooling smile. Her fingers, thick as eels, were fiddling at her arm-pit, picking off the bobbles of grey cotton sprouting from her towelling house-coat. Mitya shuddered and muttered something about being very busy just now.

'You think yourself better than the rest of us, don't you, Mikhail?' The smile had dropped off her face.

'I don't know what you mean.'

'Keeping yourself to yourself. That door: always shut. You never come to Andrei's parties, do you?'

Mitya knew it would be undiplomatic to answer with honesty. He glued his tongue to his palate and tried to smile.

'You never show an interest. I've seen you in the kitchen five or six times – six, I think it is: you never say hello.'

Mitya shrugged slightly and looked at the floor. 'I'm not a very good cook. I have to concentrate on what I'm doing when I am in the kitchen. Distractions lead to burnt food, I find—'

'I know all about you,' she cut him off. 'Mitya the Exterminator. Oh yes.'

'Really, Marina?' Again he shrugged, but the blood rushed to his neck and crept up his cheeks. 'There's not very much to know, I assure you.'

'She doesn't know, does she?' The cheese mistress smiled as she flicked a few creamy crumbs from her cleavage on to the floor.

'What?'

'Katya. She doesn't know what you do. She wouldn't spit on you if she did, you know.'

'She knows I'm an exterminator.'

'Yes, Mikhail, but she doesn't know what, does she? I found out – she thinks you kill cockroaches. But I think I'm going to have to put her straight.'

207

'No, cousin Marina, please don't do that.' He moved back towards her door with quick steps.

'She ought to know.'

'Yes, citizen neighbour, but I'll do it.' Mitya was trying hard not to become annoyed.

'She's going to find out, you know.'

'I will speak to her.' His voice was earnest.

'You'd better do it soon.'

'Yes, I—'

'She'll hate you.'

'I will explain.' He could feel a gelatinous film of sweat forming on his brow and upper lip. The effort of trying to persuade, and not simply going for his dog pole and containing this bitch, was becoming more than he could bear.

Cousin Marina smirked. 'That will be a fine conversation. And a short one! You're a loser, Mikhail Plovkin! There's nothing here for you!' She slammed the door in Mitya's face. He blinked hard, took a deep breath in and tried to relax his fingers, which had curled into claws at his sides. Cousin Marina was formidable, and slightly scary. And she had told him something he already knew. He gazed at the door for some moments, and then shook himself slightly. He raised his chin, and headed for the stairs and his van outside.

As usual on a sunny afternoon, there was a group of children going about their business in the courtyard, trailing sticks through dust and making pies out of sand, spit and leaves. Their babushkas lined the benches in a higgledy row, soaking up the sun, their wrinkled faces resembling walnuts. Mitya remembered his own babushka and her *dacha*. He hadn't thought of her in years. He could hardly remember her face. But he could recall her voice as she scolded him for eating strawberries straight from the bush. Her garden had been a safe haven for him. He smiled, and embraced the feeling, his steps light on the path as he made for his van. How they'd enjoyed those days in the garden, he and his best friend.

'Murderer!' The screech was like a slap in the face. His head jerked up and he was surprised to see a small girl with brown pig-tails and a dust-smeared face standing directly in front of him, blocking his path. She had a large stick in her hand and was trailing its end across the clean paintwork of the van, leaving smudges that set Mitya's teeth on edge. She looked vaguely familiar.

'Citizen Small Girl, please remove yourself from my van.'

'You're a murderer!' the small girl persisted.

'I don't know what you're talking about, but please—'

'You're the Exterminator. I know you! My babushka told me about you. And you killed Boroda!'

'I remove canine infestations, or I have done in the past, as a service, that's—'

The girl smacked the stick against the side of the van and shrieked.

'Murderer! Boroda wasn't stray! Baba Galia loved her. And she only had three legs.'

'Ah, you're referring to that tri-ped, aren't you?' he muttered, more to himself than to the little girl. 'Look—'

'She wasn't a tri-ped, she was a dog!' the girl smacked the stick against the van again.

'Yes, look, stop doing that.' Mitya made a grab for the stick and missed as the girl jumped backwards.

'And now Baba Galia has gone to Moscow to tell the Minister.'

He cocked his head to one side and looked at the girl with surprise.

'Really? She's gone to Moscow?'

'And you will go to hell.'

The girl threw the stick at him and ran off to join her gang under the birch tree. They thumbed their noses at Mitya and mimed horrible deaths, while their babushkas looked on in mute approval. Mitya stared after her open mouthed. Had the Elderly Citizen really gone off to Moscow to make a complaint? Shouldn't she be dropping off parcels for . . . for the old man, Volubchik? He'd been in the SIZO for several days now, and must be in need of additional sustenance. Had she just abandoned him to go complaining about a dog – a dog which, whatever way you looked at it, whoever was in the wrong or in the right, must surely be dead by now? He unlocked the van and slid carefully into the driver's seat. The sun-baked interior stank of faeces and matted hair, and took his breath away for a moment. He wound down the window and looked out over the courtyard. Had the old woman really gone all the way to Moscow about a dog? He looked into the wing mirror and caught sight of the children in the background, still miming horrible deaths and gesticulating crudely. They were laughing and daring each other to come closer to the van. Mitya turned the key and pressed the gear stick into reverse. The children scattered into the dusty courtyard, howling and shrieking to each other, as the radio belched on: they were playing Depeche Mode, 'Walking in my Shoes'. If Mitya had understood the lyrics, he would have found them apt.

* * *

Petya Kulakov had endured a tiring morning dealing with other people's shit. His landlady had failed to do his washing, as her sister had died (or so she claimed), so his uniform today was crispy with yesterday's sweat. He didn't care: sometimes a stinking policeman was worth more than a fresh

210

one. Not that Petya Kulakov ever made 'fresh': what was the point, when you only got dirty again? At the kiosk that morning, where he habitually indulged in a little 'hair of the dog' over a breakfast bag of biscuits, there had been nothing but grumbles and bad omens, complaints over bad business and lack of protection. And the final nail in the coffin of the day was the news from his dentist. Oh, Kulakov had been struggling with his mouth. For weeks, he had resisted the dread conclusion, but now he could resist no more. The rotten tooth tormented him by lying low for several hours with not so much as a murmur, and then bursting into full-blown pulsating agony that made his eyes water and his fists punch whatever was close. Oh yes, he'd had two caps punched out last night by that Plovkin bastard, but if he'd only aimed a little to the left, the rotten incisor would have been smashed out instead. He might even have thanked him. And now the news was awful: he had finally called the dentist, and was disturbed to learn that she had emigrated to Israel. Israel! He'd been having his teeth seen to for free by a Jew for all this time, and he didn't even know. He winced.

Now, at lunchtime, he couldn't face chewing. He'd snuck off a couple more vodkas to ease the pain, and tipped back in his office chair, sockless feet on the desk, his mouth wide open as he dozed. Occasionally he was aware of a buzz near his face: his only concern in this moment, and it was a slight one, was that he might swallow a fly. There were plenty of them in the office, attracted by something under Kulakov's desk. But then, it wouldn't be the first time, and he'd suffered no ill consequences on the previous occasions when this had happened.

'Kulakov!' The word was accompanied by a rap of knuckles on the desk, and a sharp intake of breath. The policeman did not stir. Mitya remembered his knuckles, and this time kicked his chair.

'Hey, Petya! Wake up! I have a bottle for you.' Mitya kicked the chair leg again, and waved the spirit in the policeman's face. Kulakov shut his mouth and opened first one bleary eye, and then the other. He surveyed the vision of the proffered bottle cloaked in its dewy blanket of coolness. He surmised that it must have come straight from a freezer. He wondered if he had any gherkins left in his drawer. Then he wondered why that bastard Plovkin was waving it at him.

'I just came to say . . . no hard feelings about last night.' Mitya cleared his throat and leant against the desk slightly.

Kulakov sat motionless, eyeing him suspiciously but hungrily. He licked his cracked lips, and wondered where Big Vova was, just in case he was needed.

'I don't know what came over me.' Mitya couldn't quite meet Kulakov's eyes, but fixed his gaze as close to his face as he could: his left earlobe seemed about right. 'I'm not usually a violent person.'

Kulakov's smile oozed across his face.

'Well, Mitya my brother, this is a surprise.' Kulakov sucked at his teeth, and found that at present, they did not ache. 'I didn't think I'd see you for a while after the beating I gave you last night. You caused me a great deal of offence, you know. I was only trying to help you.'

Kulakov reached out and fingered the glass neck of the bottle. The cold kissed his fingertips and he swallowed hard. 'Apology accepted. You can leave the bottle on the desk.'

'There's another matter, Kulakov. I wanted to tell you . . . I'm withdrawing my complaint against the Elderly Citizens we dealt with on Monday night. I won't be giving evidence. I've filled out the form; you'll find it in here.' Mitya pointed to the ten-page document on regulation grey paper which now resided, like a dead fish, in the net of the policeman's in-tray.

'Well, get you!' Kulakov slid his feet from the desk and thudded his chair back on to the concrete floor, the impact jolting his incisor into action, and pain roaring through his face like molten lava. 'Arrghh!' His hands flew to his face.

Mitya peeled the thin metal lid from the vodka bottle and placed it to Kulakov's lips.

'Drink, Petya. It will help.'

The policeman took a swig, and then another one, vodka spurting on to his collar and cheeks as he choked slightly with the force of the spirit travelling up his nose and down his throat, as Mitya raised the bottom of the bottle. He gasped slightly, and then giggled.

'You're a joke, Plovkin. But you can do what you like: I've processed the paperwork. I don't need your evidence. I can give plenty of evidence. I always do!' Kulakov took another swig. 'You can't stop this wagon, brother. He's going to rot in jail, and the dog's already cat meat.'

Kulakov's jowls wobbled as he began to giggle. Mitya looked down at the stained concrete floor and nodded slowly. It was too late. There was no reason for Kulakov to help him, and there was no more that he could do here. He turned and started to walk away, every bone in his body suddenly aching and heavy.

'Don't you want to know how I found out?' Kulakov's shout held him back from the door.

'Not really.'

'He told me! The old goat just went and told me. How about that? I didn't have to do anything to him at all!'

'What do you mean?'

'We were sitting in the car – I was sobering up a little,

213

you know – I had paperwork to do. So I gave him a nip of vodka, just to settle him down. I don't think he drinks much – unlike some fathers we could mention, eh? And he told me he was sorry . . . sorry you turned out so bad.'

Mitya turned and pushed through the grimy grey door into the bright light of the station courtyard beyond.

18

The Third Way

'This isn't going to work.' Kolya stood in the hallway, jaw slack, surveying the three elderly Bohemians before him. 'OK, so it's not one of those glitzy places that charges you thirty dollars just to get in and makes you feel like it's your privilege, but still – they have standards. Ladies, Grigory Mikhailovich, with all due respect, you look like you have escaped from a lunatic asylum. Why don't I just put the kettle on and make us all a nice cup of tea and then perhaps I can fry some potatoes—'

'Insolent pup! We have to get in to The Third Way. We have to speak to the Deputy Minister about this lady's dog and boyfriend—'

'He's not my boyfriend.'

'Potential boyfriend.'

'No.'

'Man friend?'

'Well, that implies something more, don't you think?'

'Acquaintance?'

'That's a little cold.'

Kolya rolled his eyes and snorted. He felt he knew how

215

to handle Grigory Mikhailovich, difficult as he was, however three of them was just impossible. He had been looking forward to a pleasant evening of flirting with the girl next door, if she would let him in and he could get past her damned dog, but now things were looking decidedly more irritating. The old man was clearly delusional, as usual, but the fact that tonight he had two female accomplices was most peculiar. And they seemed relatively with it, although the small one with no hair was a bit odd.

'Shall we get back to the subject now?'

Galia shifted her headband further up her forehead and focused on Kolya, trying not to rub her itching eyes. The mascara that Zoya had applied had tickled like madness at first, and now felt like diseased growths weighing down her lashes. She could see the fibres in the periphery of her vision and kept thinking they were blue-bottles buzzing her. The jodhpurs, found in the bottom of an old army trunk and smart enough once the wizened spider corpses had been removed, fitted her quite well, although as she was unaccustomed to wearing trousers of any sort, they did seem to chafe a bit. There was consensus that they didn't really go with her sandals, but that couldn't be helped. She hoped that the green-and-yellow striped shirt draped over her top half gave her an artistic air, but wasn't entirely sure. She hadn't had much experience with Bohemians, so it was all guesswork.

'Ladies, what is this nonsense about the Deputy Minister. Which Deputy Minister is it, and why do you think he is at The Third Way? I have been to that club, and I can assure you, there are no Ministers there. Not even the Minister of Culture, or the Deputy Minister of Music.'

Kolya laughed through his nose a little, and Galia decided that she didn't particularly like him.

'Grigory Mikhailovich gets a bit confused. Maybe you, too, get confused sometimes, ladies? A nice cup of tea and a sit-down—'

'We do not, ever, get confused. We are perfectly in control of our faculties. We simply need to get in to the club, and you will help us do it.' Zoya said, leaning in towards Kolya and pinning him to the wall with her bright, beady eyes.

'I have no money,' said Kolya softly, with a smirk, 'I am a student.'

'I have money. Here – 50,000 roubles. Now, we need to get to Novokuznetskaya, and quickly, so please step outside and hail us a cab, and we will join you on the pavement presently.'

Kolya made for the door with a petulant sigh, and the others stooped to collect their bags and other accessories, which on this occasion included a pallet and brushes, the ladies' opera glasses and a packet of biscuits, to keep Grigory Mikhailovich going.

'Is he really your flesh and blood, this Kolya?' asked Zoya with a frown.

Grigory Mikhailovich nodded and belched quietly behind his great paw. 'It hurts me to say it, but . . . yes. He is something of a disappointment. I wouldn't mind so much if he were wicked, but as you can see, he is just rather wet.'

The sun was setting as the three ghoulish Bohemians and a furtive-looking Kolya fought their way out of the close confines of the Zhiguli cab and on to the street at charming, old-world Novokuznetskaya. Clouds of starlings undulated in the heavy, rose-tinted air. They were in an ancient part of the city, still quite central, but seemingly miles away from the wide busy boulevards and the Stalin towers. Here the crooked lanes clotted around gentle, tree-lined squares and the apartment blocks huddled meekly at a meagre three storeys. Small art galleries and silver-smiths nestled in clumps along the narrow road. To Galia's eyes, it didn't look like the kind of place a night club would be found, but then, her experience was very limited: she had once visited a discotheque in the basement of a holiday camp – during the holiday to Chelyabinsk, in fact. She remembered red plastic cups, juice that tasted like it came from Mars, very loud oom-pah oom-pah music and a dance trainer who had fuddled her mind by urging the sweating, red-faced dancers to build a perfect Communism while struggling to avoid tangling their limbs in a double-quick samba. It hadn't been a pleasant evening. Galia's first-aid skills were called on many times and although she didn't have to set any serious breaks, the iodine and ice had been free-flowing. Galia wasn't much for dancing.

'Kolya, lead on. Where is the place?' rumbled Grigory Mikhailovich, adjusting his beret to what he imagined was a more jaunty angle, and pulling up his voluminous red satin Cossack trousers, at the same time pulling them out of the tops of his shiny green boots. 'These damn things will be the death of me. I say, Galina Petrovna, would you mind tucking them in to my socks a little more firmly?' Galia wrinkled her nose, but complied with the request as best she could.

'Follow me,' said Kolya, with the look of a child being forced to take his parents, or maybe even maiden great aunts, along to youth rock club. They walked a hundred paces or so up the quiet street, until they came to a broad metal door in an anonymous-looking apartment building. At the door there stood a girl of about sixteen with long, dark hair, a lot of eye-liner and a mouth that must have been born sulky. She was ignoring an earnest-looking young man with straggly facial hair and dirty glasses. The young man's mouth dropped open when he looked up into Galia's eyes and realized that she wanted to gain entrance to the club. Nothing in life could have prepared him for this shock. His world had shifted on its axis, and would never be the same again. Bouncers at The Third Way were not your usual sort.

'How much?' asked Zoya in her best, shrillest bird voice.

The young man's mouth opened and closed silently, and then did it again. His round eyes ran from Galia to Zoya to Grigory Mikhailovich and back, and finally rested on Kolya, who was standing behind the three elderly clubbers, trying to pretend he was not there at all.

'Well?' pressed Zoya.

'Ah, citizens, I'm not sure . . . you know, we're a friendly bunch, but you—'

'Face control?' asked Grigory Mikhailovich, pressing forward and pushing his great shaggy head towards the lean young man.

'Well, it's not exactly face control, sir. It's just that . . . well, you know, we want everyone to enjoy themselves at The Third Way. We love everyone; there are no bad vibes here. But . . . why do you old guys want to come in?'

'We want to dance!' said Zoya, indignantly.

'Dance?' The young man raised his eyebrows as his gaze travelled down her tiny, sparrow legs, every joint, vein and tendon of which was being thrown into eye-aching relief by the wet-look purple leggings she had purchased and put on (much to Galia's embarrassment), at a kiosk on the corner outside Grigory Mikhailovich's apartment block. Zoya had paired the leggings with the Brezhnev toga worn the morning before and a pair of girl's ballet points found in the back of Grigory Mikhailovich's fridge. Galia thought the leggings were preferable to Zoya's own bare legs, which had been the initial proposal, but fully understood the earnest young man's consternation.

'We're from Chelyabinsk,' lied Galia, and smiled encouragingly.

The earnest young man nodded slightly, and gave a half smile of his own, as if this was sufficient explanation for the trio's bizarre appearance. At this point, the young girl finally looked up from a long inspection of her shoes, and dropped a shiny grey knob of chewing gum on to the pavement as it tumbled from her open mouth.

'They are from Chelyabinsk,' Kolya repeated in his nasal whine, wincing slightly.

'Jesus,' the girl whispered, 'the circus must be in town.'

'OK guys, you can go on up, but I really don't think it will be your thing. Try not to scare anyone, eh?'

Zoya clutched Kolya's arm as he attempted to melt away down a neighbouring alleyway, and propelled him through the door and up the dark, narrow stairs in front of them.

Galia wondered to herself whether the Deputy Minister Glukhov, Roman Sergeevich, was really going to be found in a place like this. It seemed like a normal old ramshackle apartment block, apart from the loud thumping beat that shook the staircase ominously and, to Galia's mind, threatened something both thrilling and unwelcome, like thunder on a summer afternoon, or a brush with a nasty infection of some sort. At the top of the stairs they came to a wide wooden door, dented and poorly covered with something similar to silver foil. Kolya pushed the door open slowly, and all at once Galia's fears were realized.

The massive room, once no doubt an elegant boudoir, pulsed with light and sound. The ceiling seemed to undulate as fronds of music sprouting from speakers the size of tractors beat gently against it. There were a few young people dancing, making weird angular movements with their arms and barely moving their feet. Their faces were sweating profusely, eyes clouded with joy or pain; the on-lookers weren't sure which. A youth wearing yellow trousers huddled over a collection of boxes, wires and small blinking lights on a home-made platform at the far end of the room. Galia wondered what he was doing: he appeared to be fiddling with a set of small knobs. Around the walls, young people lounged in small groups, their glassy eyes reflecting the pink, orange and green hues of the dance-floor lights.

Grigory Mikhailovich stood gigantic in the doorway, looking for all the world like he had just woken up, and found himself in a dream. Galia put her hands over her ears and tried to keep a track of where Kolya had got to: the boy was striding across the room, heading for a doorway and a darkened corridor beyond it. Zoya stood at the edge of the dance floor transfixed, eyes shining, staring at the bright projections on the wall and nodding her head in approximate rhythm with the scintillating beat. Galia grabbed her friend's hand and tugged her along through small shoals of warm bodies with googly eyes, following Kolya as he made his way through a maze of corridors and antechambers towards his ultimate goal: the bar. Grigory Mikhailovich remained shipwrecked in front of one of the speakers, the hair on the back of his neck standing up as he felt the noise of the speaker behind him thud through his chest and into his heart, but didn't understand why.

'Have you seen him yet?' yelled Galia to Zoya over her shoulder as they waded towards the bar.

'Who?'

'Deputy Minister Glukhov, Roman Sergeevich, of course!'

'I don't know what he looks like.'

'Well, does Grigory Mikhailovich know what he looks like?'

'I doubt it, my dear. Don't think he's ever met the fellow.'

'What about Kolya?'

'Don't be ridiculous.'

'Well how on earth are we going to find him then?'

'A Deputy Minister of the Russian Federation will be quite easy to find in a place like this. Look around you Galia: use your brain. I intend to. But first, I think a little drinkie is in order. To increase the synapse connections, and all that. And put a fire in your engine!' Zoya was chirruping at full throttle.

They reached the bar, and Galia clung on for dear life. Zoya bobbed by her side and ordered four vodkas from the midget bar tender. Then she sent the reluctant, shrinking Kolya back to reclaim Grigory Mikhailovich from the speaker's grasp. The boy looked sulky, but did as he was asked.

'Look, Zoya!'

The drinks had arrived in crystal glasses shaped like winter felt boots. Galia smiled: she had once had the very same set, a very long time ago.

'Down the hatch, and bottoms up!' Zoya grinned.

Galia chinked glasses and downed her vodka in one, returning her little glass boot to the bar top with a thud. Usually, she would have demurred, but on this occasion the fiery cold was most welcome. Its effect was almost instantaneous: her belly burnt, her cheeks flamed, and each limb relaxed, disengaged from her core and floated off in a different direction. Her brain buzzed, and a light sweat broke on her forehead.

'Hey, maybe that's him!' she giggled to Zoya.

A serious-looking, middle-aged man wearing a polo-neck and smoking a pipe was sitting at a mushroom-shaped table in a side-room off the bar, playing chess with a small, bored-looking dog. Apparently, the dog was losing. As the ladies watched, it began the careful process of chewing its own king's head off.

'I never met a Minister who could play chess, even against a dog,' was Zoya's response.

'Have you met many Ministers, Zoya?'

'That's classified,' replied Zoya smugly.

Galia was pondering this response with a slight frown when she witnessed Grigory Mikhailovich's approach cutting a swathe through the revellers like hot dog pee through snow. Young women recoiled, spilling their drinks over themselves, and young men turned to stare, incredulous, earnest discussions forgotten. He had removed his ruffled shirt and the filthy vest beneath to reveal his chest, tufted in curly grey hair, bread-crumbs and scraps of yellowed newspaper, and it glistened in the heat. He was roaring, singing some long-forgotten song, as huge tears rolled out of each of his bright-burning eyes.

'Goodness me, Kolya, what has happened here? Grigory Mikhailovich hasn't even drunk his glass yet.' Zoya hopped around her cousin, examining him for evidence of foul play or injury.

'Oh the road is long!' sang Grigory Mikhailovich in a full bass voice.

'I think, Zinaida Artyomovna, that someone has been sharing their drink with Grigory Mikhailovich, and that it hasn't entirely agreed with him,' Kolya smirked, and man-oeuvred the old man slowly and carefully backwards into a vacant armchair covered with an enormous furry throw.

'With dust and fog, and hardship,' continued Grigory Mikhailovich, before looking around wildly for a second, and then relaxing. He started to stroke the chair with the back of one hand, as if it were a cat.

'I have but one true love.'

'What are we to do with him?' asked Kolya querulously and obviously displeased.

'Good boy, good boy,' murmured Grigory Mikhailovich, looking intently at the chair arm, and giving it a little tickle under the chin. Kolya tutted and rolled his eyes skyward until Zoya and Galia fixed him with glares that promised physical harm if he continued.

'You are impudent, young Kolya,' snarled Zoya.

'But people are laughing,' whined Kolya indignantly.

'Zoya, my dear, I don't think he is going to be up to recognizing anything very much, for a little time,' said Galia, with a sigh, 'the music seems to have had a strange effect on him. Grigory Mikhailovich, can you hear me?' Galia shouted into the old man's ear, her lips only centimetres from the waxy orifice, but there was no response. Grigory Mikhailovich continued to stroke the chair and sing, his eyes distant and dark.

'On this occasion, Galia, I fear you are entirely right: he is of no further use to us at the present. But we shall not give in! One of these men is the Deputy Minister Glukhov, Roman Sergeevich. We just have to deduce which one. We are clever women: we will do this. Once more unto the breach, dear friend!'

Galia nodded quickly, her headband slipping into her eyes, but her spirit fortified by the vodka and a pickled gherkin proffered by a midget hostess on roller-skates who just happened to be rolling by.

'Let us commence our detailed search, Zinaida Artyomovna,' said Galia.

They marched from room to room, looking into each and every face, some smiling, some glowering, but most just hugely puzzled, trying to spot some evidence of another life. The life they were trying to spot was a life spent in dusty corridors: a life of endless dry meetings concerning ruddy-cheeked citizens, or arguments with *Duma* representatives from the far-flung icy reaches; a life receiving and giving back-handers, in place of any real work. They looked for evidence of a wearer of cheap and unclean suits, someone who had spent his school days unpopular yet reasonably bright, never the best or the most industrious, but one who knew how to play the system and get good scores in end-of-year exams. One who had got in to university at the right time and got through the Soviet system, to be in place at the ministry once that whole edifice had been dismantled, ready to step in under a democratic banner and seize promotion to Deputy Minister, Internal Affairs (Southern Non-Caucasus). One who might be a friend of Yeltsin, or the oil barons, or the new breed of bankers who seemed to rule the capital, if not the provinces just yet.

Their gaze scoured every corner of every room, but each glowing face they saw just spoke of vodka, and beats, and ecstasy, and love. In one of the winding corridors, a young woman dressed as a tiger stroked Zoya's hair and murmured something in her ear. Zoya's eyes widened, and she nodded suddenly, before disappearing to the dance floor. Galia almost followed, but something held her back. She didn't know quite who the lady was, but she was pretty sure the tiger woman was not a lead to the Deputy Minister. She looked at her watch: it was ten p.m. already, and suddenly she felt a panic that grasped her throat: the evening was slipping away, and nothing had been gained. Ten p.m. in Azov too, but poor Boroda and Vasya weren't kicking up their heels in a night club with vodka and tiger ladies. An image of noble Vasya surrounded by murderers and rapists, and noble Boroda surrounded by snarling street dogs, crept before Galia's eyes. She had to stay focused. She had to find the Deputy Minister and plead their case. Even if Grigory Mikhailovich and Zoya were now . . . otherwise engaged.

Galia roamed back through the club, studying each room as best she could: the chess room, home to mushroom tables and weird paintings on the walls whose multitudinal eyes followed you as you moved: the bar, now raucous and overflowing, even the walls wet and warm to the touch: the dancing room, still pulsating, a myriad of rainbow colours; the corridors that laced their way endlessly up and down, in and out, full of people lounging against walls, sitting on floors, all deaf, all wordless, all moving in slow motion or not at all; the toilets, dark and forbidding, at the top of a winding staircase that threatened to topple any unsuspecting, over-zealous reveller. Finally, Galia made her way back to the corner of the bar where Kolya had left Grigory Mikhailovich in the cat-chair. She hoped he had recollected himself and would now be able to at least give her a hint of what the Deputy Minister Glukhov, Roman Sergeevich might look like. However, when she returned to the chair, he was nowhere to be seen.

In his place there sat a slim young man with sly, tilted eyes, high cheekbones and an interesting scar across one cheek. His fingers were interlaced in his lap and his eyes were half-closed, as if he were on the edge of slumber. The fur of the cat-chair caressed the silk of his plain black shirt.

Galia looked at him for a few seconds, hesitated, and made to turn away.

'Madam, are you looking for Grigory Mikhailovich?'

Galia turned back to the young man, somewhat surprised at his melodious voice and the fact that she had been able to hear it over the revelry.

'Oh, er, yes, I did leave him here. He was feeling a bit . . . unwell.'

'He's fine, madam, just fine. In fact, he's gone for a dance.'

'What?'

'He's on the dance floor. Your friend Zoya, I believe, came and collected him, but he wasn't unwilling, to be honest. I think the music is good for his soul, as it is for all of us, wouldn't you agree?'

'Er, yes, I suppose so,' Galia agreed, but wondered at her agreement. This sort of music didn't really seem to be doing her soul much good, she had to admit.

'Would you like to sit down – please, go ahead.'

The young man stood suddenly, and Galia gratefully sank into the cat-chair. She could almost hear it purr as she leant back into its folds, but resisted the temptation to tickle its whiskers. She had the distinct impression it had stray fish scales on its chin, however.

'Let me introduce myself. My name is Roma.' The young man squatted beside her chair and offered his hand. His smile creased one side of his not-quite-handsome face as his eyes almost disappeared into his cheekbones. Galia liked the smile.

'I am Galina Petrovna. Very pleased to meet you. And how do you know Grigory Mikhailovich?'

'Well, Galina Petrovna, I would have thought that was obvious?' Roma replied, lifting his eyebrows high and pretending surprise.

Galia was trying to decide how to respond to this perplexing statement, when a thought struck her like a shock from a cracked plug socket: this man's name was Roma, short for Roman . . . and possibly, just maybe, short for Roman Sergeevich Glukhov. He didn't look like a Deputy Minister, but then, these days, in this life, who could tell?

Galia screwed up her courage, and took a punt on using his first name and patronymic. If it were wrong, the offence caused to the young man would be searing, but she had to try.

'Roman Sergeevich, which way did Grigory Mikhailovich go?'

His eyes did not flicker. He looked at her sardonically, still smiling half a smile. 'To the dance floor, Galina Petrovna, that way – see, there he is! Quite safe! Having a ball, in fact.'

Galia's eyes followed Roma's gesture: sure enough, there in the next room, visible through the archway, was the massive form of Grigory Mikhailovich, twitching in time to a beat that Galia felt through the floor but could not distinguish with her ears. The old man was still glistening, bare-chested, but now appeared to be wearing some sort of garland round his neck. His eyes were closed, and he was using his hands to conduct some symphony that no-one could hear except him. Young women were circling him, curious, and unafraid now that he was clearly harmless. Zoya was also nearby, dancing opposite a young man with short back-and-sides, thick glasses and an Adam's apple the size of Venus. She looked contented enough, and the young man was clearly enthralled. The Brezhnev toga had been removed and was being passed from dancer to dancer to try for size: Zoya was dancing in her bra, girdle and purple lycra leggings. Galia shuddered.

Roma gave the cat-chair a stroke. 'Galina Petrovna, I have to tell you, I couldn't really make head or tale of what Grigory Mikhailovich and his cousin, the little sparrow lady there, were telling me. However, I understand you wanted to speak to me about a spot of bother that a friend of yours is in?'

Galia nodded long and vigorously, so much so that her bandana flew off her head and plopped in to Roma's drink.

'It's no bother, really, don't worry. There's more beer. But I'm afraid your bandana is ruined.'

'I don't care about the bandana, Roman Sergeevich. You see, I'm not really a Bohemian. I just want my friend, Vasily Volubchik, to be freed from the SIZO: he's an old man, and he's never done anything wrong. He's an ex-teacher, and he has four grandchildren! Goodness knows, he's done so much for Azov's elderly people, with his club and his Lotto and his talks on vegetable matters—'

'Calm yourself, Galina Petrovna. Perhaps another vodka, and a small beer to go with it? And a gherkin or two: let's have some gherkins!'

Roman Sergeevich Glukhov raised his hand imperceptibly, and the midget hostess on roller-skates was by his side instantaneously.

'So, tell me more? This is all happening in Rostov, is it?'

'Azov, Roman Sergeevich. Much nicer than Rostov. And better cabbages,' said Galia.

'I'm sure the cabbages are fine. But I hear a dog is involved in this story, unless I am much mistaken, and I am a serious animal lover, Galina Petrovna. I myself have a dachshund called Eric.'

'No!'

'Oh yes. So I want to hear everything, my good lady, from start to finish.'

The drinks and gherkins arrived, and Roman Sergeevich pulled up a chair. He then stood and raised a toast to long life and faithful animals. Galia echoed the toast, downed her vodka and blotted her mouth delicately on the end of her bandana.

'Everything,' she nodded, somewhat in awe. 'Well, let me

tell you about my dog Boroda, so named because she has a fine, pointy beard—'

'It is important to know every detail.'

'Oh it is, Roman Sergeevich, it is. The devil is in the detail, I find.'

'Oh yes,' concurred Roman Sergeevich with a smile, 'that's what I always say to my bureaucrats.'

'Quite. Anyway, I found her a few years ago, outside the station. Well, she found me, to be honest, in that way that dogs have . . .'

And so the elderly jodhpur-wearing Bohemian told her story to the charming Deputy Minister with the interesting scar, and together they sketched out the whole history of Azov, dogs, humans, the Great Patriotic War, Volgograd, the factory, thousand-eyed serpents, crooked policemen, annoying husbands, cabbage root fly and old ladies with sickles as big as the moon. In a room full of goggle-eyed fish-humans who danced on legs only recently evolved for that purpose, they made sense of the world, and set out to right a wrong.

And in another room, Grigory Mikhailovich, gyrating as best he could to the beats, winked conspiratorially at Zinaida Artyomovna, and the latter winked back.

19

A Dog's Life

A dog's life is not all bad. It's not all good, but it generally has a balance, depending on the humans around, the time of year, how many toes you've got to scratch with, and what kind of woof you can produce.

Boroda had enough toes to scratch with, enough legs to run with and teeth enough to eat with, so she counted herself a contented dog, in the greater scheme of things. She had had a life: she had warmed her bones by radiators thick with green paint; wrapped her tongue in sticky-sweet fudge wrappers; contemplated the wide southern skies and enjoyed the exquisite squeak of the refrigerator door opening. At some point there had been rats as big as cats to chase, and deep cool rivers to swim in. There had been different humans, and different boxes to sleep in. At times there had been no box at all, and occasionally no food. She licked her paw.

Life on the farm had been energetic and loud. The other farm dogs had shown her a trick or two, and she had done her best to get on and do as expected. But she was a gentle soul by nature, and not particularly clever: they quickly saw that she was no good as a guard dog, and not much of a

231

hunter. She followed the pack, and kept her nose clean, but she was not a prized canine. She liked the women and children, but at the farm they were kept quite separate: she would occasionally receive a pat from a chubby pink hand, or a crust thrown over the fence, sometimes butter smeared, but there was none of the cosy comfort that she had grown to love as a mature dog. The farm had meant work.

The farm had also been full of machinery and sharpness, thumpings, scrapes and clankings. Boroda had often hidden among the calves when the machinery was being used: their black softness made her feel protected, and safe. Maybe it had always been her fate: maybe it was meant to be. But the machinery had been her downfall. She'd learnt the hard way that it was not to be climbed upon, no matter whether it was still and cold, and no matter how excited you were about the rats running around the grain store.

Boroda didn't know what order her life had happened in; she could remember people and places, but not when they were. She remembered train tracks and kiosks, cold winds, fleas and ticks in her coat. And warmth: a quiet flat with sunshine and lino and plenty of bacon fat to eat and clear water to drink. Oh, treacherous bacon fat! Although she loved it, she knew it was not her friend. Bacon fat tempted her, made her move when she knew she should be still, and had, in the end, made her old lady very sad.

And now there was no old lady, and no bacon fat. Now there were just cages ranged along a long, dark room. She could stand up in hers and stretch her legs a little, the muscles shaking with the effort, but some of the other dogs were not so lucky. Every so often a pair of large black boots would beat down the corridor and dogs would be taken from their cages. They howled and barked, and some whined. But they never came back. Maybe they were moving on to new homes: new old ladies. Maybe the new homes were being rationed, and that was why it was so slow. There was certainly nobody here to give a tickle behind the ear or compliment a dog on a waggy tail. She sighed and turned around in her cage, and hoped that her turn for a new home would come soon.

She missed the kitchen table and the old lady. She could hear a radio somewhere far away, the sound muffled by several thick walls and windows. A clock was striking the hour. It reminded her of home. Her companions in their cages were getting restless: they had water, but no food. Some had been here since before she had arrived. Boroda's belly had long since shrunk to a tight ball. She wasn't hungry now. She yawned and let out a soft whine. She wanted to see her old lady: to sniff her floral skirt, and give her toes a gentle lick.

Footsteps echoed down the corridor, and Boroda stood as the now-familiar black boots stopped before her cage and a hand reached down to draw back the bolt. It hesitated, and then moved away again. Through the bars she could make out a shambolic human form, wad of papers in one hand, and broken eye glasses in the other. The human scratched its head, and tried to read what was written on the papers.

'What the . . . where are the papers, dammit? They've sent the wrong ones!' There was a scuffling of skin on paper, and then paper on concrete as the wad slipped from the fingers and cascaded on to the floor.

Boroda whimpered in response. She knew nothing about papers. The human bent to scrunch up the papers from the floor and let out an 'argh!' as its spine clicked painfully.

'Why can't they, just for once, do their jobs properly?' the human snorted and straightened up gingerly, before stomping

20

The Return

'Olya will be angry.'

The taxi driver hunched forward in his seat, and took a prolonged and emphatic chew on his stubby yellow finger-nails. The rough edges hurt the end of his tongue, but it was as nothing compared to the turmoil in his psyche. It had seemed like a good job at the time: in the dead of night, a group of past-it out-of-towners needing a lift home. But now he wished he hadn't started.

He looked at his watch again, and muttered to himself: it was almost six in the morning. The three elderly revellers in the back had been asleep for some time, sprawled, as best they could, across the shiny black plastic of the seat. Their mouths were endlessly puckering and twitching, and in the rear-view mirror, to the driver's tired and distracted eyes, they had looked like a row of ghastly, wizened babies, sucking up the last sleepy milk from the swollen teats of the night, while the lights of Moscow had twirled by, hour after hour, mile after mile. Occasionally they had made slight mewling and burping noises. The driver had felt a certain affection for them at first, but it had soon disappeared: now he just

235

wanted to be rid of them. He had driven, and enquired about direction, and received no clear instructions one way or the other. The younger man with the scar who had got in with them had been more forthright: he had known exactly where he was heading to next, and had alighted quickly outside a smart block in the diplomatic area. But then, then it had got difficult. The old man had occasionally roared something very insistently, but completely unintelligibly. And the two old women seemed to have no idea who they were, let alone where they were.

He'd been paid to take the old ones home, so he hadn't wanted to be fierce with them, but they had steadfastly refused to tell him where home was. Now they had made him late, and made him run out of petrol, and it was miles to the nearest garage. Olya was going to be so very, very cross. The taxi was beached, washed up on the edge of the grand weed-riven pavement, its fuel gauge stark, staring dead. It had coughed its last just as it was making its way, slowly and for the third time, around the great edifice of the Moscow State University. Up, up towards the sky the spikey towers of the university stretched, and down, down the needle on the gauge had fallen, unnoticed by the driver, who was too much in a quandary what to do with his sleeping passengers to see how his night was going to end.

The three on the back seat continued to snore.

'Olya will be so angry! You . . . lazy old bastards!' With shaking hands, the driver picked up his water bottle and, with a fierce squeak of trouser on plastic, turned and gave the three passengers a good, hard squirt.

'Everybody out! Out, I say! I have to go for petrol, you've made me late, and you're a lot of stinky old lazy bastards. Olga's going to kill me, and it's all your fault!'

The three on the back seat squirmed slightly as the water drizzled them, and a floppy hand was raised, vaguely, to fight off the drops.

'Ha! Yes, that wasn't nice, was it? And there'll be more of that, too, if you don't get out of my car! Go on! Shoo! It smells like a brewery. She can't stand booze – especially in the morning! She'll be so cross! And I'm late!' The driver turned in his seat again and started flailing at the sleepy OAPs with his gnarled hands, tugging at their togas and pushing at their swollen, pinky-purple knees.

Galia batted away the water, and her hand came into contact with Zoya's nose with a hard slap. Zoya squawked, and thrashed her head away from the blow, head-butting Grigory Mikhailovich, who stirred like a long-dormant volcano on a tropical island. A trickle of blood escaped the end of his bulbous nose, and the driver crossed himself.

Grigory Mikhailovich emitted a vodka-soaked roar and, in slow motion, raised both massive fists before his face, as if about to tear off Zoya's head.

'Oh Saints preserve us! Now there'll be trouble. Get out of my car!'

The driver shrieked, and Grigory Mikhailovich opened his eyes, one and then the other, and fell silent, fists still raised, but looking about slowly as if the movement of his lead crystal eyes caused him great pain. Galia also finally prised open her eyes, which had up to now been glued shut with an earthy cocktail of Zoya's mascara, Moscow air and her own sleepy dust. She tutted, blinked rapidly, and tried to recall where she was, and how she had got there. Grigory Mikhailovich let out a loud, hacking cough, and opened the car door to spit plentifully. Zoya slept on between the two wakeful monoliths.

'Get out of my car, or I'll call the police! Really, this is enough. You've had all my petrol. You've had your tour. Now get out! I'm an honest man, and I have business to do. I have to get to the market. Olya will be so cross . . .'

Galia struggled with the door handle on her side, if only to get away from the screeching farmer, or driver, or whoever he was, but her hand did not seem to be part of her own body any more: momentarily, she couldn't really remember what she needed to do to make it move, or why she wanted it to move. Eventually the door fell open of its own accord and Galia pitched forward, steadying herself by grabbing hold of Zoya's bony knee, which caused the latter to emit a piercing scream and slap the driver in the face, which he happened to be poking through the gap between the two front seats.

'Out! Out!' Blood-pressure mounting, he was working himself into a frenzy, now producing a yellowish froth at the corners of his mouth. Galia could tell it was time to go.

She tugged Zoya out of the car, mostly by the hair, and then stood still, looking down at her feet for a moment. She was missing her left sandal, and had acquired a child's pink plastic slipper instead. It was not comfortable. She breathed in deeply through her nose, and shut her eyes. Her head was full of helicopters and the angle of the ground beneath her just wasn't right. Her stomach seemed to be making an attempt to crawl up to her throat, and she felt the wrinkles in her face deepening, forming some sort of relief map of the Himalayas, even as she breathed. She was aware of the sound of Grigory Mikhailovich being levered out of the back of the taxi by the driver, and could hear him coughing and swearing on the other side of the car. She was almost tempted to sit down on the tarmac where she stood, wavering slightly, but then something in the air, not as solid as a smell but something like it, made her stop.

238

The quality of the light touching her still-closed eyelids made her heart miss a beat and she looked up, squinting for a moment.

'Let's get away from the car, shall we, Zoya? That driver is rude. There's no need for rudeness.'

Zoya cawed a vague affirmative, and the two ladies stumbled forward, away from the car and on to the grey expanse of empty pavement.

'I'm going to crawl,' whispered Zoya, bending her knees stiffly and stretching her fingers towards the infinite grey slabs.

'No, you're not. You'll be arrested, and then where will we be? Just breathe, and put one foot in front of the other.' Galia hoisted her back up.

'You're a fine one for . . . perambulatory advice,' muttered Zoya thickly, as Galia's plastic slipper flopped about on the ends of her toes like a dead fish, threatening any moment to send her plunging to the ground. 'That'll teach you to bet your shoes,' she added, spitefully. Galia had no recollection of betting anything the previous night, but felt it was wiser, at this stage, to resist further questioning. They staggered across an acre of grey, before coming to a barrier: a parapet.

As Galia's eyes accustomed to the zesty lemon light, she raised her gaze and, with a little gasp, surveyed the view that spread from her feet to the far horizon. Her fuddled brain gradually focused on the jumble of colours and lights before her. She breathed deeply, and with each breath, her head raised a little higher from her shoulders, her chin lifted slightly from her chest, and she began to feel a little more like a person, and a little less like one of the living dead. Zoya leant against her slightly, whimpering, and she put her arm around her friend's sharp shoulder. The car

239

had come to a halt on a terrace that marked the edge of a huge green escarpment. The ground in front of them dropped away in green undulations towards the banks of the wide, deep river below. Their vantage point was complete and unspoilt. Laid out at their feet was the entire city of Moscow, bordered by the silver-green Moskva River, and stretching out languidly in all directions into the hazy morning. In the pink distance she could just make out the Ostankino TV tower, famous across the federation: a symbol of progress, homogeny and mediocre state-run TV. She counted the Stalin sky-scrapers, and could see six. Everybody knew there were seven. She tried again, and still only saw six. She couldn't believe she was wrong. And then some sense made her look back, and up, over her shoulder, and she tutted to herself. Turning to face the opposite direction, she witnessed the majesty of the Moscow State University looming over her. It made her heart flip over, and then thud with a mixture of pride and fear. The seventh of the seven sisters was breathtaking and very close, almost hunching over her. She nodded to it, and then slowly turned back to her private vista. She caught the glint of the Kremlin's golden roofs, and the vague ice-cream outline of St Basil's cupolas. A patch of mottled green dotted with bright fairground rides must be Gorky Park. And at their feet, much closer, lay the Luzhniki Olympic stadium, huge and dark and empty. And to set it all off, to their right, slightly surprisingly in the green of summer, a ski-jump lounged.

The new blue sky still sported a smudge of rose at the horizon, and the air itself felt alive with dew and promises. In nearby streets, Galia could hear the approach of teams of cleaners, washing down the pavements and the previous night's spillages, and bagging up the waste and dust and grime. Making the city clean and bright, ready for the new day.

'Look at that Zoya!' said Galia, smiling. 'It just makes you feel like everything will be all right with the world. Such beauty!'

Zoya said nothing. Galia wondered if she had gone back to sleep in a standing position, and wriggled her shoulder a little beneath her friend's head.

'Hey, Zoya, look at the view. It's magical!'

'Stuff the view,' said Zoya in a thick rumble, before gently lowering herself to the pavement.

'But look!'

Zoya refused to look and laid down on the pavement with her hands folded under her head. She was just about to nod off, when with a sudden snort, a regiment of fountains laid out before the university shot plumes of silver water into the dawn air, covering all three revellers with a cold, wet dew. Galia clapped her hands and laughed. Zoya's response did not bear reporting.

'Muph stuffun.'

'What was that, Grigory Mikhailovich?' laughed Galia.

The old man, now wearing an orange boob-tube borrowed from a large young lady the previous night, was trying to get some words out, muttering and gesticulating towards the east with a puffy but insistent finger.

'Muph stuffun!'

He coughed loud and long, and struggled for breath, but still pointed.

'I don't get it, Grigory Mikhailovich. Can you mime it?'

Grigory Mikhailovich regarded her blankly for a moment or two, and then, very slowly, held his hands out in front of him, parallel, palms facing each other, and rotated them, in a single motion forward, round and round. He began

241

slowly, but gradually picked up speed. As he did so, he began to shuffle his feet.

'Is that some kind of burlesque he's doing?' asked Zoya, opening one eye.

'Really, my dear!' said Galia.

'Woo woo!' said Grigory Mikhailovich in a deep baritone.

'It is a burlesque!' and Zoya began to giggle uncontrollably. 'Is there no end to his talents? He's almost as good as that young lad last night!'

'What young lad?'

'The one you offered to take home!'

'You're hysterical,' Galia snapped and sucked in her lips, turning her back on Zoya.

'I think he's miming a train: is it a train, Grigory Mikhailovich?'

He didn't hear, so busy was he with his woo-wooing.

'Grigory Mikhailovich, is it a train?' Galia bellowed as loudly as she could, standing in his path and scaring a cloud of pigeons into the air.

Grigory Mikhailovich stopped, thought for a moment, nodded, and then winced. In the middle distance, Galia could just make out the grand silhouette of the Southern Station.

'We need to get a train? Well, of course, of course – Zoya, get up! We need to get a train! What was I thinking, standing here, looking at the view . . .'

Galia broke off, and with a yelp, shoved her hand deep in to her jodhpur pocket. Her fingers scrabbled about in the rough material as her heart stood still. It wasn't there! She tried again, fingers digging as deep into the pocket as they could reach. And then, right at the bottom, folded several times and crumpled under her loose change, her fingers closed around it: the VIPP – Very Important Piece of Paper, signed by Glukhov, Roman Sergeevich, and sealed with his official seal. As far as she could recall, it set out, in official terms, that the dog, Boroda, and the man, Vasily Semyonovich Volubchik, should be freed immediately as they were friends and comrades of the Deputy Minister, Southern Section, and the State in general. Galia curled her fingers around the paper, and lifted her chin.

'Come, Zoya, rouse yourself. We must go. We have to get to the station. We must get back!'

'Muph . . .' wheezed Grigory Mikhailovich, before erupting into a coughing fit that blew a great blob of bloody phlegm into the morning air, where it briefly shone like a ruby star on the top of the Kremlin roof, before disappearing over the parapet and into the shady greenery below.

'That's better!' Grigory Mikhailovich wiped his face on the back of his hand and leant on the parapet for support. 'I find . . . sometimes, the airways . . . are a little . . . stiff in the morning.'

'The station, Grigory Mikhailovich?' asked Galia.

'Galina Petrovna, time is too short.'

'But we must try!'

'No, too short for trains! My advice is to fly. Time is of the essence, especially for the dog, and . . . what day is it?'

Galia thought for a moment.

'Saturday, I think. Yes, Saturday.'

'Well, that settles it. You have to fly. You must get back today. Tomorrow is . . .'

'Sunday,' Galia filled in for the old man.

'Sunday, precisely. Sunday is no good to man or beast. You won't get access to anyone on a Sunday. You must hurry; I can get you the tickets. But it must be today.'

'Fly,' murmured Zoya, 'I love to fly.'

'Do you, my dear?'

'Fly! Weeee!' Zoya leapt up from the pavement and thrust out her arms, dive-bombing Grigory Mikhailovich and scattering the poor pigeons once more.

'Weee, weeee, up and down, over the clouds! Up, up and away!' She stood still suddenly and wobbled slightly, all the meagre colour draining from her face in an instant.

'Ooh, oh, actually, I don't feel at all well.'

'Oh goodness, Zoya, don't heave up here, not in front of the university! It's a seat of learning. Oh heavens!'

It was too late. The rose bushes received a direct hit, and the taxi driver, just returning with his petrol can to the dead car, clucked monstrously.

'You old people should know better! You're a disgrace!'

'Mind your own business!' said Galia, as she rubbed Zoya's back, and wondered how she was ever going to get her friend on an aeroplane that morning.

'Come, Zoya, collect yourself. We must get back to the flat and get our things, the plane won't wait for us, and Vasya and Boroda are relying on us.'

'We can't let them down,' mumbled Zoya, before vomiting over the unfortunate flowers a second time.

'No, my dear, we can't let them down. So come on, stop that, we don't have time.'

'I would if I could, believe me, Galia. Something must have disagreed with me. This is most unusual.'

'I'll hail us a taxi,' said Grigory Mikhailovich, and set off, with extreme slowness, for the main boulevard.

* * *

Contrary to all their expectations, the trio arrived at the airport while the morning was still dewy, the air still fresh, the day still early. Galia had thrown together whatever contents of the travel bag that she could remember and locate within the trembling darkness of Grigory Mikhailovich's cave-like dwelling. Zoya had spent a long time looking for something, but she wouldn't say what: she just scratched about in all the corners, like a cat that had been shut in for too long. The object, whatever it was, was never found, and this produced a deep crease on Zoya's papery skin that ran from the crown of her head to the bridge of her nose. Grigory Mikhailovich sat in his armchair and ranted, occasionally, about how Lenin would have appreciated electronic music had he been alive today, and asked the ladies if they thought it would be possible to resurrect their former leader, like Frankenstein's Monster, if the right kind of replacement parts could be found. His raves were interspersed with a silence broken only by his wheezing.

Towards the end of the process of packing, Kolya surfaced briefly from a room at the far end of the hallway, just as they were gathering their strength to leave. He tried to squirm back into the room when he realized they were still there, smirking and congratulating Galina Petrovna on having correctly identified the Deputy Minister Glukhov.

'It's a shame you didn't introduce me though, Galina Petrovna. I could have made a connection. Students need connections. But well done on getting home on your own, and changing out of those ridiculous costumes.' And with that he disappeared behind the door.

The taxi ride out to the airport was thankfully uneventful. Zoya seemed to have spent all her forces on the unfortunate rose bushes, and simply dozed, ashen-faced but with a frown still in place, as the car bumped its way through the outskirts of the city, regularly taking crazy detours across the dual-carriage way to avoid potholes that could swallow a whale. The silver birches wavered gently in the summer breeze as

245

they crossed the city limits, passing the impressive memorial of giant iron exes that marked the limit of the Nazi's progress during the Great Patriotic War. So close to the capital, so close to the seat of power: despite herself, Galia couldn't help the shudder of respect that passed down her spine as she thought of Stalin pacing in the Kremlin, hands behind his back and moustaches twitching, refusing to be evacuated, refusing to be moved from Moscow even though the fascists were almost at the city gates. Thank God for the Russian weather, and the Soviet soldiers who fought on, ill equipped and barely fed, to defend their motherland.

And therefore, perhaps, thank God for Pasha too, long half-forgotten, but not quite invisible in her past. Pasha, who had fought after a fashion, and fed the soldiers what he could find. Pasha, who had lived with her in that flat, shared a bed with her, had sat at that same kitchen table, but who left only empty shoes and grey shirts with frayed collars when he died.

Galia eased her shoulder under Zoya's nodding head, and observed her friend's sleeping face. She wondered how this old friend, well known, whose hand she'd held in adversity, and whom she'd shared a laugh with at least every week for the last forty years, could still present her with mysteries. She was an enigma, this Zoya. But an amusing one, Galia had to admit. She examined the back of Grigory Mikhailovich's head as he sat, grey and monumental, in the front seat of the taxi. She should thank him for his part in arranging Pasha's visit to the sanatorium at Kislovodsk, long ago and unsuccessful as it was. It didn't feel right not to mention it. He had been kind, in his own way, and now that they had achieved their mission of meeting with the Deputy Minister, or Roma as Galia referred to him in her head, she had time to feel thankful.

They made their way through the departure terminal, squinting in the sunlight at the huge and puzzling information boards for a clue as to which direction to shuffle in and at what time. The whole airport was high and airy and full of chrome and bright electric light. It was totally alien. Zoya was suffering and could barely lift her eyes from the shiny tiled floor. Galia had to guide her as a mother leading a small, slightly straggly, purple-haired child. They drew no quizzical glances though: the airport was full to the shiny chrome gills with the odd, the unusual and the slightly bizarre. This building was no homage to internal flights only: from here, you could get to all four corners of the world, and meet any kind of person you desired to. And suddenly, Galia had had enough of the bright lights and the noise and the odd people, and dearly, dearly wanted to get back home, to normality.

'Grigory Mikhailovich! It's Rov Avia, I believe, for Rostov on Don, and the ticket booth is over there, in the far corner. You see, with the red-and-white signage?' Galia needed to take control and get home, otherwise she could see the three of them still bumbling around this shining monstrosity for days to come.

Grigory Mikhailovich nodded dumbly and set off across the concourse at the pace of a dead goat. Galia plonked Zoya down in a very uncomfortable-looking shiny chrome-and-plastic chair, and examined the departure board as her friend began to slide gently towards the floor. Only one hour and she would be on the way home. She crossed her fingers for luck and then crossed herself with the crossed fingers for yet more luck. Galia heard Zoya squeak as she slipped from the chair on to the floor. She scooped her friend back up and propped her more firmly into the seat by wedging the travel bag in between her and the wall.

'Thank you, Galia. When do we fly?'

'One hour, Zoya.'

'Excellent. I shall sleep, sleep perchance to dream,' and with that Zoya curled over the travel bag and fell into a deep and dark sleep that was immediately more impenetrable than the deepest mediaeval forest or darkest well. Galia wished her goodnight and, with a sigh, looked around for Grigory Mikhailovich.

She eventually located him resting on a kiosk selling girly magazines, hairnets and yoghurt pots containing the cheapest vodka known to man.

'Hair of the dog, so to speak, Galina Petrovna.' He wiped his mouth with the back of his hand and dropped the two empty pots into the over-flowing waste bin, before straightening the red-flag pin in his lapel and allowing Galia to frog march him gently to the Rov Avia desk.

'Buy the tickets, please, Grigory Mikhailovich: Zoya and I have a plane to catch.'

'Yes, madam. My pleasure.'

He began the laborious process of ordering the tickets, from a lady who seemed not in the least interested in providing him with anything at all, apart from evil looks with a side-order of rasping sighs.

'Grigory Mikhailovich—' Galia began, but broke off.

He turned to her slowly, frowning a mild enquiry at her hesitant tone. His blue eyes looked in to hers.

'I'd like to thank you, Grigory Mikhailovich, for a favour you did for me a long time ago. You probably don't remember—'

He raised an eyebrow and waited for the question, his face otherwise as blank as an empty desk.

'You organised a visit to the sanatorium at Kislovodsk, for my husband, a long time ago. It didn't save him, in fact

248

he came back worse than before he went, but it was still a kind thing to do. I never knew until the other day that you and Zoya were involved in organising it.'

'Kislovodsk? Your late husband, good lady? I have no clue what you are talking about. I am here to buy your tickets, and that is all, I believe.'

'Zoya told me, Grigory Mikhailovich. Zoya told me . . . well, she said it was classified information, but she said you fixed it. It was kind.'

Still he looked at her blankly. 'What year are we talking about, madam?'

'It was 1956, Grigory Mikhailovich, forty years ago. Another lifetime ago. I hadn't thought about it for ages, but then, she mentioned it, and it came back, like it was yesterday.'

Grigory Mikhailovich pulled a dirty yellow handkerchief from his trouser pocket and coughed into it, but said nothing. The woman behind the desk thrust various bits of paper at him, and he signed them with much deliberation and an unsteady hand. He handed them back and turned to Galia, about to speak.

'No, Elderly Citizen! You've signed in the wrong boxes! I'm going to have to do the whole form again.' The woman behind the counter pounced on the pen, tearing it from Grigory Mikhailovich's slackening grip, and started shredding the offending papers with a ferocity that sent strips of mangled paper high into the air. 'You old Commies, you're all the same: can't cope with modern life. You need to get your lives in order! There's no Lenin now, you know!'

'Lenin? Where is he?' He looked around wildly for a moment, his chins wobbling with the effort. 'We must call to Comrade Sasha, if Lenin is—'

'No, no, Grigory Mikhailovich, we're only here to buy the

249

tickets. We don't need to call anyone,' Galia broke in, concerned that they were about to get side-tracked by searching for Lenin.

The old man looked her in the eye.

'You are here to buy our plane tickets. Remember?'

There was a long, long pause as he thought.

'In 1956 you say?'

Galia was startled, but nodded. 'Yes, but—'

'That was an interesting year for us, yes. We had a number of projects going on. I remember it well.'

'Well, that's wonderful, Grigory Mikhailovich. They were health projects? My Pasha had . . . well, he had cancer, so a holiday in the fresh air at the sanatorium was our only hope, really.'

'Good lady, I don't remember sending anyone on a "holiday" in 1956. In 1956 I was gathering volunteers for a programme of experiments.'

'What kind of experiments?'

'Medical experiments.'

The woman behind the counter raised her head and tutted at the mention of medical experiments. Galia felt the blood in her veins turn thick like gravy, weighing down her limbs. She drew in a breath. 'So my husband was a volunteer for a medical experiment, Grigory Mikhailovich?'

'Well, Galina Petrovna, it depends on how you define the word "volunteer". Our subjects were volunteered on their own behalves, by the State, if you see . . . they were generally people of . . . poor character.'

Galia's eyes rounded. 'And what about my Pasha?'

'Well, I don't remember his case, obviously, but most likely he was a snitch, you know, not one of *ours*,' Grigory Mikhailovich stressed the word with a deep bass note, 'doing things that . . . brought him to our notice. I don't know, I can't recall. But it must be true.'

He proceeded to pick a piece of old biscuit out of his coat pocket and put it in his mouth. The woman behind the counter handed him a sheaf of pieces of paper and withdrew her hand quickly. Again he signed in a series of boxes with his large, unsteady hand.

'My husband was no snitch, Grigory Mikhailovich. That is one thing I know.' Galia's hands were shaking: in fact, her whole body was shaking, very slightly.

The old man paused, and looked around himself, and up at the high glass and chrome ceiling, and down at the polished tiled floor, where his drooping jowls were reflected back at him. He scratched his head.

'Well . . . good lady, I think if I sent him to Kislovodsk, it must have been for a reason. And if Zoya referred him to me—'

'What did Zoya tell you?'

'I have no idea, my dear. But it must have been something. A spy, perhaps? That's how it was, I expect. Although I really don't recall.'

Grigory Mikhailovich made to pat Galia's hand, and she jumped backwards, as if burnt. The tickets were placed on the counter, followed swiftly by a 'position closed' sign.

'Here we are,' Grigory Mikhailovich bellowed brightly. Galia began to open her mouth to speak, but her dry tongue rustled like a mouse in the summer grass. She could only stand and stare, and feel a thrill of anger rush through her to the tips of her fingers. Her hands clenched into tight fists and she thought that she might just punch Grigory Mikhailovich.

'What's the matter, Galina Petrovna? There's no shame on you, my dear. We are all part of progress. And there is no progress without science. You'd be surprised what those boffins can brew up, Galina Petrovna, when they put their throbbing old brains to it. Did you know how many boffins they've got under the Kremlin keeping Lenin together? Hundreds, literally! You would be shocked at the—'

'Grigory Mikhailovich! I am shocked . . . shocked at your experiments! What gave you the right—'

'We were the Soviet Union, madam.' He cut her off. 'We were never wrong! We worked for the common good! Lenin knows that!' Grigory Mikhailovich was shouting suddenly. A silver thread of saliva looped from his wide, purple mouth down on to his coat front and touched the red-flag pin.

A shiver trickled down Galia's back and for the first time, she felt a little afraid of Grigory Mikhailovich.

'He was a sick man, Grigory Mikhailovich. He needed a holiday. Even Lenin would have recognized that.'

'We needed bodies! I needed my human mice! We were building Communism! We still are! And they all served very well, our mice. If only my experiments could have continued—'

Galia snatched the tickets and tags from the old man's hand and fled across the concourse, desperate to get away from his booming voice and mad ideas. Weaving her way through the sun-kissed, dazzling crowds, she worked back through the maze of chairs, shrink-wrapped cases and bulk boxes of imports, back to Zoya, still slumbering on her slippery chair, unaware of the grubby fingers of history clutching at both her scraggy neck and that of her cousin. Galia shook her roughly by the shoulder.

'Come on, we're going to the gate. We have to go. I have to get home. I've got a dog to free. And an old man to rescue. We don't all have to die.'

'Die?'

'Well, we do all have to die, but not before our time. And it's not our time. Come on!'

252

'Will there be beer?' mewed Zoya.

'On the plane? Of course. And nuts.'

'And little hand towels?'

'Of course little hand towels. Grigory Mikhailovich has arranged it all. Come now, we must hurry, my dear. He says goodbye, by the way.'

And Galia shuffled Zoya towards the gate as fast as she could, allowing for the latter's dazed state and tiny steps.

They left Grigory Mikhailovich in the middle of the concourse, alone, and very confused. He stood on the concourse for ten minutes, twenty minutes, half an hour, trying to remember why he was there, and who he was with, repeating over and over again 'My mice! Where are my mice! Where are my mice?' muttering the words under his breath. Eventually, another vague thought crept into his head and the mantra changed. 'Kolya!' he rumbled, at first under his breath, and then getting louder, and more insistent, until it became a shout, and then a roar.

'Kolya! Kolya! We must go . . . Kolya, where are you? Kolya! Kolya!'

Navy-shirted security guards were called by an unseen hand responding to an unseen eye to deal with the old fella making a noise like the end of the world in a dustbin. A scuffle ensued, and the old man wet himself as he was bodily restrained. The two younger guards laughed as they put his hands behind his back and began to push him forward, out of his puddle, and towards the doors that led to the bowels of the building and the security guards' office. He begged them in a mewling voice not to take him away, asking if only they wouldn't take him, they didn't need to worry, he wouldn't tell a soul, and he'd never been involved with *them* anyway. He just wanted to return Lenin to his proper place.

The youngest security guard winked, and told granddad not to worry. They would take care of him.

As they passed through the door a loud buzzer shocked the air: the metal detector had been triggered. Zoya's gun was to do Grigory Mikhailovich no favours today, it seemed.

21

Of Butterflies, Dogs and Men

In the southern morning sunshine, the cloud of dust kicked up by the little car as it bucked along the track gave it the aura of a glittering tumble weed speeding through scrubby, empty fields. Mitya could hardly see the road ahead: partly because one of his eyes still wouldn't fully open, but mostly because the entire windscreen was coated in a thick layer of summer meadow dust. Every so often Katya, kitted out with a pair of men's leather driving gloves, a red-and-green checked headscarf and the biggest sunglasses Mitya had ever seen, stopped the car and wiped down the glass with an old and yellowing copy of *Pravda*. Mitya was not sure he approved. True, windscreen wiper blades were still a highly prized commodity in modern Russia and therefore open to theft, but he wished the girl had removed them herself to ensure they weren't stolen. Her lack of foresight meant today's journey was going to be unnecessarily elongated and uncomfortable. But on reflection, Mitya didn't care. He would forgive her anything.

He had tossed and turned for hours the previous night, his head full of doubts, but then he had come to some conclusions, and once that was done, he had slept like the dead, straight through. It was only Katya's knock around ten a.m. that had brought him to a gluey consciousness. He was aware that he had dreamt and that the dreams had been deep and threatening, but the details scampered away like mice from a hungry cat when he awoke. He had washed, shaved and combed his hair according to his usual schedule as best he could, but the results were patchy and not at all pleasing: stubble remained in red raw clumps on the tender bruises about his face, and a ridge in the middle of his hair stuck up like a little coxcomb no matter how much water he applied to it. He had dressed, slowly and painfully, in the new clothes bought at the commission shop the previous afternoon: blue T-shirt, white knee-length shorts, white socks, and then his brown lace-up casual shoes. He had a vague suspicion that the shoes didn't go. He would have liked to have asked Katya, but felt he shouldn't. She had not said anything about his attire: but then, she did not know that it had all been bought with her in mind.

Mitya still ached. In fact, every particle in his body seemed to be raw and swollen. He could not fit sunglasses over his bruised eyes, so he opted for a sunhat, leant to him by Katya. He would take it off upon their arrival at the remand institution: it was orange, purple and white and bedecked in psychedelic swirls, and Mitya suspected it was too small for him.

'So!' said Katya with a brightness to challenge the sun. Conversation in the car had been a little lacking.

'So,' croaked Mitya, looking out of the window at nothing.

'We're going to the SIZO, puppy, like you wanted.'

'It's not something I want, Katya. It's just . . . necessary.'

'OK. Can you tell me why?'

'Well . . .'

'Give me a hint?'

'It's a long story. I have some unfinished business.'

'Is it a crim, who owes you something? Are you going to threaten him? Blackmail, maybe? You have to know, I'm not sure I like that kind of thing. It's not very nice. It can get you in to trouble. Believe you me, I've—'

'Blackmail?' Mitya looked at a cow, standing forlorn in a parched field, flicking its ragged tail among the flies that buzzed around its haunches. 'Well, that's a fine idea.'

'But, you know, you shouldn't really get involved in that kind of thing, I don't—'

'There's always money to be made, Katya. It's just that old Mitya here never seems to be at the money-making end of things. Maybe I should give it a try, I don't know: it seems to work for policemen, after all.'

'But technically, puppy, I think it is illegal.' Katya was frowning. 'Blackmail, that is. I know everyone does it, but I'm just saying. It's not a friendly thing to do.'

'Katya, I'm teasing you! I'm sorry, you didn't get my joke.' Mitya looked forlornly at his knees.

'Oh, OK – you were joking? Ha! Well, Mitya, good for you!'

Mitya smiled, then stopped, as his bottom lip split again and his tongue curled under the metallic taste of blood. The little car traversed a pothole the size of Siberia and flung both its passengers up in the air till their heads touched the roof, and then back in to their seats until their coccyxes kissed the floor. Mitya bit his bleeding lip as pain lurched from his buttocks up through his stomach and all the way to his aching head.

'Oops!' said Katya, struggling to keep her hands on the wheel.

'OK, stop the car. I think I have to stretch my legs. Right now, Katya!'

They pulled over on to the side of the track, into the cool shade of a linden tree. The sudden stillness washed over them, until Katya began to speak.

'It's beautiful here. We should have brought a picnic. That would make you feel better, puppy. Some sausage and black bread, hard-boiled eggs, tea. Maybe a little bonfire and some shashliks? You know, when I was little, my Uncle Borya took us to the woods every week and . . .'

Mitya nodded absently and made his way into a little green copse to pee in peace. Katya liked to chat, and he liked it too, but this morning he needed a little quiet to clear his head. He felt the summer all about him in this little copse, verdant and seething. A small blue butterfly landed on the back of his hand as he stood, swaying slightly, peeing into the vegetation. He felt the vague tickle of its body on his skin and looked closer, his eyes taking in its tiny papery wings and bobbing antennae. Instead of brushing it off, he gently raised his hand to eye level and looked at it, face-to-face, man-to-man . . . being-to-being.

'Why?' said Mitya. 'Why are we here?' The butterfly opened its wings, and then slowly closed them. 'What is it all for?' The butterfly uncoiled its proboscis slightly on to Mitya's damp skin. He was filled, all at once, with the strong impression, strong like the smell of lavender in clothes drawers, or bleach on toilet floors, that he had met this butterfly before. There was something familiar in its gaze, in the way it licked his hand, something that spoke to him through its silence, through the deliberate opening and closing of its wings, the uncoiling and re-coiling of its proboscis. The butterfly cocked its head slightly, and raised one tiny leg.

258

'Sharik?' breathed Mitya, and his swollen eyes filmed over with tears. The butterfly opened its wings, caught the breeze and gently fluttered into the air above his head. Dancing for a few moments before his eyes, it gained height, bobbing towards the branches of the tree as they, in turn, nodded downwards to meet it. The sunhat fell from Mitya's head on to the wet grass. His eyes searched the branches for the butterfly, but it had disappeared into the green canopy above. Sunlight filtered through the branches and enveloped Mitya in a warm honey glaze. His heart swelled and filled his chest.

The butterfly silence faded as Katya's story-telling broke through the skin of his consciousness like a pebble into a woodland pond. Her voice called him back. Mitya shivered slightly in the sunshine, picked a frond of long green grass to chew, and followed Katya's call out of the copse and back towards the dusty dirt track.

'—And do you know what? She was never the same again! Just the sight of a melon was enough to do it! Of course he apologised, but still. Are you OK, puppy?' Katya stopped talking and eyed him quizzically. 'Where's your hat?'

'Who says we're better than butterflies, Katya?'

The girl was stumped by the question for a moment.

'Who says a man's life is worth more than that of an . . . an ant, for example? Why is a human worth more than a dog? Why are there different rules for the animals and us, Katya?'

'Are there different rules, Mitya? Just treat everything and everyone properly, and everything will be OK, puppy.'

'Everything and everyone?'

'Yeah, well, you know. Just be good, I guess.'

'Be good. Yes. But what about dirt?'

'What about it, Mitya? It's kind of in the eye of the

259

beholder, isn't it? Well, it's not actually in your eye, obviously. Pigs love it, old ladies mostly don't. Whatever makes you happy, I guess, as long as you hurt no-one else. Where's my hat, hun?'

'But animals make dirt. Disorder. That's what I . . . I can't abide. Can animals be orderly, do you think?'

'Animals have their own order, Mitya: they're animals. They have their own code. They do what comes naturally, until humans get in the way. It's only humans you have to watch out for. It's only humans who murder and torture, after all.'

They stared at each other for a moment across the bonnet of the car.

'That's very clever, Katya.'

'I'm a clever girl, puppy. Now, where's my hat?'

'I left it in the copse. It fell off. I couldn't bend down to get it. I'm sorry.'

Katya leant over to ruffle his hair, her fingernails light over his scalp. Then she set off to the copse to retrieve her hat. Mitya looked up for his butterfly in the branches of the linden, squinting in the sun as it prodded at his eyes through the protective green leaves. He couldn't see it, but he knew it was there. He could feel it.

'It's wet, honey. What did you do to it? Did you pee in it? There was really no need—'

'Katya, I need to tell you something.' Mitya's tone was urgent

'What is it? Did you pee in it? You didn't!' Katya giggled, one hand to her mouth.

'No, listen. It's something . . . important.' Mitya swallowed. His hands were shaking as if an internal earthquake were taking place.

'OK, puppy. I'm your friend: you can tell me something

260

important.' She looked at him with her clear, wide eyes and a slight frown.

'You know I'm an exterminator, right?'

'Yes, I know that.'

'You think I kill cockroaches and things, don't you?'

'Yes.'

'That's not right.'

'Oh?'

'Actually I . . . er . . .'

'What?'

Katya stopped, and turned her head slightly as she heard a distant but rapidly nearing roar. Something big was coming along the track towards them, from the direction of town, kicking up clouds of dust and flies.

'I kill dogs.' It came out as a mutter, completely lost under the roar of the approaching engine.

'What did you say?' Katya turned back to him, mouth open.

Mitya lurched towards her and grabbed her arm just as an ancient red tractor rounded the corner behind them.

'I kill dogs!' he shouted at the top of his voice.

The tractor roared round the bend and lurched up the track, throwing dried mud and husks over the little car and scattering wildlife as it went.

'Dogs?'

'Dogs . . . I am . . . a controller . . . of canine infestations.'

There was a long pause. Katya shook her arm free of his and twisted her hands in front of her, then picking at a hangnail, and then biting it sharply.

'But you—'

'I'm sorry, Katya. I tried to tell you.'

'Oh, really?'

'Look at me?'

261

She looked at him with eyes that burnt.

'All my life, it seemed like the right thing to do. Well, not quite all my life. But it seemed to be . . . my calling. I couldn't bear to see dogs roaming the streets. Dogs, for me, meant disease, pain, fear.'

'But you were saving those puppies the other night.'

'Katya . . .'

'You *were* saving them, yes?'

Mitya looked up into the tree and saw a flutter of blue wings.

'Katya, I . . . I wasn't saving them. I was going to gas them.'

She let out a small 'Oh!' and turned away from him.

'But I didn't, Katya! I saved them . . . because . . . something changed. I can't explain.'

'Try, Mitya. Try very hard to explain.' Her voice was hard as winter, the soft lisp all gone, her eyes like chips of ice.

'You were so tender with them. They reached for you like . . . like furry babies. And it reminded me about . . . things I haven't thought about for years. When I was a child. And I remembered what it's like to care. And suddenly I felt sorry for them. And I realized that it's not their fault.'

'You're right. It's not their fault. It's ours.'

'Katya, please . . . be my friend. Forgive me. I'll explain everything to you properly later; I'll answer all your questions, but just believe me: I won't do it anymore. I'll give up being Mitya the Exterminator.'

Katya frowned, 'Well, that's a fine aim, Mitya, but who will you be instead?'

Mitya thought for a moment, eyes probing the leaves and branches of the swaying tree above them.

'I will be . . . a defender of animals. I will become . . . a defender of human kind, Katya, and of human kindness. I will . . . I will become a vet.'

'A vet? Really?' Katya squeaked, a smile splashing across her face despite herself, before it disappeared just as quickly. 'You're not serious. You're trying to fool me. You don't really want to be a vet.'

'No, really. I am serious. I can do it. I was thinking about it all last night. My teachers always told me to use my skills for good . . . it's not too late, is it?'

'Well . . . I don't know. Perhaps it's never too late, Mitya? We all have to hope.'

'Will you . . . can you forgive me, little girl? I promise I will never mislead you again. It is not something I wanted . . . to hurt you.'

'Do you swear? That you will help animals, not hurt them?'

'Yes I swear.'

'And are you really my friend, Mitya?'

'Yes, I swear, I'm really your friend.'

Katya took Mitya's face in both her hands.

'Then I am your friend. I forgive you. But don't ever take me for a fool again.'

Mitya took Katya's hands from his face and kissed both palms. 'Thank you.'

'OK, well, we'd better . . . we'd better get on for the SIZO. It's nearly midday. And you have business.' Katya led Mitya back to the car, and climbed into the driver's seat. She spun the wheels, and the little car hopped back on to the dusty track, a plume of brown rising into the summer sky.

High up in the linden tree, the butterfly opened its wings, and closed them again, and sighed.

22

Rov Avia

'So, Zoya, are you feeling better?'

'Yes, Galia, dearest, a little better, thank you.' Zoya nodded carefully and shuffled her shoulders further into the nylon embrace of the aeroplane's seat, looking small and old and frail.

It is true to say, Zoya had milked her indisposition for everything it was worth upon embarking on the process of taking her flight. She insisted on being provided with a wheelchair to bump her across the tarmac to the rather dog-eared Tu-154 that awaited them, and Galia thought at one point that she was going to insist on being carried up the steps to the plane's passenger door too. However, happily for all concerned, a large and jolly baggage handler with last-night's vodka still in his eyes had gently taken her arm and floated her up the stairs before she realized what was happening, popping her in through the passenger door rather like a magician producing a coin from behind an unsuspecting audience member's ear. She had been left temporarily speechless, much to Galia's relief.

Once on board, contrary to Galia's promise, there were

no little paper hand towels, or nuts, but there was beer, and Zoya availed herself of it as soon as the 'fasten seatbelts' sign had been snuffed out and the stewardess had squeezed herself along the gangway. The other passengers were mostly businessmen returning to the south following long-winded negotiations, or bare-knuckle bar fights. Galia was relieved to see that there was no livestock in the cabin on this flight. She had never forgotten one experience on the way back from the Urals when a number of geese had escaped their cage, which had been on the luggage rack above her head. Her hair had taken weeks to recover, and she still couldn't look a goose in the eye. But times had moved on. Geese were now confined to the hold, or the toilet, depending on the airline.

'So, my dear, if you are feeling a little restored, I need to talk to you: about Pasha.'

'What do you mean, my dear?' Zoya replied, eyes watering as she put down her can and burped delicately on to the back of her translucent hand.

'I had a talk with Grigory Mikhailovich, Zoya, at the airport, and it wasn't very nice.'

Zoya was utterly still for a moment. 'Why not?'

'From what I could make out, Zoya, he said,' Galia paused, not quite believing she was saying the words, 'he said, you told him that Pasha was a spy.' Her friend's head vibrated slightly on her neck with a slight cracking noise.

'I didn't!' Zoya's answer was immediate and firm.

'A spy!'

'No, Galia, that's nonsense!' Zoya began to laugh, and then the laugh became a cackle, and her tiny bony fingers made little crackling indents on the can of beer in her hand. Her eyes disappeared within a nest of wrinkles beneath her brows and she guffawed so hard that the rows of grey heads

265

in front began to turn towards them with curiosity and some annoyance.

'It's not funny, Zoya. That's what Grigory Mikhailovich said.'

'Oh, Galia, can't you spot an old fool when you see one? He can hardly remember what day it is, let alone anything else.' Zoya continued giggling, and wiped her eyes with the back of her hand. 'And he is also a Scorpio, Galia: supposed to be wise, but mark my words, they are generally bullshitters of the first order, my dear.'

'So now you're saying he's lying?'

'Not lying, Galia, that is an awful word. But quite possibly . . . very confused.'

'Demented?'

'Well, maybe. Oh look – some houses, with little piggies running in the yard!' Zoya leant further towards the window and away from Galia, tapping her gnarled finger on the Perspex.

'This is serious, Zoya! Be quiet about piggies!'

'Don't take that tone with me, Galia. It doesn't become you. And I like piggies.' Zoya took another gulp from her can of beer.

'Two days ago, Zinaida Artyomovna, your cousin was going to be our saviour, then he neglected to come to the ministry to meet us.'

'Now, that's not strictly, true, he—'

'And now, now he's a demented old liar. That's a startling turnaround, isn't it? What is he, Zoya?'

Zoya harrumphed a little and continued looking out of the window, her beady eyes constant on the middle distance. Eventually, she spoke.

'Had there been mention of Lenin, when he said that Pasha was a spy.'

'What do you mean, mention of Lenin? We were booking tickets at an airport, in the 1990s, not sorting cabbages on the collective farm in 1930.'

'Yes, I know, but sometimes mention of Lenin sets him off, on a bit of a flight of fancy. I have seen it before. Was there talk of Lenin?' An odd sincerity in Zoya's eyes made Galia pause, and think back over the conversation in the ticket hall.

'Ah, well, yes. Oh . . . yes. The woman behind the desk: she was a bit disparaging about Lenin, actually. I didn't really pay it any attention, and neither did Grigory Mikhailovich, I thought—'

'Oh, Galia, it doesn't need to be much. But it can have a terrible effect.'

'But he was so clear, Zoya. He said you must have referred Pasha to him . . . because he was a spy. He said he did medical experiments on him! Pasha was no spy, Zoya. He was weak, yes; difficult, in fact quarrelsome sometimes. Annoying a lot of the time, mildly dishonest, not very clean, lazy in the garden . . . but he wasn't political.'

'Yes, Galia, I know. Do you really think I'd report your husband as a spy and then never mention it, for forty years? I am not a bad person, Galia.' Zoya gave her friend an unwavering look. It pierced Galia's defences, and had her looking down at her own hands and fumbling in her pocket for a boiled sweet.

'Well, Zoya, that's as maybe, but you didn't mention arranging the trip to Kislovodsk. You didn't mention that for forty years.' Galia found the last of her reserve of barley sugars and sucked on it for all she was worth.

'That's different. I told him Pasha needed a holiday.'

'Really? Is that all?'

The aeroplane buzzed high above the fields and trees, the

factories and farms, following the River Don southward. Zoya looked away through the window.

'Yes. I may have expressed some doubts as to the qualities of Pasha's character, at some point. But that was all. It was just in conversation, nothing more. I made no . . . report. My cousin was looking for people to try out new facilities at the sanatorium at Kislovodsk, and I told him Pasha needed a holiday and said some words to the effect that he was a difficult sod, I believe.'

'Grigory Mikhailovich told me that Pasha was part of an experiment, Zoya. He was there as a guinea pig. Did you know that?'

'You're not hearing what I am saying, Galia,' replied Zoya with a squeak, blinking rapidly. 'Grigory Mikhailovich is deluded. There were no medical experiments. Galia, my dear, I knew you were struggling with Pasha at home.' Zoya stopped for breath, wheezed slightly and thumped herself on the chest twice. 'Remember, Galia: there was no love lost between you two then. I thought a few weeks up in the clear mountain air, with the natural spring waters and plain food, might do him some good. And I thought the break would do you good too.'

'But why, Zoya? And why not tell me?' Galia lifted an eyebrow.

'Oh Galia, he didn't deserve you! Ever!' Zoya grabbed Galia's hands and looked into her eyes.

'He was my husband!'

'Yes and he was weak and mean and paltry and . . . you know that wasn't all.' Zoya ended her sentence with a small sigh, and dropped her friend's hands. She reached for her smelling salts and inhaled deeply, shuddering slightly.

'What do you mean?' Galia may have regularly thought these things about her husband, but she was not entirely prepared to hear them from somebody else, and especially not her friend.

'Wait . . . I can't breathe.' Zoya's eyes rolled back in her head and her tongue protruded slightly.

'Stop that at once,' said Galia firmly. 'You're play acting. Breathe, and speak.'

'Oh . . . you're so harsh! Just wait,' Zoya finished off her beer with a gulp and hiccuped slightly back in to the can. The fleshy man in the row opposite tutted loudly and quickly put his head back in his copy of *Pravda* when Galia caught his eye. 'He was . . . an odd fish . . . Oh, you know. You must know!'

'Know what?' Galia was flummoxed.

'Don't be dumb. You know what I mean.' Zoya folded her arms and looked out of the window again, her cheeks now restored to pale lilac by her smelling salts and the beer.

'I don't know what you mean. What must I know?'

'Oh, Galia . . . come on! That . . . he was one of them.' Zoya hunched over in a conspiratorial manner and hissed the words quickly.

'One of *them*?'

'Yes.'

'A spy? But I told you just now—'

'No! Not one of them, one of *them*!'

'One of who?' Galia was confused.

'Keep your voice down! You know . . . one of *them*!' Zoya looked about her in a way that unnerved Galia, but gave her no further clue as to what she was talking about.

'No, I don't know! Would you please explain yourself?'

Zoya rolled her eyes and began to look about for the stewardess for more beer.

'Spit it out, Zoya.'

269

'Oh, for heaven's sake,' the bird's-nest head leant towards Galia. 'A gay!'

Galia's jaw dropped. It seemed to her that time had stood still on the vibrating jet as she gazed into her friend's face, which had now turned an odd shade of ox blood.

'Have you gone mad?' Each word was very carefully enunciated by Galia's lips.

'You must have known.'

'What are you saying?'

'Well, I just said it.'

'You're not serious.'

'You mean you didn't know?'

'How dare you!' Galia had the awful feeling she might slap her friend.

'You must have known?' Zoya's look was all concern.

'But it's preposterous!' Galia slapped her own forehead instead, and Zoya quivered.

'How can you not have known?'

'But he was married to me!'

'That means nothing, Galia . . . you know that. People get married for all sorts of reasons: to get a flat, or get their dinner cooked, or just because it's a thing they think they should do. I'm sure he liked you . . . at some point, and thought it was a good thing to do.'

'Well that's big of you to say so, Zoya!' Galia turned her head away and stared down the gangway at the backs of the rows of grey heads and the shafts of sunlight that picked out the dandruff on all of them.

A long silence ensued.

'Galia, it's not as if you were desperately in love with him, was it? You couldn't stand him after a while, that's what I seem to remember. There was always trouble and silence at your flat. It wasn't a . . . a happy home.'

270

'For what it's worth, that's not strictly true, Zoya. I think I loved him at the start. Well, I'm not sure . . . but I definitely needed him. He was there for me and, yes, well . . . maybe we needed each other. Sometimes.'

'Exactly! He needed a wife to cook and clean, and you needed a man to do whatever it is men do. Although in view of the fact that he—'

'Enough, Zoya! How dare you! This is just gossip! You think you knew him better than me?' Galia's chest heaved with indignation.

'You asked for the truth, so here it is. It is my truth. I thought you needed a break, and I thought it might do him some good. I knew that Grigory Mikhailovich could book people in to the sanatorium, so I used my connections.'

'He wasn't gay, Zoya.'

'Well, you choose to believe what you like, Galia. It doesn't really matter now. I wanted to help . . . but it seems that I actually may have made things worse.'

'Ha!'

'But I am sorry, Galia, if what I've said has upset you.' Zoya reached out a shaky, wizened hand and clasped Galia's arm.

Galia looked away from her friend and out of the small, oval windows across the gangway into the deep blue sky. She could see the ghost of last night's moon still hanging there.

'I thought you were a seamstress, Zoya. Through all these years of being friends, you told me you were a seamstress. Were you a seamstress, Zoya?'

'Partly.'

'And what was the other part?'

'To know things, Galia. To keep my eyes and ears open, and to know things.'

271

'Oh, Zoya!'

'It was the right thing to do at the time.'

'Keeping tabs on everyone.'

'Helping to build Communism. And it was nothing compared to what my cousin used to do.'

'Ha! And I thought he was just a harmless old man.'

'He is – now. Just a bit confused.'

'Confused? That's one way of putting it.' Galia shifted in her seat and began to twist the air-conditioning nozzle, trying to coax the tiny stream of cold air to reach her over-heating body. 'Well, how do you like your Communism now, comrade Zoya?'

'It was a good theory, Galia, but the execution was lacking somewhat. And the beer is better under capitalism.' Zoya's eyes strayed again towards the broad and sweating air hostess, who was bearing down on them with a little silver trolley that refused to run in a straight line and clipped each passenger's toes in turn.

'You're unbearable,' Galia muttered, and signalled to the stewardess for a beer. She poured the golden liquid into a soft paper cup and took two large mouthfuls. The bubbles bit at her tongue and sent froth up into her nose. She sneezed loudly, eyes watering, and tutted.

'Galia, think about it. Everyone was doing it. Snitching on their friends, keeping tabs on their neighbours, using their connections—'

'I wasn't doing it, Zoya.' Galia's voice was flat. 'And Pasha wasn't doing it either.'

Zoya carried on, seemingly not hearing the words. 'It was just . . . part of the times. It was almost expected, I think. It did no harm. And it was interesting!' Zoya added quietly, the hint of a smile playing across her thin lips.

'Interesting? But don't you see how meddling and gossiping

makes things worse, Zoya? Interfering and making your mind up about people with absolutely no foundation or proof?'

'Proof? Well . . .' Zoya muttered the words to herself, and was thankful that Galia did not hear. In a louder voice, she added, 'I thought the Kislovodsk trip would do you both good, my dear. I didn't realize his cancer was so advanced. I only wanted what was best for you.'

'But you sent him there because you thought he was gay! You didn't think to speak to me about it?'

'You would have been upset, Galia.'

'Well, yes, Zoya, well spotted! You just thought you knew best, but you didn't.'

Galia took another gulp of her beer. On her empty stomach, it was going straight to her head. The aeroplane whined as it banked right, tipping one wing into the air as fields and farms came into view ground-ward on the opposite side. The motion made Galia feel a little nauseous, and the nausea made her feel very tired.

'What nonsense! One minute he's a spy, the next he's gay! You and your cousin – you think you know about these things. You don't know anything. You're both just confused old baggages.' Galia's tongue felt thick in her mouth and the words spilled out on top of themselves.

'Sometimes the past is better left buried, my dear.' Zoya patted her hand.

'Baggages with brains like cabbages, ha!'

'We have a busy morning ahead of us, my dear. Maybe you should get some sleep?'

'With your connections and your ministries and your limos. But it was me: I did the deal with Roman Sergeevich. And I know the truth – about Pasha, about me, and about you now, Zoya,' Galia tapped Zoya's chest with her broad, brown fingers.

'Yes, my dear. You know the truth. And you need to be on top form, now, too.'

'Oh I know, I know. I can't leave it to you. You'll be making up stories about Boroda next. You'll be going to the SIZO asking them to take her in too!'

'Now, Galia, you're being silly. I don't think beer agrees with you.' Zoya was becoming indignant, but trying not to become impatient. She would have loved another beer, but felt it would be imprudent to ask.

'Did you know she was a deviant? Oh yes, better run and tell Grigory Mikhailovich. My dog needs to go to the sanatorium too.'

'I'm not going to discuss it further.'

Galia crumpled her beer can with one brown hand and shoved it in the pocket of the seat in front of her.

'Think of the living: the here and now. Think of Boroda, and Vasya: they need you, Galia. So get some sleep.'

'I don't feel like sleeping, Zoya. I'm too angry.'

Thirty seconds after those words were muttered, Zoya heard Galia begin to snore quietly, her head nodding to her shoulder, hands loose at her sides. Thirty seconds after that, Zoya too was sound asleep, dreaming of ballet, and old friends, and policemen, and secrets.

23

Vasya's Pussy

Vasya Volubchik eyed his porridge with caution. He had had a difficult night. It wasn't so much the constant bad air making his clothes damp and sticky, or the droning noise of his fellow prisoners as they shuffled backwards and forwards, occasionally swearing and cursing, or crying out in pain or anger. It wasn't even his neighbour Shura, whose curiously attentive stare infiltrated most of the two men's shared waking moments and seemed to slither into his very soul. It was the blurred line between day and night, the twilight of existence here that really got to him. His reality, the brightness that had been Vasya Volubchik's life with its club meetings, kitty cat, veggie patch and well-pressed trousers, seemed to have been completely extinguished. Sometimes, at moments of horror, he wondered if he had made it up: maybe he was mad, and perhaps it had never happened at all. Maybe he had been here for too many years, a petty criminal and hoodlum, who had simply dreamt up another life outside this cell, and was destined always to remain within these dank walls, always eating thin porridge and listening to the ramblings of his fellow prisoners, hearing their bellies rumble and their farts pumping out in to the shared air like fumes from rotting cadavers in a morgue.

Still Vasya eyed his porridge. His spoon hovered in mid-air, and then rested on his knee again. The waking days he could cope with, even given the twilight and stench. But at night things really got to him. The empty night, when he could not sleep, and tossed and turned on his narrow bed, aware of all those around him, above him and below him. And worse, the stinking dreams his mind presented before him when he did finally drop off.

The previous night he had dreamt he was lying in his bed at home. It was so real and familiar; it was comforting like an old quilt, or a favourite meal. Everything was as it should be: the sounds were right, the smells were right. He could hear his neighbour, Petr Grigorievich, singing along to Shalyapin in a rich baritone and occasionally arguing with his wife in that good-natured way that some old couples manage. The smell of apple blossom and fresh rain made his nostrils flair, as a warm breeze wafted in through the balcony window. He knew, deep in his heart, that the fridge in the kitchen contained a bowl of cherries waiting for him, picked the previous day by his own hand. He felt the cool clean cotton of his favourite navy spotted pillow case beneath his face, and scraped his stubble across it gently. Best of all, little black-and-white Vasik was curled up on his special cushion in the corner of the room, fast asleep. He took it all in, and then looked again at Vasik, calling the cat over to him.

'Vasik, Vasichka! Come here, tiddles!'

The cat did not move. In fact, not a feline molecule appeared to be moving. Vasya raised his head off the pillow, leaving a slight wet smudge where his sleep dribble had escaped, and placed his feet thankfully into his ancient, soft leather slippers.

'Vasik! You funny little cat! Come here and give your papa some cuddles!'

He approached little Vasik, but the cat hadn't heard. The cat was a black-and-white pool of silky stillness.

'Vasik! What a lazy pussy!'

And the old man leant down to give the cat a tickle. At that moment, the cat's head lifted and turned towards him, clicking as it did so. The old man withdrew his hand as if he had been bitten.

'No! No, pussy, no!'

Where Vasik's eyes should have been, there squirmed twin balls of worms. Vasik opened his mouth, but in place of a meow, the cat spewed out pint after pint of porridge. The thick liquid spread out in a grey puddle until the entire floor was covered, and Vasya's ancient slippers became cold and slimy beneath his toes.

'Get out!' shouted the old man, backing away in fear. But now the zombified cat began to scream, scream like a soul in torment, arching its back and making a noise that surely could be heard in both heaven and in hell. Vasya went to kick it and found that his legs were tied, bound at the ankle. He struggled for a moment, reached out his arms in a desperate attempt to steady himself, and then fell like a tree in the forest, landing face-down in the porridgy cat vomit, the shock of the movement jolting right through his body, but the sticky sick covering his nose and mouth, making it hard for him to breathe.

'Help me, pussy!' he cried thickly. 'Help me, pussy!'

At that moment, Vasya awoke as if breaking the surface of the sea, to find an intent, personal stare being directed at him from not more than twenty centimetres away. Shura was so close he could feel his heartbeat thudding through the bedclothes. Behind him, he could see the bunk was surrounded by curious on-lookers.

277

'You calling me Pussy, oldie?' Shura murmured the words, and Vasya was unsure what was going on. 'You want my help?'

'Er, no, Shura, I was dreaming. About my pussy.'

Shura eyed him doubtfully, a smile playing around his greasy lips.

'Your pussy?'

'Yes, my pussycat, Vasik. I'm sorry if I disturbed you.'

'Your cat? You were screeching and writhing like that while you were dreaming about a cat?' Shura laughed, and the other prisoners standing around the bed did the same, all looking down at Vasya, their mouths open, salivating, laughing at him. Vasya was mightily relieved to be a source of mirth rather than offence . . . or anything else.

'He's black and white, with a little red collar. Oh yes, I always make sure he's got a collar on. He's a very good cat, generally. But in my dream, he was being very odd indeed. He appeared to have eaten a surfeit of prison porridge, and was feeling unwell. Oh yes, it was quite a dream, and not one that I would like to repeat in a hurry. Oh my, I do wonder how he's getting on without me.' Vasya was conscious that he was rambling, but felt safer as long as he was talking.

'Probably been eaten by now, oldie.'

'By a dog, you mean?'

'By a neighbour, more like. But maybe your neighbourhood is better than mine: less hungry?'

'I've never heard of a cat being eaten for dinner, Shura. Well, not since the war.'

'No? It was staple diet where I came from.'

The other neighbours laughed, and made cat noises, and picked their noses, and gradually drifted away.

So now in the beige light of morning he sat on his bunk with his spoon hovering over the porridge and an image of gushing zombie cat sick in the forefront of his mind. His fellow prisoners were restless; the awake half shifting and muttering and kicking the walls, and the sleeping half sweating on rough mattresses or the floor. Vasya knew sunbeams were beating against the shuttered windows, but only vague ghosts of the light made it in to the deep of the room.

A commotion in the corner of the cell gradually impressed itself on his senses and he turned his grey eyes towards the door, where it seemed the noise was coming from.

'Stand back, stand back!' Two prison warders, one very old and one very young, stood in the cell doorway, each wearing an equally ill-fitting khaki uniform, evidently designed for some species of being that wasn't actually encountered on earth. Vasya could make out the pimples on the chin of the young one: they glowed with an unearthly light and rivalled his Adam's apple in size. 'Bad diet,' thought Vasya. 'Needs more green vegetables, and jam.'

The commotion quickly subsided and the prisoners stood about expectantly, and largely in silence.

'Something's going on,' murmured Shura behind Vasya's ear. 'They never come in in the morning like this. Maybe we're on fire.'

'Fire?' Vasya echoed, loudly.

It was enough. The awake half of the prisoners started echoing 'fire' and woke the sleeping half. The shouts multiplied and bodies began to stomp their feet and stumble towards the open door. The two wardens were lost in the crowd for a moment as the men began to move forward as one. Then a crack rang out.

'Get back! There's no fire! There's no fire, damn you! Silence!' The extremely elderly warden held surprising authority, and brandished in his hand, ready for use, a regulation hand gun.

His school-boy chum held a whip, and cracked it on the wall behind his head.

'Now calm yourselves. There's no emergency. Do you think we'd be here if there was a fire?' The younger warden sniggered.

'We've come to collect a prisoner. What was the name, Ponchikov?'

'The name is Volubchik, Vasily Semyonovich,' replied Ponchikov, sniffing.

'Volubchik, come along. We demand immediate obedience.'

The prisoners shifted and parted, forming a tunnel-like gap for Vasya to walk uncertainly through, immediately obeying, but wondering what he was letting himself in for.

'*Blin!*' muttered Shura, 'what have you done, old man?'

Vasya didn't reply, but shuffled towards the orange light of the corridor.

'Are you sure it's me you want?' he asked the elderly warden when they were face to face.

The cloudy eyes looked in to his, and the hunched shoulders shrugged.

'If it's your name, it's you we want. Ponchikov doesn't mistake names. Follow me. Hands out of your pockets, back straight, eyes front.'

The cell door slammed behind them, and they set off on a ragged march down the corridor, the sound of their footsteps echoing off its dimly glowing orange walls.

24

The Sunshine SIZO

'So, anyway, enough about you already. I've been thinking. We need a make-over. Oh yeah, no really! It's three months since I took over here, and I've had a really good look around, and well – the place is a mess, you know? Yeah, it's like we have a bad reputation, and people don't like us. The staff don't like it here, and the prisoners sure as hell don't. I know it's a bit left-field and some of the old fuddy-duddies at head office won't like it, but, Grisha, I want to make my mark, and I want this SIZO to be somewhere that Azov District can be proud of. A centre of excellence. I want to see our name in lights!'

Kommandant Krapivin was having a good day. He'd been in the office since seven-thirty that morning and had already had over a dozen Good Ideas that had been met by amazed silence by most of his staff. Some of the Good Ideas he knew they just would never grasp, given their poor educational background and lack of general knowledge, but others he thought would just take a little time to sink in – like the idea for a staff talent show, and the one about growing free-range marrows for distribution to the poor. Kommandant Krapivin liked to talk to his friend Grisha, Kommandant at another SIZO down the river, every morning at about eleven while he sipped his Turkish coffee and tucked in to a piece of fresh, ripe fruit picked from the SIZO garden.

'Oh, and that reminds me. I know we have to stick with the old SIZO No. 24 Southern Section title, but I want a strap-line, and I've thought of a great one. No, hang on, wait, you'll love it . . .'

Kommandant Krapivin's secretary flounced into view on the other side of the little glass hatch that kept her separated from his office, and tapped viciously on the pane. She was waved away with a white hand, a smile and a cheeky wink. Krapivin would deal with the hum-drum of typical SIZO business after his coffee and fruit: nothing was allowed to come between him and his elevenses ideas fest. He inhaled deeply and meditated for a second on the warm scent rising from under his collar: lavender soap, made with home-grown lavender and tallow from the SIZO's own stock of cows. Who knew such wondrous scents could be produced from a bunch of cows and herbs: Kommandant Krapivin knew.

'Anyway, the strap-line is . . . *The Sunshine SIZO!* Oh yeah, you love it, don't you? I can tell you love it. I love it too! I think it sums up our ethos here: we're in the sunny southern region, but that's not all: our remand prisoners and staff totally embody the positive energies of the sun. Oh yeah – you know, it's the sun that makes things grow, it's the sun that gives life, and we can be the same: restorative, regenerative, happy, you know! And yes, Grisha, that is a word: regenerative. Go look it up if it's giving you a headache.'

Again the secretary tapped on the glass, this time pressing her face into it and rolling her eyes wildly. The glass steamed up. Kommandant Krapivin shooed her away and swivelled in his chair to face the window and the SIZO garden, where trusties were scraping hoes across bone-dry soil in a less than energetic manner.

'Grisha, you wouldn't believe the size of the grapes these guys can produce! No really, they're the size of golf balls! And so juicy! We're missing a trick: we could supply farmers' markets, or have our own farmers' markets right here at the Sunshine SIZO! How about that then? And maybe have orphans—'

Kommandant Krapivin broke off and swivelled round on his chair as his secretary minced into the room, coming to a stop right in front of him, and glowering.

'Kommandant, there are people waiting to see you and I cannot contain them any longer.'

'People? What people? I'm on the phone to Grisha, we're talking fruit—'

'Kommandant, really, they're upsetting me!'

'OK, OK, I can tell when you're cross with me. Grisha, listen, I'm going to have to go, there's some sort of visit going on here and I'm needed to smooth a few furrowed brows, it seems. I'll catch you later. Ciao!'

Krapivin replaced the receiver on the white Bakelite phone and turned to his secretary.

'OK, Masha, what's the problem here. Who are these visitors?'

'Kommandant, my name is Julia. JULIA.'

'Oh yeah, I'm sorry, chick, you just look like a Masha. I'll get it eventually.' Kommandant Krapivin paced the room as he spoke. 'Anyways, what's the beef?'

'Well, Kommandant, there are two old ladies—'

'Two old ladies? Marvellous!'

'You haven't met them yet! They appear to be mad, or at

283

least senile. They smell of booze, and they keep clucking and tutting and talking about the Deputy Minister, Southern Section Non-Caucasus—'

'Glukhov?'

'Roman Sergeevich, uh-huh.'

'Interesting. Go on – what do they want?'

'They say they are here to free a prisoner.'

'Oh really? How fabulous! Which one?'

'Volubchik.'

'Volubchik? I've never heard of him.'

'He only got here on Tuesday.'

'Is he trouble?'

'No, Kommandant, he is old.'

'Old! Another old person: terrific! But he's a prisoner: what is he supposed to have done?'

'Attempted to bribe a police officer, and had a dog dangerously out of control.'

'Oh, you're kidding me! No! Seriously? I don't believe it. Bribing a police officer! He must have been out of luck that day. Who was the arresting officer?'

'Officer Kulakov, Kommandant.'

'Oh, now you're killing me! That's hilarious! OK, well, so you don't know what they want to see me about, but it is all to do with this old fella, Volubchik.'

'Er, yes Kommandant. And a dog.'

'We don't have dogs in here, do we?'

'No, sir.'

'Well, I can't deal with the dog issue then. But actually, that gives me a fabulous idea, Masha! We should have dogs here! Oh yes, we could breed them. Pedigree dogs, and train them. Oh yes, I can see that catching on. With the rich and influential up in Rostov, or even, you know, up in Moscow: ex-con dogs, trained to protect. And they could have tattoos.

Oh yeah, they're really going to be something. Write that down, would you, Masha—'

'Julia.'

'Yeah, for tomorrow's call to Grisha: ex-con dogs with tattoos and attitude.'

Kommandant Krapivin sat back on his chair and took a few spins, chewing on a pencil as he did so.

'Yes, Kommandant. But can we get back to the visitors now, please? They are cluttering up my reception and, well, they smell.'

'Ha, Masha, you're a scream. They smell! In that case, you better show them in. I'm fascinated. And have them fetch Volubchik from his cell, just in case. Keep him down the corridor for the moment.'

'Yes, sir, I thought you might say that, so I've sent for him, sir.'

'We'll see what the Sunshine SIZO is going to bring us this morning, Masha. God, I love this job!'

'Julia.'

'Whatever you say, boss!'

* * *

In the waiting room, the thick air hung between the elderly visitors like shrouds of lead. Galia sat with a fist on each floral knee, breathing steadily and deeply, and keeping her eyes fixed on the polished floor in front of her. Zoya, hangover now a fairly dim memory, paced to and fro, her tiny feet tapping out a staccato rhythm as she went. The two ladies had said little to each other during the taxi ride from the airport: Galia had decided to save her strength for the coming meeting, and Zoya recognized that any further discussion of Pasha was probably unwise. Galia slapped a mosquito on her calf and launched Zoya into the air with the shock of the noise. The latter took a deep draw on her smelling salts.

The red door at the far end of the room was pulled inwards violently, and a young woman approached them with quick steps, before fairly yelling at them, from a distance of three feet.

'Kommandant Krapivin will see you now!'

The office into which they were ushered was light and airy compared to the waiting room, and the ladies felt, if not at ease, at least less unnerved. The smell of dirt that had hit them as soon as they had come through the first SIZO gate was barely detectable in this room, and the colours in it seemed more in line with the natural spectrum, rather than the dirty yellow that seemed to infect every animal, vegetable and mineral in the rest of the building.

'Ladies, ladies! Welcome to the Sunshine SIZO! Please, be seated! Would you like a lemon tea? It's home produced – right here, by the prisoners' own hands!'

Galia and Zoya eased themselves into the tiny leather tub chairs offered by Kommandant Krapivin.

'Snug, aren't they? I'm hoping we're going to start producing those here, ourselves, in the near future. I'm all about innovation, ladies, as I'm sure you've heard.'

Galia nodded vaguely and smiled, 'Er, yes, Kommandant. As it happens, I think I have heard about you and your innovations.'

'Was it Glukhov? He and I go back a long way. Oh yes! Of course, he ended up in the ministry, poor soul, but I ended up with the best job in the world! I bet he's quite green about it, but hey, what can you do?'

Zoya snorted loudly and then tried to disguise the sound by turning it in to a cough, which then became a real cough, which then threatened to shake every bone in her body to dust.

'Oh my, that's a nasty one. You should have some lemon tea. Definitely, it will really help. Masha, oh Masha!'

The secretary opened the hatch between the two offices.

'Lemon tea all round please, and quick!'

The hatch slammed shut, and Galia was sure she heard the wooden frame splinter as it did so.

'Kommandant Krapivin, I'm afraid this isn't a social visit.'

'Well no, good lady, I was sure that was the case. What can I do for you?'

'We have come to free our colleague, Vasily Semyonovich Volubchik.'

'I see. What makes you think you can do that, er, sorry, what was your name?'

'Galina Petrovna Orlova.'

'Well Galina Petrovna, that's a very noble aim. I'm assuming it is – you do think the old bird is innocent, don't you? You're not into organised crime or anything like that? You don't look like it but, jeepers, we have to be careful! You wouldn't believe some of the gangsters around here!'

'No, Kommandant Krapivin, we're not gangsters.'

Galia gave Zoya a sidelong look, to make sure that her friend wasn't about to contradict her and claim to be a mobster, or that anyone else was of that inclination. Zoya was looking relaxed, her eyes half closed and her beak firmly shut, awaiting her lemon tea.

'Kommandant, I have in my pocket a Very Important Piece of Paper, which I have brought all the way from Moscow, this morning.'

'A Very Important Piece of Paper? My, today is really hotting up. May I see?'

287

Galia squeezed her buttocks back out of the bucket chair so that she could stand, and therefore get her hand into her dress pocket. She pulled out the Very Important Piece of Paper, and handed it to the Kommandant.

'You will see, Kommandant, that it is signed by the Deputy Minister Glukhov, Roman Sergeevich himself, with today's date. Vasily Semyonovich Volubchik is no criminal, Kommandant. He is just an old man who was trying to help his friends. He does not belong in jail: he belongs at home, with his kitty cat and his friends. And this paper proves it.'

Galia had been standing over the Kommandant, but now she bent carefully, bringing her eyes into line with his and looking squarely into his face.

'He is a fine upstanding citizen: he runs the Azov House of Culture Elderly Club, and we would be at a loss without him. Over forty elderly women are reliant on him, Kommandant. Don't let us down. Free him, Kommandant, so that the club can, once more, meet and discuss vegetable matters, and celebrate Fridays with the weekend Lotto and a film!'

Kommandant Krapivin wiped away a small tear from the corner of his left eye as Galia finished her speech.

'Yes, and aside from all that, he is Galia's only hope of a man friend in the few years that she's got left. She's waited long enough, Kommandant: don't deny her of a bit of love in the autumn of her days!'

Galia turned and issued a sharp hissing 'Shh!' in Zoya's direction.

'I'm only trying to help! And anyway, it is the truth!'

'Ladies, you are adorable. Where have you been all my life? This is just perfect. And yes, you are right: it is all here, in black and white, complete with his signature and his

288

official stamp. I see no reason to keep this Vasily in the SIZO any longer: we'll get the wardens to go fetch him.'

The Kommandant returned the paper to Galia and she almost kissed it, breathing a sigh of relief that felt like the first free breath in her lungs for a lifetime. Her shoulders lifted and her spirit felt as light as smoke.

'Kommandant Krapivin, I can't thank you enough—'

She broke off as his secretary knocked on the door and entered simultaneously, her mouth dropping open slightly at the sight of Galia almost on her knees in front of the Kommandant.

'Er, I am sorry for the interruption, Kommandant Krapivin, but there are yet more visitors for you, and they're here to save this old Volubchik too. And to be frank, they're even worse!'

'Whoah, Masha, take a second!'

'It's Julia.'

'Yes, of course Julia, I was just kidding. More visitors, you say?'

'Yes.'

'Also here for Volubchik.'

'Yes.'

'You seem upset. Are they dangerous? Do they smell?'

Julia looked momentarily uncomfortable.

'They do look dangerous, sir, yes. One of them is all beaten up, and is wearing a woman's sunhat. And the other has a smile like a Cheshire cat and smells of cheap perfume.'

'My secretary is so sensitive; she doesn't like smiles or smells. Anyways, do you know who it could be, ladies?'

Galia and Zoya looked mystified.

'How fabulous! Show them in! Show them in! We're all friends here, let's not stand on ceremony.'

* * *

289

Mitya the Exterminator, his appearance greatly changed since Galia had last seen him, and not a little peculiar, limped into the room. When she had last seen him, as he dangled her beloved dog by her scruff over the stairwell, she had thought, if she ever saw him again, that she might shout at him, maybe even box his ears, and perhaps might hate him. But what she felt, when she saw him, was a sharp pang of pity: his face was swollen and bruised, as were his arms and hands. He walked stiffly, and with a stoop, and seemed to have shrunk: in some ways, he resembled an old man, but with the eyes of a boy. He caught her stare, and much to her surprise, nodded to her.

'Galina Petrovna, I should have known that you would be here.'

The girl with him was pretty but seemed slightly asymmetrical: she smiled at the old ladies and the smile was slightly goofy, slightly lopsided. She carried one shoulder slightly higher than the other, and seemed to walk on the toes of her left foot. But despite the couple's odd appearance, they seemed, to Galia's tired senses, to radiate something calm: was it happiness, or tenderness?

'Well, young people, nice to see you! Masha, where's that tea? Would you like lemon tea, young people? We make it ourselves.'

'Yes please, Kommandant, that would be lovely,' replied Katya with a slight lisp, and a wide grin.

'Not for me, sir,' said Mitya in a low voice.

'OK, we'll get that ordered and then we'll all be right as rain. So, you're here about Volubchik too, this old rascal, eh? You can't be fellow members at the Azov House of Culture Elderly Club, can you, so, you know, what's the link?'

'Yes, Mitya, what's the link?' Galia fixed him with a surprisingly beady eye and leant forward in her chair, the creaking of her thighs against the plastic-leather loud as thunder in the silent room. 'You were the last person I was expecting to see here today.'

Mitya cleared his throat, and clasped his hands in his lap. 'Well, Galina Petrovna, Kommandant and other Elderly Citizen, this week has been a very strange one, for me. You could say that it has been one of revelation, and on many levels.'

'Don't tell us you've found religion?' broke in Zoya with a croak. 'Because we won't believe it. You're bad, through and through. It's a well-known fact.'

'No, not religion as such, Elderly Citizen, but the things I thought were true, well, I can see now that they are not.'

'This is fascinating,' chipped in the Kommandant. 'But young man – who are you?'

'I am Mikhail Borisovich Plovkin, Kommandant, and I am a . . . a canine exterminator, by profession.'

The Kommandant recoiled slightly as Mitya said the words.

'You want us to believe that you've changed, Mitya?' Galia's voice wavered as she addressed him. 'But I saw your eyes when you came to my door. They were empty.'

'Galina Petrovna, I am sorry for my conduct. I realize that I removed your loyal friend, and it was the wrong thing to do.'

'That's putting it mildly!' said Zoya. 'Were you born without emotions, young man?'

'I don't think so, Elderly Citizen, but somehow they got buried. But I can change.' Mitya glanced at Katya with a half-smile. 'I can change.' He pushed the words out, hoarse and low. 'I went to see Kulakov, to get the charges dropped, but he refused to cooperate. And now I—' Mitya broke off with a jerk as Julia kicked open the door, a tray of tea

291

cups in one hand, and a grey tabby cat in the other. She jumped into the room as the door slammed shut again behind her.

'My goodness, Masha, you pick your moments. Ladies, gentleman, this is Tabby, the SIZO cat. Say hello, Tabby.'

The cat said nothing, flicking its tail viciously while swinging from Julia's arm as she offered the tray of drinks around. 'For the last time, my name is Julia.'

'She's right, her name is Julia,' Zoya piped up, having taken a slurp from her lemon tea.

'Julia, Julia, I am so sorry. You know what I'm like.'

'Perhaps I should change my name to something more memorable, Kommandant?'

'Oh Julia, you kill me. That's funny. Anyway, was there something else?'

'There is another visitor for Volubchik out in the waiting room, Kommandant. That's why I've brought the cat in.'

'Oh really? Wow, this is unbelievable. Is the visitor a dog or something – I don't get the cat connection?'

'No Kommandant, the visitor is—'

The door flew back on its hinges as again it was kicked open with considerable force.

'Dyeh! Dyeh!'

The shrill and indecipherable shriek emanated from a tiny, frail figure, silhouetted in the doorway. The figure wore a huge, orange headscarf, and carried a sickle.

'Mum!' whispered Mitya.

'Saints preserve us!' whispered Galia.

* * *

'OK, well, now the gang's all here, maybe we can start again. Erm, Elderly Female Citizen, maybe you could put the sickle down for a moment, just on the coffee table, that's fine – and take a seat over there: yes, on the beanbag maybe? It is very comfortable.' Kommandant Krapivin took the situation in his stride and eyed the new old lady closely.

Baba Plovkina laid her sickle down as requested and, after a moment's pause surveying the room, edged on to the sagging beanbag, but was obviously not comfortable. She could not rock properly while seated on a beanbag: it made her anxious. Her head rustled slightly under the bright orange headscarf as she worked her gums together, and her beady eyes darted from window to floor, to door, to her feet, to Mitya's feet, and to the framed photograph of President Yeltsin on the wall opposite. All the while, her small, red-raw hands twisted a handkerchief in her lap. Her jaws moved, but she did not speak any decipherable words. And every time Mitya cleared his throat, she jumped slightly and glared at him for a moment.

'Baba Plovkina, would you like a glass of water, or a cup of tea?' Galia broke what had become a rather strained pause.

'Nya!' was Baba Plovkina's response. Galia looked at Mitya, and caught his eye. She shrugged her shoulders, questioning. He hesitated, looked away and said firmly:

'No water. She doesn't drink water. Or tea. Ever.'

'No tea?' Galia's eyes crinkled at the edges and she shook her head slightly. Katya watched Mitya looking at the old lady, and tried to spot a family resemblance between the two. There was none. He didn't return her gaze: he watched his mother for a few moments, and then returned his eyes to the opposite window, refusing to peel them away from the bright light of the garden and the grapevines. Katya returned her gaze to the old lady, and squinted slightly. Baba Plovkina caught her stare.

'Shtrumpeth!' she called out clearly, tiny eyes wide and glittering, before snapping her jaws shut and again fastening her eyes on the framed photo of President Yeltsin.

Katya laughed, the sound tinkling like a bell in the still air, and Mitya closed his eyes.

'Mother, please . . .'

Kommandant Krapivin sat down behind his desk and swivelled gently from side to side on his chair.

'Well, we're all a little quiet suddenly, aren't we? Don't let the SIZO get you down! This is the Sunshine SIZO, did I tell you? Don't let it intimidate you. Be at ease. Come on, everybody, how about a big breath in, and a big breath out, all together one-two-three.'

And the Kommandant led the group in a big breath in, and a big breath out.

'There, is that better? Now, I think you all know who I am, but I'm not sure you all know each other, so maybe we could go around the room and all introduce ourselves, and tell the gang one little secret no-one knows. You know, a bit of an ice-breaker? I find it really helps break down barriers . . .'

'Yeah, that sounds good,' chirruped Katya, as the other members of the group either stared at the floor or glared at her. 'Sometimes people can be so closed. It will help us all to trust each other.'

'But, Katya—' Mitya began.

'Oh, good! Right, well, shall I start?' the Kommandant didn't need any further encouragement. 'My name is Sasha Krapivin. I'm from Moscow, and when I was little, I wanted to join the circus! OK, you go next.'

He indicated Katya to go next.

'OK. Well, my name is Katya, I'm from Azov, and I have a psychological condition that makes me lie a lot.' Katya giggled slightly, and then went quiet and cleared her throat.

'I'm sorry, that was a lie. I don't know why I said it. I'm nervous. I can't think of anything interesting about me that nobody knows.'

'Oh, you must do! Try harder!'

'OK. Um, well . . . I once drank human pee by accident.'

This time a murmur went round the room.

'Oh really? How fascinating, you must tell us more, but not now. We have to move on. Next, you, er, Elderly Sickle Lady?'

'Yevgeniya Kirpichovna Plovkina, and I am that one's mother, for my sins,' and she pointed a crooked finger in Mitya's direction.

'And something nobody knows about you, Yevgeniya Kirpichovna,' prompted the Kommandant softly.

'I once stole apples from the collective farm!'

Again a murmur went around the room, but all eyes remained on the floor. Outside the door, coming slowly along the corridor, the echo of footsteps could be heard.

'Oh my goodness! What an adventure we're having, and it's not even midday! I must say, usually we aim for some sort of, you know, light-hearted kind of secrets. You know! Like, when I was young, I had a crush on Yuri Gagarin. No, I don't mean me, obviously, that would be silly – but that kind of thing. Madam, you're next,' and the Kommandant turned to Galia expectantly.

'Very well, Kommandant. My name is Galina Petrovna Orlova, and I'm from Azov too. My secret is that there is no secret: I was married to a man who was not a spy, or a homosexual, or an alcoholic. But he was annoying. That is all.'

There was a short silence.

'Is that really a secret?' asked Kommandant Krapivin looking around, a little crest-fallen.

295

'It appears to be something that precious few knew. It appears to me that sometimes, when people don't know, or can't remember, they make it up. I don't know why they make up nasty things, Kommandant,' all of a sudden, Galia could not stop talking. The words rushed out in a torrent. 'Why not make up good things? Like the fact that they made nice tea, or were always punctual, or didn't take more than their fair share of the cheese?'

'Well, Galina Petrovna, let's move on—'

'No, Kommandant! Really: I want to know – why don't people make up nice things?' Galia leapt to her feet, bucket seat still firmly attached to her backside, and stood before the Kommandant, waiting for an answer.

The Kommandant was silent.

'It's something peculiar to humans, Galina Petrovna. Making ourselves feel better, by being nasty about others: making up stories – giving ourselves reasons to hate.' Mitya spoke the words in a soft voice, but did not look away from the window and the bright sunlight beyond.

Galia nodded and smiled slightly, and sat back down with a sigh.

'Right,' the Kommandant turned to Zoya, with an oily smile on his face. Zoya looked like a sparrow at the end of winter: fragile, ruffled, and very sorry for herself. She sighed.

'My name is Zinaida Artyomovna Krasovskaya. And I have to tell you that I used to be an informant to the KGB.'

Everyone in the room sucked in their breath.

'Ah!'

'Shall I get more tea now, Kommandant?' Julia the secretary broke the silence.

Mitya scraped his shoes on the floor and cleared his throat.

'I haven't had my turn yet. Do you mind? My name is Mikhail Borisovich Plovkin, I am from Azov.' Mitya's face turned pale and his eyebrows rose, corrugating his forehead as he hesitated. Not a particle stirred in the room as the assorted group waited for him to speak.

'You want something that no-one else knows?' Mitya began in a husky voice and wiped his hands on his shorts. 'Well – until this week, I never knew who my real father was.'

There was a hollow knocking on the floor as Baba Plovkina fell off her beanbag and landed at the Kommandant's feet. He bent down swiftly and propped her back up with deft hands, making sure her headscarf was straight and that she was breathing.

Zoya let out a low laugh. 'Well, Baba Plovkina, some chicks have come home to roost?'

Galia prodded her pop-socked toe into Zoya's shin as Baba Plovkina growled, the sound not a little unnerving, given the proximity of her sickle.

'So where is he?' squawked Baba Plovkina.

'I'm sorry, *Babushka*, but I should explain a few ground-rules here—' the Kommandant tried to break in.

'Shut your mouth! Where is he, the old bastard?' She propelled herself out of the clammy embrace of the beanbag with surprising speed and began to prowl the room, as if expecting her quarry to be hidden somewhere among the tea cups and bookshelves. All the while, her joints clicked slightly like knitting needles, and her jaws worked beneath her sharp cheekbones and tiny, glistening eyes.

'Who are you after, Mother?' Mitya too rose out of his chair.

'Volubchik: I'm here to rescue him.'

'No, no, no!' Galia began. 'What are you talking about,

Baba Plovkina?' she continued. 'We're here to rescue Vasya Volubchik. You have no business meddling with that. We have an official letter.' And she squeezed herself out of her seat and raised her hand to waft the Very Important Piece of Paper in the air.

'No, Galina Petrovna, you are mistaken,' said Mitya, 'I am here for your old goat Volubchik. We have to have a . . . very serious conversation, him and I. No harm will come to him, I can assure you.'

'What, like the dog?' crowed Zoya. 'You're not human, Mitya. We don't trust you. Don't trust him, Galia. A leopard can't change its spots, and neither can a Taurus.'

'No, Zinaida Artyomovna, I am human. But I'm only just finding out . . . what sort of human.'

'Bring him to me!' screeched Baba Plovkina, pushing Mitya to one side and reaching for her sickle.

'Oh my!' exclaimed Kommandant Krapivin. 'A transformation story!' and he propelled Baba Plovkina away from her instrument and back towards her seat with the dexterity and panache of a lion tamer.

*　*　*

Out in the corridor, Vasya's ears were beginning to burn. He still wasn't sure who it was who had requested to see him, but he was hoping against hope that it was Galia, and not the police for further questioning, or any of his former teaching colleagues: the shame would be unbearable. He sat on a wooden bench between the two guards and enjoyed his first glimpse of the sky for four whole days. He could almost taste the sunshine, and as he spied a corner of the gardens below, the scent of green peppers, garlic and apricots mingled in his nostrils. He thought he might be able to smell freedom, or maybe it was the smell of the future. Whatever it was, he liked it very much, and it filled his heart with the warm honey of hope.

25

Chickens Roost

In a dank kennel, a dog with a narrow face and delicate limbs tufted with wiry grey hair sat very still. A noise somewhere far off to the left of her had startled her. It had wrenched her from a welcome dream, where she had padded gently around a clean, bright apartment with sunshine streaming in golden rays through netted curtains. Her dark eyes, tilted over high cheekbones, rested on her cell door. Through the bent and torn metal bars she sensed the corridor black as pitch, which stank of fear. All was quiet on the corridor. She was the last dog on the row. Her hopes of rehoming and a new old lady now seemed misplaced. She had realized, slowly, that nothing good could happen in this place. Boroda licked her forepaw and chewed at a flea for a second, and then rested her chin on the clean patch of fur. Despite the lack of exercise, she felt tired: bone tired.

She shut her eyes again, and remembered her home, and her mistress, and the stars that speckled the southern night sky. She remembered bacon fat, and her cardboard box, and the children who made her little leaf headdresses and tickled her ears as they sat with her beneath the trees. She remembered the smell of cats, the scamper of rats, and the joy of finding a bread crust trapped between the flagstones. She remembered Galia, and her food bowl, and the pool of green light under the kitchen table as meals were being prepared. She remembered the quiet, and the clock ticking, and the sound of the front door clicking shut. She heard footsteps in the corridor, and a small whine squeezed out of her parched throat.

She stood up as best she could in the tiny cage, and hung her head towards the cage door, listening intently. The footsteps came to a halt in front of her, and she could see the outline of the decrepit black boots again, close to her nose. They were coated with disinfectant and other liquids too terrible to name. Her back legs began to shake violently as the bolt to her cage was drawn back with a sudden jerk. She backed away from the rough gloves that reached for her, pressing her tail into the bars behind her, and bearing back with all her weight. She growled slightly as she was dragged forward and her claws caught on the wire mesh beneath her, etching the air with a sharp scratching sound. The human cursed and caught her roughly by the scruff.

A rope collar was placed over her head and tightened around her neck, and then she was tugged slowly along the long dark corridor. The human smelt strongly of spirit and decay: it filled Boroda's nostrils, and she sneezed loudly as she walked hesitantly beside him. The man seemed to wobble as he walked, taking a zig-zag route and hiccuping as he went. He was talking to no-one, and seemed somewhat distracted. Towards the end of the corridor, his shoulder hit the wall with a smack and he swore as the impact swivelled his body and snapped his face into the concrete with a loud, wet sound. He dropped the rope lead as he reached up to stem the blood now dripping from his nose all over his black boots. Boroda felt the weight of the rope hit the floor, and saw the door at the end of the corridor standing ajar.

* * *

'Mitya, what sort of conversation can you need to have with Vasya Volubchik? Surely the business of my Boroda is being dealt with by the police? You're not going to press separate charges, are you? He didn't touch you, Mitya, you know that he didn't. And I have a piece of paper—'

'No! No, Galina Petrovna, nothing of that sort. Please, just wait a moment. Perhaps I can explain.'

'Oh, I wish you would!' Kommandant Krapivin leapt from his chair and hopped around the desk to sit on the front edge, the better to hear Mitya's words.

'My father . . . my father—'

Mitya was interrupted by an extended groan from his mother as she crossed herself twice.

'My father—'

Again the old woman groaned and crossed herself.

'Is that strictly necessary, Baba?' Kommandant Krapivin gave her a stern look.

The old woman put her hands in her lap and clamped her toothless jaws shut.

'My father was a chronic alcoholic.'

'Well, that goes for half the country, Mitya,' said the Kommandant breezily.

'I accept that, yes, but that doesn't make it right. That is how we end up with people like Petya Kulakov and my neighbour, Andrei the *Svoloch*.'

'Is that really his name?'

'No, Kommandant.'

'Kommandant, please be quiet. We need to hear from

302

'Mitya.' Galia turned to the Exterminator. 'Go on, Mitya. We're listening.'

'Thank you, Galina Petrovna.' Mitya looked down at his fingers, still swollen and sore, and took a breath. 'Well . . . it's like this. My father beat both me and my mother, often. Many things made him angry. If we made any noise, or the dinner was not on the table at the right time, or we attempted to hide his home brew, we were in for it.'

'We got it!' The old woman nodded her head, and started to weep silent tears that got caught up in the wrinkles around her eyes.

'My only consolation, my only joy, at this young age, was my dog, Sharik.'

An almost visible shockwave travelled around the room, bringing tears to Galia's eyes and wobbling the hairs on the top of Zoya's head.

'But, Mitya, I don't understand. You . . . you hate dogs. To you they are vermin, to be exterminated: that's what you said? You wanted to kill my Boroda – you probably have done . . .' Galia broke off, unable to continue.

Mitya bit his lip, and caught Katya's eye. She was serene, swaying in her chair slightly, slowly twirling her hair around one narrow finger and smiling slightly to him.

'We lived in a little wooden house: a hovel, really. We hadn't qualified for modern housing, mostly because of my father's drinking. One day, he came home late, and in a terrible temper. He was already drunk, but demanded more when he got home. He had drunk us dry; there was nothing in the cupboard, so Mother sent me round the corner to one of the neighbours to beg some spirit. I had to try many doors: we were well-known already, and most wouldn't give us the time of day. Eventually, I managed to borrow half a bottle, and Sharik and I made our way back.'

'What's this got to do with Vasya?' croaked Zoya.

'Sshh, you old goat!' whispered Galia in return.

'Go on. Here, would you like a piece of fruit, perhaps?'

'No fruit, Kommandant. On returning to the house, we heard a commotion in the yard: my father had my mother by the throat, and was attempting to strangle her. Old Sharik couldn't bear it, and leapt on my father, snatching at his neck with his teeth, and barking like a mad thing. I can still hear it now.'

'Brave dog!' said Galia. 'Like my Boroda! Brave and loyal.'

'Brave, yes, Galina Petrovna, but also old. He did his best, but Father was too strong for him. They wrestled in the yard, on and on. But Father was possessed by the devil. Sharik became exhausted, but Father wanted total victory. He couldn't abide disobedience. He staggered across the yard, the dog's scruff in his hand . . .'

'And?'

'And, I have to tell you, that he threw my Sharik down the well. We heard the splash when he hit the bottom. We heard him swimming for dear life, around and around in that awful pit. And later . . . howling, for hours, treading water. Father wouldn't let us near: he made us sit on the bench in the kitchen, made Mother cook his dinner, and all the while we could hear our beloved Sharik calling to us. Father sat in the yard all night, listening to him suffer, making sure we couldn't save him. It took him all night to drown.'

A silence thick as felt fell across the room.

'And the next day, he was gone. I . . . I went to school, and hated everybody. I couldn't bear to look at anyone. I couldn't bear to think. Mother never drank water again, and me – I made sure I would never be close to anyone again: not animals, and not humans.'

304

A large tear rolled down Kommandant Krapivin's face, and he drew an unsteady breath.

'That is very sad, very sad indeed. You know what I felt, then, when you held my dog over the railings?' Galia leant forward and looked into Mitya's eyes.

'But I still don't see how this connects with Vasya Volubchik?' broke in Zoya, from her corner. 'Your daddy was a bad one; that seems clear. He killed your dog, which was unforgivable, but that doesn't explain—'

'No, well, let me enlighten you, if you don't already know, Comrade Krasovskaya. The thing is . . . the thing is that I remembered who gave us Sharik in the first place. All this week I've been remembering things. Something sparked the memories off: maybe it was . . . maybe it was love,' he turned to Katya, 'or maybe it was rescuing those puppies in the park, the way they cried . . . or maybe just concussion . . . I don't know. But I remembered what happened to Sharik, and the reason I'd started hating animals. It was tucked away, in the back of my mind, in a place I didn't know was there. I remembered Sharik, and how he'd been my best friend. How I'd laid beside him at night, his warm fur keeping me cosy even in wintertime. How he'd always walked to kindergarten with me, and then waited for me at the gate. And I realized that I'd dealt with my loss by closing my heart and turning what I'd loved so much into something to hate.'

'That's a terrible thing, Mitya,' said Galia, kindly.

'And when I was lying in a pool of my own blood and vomit outside the Smile Bar!, after a disagreement with Kulakov, I had a vision. It was very vague – just scraps of memory, like jigsaw pieces, but on one piece there was Sharik, full of life and playing with a new red ball, and on another piece, there was a kindly man with a big smile who held my hand while we patted the dog and played. And that man . . . I realized that man was Vasily Volubchik.'

'Hell and damnation!' Baba Plovkina cried out and then got back to grinding her gums and mashing her handkerchief in her lap.

'And he gave us that dog, I think, because he felt guilty.' No-one breathed a word.

'He felt guilty, because the man who I'd been calling father, was actually nothing to do with me. The man who was actually my father, was the one who gave us Sharik.'

'Oh Vasya!' said Galia, with a low, sad note to her voice.

'But why now, Mitya?' Zoya was fascinated.

'I had had my suspicions for a long time. I knew I couldn't be related to that drunken bum that I called father. Mother was . . . well . . . reticent about it. But then, this week, that filthy Kulakov . . .'

Katya put her hand on his arm, and he took a moment to breathe.

'The reason for our fight at the Smile Bar!, was that he told me my daddy was in the SIZO. And then he told me his name. And tried to blackmail me. I punched him, of course.'

'And took a licking yourself,' observed Zoya.

Galia was watching Mitya, open-mouthed. His story was almost too weird – to think that he loved dogs! But deep inside her, she felt that maybe it was true. Sometimes when you were really hurt, you shut off part of yourself and put all your energies into something else, be it marrows or chess, or direct self-destruction, or something somewhere in-between.

'To my shame, I worked out my anger on those most innocent and blameless of creatures: domestic dogs, abandoned dogs . . . I could not bear the presence of animals.

Not even butterflies. I came to believe that I had a calling to rid the community of canine vermin, and I fear that it contributed to my mother's . . . madness. But enough, really, I have to speak to Volubchik. I have to start making amends, and he is here, because of me.'

'No, Mitya! No! It's not you that needs to speak to him: it's me!' Baba Plovkina spat the words out, and her eyes glistened with challenge.

'No, Baba Plovkina! What's the use? I have the paper, comrades, that will get him freed,' Galia broke in, feeling confused, flustered, not at all sure what to think about Vasya Volubchik, but still all the same, having the VIPP in her hand, and wanting to make the most of it.

'But I have to see him – we have so much to discuss!' said Mitya, again jumping to his feet.

'Let him see Volubchik, please, Kommandant!' Katya took Mitya's hand and stood to face the Kommandant. 'You don't know what he's been through. It means such a lot.'

'Look, guys, can I make a suggestion?' The Kommandant attempted to take charge. 'You all seem to be here to talk to this fella Volubchik. I guess he's quite a guy? So I tell you what, why don't we get him in here, and then maybe he can tell his side of the story – straighten things out a bit? I think we need him in here, don't you?'

All the heads nodded slowly, agreeing finally that what the party was missing was Volubchik himself. The Kommandant nodded to Julia, and she called through to the corridor. Seconds later, there appeared in the doorway a rather tall, very old man, grey-stubbled and creased, with a prison warden at each shoulder. Vasya Volubchik stopped in the doorway, and looked around the room, his mouth open. The sweetness of impending freedom, and future, and the nectar of happiness bled from his bones. As he took in

307

26

The End of the Beginning

'So!' Kommandant Krapivin surveyed the room with a piercing glance, and then settled his attention on Vasya, now seated in the middle of the room on the only piece of sitting furniture left: a tall, narrow, brushed steel bar stool.

'Prisoner Volubchik? Well, it's good to meet you, Volubchik. Can you believe all these fine people are here, waiting to rescue you? I'm not really sure what they think they're rescuing you from.'

'No, well—' began Vasya.

'No really – as you know yourself, this SIZO is actually not bad at all. In fact, this place is really much nicer than many cheap hotels, don't you agree?'

'Well . . .' Vasya began uncertainly. 'Kommandant, it certainly has a lot of character.'

Vasya caught Galia's eye and tried to smile a reassuring smile, but his lips trembled, and Galia's eyes slid away from his to study her own knees peeping out from beneath her blue floral skirt. Vasya clasped his hands together to keep them still and tried to avoid further eye contact with anyone.

'Yeah! It has a lot of character. You haven't really been

here long enough to get to know it properly. If you gave it a few months, you'd really settle in.'

'I don't doubt it, sir.' The words 'a few months' sank like lead into Vasya's belly, draining the blood from the rest of his body. He felt he might fall sideways off the stool and into the beanbag. He pressed his hands together more firmly.

'So, Vasily Semyonovich Volubchik, is there something that you want to tell us?'

Vasya hesitated and began to shake his head, before plucking up the courage to look around the room again, not quite able to believe that Galia, Mitya, Baba Plovkina, Zoya, and a girl whom he didn't know were all there, waiting for him. He shivered slightly, and blew on his clasped fingers.

'Erm, well . . .' he remembered the promises to himself that he had written down while in the cell, cleared his throat, and started again. 'It is quite a surprise, but of course lovely, to see you all here. I had almost given up hope of ever seeing you again. I know it sounds a little melodramatic, and I know it hasn't really been that long, but . . . but well, I am a coward, as you all, I think, know, and these days have been a terrible trial for me.'

Vasya paused, and coughed softly, waiting for any acknowledgement, or denial, of his statement. A heavy silence dropped into the room, reminiscent of a snowy Sunday. He looked towards the window, and was stabbed in the eye by the sun reflecting off a prisoner's spade down in the vegetable garden.

'Ah! My eyes!'

'Come on now, Volubchik, you're hardly the man in the iron mask! You're embarrassing me here!' Kommandant Krapivin laughed, although he looked a little concerned.

'I am sorry, Kommandant, but I think I can truly say that my experience here has been dark.'

310

'You ain't seen nothing yet!' muttered Zoya to herself.

'Yes, it has been terrifying. But it also gave me some time for reflection, and contemplation, if you will. I reflected long and hard, and decided now was probably the time, if I ever got the opportunity, of course, of ceasing cowardship, and putting things right. And, dear friends, I come here this morning and find you are all here, giving me that opportunity. Please bear with me, but if I may, I must.'

Vasya stood slowly and swayed a little in the warm morning breeze. Again, he looked slowly around the room, studying the faces of his friends and acquaintances.

'Zhenya Plovkina, to you I owe an apology from the heart. I have treated you abominably, and for a long time. You have withstood it as well as could be expected. I know you are not the woman you once were.'

Baba Plovkina squirmed on her beanbag and coughed into her mashed handkerchief.

'When we were young, our hearts ran wild, and so did we. I remember corn fields and tree-houses, and love among the buttercups and daisies when the tractors ran out of diesel. You were but a child, Zhenya, working on the collective farm, and I was little more, just starting out at the school. You were the joy of my heart, and the treasure that I thought I could never lose. But lose you I did. No, that's not true! I didn't lose you. I left you behind, like a forgotten handkerchief on a trolleybus: I know. I betrayed my own heart, Zhenya, and I betrayed you.'

'Oh my, Vasya, you bad boy! Did you leave her? Why? Tell us more! It's good to talk, really.' Kommandant Krapivin could not contain himself.

'I was young and confused, Kommandant. I was already engaged to the lady who went on to become my wife, and I was not strong enough to make the right decision. I let

311

fate carry me along, and I pretended that there had been nothing between us, didn't I, Zhenya?'

Baba Plovkina said nothing, but ground her jaws lightly and looked towards the window with a glare that threatened to puncture the air as it wavered in the heat.

'Zhenya came to me, a few weeks before my wedding, and told me some news . . . she told me that . . . she told me she was expecting a baby. I was thrilled, but also petrified, and . . . I couldn't cope. I couldn't call off my own wedding, I couldn't bear to upset my fiancée, and to be honest, I could not face the scandal. So instead, I sent her away, but decided to support her in secret. It was our secret. I visited her often, both before the baby came, and afterwards. I gave him little gifts, that sunny little boy. But then . . . I watched her marry that sorry excuse for a man, and Zhenya, I saw how he mistreated you over the years. I knew things weren't right, and I knew the boy was suffering, but I turned a blind eye. I pretended to myself that there was nothing I could do.' Vasya paused and, after a short struggle, produced a handkerchief from his trouser pocket and blew his nose into it, long and loud. The sound echoed off the window frames.

'Oh, stop!' Baba Plovkina suddenly exploded like a firecracker off the beanbag and stood at her full, tiny height in the middle of the room. 'Stop, stop, stop! I can't bear it!'

'I'm sorry, Zhenya!' Vasya thrust his handkerchief back into his pocket and fell to his knees before the tiny old lady, burying his face in the hem of her floral skirt. Zoya sucked in her breath loudly as Galia bit her lip and looked away.

'Get up, you old fool! Why do you think I'm here?'

Vasya slowly raised his head, his grey eyes looking nonplussed, and gave a vague shrug.

'Erm . . .'

312

'It's not just you who has a confession to make.'

'What, more?' whispered Galia incredulously, and blotted her forehead with her handkerchief.

'There's always more, Galia. These peasants . . .' and Zoya shook her head towards Baba Plovkina.

'Vasya, you old fool, you old . . . treasure. I . . . I . . .'

'Go on, Mother, say your piece,' encouraged Mitya with surprising gentleness.

'Vasya, I . . .' and with those words, Baba Plovkina also dropped to her knees. Vasya took her brittle, red hands in his and looked into her cherry-pip eyes.

'Vasya, my pigeon, understand,' her voice was soft, whispered, 'I lied to you. It wasn't true, you see. I told you that you were Mitya's father, maybe, because I really wanted it to be true. But it wasn't. It was that old scumbag who I married, for my sins. But once I had lied to you that night, I couldn't stop. I wanted you to visit. I wanted it to be you.'

Vasya dropped her hands as his face first faded into white, then shot through with purple, then became tinged with green. His breath came in short, understated rasps, his mouth working with a twitching motion, but no sound coming out. Galia feared that this time a stroke, or even worse, was totally unavoidable. She pushed herself to her feet to fetch water, but found Julia the secretary already several steps in front of her, clinking glasses and fruit bowls, while Kommandant Krapivin drooped by his desk open-mouthed, eyes glistening.

Vasya closed his mouth slowly and his eyes, shiny and wide as those of a small child, looked into the depths of Baba Plovkina's shrivelled irises.

'All those years?'

'All those years. Yes.' Baba Plovkina looked away and shrugged her shoulders. 'I came to say sorry today. I heard

313

you'd been arrested, and that my so-called son was involved, so I thought . . . in case you die in here, you know . . . I should put things right.'

Vasya nodded slightly. 'Put things right. I see. In case I die here.'

'So, I'm sorry, Vasya. There, I've said it. You'll get nothing more, mind.' Baba Plovkina gave Vasya a long, hard look, and then jumped to her feet. She arranged her headscarf, took up her sickle from the coffee table, nodded to the Kommandant, made a disgusted, tutting sound at her son and Katya, and scuttled for the door.

'Zhenya, wait! We need to talk!' Vasya struggled to push himself to his feet, wallowing in the clutches of the beanbag and flailing with desperate hands.

'Mother!' Mitya leapt from his chair, but stopped as she turned in the open doorway, held frozen in the air by her stare.

'We've talked. The truth is known. That's all there is! Don't trouble me more!' and with that, the elderly little citizen slammed the door behind her.

'All those years,' said Vasya again, and collapsed face down into the recently vacated, still-warm beanbag, gasping like a landed carp.

'All those years,' echoed Mitya. 'I can't believe it. He really was my father. It's just . . . so wrong. I was ready . . .' Mitya remained a statue in the centre of the room.

'Kommandant Krapivin, I think we need more lemon tea, quickly. Please, could you provide some? I'm worried about my . . . comrades, here,' as Galia spoke she motioned Katya to help her raise Vasya from where he had fallen. Together, the two women gently drew the old man back to his feet, straightened his shirt and shuffled him across the room to Galia's leather tub chair, carefully folding him into it. He whimpered slightly.

'There, there, Vasya, a little sit-down and a cup of lemon tea will soon have you right.' Galia didn't know whether this was really the case, but the words had to be said on an occasion such as this.

'My goodness, this morning has been so . . . emotional! I feel drained – but exhilarated. Do you find it cathartic, Galina Petrovna, this kind of thing?' The Kommandant was almost frothing at the mouth and Galina was glad when she heard the door slam after him as he went to fetch the tea.

Mitya still stood by the red door, staring at the space where his mother had briefly stood. Katya took his hands in hers and softly moved her thumbs over the sticky brown scabs that decorated most of his knuckles. 'It's OK, puppy. Does it matter who your daddy was? It's you who makes you.'

'But I was ready to think . . .' Mitya couldn't complete the sentence.

'Did you really want Vasya to be your daddy?'

'I don't know. I just thought . . . that was the truth. It felt right! It felt better than . . .' Mitya stopped and turned his face away. 'He killed my Sharik, Katya. He put him in the well.'

She gently led him away from the door and laid him down on the warm beanbag, sitting down beside him and cradling his face in her hands.

'I know. Sharik must have been a very brave dog. But the brave are always with us, Mitya. He's always been there, in your heart. Can you feel him?'

'I don't know. For a long time there was nothing, Katya: nothing at all. But now – I think I can feel him. I'm sure I met him this morning, you know, when we stopped to pee. Sharik came to me – in a butterfly. Under that tree.'

Katya put her head on one side and probed Mitya's eyes with her own velvet gaze.

'Well, that's lovely, Mitya. He's still there for you, then.'

'My head hurts.' Mitya closed his eyes and nuzzled his face in to Katya's armpit. She smelt of soap and cigarette smoke and the sea.

'OK, everyone, here's the tea! And I want everyone – no exceptions – to have some this time. Julia, you be mother, and give everyone sugar too: we could all use a sugar hit. I know I could.'

Julia beamed as she handed out the grey regulation SIZO cups and saucers. Today was so much more entertaining than usual.

Vasya, from his perch in a leatherette tub chair, reached down a gentle hand to Mitya's shoulder, and pressed it slightly. 'Mitya, I want you to know that I am sorry. I'm sorry I never could help you and your mother. It's not important . . . that I now find out that you weren't, technically, erm, my son. I always thought that you were, and I always regretted failing you.' The hand began to shake, and Vasya made a slight sobbing sound.

Mitya pressed the hand on his shoulder and looked up in to the old teacher's face. 'It wasn't your fault, Vasily Semyonovich. You did your best. For what it's worth, I am finally going to take your advice.'

'What advice, my boy?' Vasya looked slightly perplexed.

'I'm going to become a vet.'

*   *   *

'Right, ladies and gentlemen, now you've all got your tea, I'd like to say a few words. We've had disputed parents, government ministers, madness, sickles, alcoholism, someone who was just pretty annoying (and not a spy or homosexual), and somewhere along the line we've had lots of mention of dogs—'

316

'Oh my God, Boroda!' Galia dropped her regulation SIZO cup and saucer on to the lino with a thud.

'If you don't mind, Galina Petrovna, I was speaking—'

'We have to rescue Boroda! We've been fussing around here about babies and fathers and all that nonsense, and we've got a dog to rescue! My dog!' Galia's chest heaved as she started to gather up her bag with shaking hands and elbowed her friend in the face, somewhat forcefully. 'Come on, Zoya!'

Zoya had been napping quietly in her bucket chair for a good five minutes.

'Faggots with jam!' she yelped, before blinking rapidly as the room came back in to focus, and wincing at the brightness all around her. She had stood to attention immediately at the steely tone in her friend's voice and now wavered slightly in the breeze. She waved away the lemon tea proffered by Julia.

'I thought I was somewhere else. Have you got any beer?' she croaked. 'I was having ever such a funny dream.'

At the mention of Boroda, Vasya had stiffened.

'Rescue the dog . . . of course, Galina Petrovna, I must help you! I feel, it is my duty . . . no, not duty, my honour, to help you recover your valiant dog. Please, Kommandant, may I be released to help rescue the dog? I beg you – I will come back afterwards to serve out my time.'

'Valiant dog!' Mitya echoed, replacing his teacup in its saucer with a solid, regulation tinkle.

'It is also my honour to help you rescue your dog, Galina Petrovna, if it is not too late, and if you will allow. It may, I hope, start to make amends for my inhuman behaviour of the past. "*Pipple ar pipple*", Galina Petrovna!' And Mitya winked at Galia. She had no idea what he was talking about, but he seemed to be on her side, and seemed to mean it.

'Yes, Vasya, yes, Mitya. Yes, Kommandant, she is a valiant dog. She only has three legs, but she is a brave, and very polite, dog.'

'Was it this guy put her in the clink?' the Kommandant pointed at Mitya.

'Yes, it was. She bit him, you see, and Officer Kulakov. She was defending me. She wouldn't normally dream of biting anyone.'

'Do you have a piece of paper from Glukhov exonerating her as well as this Volubchik?'

'Oh yes, she is included in the VIPP, Kommandant.'

'Tremendous!'

'We must go to Plovsk, Galina Petrovna. That's where the . . . er, the canine facility is.' Mitya looked uncomfortable and bit a fingernail. 'I truly hope it's not too late.'

'So, what are we waiting for? Let's bust her out of jail! Come on, gang! We can take the KAMAZ truck – we should all fit in that. It's a monster!'

The group began to gather their bags and fruit and make for the door.

'Exonerating me? Am I exonerated?' Vasya looked to Galia with hopeful grey eyes.

'Yes, Vasya, I think probably in most respects, you are exonerated.'

'Glory be!'

27

The End

In an echoing flat on a tree-lined boulevard in Moscow, a young man with a floppy fringe and tattered slippers was getting very cross indeed.

'Look, Angelika, I don't care how many toe nails you've got left to paint, come and get your damned dog from my apartment!' He flicked dead flies from the windowsill to the floor as he spoke, and felt them crunch under his feet as he paced, somewhat gingerly, to and fro.

The Chinese Shar Pei, or 'ugly dog' as Kolya thought every time he looked at it, had parked its not inconsiderable backside in front of the apartment door two hours ago, and would not budge. It sat wrapped in its sandy-coloured, wrinkled skin and kept its tiny piggy eyes locked on to Kolya, tracking his every movement from its vantage-point in the hall. He'd tempted it with morsels from the kitchen, but had been repelled with some force. He'd stood on the other side of the hallway and shouted at it, while pointing in the direction he wanted it to go. It did nothing but let out a small, noxious fart. And now Kolya was phoning its mistress.

'No, Angelika, I'm not afraid of it!' Kolya let out a whinnying laugh and gave the dog a small sideways glance as he lied to the girl next door. 'But I have to tell you it has already attempted to bite me – twice – when I've tried to shift its enormous backside away from my front door, and now I've got a family emergency on my hands.'

He listened as his neighbour's voice whined down the telephone line at him. She was explaining that she could not come and collect the dog right now, as she had a date, and could Kolya be a darling and just hold on to him till midnight. 'And he doesn't have an enormous backside, Kolya. He's a total pedigree and he cost a lot of money. You're just being rude. Are you jealous?'

'Angelika, I can't have the dog till then. My Elderly Citizen has been arrested at the airport for carrying an illegal handgun, and I have to go and get him released. I have a whole mountain of papers I have to take and—'

She replied that she hadn't a clue who the Elderly Citizen was, but that she was sure they'd keep good care of him until tomorrow. And with that, she replaced the receiver and carried on painting her nails.

Kolya replaced the telephone on the crumb-strewn table and was aware that the dog was watching him.

'Just get out of the way, will you?' he shouted across the room, a note of desperation creeping into his voice.

'Woof,' said the dog in a deep bass, followed by a gentle show of yellow teeth and a low snarl.

* * *

'Drive, Kommandant, drive!'

As soon as the Kharkov to Rostov express, also known as the Khaki Arrow, had completed pulverising the points at the level crossing, Zoya was leaning over Krapivin's shoulder, pointing the way, the fingers of her left hand digging into his shoulder.

'I'm driving, Elderly Citizen, I'm driving!'

'Galia, my dear, don't give up hope. We'll be there in an instant, do not fret. I feel it in my bones; and look – there's a black cat crossing our path! That is a good omen. Hey, Kommandant! Mind that black cat! Hey, hey!' Zoya covered her eyes with the hand that wasn't gripping the back of his seat as the Kommandant swerved hard right on to the pavement to avoid the said lucky charm, which had decided to stop and wash its bum in the middle of the deeply pitted road.

'Zoya, do you really think it's not too late? I was so full of hope when we were in Moscow but now . . . now I just feel like I've been a fool. Of course she has gone: she has been in the system since Tuesday and there's no way that the State is going to pay for dog food for five days for a dog that the President wants dead. That's so, isn't it, Mitya?'

Mitya sniffed and scraped his feet across the metal floor of the lorry.

'Galina Petrovna, I am very sorry, but you may be right. Unfortunately, it is highly unlikely that your dog is still alive. Once the canines, I mean dogs, are logged in the system, issued their papers and taken to the collective holding kennels, they are usually destroyed within a day or so. Sometimes en-masse.'

'Destroyed en-masse, eh, Mitya?' asked Zoya with a frown.

'Yes, Zinaida Artyomovna. It is more . . . cost effective.'

'So you, Katya, what do you think of your hero now? Destroying old ladies' dogs *en-masse*, eh? A fine business to be expert in.'

Katya hesitated. 'I think he deserves a second chance, Zinaida Artyomovna, as we all do.' She put her arm through Mitya's, and clasped his hand.

Zoya looked away. 'I'll tell you something: my arse is going to be black and blue after this, Galia,' and she cackled briefly like a delinquent chicken with a flick knife.

The occupants of the KAMAZ fell into silence, preoccupied with their own thoughts. Around them, it seemed that an autumn dusk was falling, as myriad downy particles twisted in the atmosphere, catching the light of the distant sun and turning it hazy, rusted and flat. Krapivin spotted Plovsk in the distance, and let out a yelp. The town squatted on a dank hillside, and as they approached they made out assorted chimneys painted in giant red-and-white checks dotting the smog that appeared to be excreted from every pore of the town. Multiple fiery suns waited to set on a dozen different knolls around the hill top, each one burning red and gold, each at the end of a crackling tube reaching out into the solid air, still and heavy as concrete, or perhaps Zoya's scrambled eggs. That air presided over the town with an unspoken threat to squeeze the life out of its inhabitants at any time it chose. There were no visible people: maybe this was why.

'Boy, this town really gives me the creeps! It's so – murky!' Kommandant Krapivin rolled his eyes meaningfully before bringing them back to the road ahead and the horizon. 'Hey, anyone know which way we go now?'

'Straight on, Kommandant, straight on,' Mitya instructed. He knew the way to the holding facility quite well. When he had started out in extermination he had been a frequent visitor, although in recent years it had been left to others to convey the dogs to their final destination. He thought about his van this week. On Thursday it had been full to the roof with dog-kind. There had even been a poodle among his catch, some mongrel puppies, and an unwanted arthritic dachshund. The latter had bitten him on the ankle at the start of the day. It had made him very angry, he recalled. He probably still had the dry remnants of the scab there, under his sock. He glanced at Katya, wanted to touch her cheek, call her kitten, have her wash him with her eyes, absolve him of his shame, but she was staring out of the window, her face blankly reflecting the desolation around her. Mitya wondered if she had ever been to Plovsk before.

'OK, after the factory on the left.'

'The glue factory?'

'Yes, the glue factory . . .'

They were just in time to witness a ragged collection of broken-down horses being fed in through the factory gates by small, mal-formed herders. One of the horses reared up a couple of feet in a last, futile act of resistance and rolled its eyes towards the heavy sky. Galia pressed her handkerchief to her mouth and stifled a slight moan. Mitya cleared his throat.

'After the glue factory, take the next left and follow the road round, until you come to a big set of black chain gates. You can't miss it.' Mitya rubbed his eyes, very cautiously, with a swollen fist, and winced. He was glad the sound of the engine had drowned out the whinnying of the horse. Why were animals boiled down into glue, but people weren't? He didn't get anything anymore. He would ask Katya about it later.

'OK, hero, I got it: whoah, here it is!' The Kommandant braked hard and swung the heavy KAMAZ around the corner, almost launching Zoya over the driver's seat and out of the window in the process.

'Citizen Kommandant!' she cawed from the blackness of the floor. 'I did not survive the Great Patriotic War, Khrushchev, Brezhnev and the others that now escape my memory in order to be sent on my way by you! Especially not in Plovsk! What would people say?'

'Zoya, Zoya, just hold on to me, I'll keep you safe.' Galia fished her friend up from the darkness and hair balls and, dusting her off lightly, wedged her back into place on the bench seat between herself and Vasya, who was mumbling something in his sleep, his head rolling against the side of the lorry. 'We don't want to lose you, especially not in Plovsk,' she said quietly. 'It's a hell of a place.'

The open gates, just as Mitya had described, came in to view and they passed under what was left of the sign before the KAMAZ slowed to a standstill in the empty yard of Municipal Incinerator No. 4. The Kommandant cut the engine and the group slowly spilled out on to the tarmac, their coughs and complaints echoing lonely in their ears against a background of almost nothing: there were no cries of birds, or children, or dogs. The only sound was a distant rumble, somewhere in the woods, or maybe under the streets themselves, a rumble and a vibration, as if something terribly huge and heavy was beating every so often against something else terribly huge and heavy, in a cave. The vibration had shaken the leaves from the trees: even in August, Galia observed, the branches were bare and grey. No wonder there were no birds.

'OK, are we all here? Mitya, you look half dead – you better buck your ideas up, buddy. Zoya – put that dream catcher away, I don't think that can help us now. Volubchik – maybe you can stay by the vehicle and guard it? I'm sorry we forgot your walking sticks and all, but you know – it's turning into one of those days.' Kommandant Krapivin paused and scanned the faces arranged around him. 'OK, so, we're clear about what the dog looks like, yeah? Three legs, long tail, brown eyes. Which way, gang? Galia? Mitya?'

'Oh, Kommandant! How should I know? I'm just an old lady from Azov.'

'Woah, where did that come from?'

'I'm sorry, Kommandant, you've been very kind, but . . . . I'm scared. Really scared.'

'Come on, Galina Petrovna, there's no need to be scared, I'll look after you!' Katya put her arm through Galia's and looked into her eyes. 'I won't let you see anything bad, Galina Petrovna, trust me. But we have to look. Everyone, let's just try! Let's look! Let's split up!'

'Yes, Galia, there is no time to be scared. We're all here for you. I will wait here by the lorry and as soon as you come out with Boroda, I will be ready to help you back into the lorry and away. Just like the last time in Azov, remember? We've done it before. Don't be afraid.' Vasya smiled at her warmly.

'Yes, Galina Petrovna,' Mitya also broke in, looking at the sky, 'yes, we just need to get searching: to give it a go. We're all tired, all scared,' he looked at Katya, 'but we have to give it a go.'

Galia nodded her head and squared her shoulders a little. 'OK, you're right. We have to do it, no matter what we might find. I'm ready, I suppose: lead on.'

They bounded away from the KAMAZ like a pack of elderly and slightly confused bloodhounds, fanning out over the site, noses into every cage, box, corridor, office and

325

hangar they could find. They lifted the lids on all the stinking bins, opened up the black trap doors leading to echoing cellars below, climbed rickety ladders in to dusty lofts and called from the windows 'Boroda! Boroda!' They checked all the skips, the holding pens, the automated lift, the underside of the inspection chambers and even the conveyor belt buckets.

But there was no sign of life: not human, and not animal. They surged into the site office to harangue the officials, but came to a sudden halt when they realized that it was entirely deserted, a browning apple-core shivering atop a huge pile of official blue papers the only sign that habitation had occurred in the room that day. They looked at each other, eyes searching eyes, and then their eyes began softly to creep away towards the corners of the room, the ceiling, the windows, their own shoes.

'Once more!' Galia cried, and again they swept through the yard and the workshops, the bins and the lockers. They poked their noses into every nook and corner they could find across the site. But there was not a sign of any dog at all. Not a single collar, or blanket, or ball of hair. And all the while the huge incinerator chimney hissed quietly in the corner of the site, coughing occasional sparks into the afternoon sky that snapped orange before dying into the grey-yellow smog that cocooned the site, the street, the town. A fine dust was settling on all the searchers. Katya smoothed a blob of soot from Galia's forehead as they stood together in the doorway of the deserted office.

'There are no dogs here. There's nothing living at all. Maybe we're too late, Galina Petrovna?'

'It seems so, Katya.' Galia's eyes were empty.

'I don't know what to say.'

'You don't need to say anything. We did our best. I blame

no-one but myself. All she needed was a collar: an owner, and not a house-mate.'

'I'm sorry, Galina Petrovna,' said Mitya. Galia pressed his hand, unable to speak.

As they slowly came back out into the yard, a slouching figure with a pot belly hanging over his belt and unruly, matted hair appeared from around the corner. He was oblivious to the collection of people standing in front of the office and continued on his way, whistling and picking his nose with a knobbled index finger.

'Hey, you, man!' Mitya called out across the tarmac as still the operative failed to look up from his boots and snotty finger.

Slowly, the man raised his head and cast dull eyes towards the office: he was stunned by the sight of the odd bunch that stood there waiting for him. Momentarily, he regretted the pickles he'd gulped down at lunchtime with the glass or two of vodka, as a sudden queasy feeling in the pit of his stomach squeezed itself down towards his colon. Had something been found out? The uniforms, those angry looking babushkas, and – was it? Yes it was: a girl.

'Hey! Stop gawping and come over here!' Mitya commanded in his best official voice, clipped and firm. There was no squeaking now, no coughing.

'I'm trying to work. And you're not allowed in here. It's forbidden. Get out!' He turned his back on the crowd, hoping they would go away if he pretended they weren't there, and made to shuffle off in the opposite direction.

'Come here and answer one question.'

'What's it about?'

'A dog for destruction. Came here this week some time.'

'We get lots of dogs coming through here.' Again he made to slope off.

'A dog with three legs, brought here accidentally.'

'Three legs?' He stopped and looked back over his shoulder. 'Was it in a wheelchair?' he sneered.

'Where is it, you waste of space?'

'How should I know?'

'You work here, man. Think!'

The man mimed the act of thinking, scratching his head and looking towards the sky.

'Nah. No three-leggers today, or any other day this week. All we had come in today was a host of mongrels – all with four legs, like any other day. And a Yorkie pup.'

'And where are they now?' asked Galia, and immediately regretted it.

'Khkhkh!!' mimed the man, drawing a finger across his neck. 'You see that dust on your collar. That's probably one of them! Yeah look – hello, Rex!' and he stepped forward as if to pat Galia's shoulder.

'You're disgusting,' said Katya, 'and drunk!'

'Yeah, and you think you're some kind of princess,' he retorted.

'Oh, guys, there's no point talking to this steaming piece of junk anymore,' broke in the Kommandant, 'I don't think he can help us.'

The operative slouched off in the direction of the offices, picking his nose and smirking to himself.

The group watched him go in silence. Katya reached out for Mitya's hand, and he held it tightly. Galia looked to the dust at her feet, and felt the pang of loss.

'She's not here,' she said.

'No, Galia, she's not. But you know, there's no need for that operative to lie: she has not been here, it seems, so maybe she's, you know, still alive somewhere. Take

328

heart, my dear.' Zoya put her arm around Galia's broad shoulders.

'Maybe, Zoya. But that doesn't really do me any good. What can I do without her? What is to become of me?'

'I'm sorry you don't have Boroda, Galia, but you do still have us, for what it's worth. And you know that I – and Vasya – love you, don't you?'

'Thank you, Zoya, my oldest friend. I know you'll look after me. And I'm sure I can look after Vasya if I put my mind to it.' Galia gazed into her friend's face, and smiled slightly. 'It's been a difficult week, Zoya. I want to go home. And I want to go to the vegetable patch.'

Zoya smiled and led her friend back across the broken tarmac to the waiting KAMAZ truck, and Vasya Volubchik, who was crying steadily.

* * *

A week or so later, Vasya and Galia were standing by the table, arguing good-naturedly over whether her tomatoes, or her cucumbers, or both, were the best this side of Kharkov. There was even talk of melons, but at this Zoya closed her ears and attempted to doze off.

'Galia, don't you think this old man deserves a little drop of beer after the hard day we've had? I swear, I've never seen such tomatoes – and those apricots!'

Vasya wiped his handkerchief around the back of his neck and then stuffed it back in his pocket. He liked to be clean.

'Old man? I see no old man, just a man who needs his dinner,' Galia smiled.

'I won't argue with that.'

A sudden noise in the corridor outside the flat, like angry

geese riding piglets, cut short the conversation. Galia bustled away through the hall and flung open the apartment door, to find out what sort of assistance might be required on this occasion. She was just in time to see the door of Goryoun Tigranovich's apartment being slammed shut, and tiny Baba Krychkova banging her forehead on it as a result.

'Ooch, Baba Krychkova, do you want a cold compress for that?'

'Stuff your cold compress! Open up you fiend!' The old lady was clearly disgruntled and hammered so hard with her tiny fists on the door that Galia was afraid she was going to snap her wrists.

'Baba Krychkova, be still! Do not upset yourself.'

'Do you know who he's got in there?'

Galia's face was blank. What could the Elderly Citizen mean?

'Do you know? Only that Drozhdovskaya woman! Yes! The merry widow herself! And he's going to give her two marrows! She told me herself! Garlic, no doubt, too! Before we know it, she'll be wearing his gold!'

'Really? Sveta Drozhdovskaya? Well, that's good, Baba. It's about time he had better company than those silly white cats, don't you think? Come away and have some *vareniki* with us, Baba. We'd love to have you. And later we'll play cards and Zoya can tell us some stories. You know her stories, don't you? They're generally quite dirty, but they're all made up.'

Baba Krychkova's face relaxed a little, and the wrinkles around her mouth quivered into a soft smile.

'Well, I don't know . . . I haven't finished my crossword yet, and I like to get them done, you know.'

'Well, why don't you finish your crossword, and then come round after that? There's plenty to spare.'

'Thank you, Galia, that's very kind.' And Baba Krychkova shuffled off up the dusty corridor with a slight twinkle in her eye.

Galia smiled to herself as she made her way back to the kitchen and to Vasya, who was gazing out of the window as his stomach rumbled like the Urals Express. She picked up her pan.

'Here we are!' *Vareniki* stuffed with mushrooms and smothered with butter tumbled from a pan into a dish that could rival the Motherland statue at Volgograd in terms of stature.

'My hero,' smiled Galia. 'Eat, eat and then have a little drink.' She sat opposite and watched as he speared the tasty morsels eagerly with his fork, almost boyish, making a mess and dribbling butter down his chin. 'We did good work today, Vasya, you and I. It's so much quicker with an extra pair of hands. I think there'll be lots of tasty treats to put by for the winter.'

'Bottled tomatoes, Galia? They are my favourite! And I do very good salted cucumbers, you know, with bay and dill – and a few blackcurrant leaves.'

'Blackcurrant leaves? Really? Well, you must show me, Vasya.'

'With pleasure, my dear.' Vasya stopped chewing and gazed into Galia's eyes in a way that made her cheeks glow red.

'Is none of that for me, Galia?' Zoya called from the next room.

'Zoya, there is plenty for you, my dear, but you must get up off that sofa and come in here to get it. I cannot feed you: you are not a child. If you come in to the kitchen we might find you a tot of vodka to help wash down the food.'

331

Zoya's response was muffled by the sudden roar of the TV. Galia sighed, and drummed her fingers on the table slightly. 'It's the wrestling: I'd forgotten – Zoya loves it.'

'Did you speak to Mitya?' Vasya asked, fork stilled in mid-air.

'Yes, he was just on his way out – with Katya. But no, there is no news.' Galia looked down at the lino table-top and breathed deeply, determined to keep her face soft.

'Well, that's it, then: she must have escaped. She can't simply have disappeared – it's not possible.'

'But she has disappeared! We have to be realistic, Vasya. We're grown-ups. Very grown-ups. The disappeared never return, do they?'

'No,' said Vasya, with a sad shake of his head.

'Life – it's not a walk in the fields, is it?' she sighed, her breath stirring the scattering of crumbs that had lain on the table since the early morning breakfast. She raised her eyes and smiled. 'But how are the *vareniki*?'

'They are magnificent, as I knew they would be,' Vasya replied. 'You are a wonder, Galina Petrovna,' and he toasted her with a forkful of dinner and a deep nod.

A little later, as they stood on the balcony watching the sun melting into the black bar of the factory walls, Vasya screwed up his courage.

'Galia, I have something to ask you.'

'Yes?'

'Well, it's a delicate question—'

'Go ahead, Vasya. I'm all ears.'

'Are these potato or mushroom, Galichka?' a plaintive voice mewed from the kitchen.

'Zoya, just take a few and see. They're a mixture. You may even find a surprise in there.'

'Not the knickers I lost last New Year?'

'You're incorrigible!' Galia laughed, the sound like water over warm pebbles. 'Vasya, do go on. What were you saying?'

'Well, I'm not sure now . . .'

'You had a question?'

'Yes, no.' The thought of Zoya's knickers had quite put Vasya off his stride.

'Oh, never mind then. Maybe later?'

'Later, yes. That's best.'

Vasya shuffled back inside the tiny kitchen to take on the task of washing the dishes, and Galia leant her elbows on the balcony railing, her gaze dipping down into the courtyard below: Masha and her gang were playing among the bushes, shrieking wildly. Rose-coloured dust clouds billowed from their heels, and their voices bounced and burst off the apartment block walls. Galia chuckled, and waved down to them as they looked up. Then her gaze floated back to the sunset, and her senses were filled with the sounds and smells of the end of the day: clouds of starlings hazing the treetops; her neighbours on their balconies, rubbing their toes and drinking cold beer; the cats and dogs and children in the yard, gradually collecting up their owners and directing their steps towards their various beds. She closed her eyes for a moment, and caught her breath as she saw, very clearly, her bearded dog lady, Boroda, turning round and around three times, and then folding her legs up neatly beneath her, ready to doze in a pool of golden-orange sunlight, just like the one on her own kitchen floor. Galia's heart squeezed slightly, and her tired face relaxed into a broad grin.

* * *

In a cool pool of dark green air under a kitchen table, Boroda licked her fore-paw and sighed. Things had been peaceful

333

for a while now, and she had put on a little weight. Her sleep was much better, although it seemed to be extending to quite a lot of the day, and night. She had just woken from a dream: she had been chasing rabbits, or were they hares? It didn't matter: whatever they were, their smell and springiness was tantalising, but their speed was too much for her, even with her imagined fourth paw. But she didn't need rabbits. What she needed, Boroda knew, was quiet. And an old woollen jumper to lie on.

This old lady didn't smell the same as the other old lady, the original old lady who had saved her when she was on the brink of starvation, but she was kind, and quiet, and had a vegetable patch just the same. This one had some small children who came around every other day, but they were no trouble. They used their sticky fingers to pat her head and smooth her coat, and their big, brown eyes gazed in to hers under the table as they muttered stubby-toed words about love and paws and princesses. Boroda eyed their grubby faces and noses sprouting glistening lemony bogeys, and felt she ought to give them a lick. But a lick was not always welcome.

She stepped from her box on to the kitchen floor with a light clatter of claw on lino, and stood for a moment by the balcony window. She observed the orange sky, the clouds of birds, and the scents of other dogs, in other apartments. All was peace. Turning several times to get her angle just right, she lay down in the patch of golden-orange sunlight that stretched across the floor, and listened with half an ear to the old lady knitting in the room next door. Every so often she sighed and tutted, admonishing herself for a dropped stitch, or chuckling over some recently remembered anecdote. In a little while, Boroda knew, the old lady would come slowly into the kitchen and reach down to give her a tickle under the chin with fingers as knobbled as sprout sticks. '*Lapochka*,' she would say, 'I am so glad that I found you.'

The sun began to set on the rooftops of Plovsk, and Boroda's eyelids softly dropped shut.

THE END

Glossary

Baba – short for *babushka*

Babushka – Granny, often used as a term of address of any
elderly woman

Blin – a mild substitute exclamation, like "flip!"

Boroda – beard, and pronounced barad*a*

Dacha – wooden country residence, ranging from a hut to
a mansion

Dedya – Grandad, often used as a term of address of any
elderly man

Duma – the Russian parliament

KAMAZ – a make of Russian truck

Kasha – porridge

Kefir – a fermented milk drink

Kroota – cool

Kvass – a fermented non-alcoholic drink made from rye
bread

Laika – the stray dog sent in to orbit by the USSR in 1957

Lapochka – sweetie, term of endearment based on the word
for paw, and used for small children and dogs

Lubyanka – HQ of the KGB in central Moscow

NKVD – the People's Commissariat for Internal Affairs, or secret police (forerunner of KGB)

Perestroika – a political movement for reformation of the Communist Party during the 1980s

Sharik – little ball, it is a common dog's name in Russia

SIZO – stands for *Sledstvenny Izolyator*, and is a remand prison

Skoraya – ambulance

Spetznaz – Russian Special Forces

Svoloch – bastard, git

Vareniki – small stuffed dumplings

Vint – a domestically produced stimulant drug, usually injected

Acknowledgements

I would like to express my thanks to the following people: Richard Samuel, for his early read through of the manuscript, valuable comments and encouragement; Greg Lawrence, for bringing to my attention The Borough Press open submission opportunity; Katie Espiner, Cassie Browne and Charlotte Cray at The Borough Press for being so helpful, decisive and supportive; and Mick James, for telling me to get on with it – without whom, I probably wouldn't have.